For Biki and Bithika Banker,
The Gemini twins.
One saved my life,
The other gave me
Two new ones.
For Ayush Yoda Banker,
Friend, son, Jedi Master,
When you were born,
I was born again.
For Yashka Banker,
Devi, daughter, princess,
You made me believe in luck again,
And, more important, in love.

KU-477-538

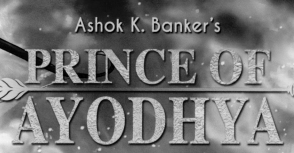

Ashok K. Banker's

PRINCE OF AYODHYA

Ramayana Series

Author
Ashok K. Banker

Artist
Sachin Nagar

Colorist
Vijay Sharma

Editors
Sourav Dutta and Shreya Mukherjee

Designer
Vijay Sharma

Cover Art
Sachin Nagar

CAMPFIRE®
www.campfire.co.in

Mission Statement

To entertain and educate young minds by creating unique illustrated books
that recount stories of human values, arouse curiosity in the world around us,
and inspire with tales of great deeds of unforgettable people.

Published by Kalyani Navyug Media Pvt Ltd
101 C, Shiv House, Hari Nagar Ashram,
New Delhi 110014, India

ISBN: 978-93-80741-92-5

Copyright © 2019 Kalyani Navyug Media Pvt Ltd

All rights reserved. Published by Campfire, an imprint of Kalyani Navyug Media Pvt Ltd.

No part of this publication may be reproduced, stored in a retrieval system, or transmitted in
any form or by any means, electronic, mechanical, photocopying, recording, or otherwise,
without written permission from the publisher.

Printed in India

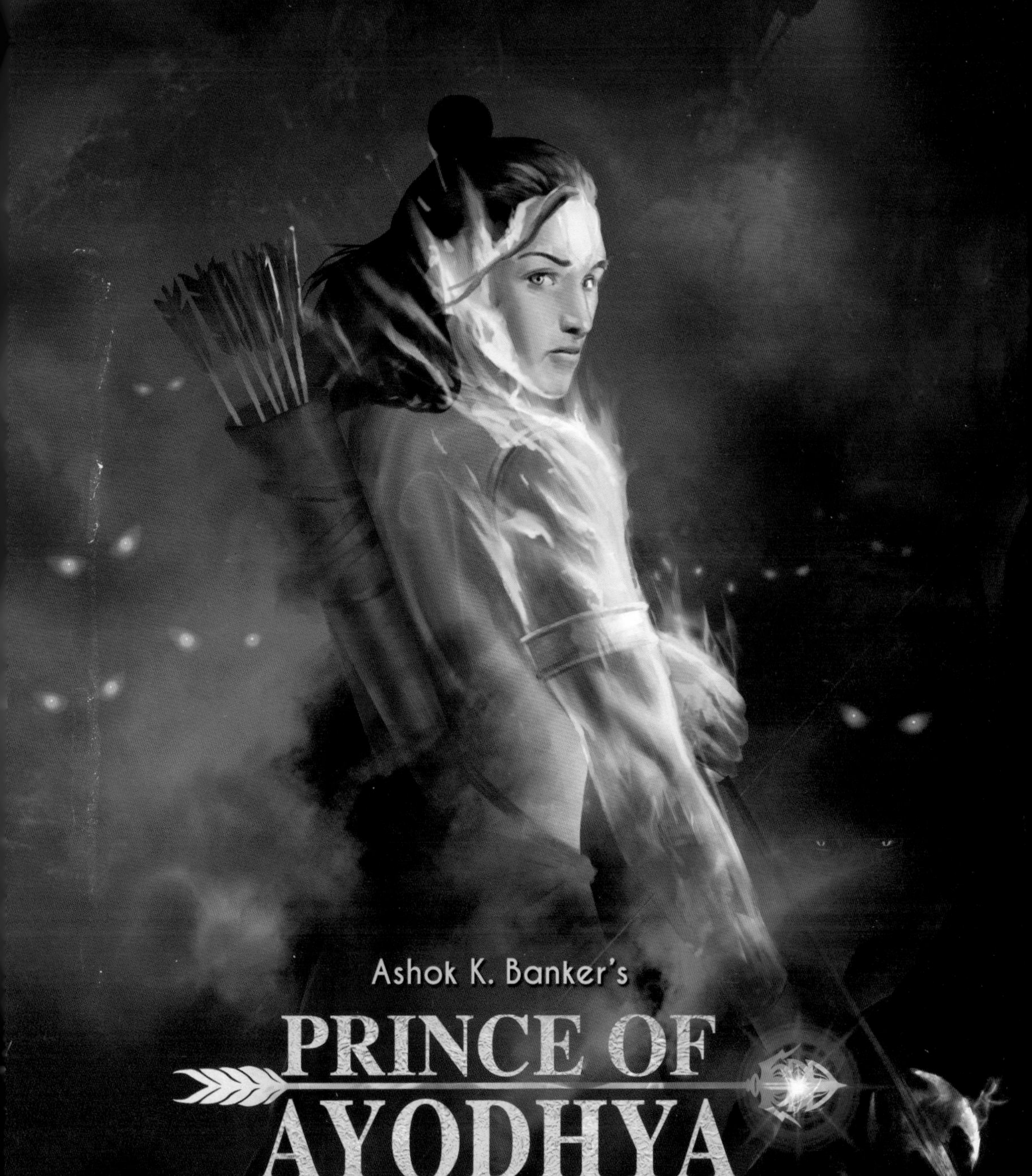
Ashok K. Banker's
PRINCE OF
AYODHYA
Ramayana Series

CAMPFIRE®
KALYANI NAVYUG MEDIA PVT LTD

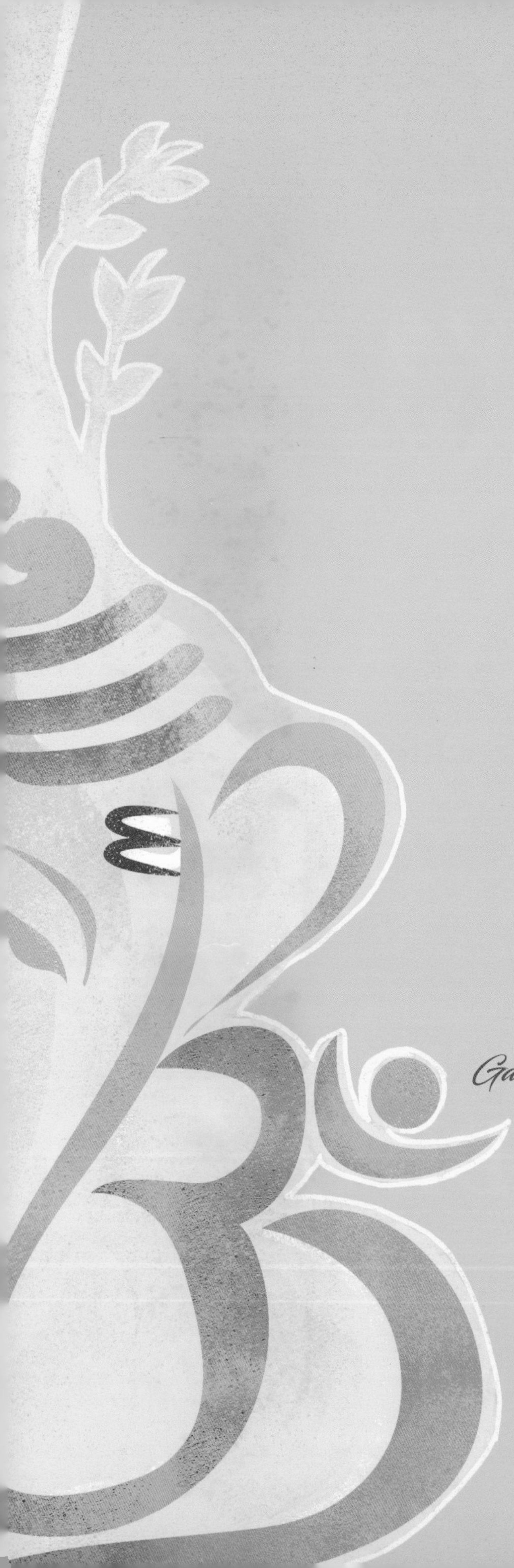

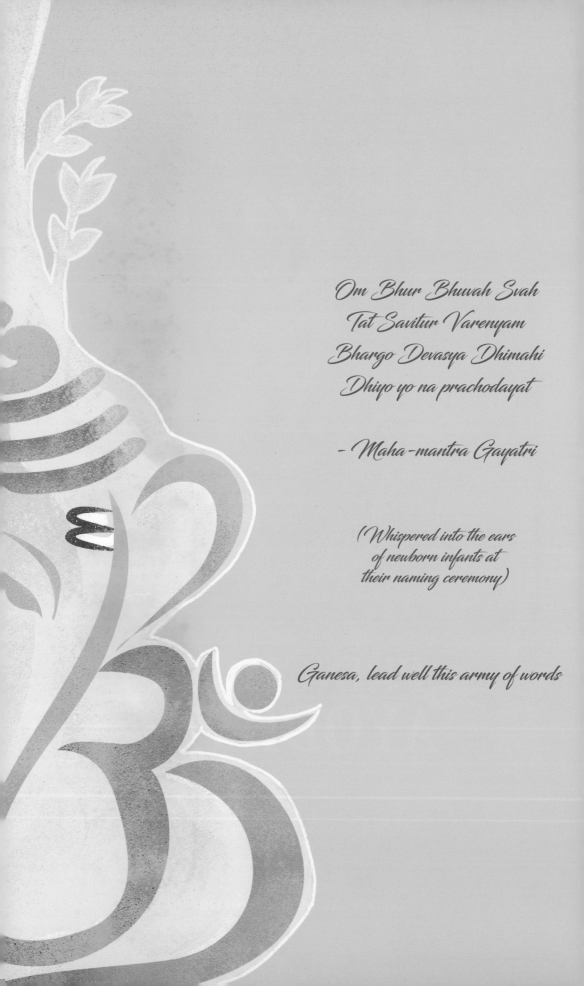

Om Bhur Bhuwah Svah
Tat Savitur Varenyam
Bhargo Devasya Dhimahi
Dhiyo yo na prachodayat

- Maha-mantra Gayatri

(Whispered into the ears of newborn infants at their naming ceremony)

Ganesa, lead well this army of words

INTRODUCTION

Adi-kavya: The first retelling

Some three thousand years ago, a sage named Valmiki lived in a remote forest ashram, practising austerities with his disciples. One day, the wandering sage Narada visited the ashram and was asked by Valmiki if he knew of a perfect man. Narada said, indeed, he did know of such a person, and then told Valmiki and his disciples a story of an ideal man.

Some days later, Valmiki happened to witness a hunter killing a kraunchya bird. The crane's partner was left desolate, and cried inconsolably. Valmiki was overwhelmed by anger at the hunter's action, and sorrow at the bird's loss. He felt driven to do something rash, but controlled himself with difficulty.

After his anger and sorrow subsided, he questioned his outburst. After so many years of practising meditation and austerities, he had still not been able to master his own emotions. Was it even possible to do so? Could any person truly become a master of his passions? For a while he despaired, but then he recalled the story Narada had told him. He thought about the implications of the story, about the choices made by the protagonist and how he had indeed shown great mastery of his own thoughts, words, deeds and feelings. Valmiki felt inspired by the recollection and was filled with a calm serenity such as he had never felt before.

As he recollected the tale of that perfect man of whom Narada had spoken, he found himself reciting it in a particular cadence and rhythm. He realized that this rhythm or metre corresponded to the warbling cries of the kraunchya bird, as if in tribute to the loss that had inspired his recollection. At once, he resolved to compose his own version of the story, using the new form of metre, that others might hear it and be as inspired as he was.

But Narada's story was only a bare narration of the events, a mere plot outline as we would call it today. In order to make the story attractive and memorable to ordinary listeners, Valmiki would have to add and embellish considerably, filling in details and inventing incidents from his own imagination. He would have to dramatize the whole story in order to bring out the powerful dilemmas faced by the protagonist.

But what right did he have to do so? After all, this was not his story. It was a tale told to him. A tale of a real man and real events. How could he make up his own version of the story?

At this point, Valmiki was visited by Lord Brahma Himself.

The Creator told him to set his worries aside and begin composing the work he had in mind. Here is how Valmiki quoted Brahma's exhortation to him, in an introductory passage not unlike this one that you are reading right now:

Recite the tale of Rama . . . as you heard it told by Narada. Recite the deeds of Rama that are already known as well as those that are not, his adventures . . . his battles . . . the acts of Sita, known and unknown. Whatever you do not know will become known to you. Never will your words be inappropriate. Tell Rama's story . . . that it may prevail on earth for as long as the mountains and the rivers exist.

Valmiki needed no further urging. He began composing his poem.

He titled it, Rama-yana, meaning literally, The Movements (or Travels) of Rama.

Foretelling the future

The first thing Valmiki realized on completing his composition was that it was incomplete.

What good was a story without anyone to tell it to? In the tradition of his age, a bard would normally recite his compositions himself, perhaps earning some favor or payment in coin or kind, more often rewarded only with the appreciation of his listeners. But Valmiki knew that while the form of the story was his creation, the story itself belonged to all his countrymen. He recalled Brahma's exhortation that Rama's story must prevail on earth for as long as the mountains and the rivers exist.

So he taught it to his disciples, among whose number were two young boys whose mother had sought sanctuary with him years ago. Those two boys, Luv and Kusa, then travelled from place to place, reciting the Ramayana as composed by their guru.

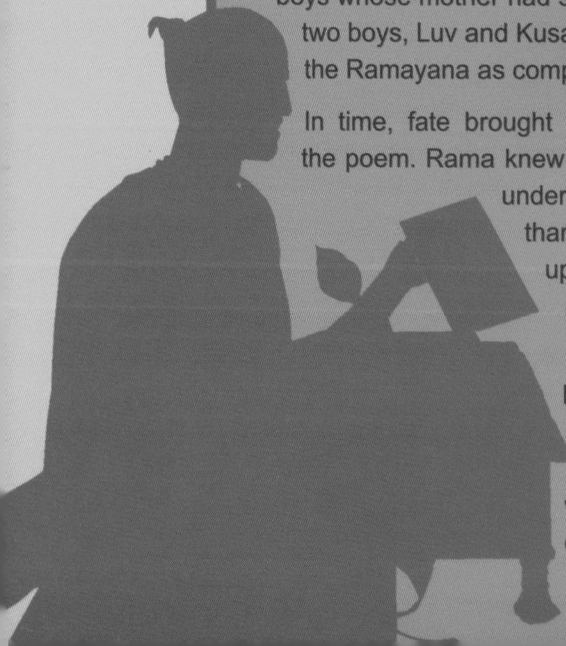

In time, fate brought them before the very Rama described in the poem. Rama knew at once that the poem referred to him and understood that these boys could be none other than his sons by the banished Sita. Called upon by the curious king, Valmiki himself then appeared before Rama and entreated him to take back Sita.

Later, Rama asked Valmiki to compose an additional part to the poem, so that he himself, Rama Chandra, might know what would happen to him in future. Valmiki obeyed this extraordinary command, and this supplementary section became the Uttara Kaand of his poem.

Valmiki's Sanskrit rendition of the tale was a brilliant work by any standards, ancient or modern. Its charm, beauty and originality can never be matched. It is a true masterpiece of world literature, the 'adi-kavya' which stands as the fountainhead of our great cultural record. Even today, thousands of years after its composition, it remains unsurpassed.

And yet, when we narrate the story of the Ramayana today, it is not Valmiki's Sanskrit shlokas that we recite. Few of us today have even read Valmiki's immortal composition in its original. Most have not even read an abridgement. Indeed, an unabridged Ramayana itself, reproducing Valmiki's verse without alteration or revisions, is almost impossible to find. Even the most learned of scholars, steeped in a lifetime of study of ancient Sanskrit literature, maintain that the versions of Valmiki's poem that exist today have been revised and added to by later hands. Some believe that the first and seventh kaands, as well as a number of passages within the other kaands, were all inserted by later writers who preferred to remain anonymous.

Perhaps the earliest retelling of Valmiki's poem is to be found in the pages of that vast ocean of stories we call the Mahabharata. When Krishna Dwaipayana-Vyasa, more popularly known today as Ved Vyasa, composed his equally legendary epic, he retold the story of the Ramayana in one passage. His retelling differs in small but significant ways.

Sometime later, the burgeoning Buddhist literature, usually composed in the Pali dialect, also included stories from the Ramayana, recast in a somewhat different light. Indeed, Buddhist literature redefined the term dharma itself, restating it as *dhamma* and changing the definition of this and several other core concepts.

In the eleventh century, a Tamil poet named Kamban undertook his own retelling of the Ramayana legend. Starting out with what seems to have been an attempt to translate Valmiki's Ramayana, Kamban nevertheless deviated dramatically from his source material. In Kamban's Ramayana, entire episodes are deleted, new ones appear, people and places are renamed or changed altogether, and even the order of some major events is revised. Most of all, Kamban's Ramayana relocates the entire story in a milieu that is recognizably eleventh-century Tamil Nadu in its geography, history, clothes, customs, etc., rather than the north Indian milieu of Valmiki's Sanskrit original. It is essentially a whole new Ramayana, retold in a far more passionate, rich and colourful idiom.

A few centuries later, Sant Tulsidas undertook his interpretation of the epic. Tulsidas went so far as to title his work *Ramcharitamanas*, rather than calling it the Ramayana.

By doing so, he signalled that he was not undertaking a faithful translation, but a wholly new variation of his own creation. The differences are substantial.

In art, sculpture, musical renditions, even in dance, mime and street theatrical performances, the story of Valmiki's great poem has been retold over and over, in countless different variations, some with minor alterations, others with major deviations. The tradition of retellings continues even in modern times, through television serials, films, puppet theatre, children's versions, cartoons, poetry, pop music and, of course, in the tradition of Ramlila enactments across the country every year.

Yet how many of these are faithful to Valmiki? How many, if any at all, actually refer to the original Sanskrit text, or even attempt to seek out that text?

Should they even do so?

So many Ramayanas

Does a grandmother consult Valmiki's Ramayana before she retells the tale to her grandchildren at night? When she imitates a Rakshasa's roar or Ravana's laugh, or Sita's tears, or Rama's stoic manner, whom does she base her performance on? When an actor portrays Rama in a television serial, or a Ramlila performer enacts a scene, or a sculptor chisels a likeness, a painter a sketch, whom do they all refer to? There were no illustrations in Valmiki's Ramayana. No existing portraits of Rama survive from that age, no recordings of his voice or video records of his deeds.

Indeed, many of the episodes or 'moments' we believe are from Valmiki's Ramayana are not even present in the original Sanskrit work. They are the result of later retellers, often derived from their own imagination. One instance is the 'seema rekha' believed to have been drawn by Lakshman before leaving Sita in the hut. No mention of this incident exists in Valmiki's Ramayana.

Then there is the constant process of revision that has altered even those scenes that remain constant through various retellings. For example, take the scene where Sita entreats Rama to allow her to accompany him into exile. In Valmiki's Ramayana, when Rama tells Sita he has to go into exile, and she asks him to allow her to go with him, he refuses outright. At first, Sita pleads with him and cries earnest tears, but when Rama remains adamant, she grows angry and rebukes him in shockingly harsh terms. She refers to him as a 'woman disguised as a man', says that 'the world is wrong when they say that there is no one greater than Rama', calls him 'depressed and frightened', 'an actor playing a role', and other choice epithets. It is one of the longer scenes in Valmiki's Ramayana, almost equalling in length the entire narration of Rama's early childhood years!

Tamil poet Kamban retells this incident in his more compressed, volatile, rich style, reducing Sita's objections to a couple of brief rebukes: 'Could it be that the real reason [for Rama not taking her into exile] is that with me left behind, you'll be free to enjoy yourself in the forest?'

By the time we reach Sant Tulsidas's recension, Sita's rebukes are reduced to a few tearful admonitions and appeals. Were these changes the result of the change in the socially accepted standards of behaviour between men and women in our country? Quite possibly. Tulsidas's *Ramcharitamanas* depicts a world quite different from that which Valmiki or even Kamban depict. In fact, each of these three versions differs so drastically in terms of the language used, the clothes worn, the various social and cultural references, that they seem almost independent of one another.

Perhaps the most popularly known version in more recent times is a simplified English translation of a series of Tamil retellings of selected episodes of the Kamban version, serialized in a children's magazine about fifty years ago. This version by C. Rajagopalachari, a.k.a. Rajaji, was my favorite version as a child too. It was only much later that I found, through my own extensive research that my beloved Rajaji version left out whole chunks of the original story and simplified other parts considerably. Still later, I was sorely disappointed by yet another version by an otherwise great writer, R. K. Narayan. In his severely abridged retelling, the story is dealt with in a manner so rushed and abbreviated, it is reduced to a moral fable rather than the rich, powerful, mythic epic that Valmiki created.

English scholar William S. Buck's nineteenth-century version, dubiously regarded as a classic by English scholars, reads like it might have been composed under the influence of certain intoxicants: in one significant departure from Indian versions, Guha, the tribal chief of the Nisada fisherfolk, without discernible reason, spews a diatribe against Brahmins, and ends by kicking a statue of Lord Shiva. To add further confusion, in the illustration accompanying this chapter, Guha is shown kicking what appears to be a statue of Buddha!

If you travel outside India, farther east, you will find more versions of the Ramayana that are so far removed from Valmiki, that some are barely recognizable as the same story. In one recent study of these various versions of the epic across the different cultures of Asia, an ageing Muslim woman in Indonesia is surprised to learn from the author that we have our own Ramayana in India also! The kings of Thailand are always named Rama along with other dynastic titles, and consider themselves to be direct descendants of Rama Chandra. The largest Rama temple, an inspiring ruin even today, is situated not in India, or even in Nepal (the only nation that takes Hinduism as its official religion), but in Cambodia. It is called Angkor Vat.

In fact, it is now possible to say that there are as many Ramayanas as there are people who know the tale, or claim to know it. And no two versions are exactly alike.

My Ramayana: A personal odyssey

And yet, would we rather have this democratic melange of versions and variations, or would we rather have a half-remembered, extinct tale recollected only dimly, like a mostly forgotten myth that we can recall only fragments of?

Valmiki's 'original' Ramayana was written in Sanskrit, the language of his time and in an idiom that was highly modern for its age. In fact, it was so avant garde in its style—the kraunchya inspired shloka metre—that it was considered 'adi' or the first of its kind. Today, few people except dedicated scholars can understand or read it in its original form—and even they often disagree vehemently about their interpretations of the dense archaic Sanskrit text!

Kamban's overblown rhetoric and colourful descriptions, while magnificently inspired and appropriate for its age, are equally anachronistic in today's times.

Tulsidas's interpretation, while rightfully regarded as a sacred text, can seem somewhat heavyhanded in its depiction of man– woman relationships. It is more of a religious tribute to Lord Rama's divinity than a realistic retelling of the story itself.

In Ved Vyasa's version, the devices of ill-intentioned Manthara, misguided Kaikeyi and reprehensible Ravana are not the ultimate cause of Rama's misfortunes. In fact, it is not due to the asuras either. It is Brahma himself, using the mortal avatar of Vishnu to cleanse the world of evil, as perpetuated by Ravana and his asuras, in order to maintain the eternal balance of good and evil.

My reasons for attempting this retelling were simple and intensely personal. As a child of an intensely unhappy broken marriage, a violently bitter failure of parents of two different cultures (Anglo-Indian Christian and Gujarati Hindu) to accept their differences and find common ground, I turned to literature for solace. My first readings were, by accident, in the realm of mythology. So inspired was I by the simple power and heroic victories of those ancient ur-tales, I decided to become a writer and tell stories of my own that would be as great, as inspiring to others. To attempt, if possible, to bridge cultures, and knit together disparate lives by showing the common struggle and strife and, ultimately, triumph of all human souls.

I was barely a boy then. Thirty-odd years of living and battling life later, albeit not as colourful as Valmiki's thieving and dacoit years, I was moved by a powerful inexplicable urge to read the Ramayana once more. Every version I read seemed to lack something, that vital something that I can only describe as the 'connection' to the work. In a troubled phase, battling with moral conundrums of my own, I set to writing my own version of the events. My mind exploded with images, scenes, entire conversations between characters. I saw, I heard, I felt . . . I wrote. Was I exhorted by Brahma Himself? Probably not! I had no reader in mind, except myself—and everyone. I changed as a person over the course of that writing. I found peace, or a kind of peace. I saw how people could devote their lives to worshipping Rama, or Krishna, or Devi for that matter, my own special 'Maa'. But I also felt that this story was beyond religion, beyond nationality, beyond race, colour, or creed.

Undertaking to retell a story as great and as precious as our classic adi-kavya is not an enterprise lightly attempted. The first thing I did was study every available edition of previous retellings to know what had been done before, the differences between various retellings, and attempt to understand why. I also spoke extensively to people known and unknown about their knowledge of the poem, in an attempt to trace how millennia of verbal retellings have altered the perception of the tale. One of the most striking things was that most people had never actually read the 'original' Valmiki Ramayana. Indeed, most people considered Ramcharitramanas by Tulsidas to be 'the Ramayana', and assumed it was an accurate reprise of the Sanskrit work. Nothing could be farther from the truth.

For instance, Valmiki's Ramayana depicts Dasaratha as having three hundred and fifty concubines in addition to his three titled wives. In keeping with the kingly practices of that age, the ageing raja's predilection for the fairer sex is depicted honestly and without any sense of misogyny. Valmiki neither comments on nor criticizes Dasaratha's fondness for fleshly pleasures, he simply states it.

When Rama takes leave of his father before going into exile, he does so in the palace of concubines, and all of them weep copiously for the exiled son of their master. When Valmiki describes women, he does so by enumerating the virtues of each part of their anatomy. There is no sense of embarrassment or male chauvinism evident here: he is simply extolling the beauty of the women characters, just as he does for the male characters like Rama and Hanuman and, yes, even Ravana. Even in Kamban's version, the women are depicted in such ripe, full-blown language, that a modern reader like myself blushes in embarrassment. Yet the writer exhibits no awkwardness or prurience in these passages—he is simply describing them as he perceived them in the garb and fashion of his time.

By the time we reach Tulsidas and later versions, Rama is no less than a god in human avatar. And in keeping with this foreknowledge, all related characters are depicted accordingly.

So Dasaratha's fleshly indulgences take a backseat, the women are portrayed fully clad and demure in appearance, and their beauty is ethereal rather than earthly.

How was I to approach my retelling? On one hand, the Ramayana was now regarded not as a Sanskrit epic of real events that occurred in ancient India, but as a moral fable of the actions of a human avatar of Vishnu. On the other hand, I felt the need to bring to life the ancient world of epic India in all its glory and magnificence, to explore the human drama as well as the divinity that drove it, to show the nuances of word and action and choice rather than a black-and-white depiction of good versus evil. More importantly, what could I offer that was fresh and new, yet faithful to the spirit of the original story? How could I ensure that all events and characters were depicted respectfully yet realistically?

There was little point in simply repeating any version that had gone before—those already existed, and those who desired to read the Ramayana in any one of its various forms could simply pick up one of those previous versions.

But what had never been done before was a complete, or 'sampoorn', Ramayana, incorporating the various, often contradictory aspects of the various Indian retellers (I wasn't interested in foreign perspectives, frankly), while attempting to put us into the minds and hearts of the various characters. To go beyond a simple plot reprise and bring the whole story, the whole world of ancient India, alive. To do what every verbal reteller attempts, or any classical dancer does: make the story live again.

In order to do this, I chose a modern idiom. I simply used the way I speak, an amalgam of English–Hindi–Urdu–Sanskrit, and various other terms from Indian languages. I deliberately used anachronisms like the terms 'abs' or 'morph'. I based every section, every scene, every character's dialogues and actions on the previous Ramayanas, be it Valmiki, Kamban, Tulsidas, or Vyasa, and even the various Puranas. Everything you read here is based on actual research, or my interpretation of some detail noted in a previous work. The presentation, of course, is wholly original and my own.

Take the example of the scene of Sita entreating Rama to let her accompany him into exile. In my retelling, I sought to explore the relationship between Rama and Sita at a level that is beyond the physical or social plane. I believed that their's was a love that was eternally destined, and that their bond surpassed all human ties. At one level, yes, I believed that they were Vishnu and Lakshmi. Yet, in the avatars they were currently in, they were Rama and Sita, two young people caught up in a time of great turmoil and strife, subjected to hard, difficult choices. Whatever their divine backgrounds and karma, here and now, they had to play out their parts one moment at a time, as real, flesh-and-blood people.

I adopted an approach that was realistic, putting myself (and thereby the reader) into the feelings and thoughts of both Rama and Sita at that moment of choice. I felt the intensity of their pain, the great sorrow and confusion, the frustration at events beyond their control, and also their ultimate acceptance of what was right, what must be done, of dharma. In my version, they argue as young couples will at such a time, they express their anger and mixed emotions, but in the end, it is not only through duty and dharma that she appeals to him. In the end, she appeals to him as a wife who is secure in the knowledge that her husband loves her sincerely, and that the bond that ties them is not merely one of duty or a formal social knot of matrimony, but of true love. After the tears, after all other avenues have been mutually discussed and discarded, she simply says his name and appeals to him, as a wife, a lover, and as his dearest friend:

'Rama,' she said. She raised her arms to him, asking, not pleading. 'Then let me go with you.'

And he agrees. Not as a god, an avatar, or even a prince. But as a man who loves her and respects her. And needs her.

In the footsteps of giants

Let me be clear.

This is not Valmiki's story. Nor Kamban's. Nor Tulsidas's.

Nor Vyasa's. Nor R.K. Narayan's. Nor Rajaji's charming, abridged children's version.

It is Rama's story. And Rama's story belongs to every one of us. Black, brown, white, or albino. Old or young. Male or female. Hindu, Christian, Muslim, or whatever faith you espouse. I was once asked at a press conference to comment on the Babri Masjid demolition and its relation to my Ramayana. My answer was that the Ramayana had stood for three thousand years, and would stand for all infinity. Ayodhya, in my opinion, is not just a place in north-central Uttar Pradesh. It is a place in our hearts. And in that most sacred of places, it will live forever, burnished and beautiful as no temple of consecrated bricks can ever be. When Rama himself heard Luv and Kusa recite Valmiki's Ramayana for the first time, even he, the protagonist of the story, was flabbergasted by the sage's version of the events—after all, even he had not known what happened to Sita after her exile, nor the childhood of Luv and Kusa, nor had he heard their mother's version of events narrated so eloquently until then. And in commanding Valmiki to compose the section about future events, Rama himself added his seal of authority to Valmiki, adding weight to Brahma's exhortation to recite the deeds of Rama that were already known 'as well as those that are not'.

And so the tradition of telling and retelling the Ramayana began. It is that tradition that Kamban, Tulsidas, Vyasa, and so many others were following. It is through the works of these bards through the ages that this great tale continues to exist among us. If it changes shape and structure, form and even content, it is because that is the nature of the story itself: it inspires the teller to bring fresh insights to each new version, bringing us ever closer to understanding Rama himself.

This is why it must be told, and retold, an infinite number of times.

By me.

By you.

By grandmothers to their grandchildren.

By people everywhere, regardless of their identity.

The first time I was told the Ramayana, it was on my grandfather's knee. He was excessively fond of chewing tambaku paan and his breath was redolent of its aroma. Because I loved lions, he infused any number of lions in his Ramayana retellings— Rama fought lions, Sita fought them, I think even Manthara was cowed down by one at one point! My grandfather's name, incidentally, was Ramchandra Banker. He died of throat cancer caused by his tobacco-chewing habit. But before his throat ceased working, he had passed on the tale to me.

And now, I pass it on to you. If you desire, and only if, then read this book. I believe if you are ready to read it, the tale will call out to you, as it did to me. If that happens, you are in for a great treat. Know that the version of the Ramayana retold within these pages is a living, breathing, new-born avatar of the tale itself. Told by a living author in a living idiom. It is my humble attempt to do for this great story what writers down the ages have done with it in their times.

Maazi naroti

In closing, I'd like to quote briefly from two venerable authors who have walked similar paths.

The first is K.M. Munshi, whose *Krishnavatara* series remains a benchmark of the genre of modern retellings of ancient tales. These lines are from Munshi's own Introduction to the Bharatiya Vidya Bhavan edition of 1972:

In the course of this adventure, I had often to depart from legend and myth, for such a reconstruction by a modern author must necessarily involve the exercise of whatever little imagination he has. I trust He will forgive me for the liberty I am taking, but I must write of Him as I see Him in my imagination.

I could not have said it better.

Yuganta, Iravati Karve's landmark Sahitya Akademi Award-winning study of the Mahabharata, packs more valuable insights into its slender 220-page pocket-sized edition (Disha) than any ten encyclopaedias. In arguably the finest essay of the book, 'Draupadi', she includes this footnote:

'The discussion up to this point is based on the critical edition of the Mahabharata. What follows is my naroti [naroti = a dry coconut shell, i.e. a worthless thing. The word 'naroti' was first used in this sense by the poet Eknath].'

In the free musings of Karve's mind, we learn more about Vyasa's formidable epic than from most encyclopaedic theses. For only from free thought can come truly progressive ideas.

In that spirit, I urge readers to consider my dried coconut shell reworking of the Ramayana in the same spirit.

If anything in the following pages pleases you, thank those great forebears in whose giant footsteps I placed my own small feet. If any parts displease you, then please blame them on my inadequate talents, not on the tale.

ASHOK K. BANKER

KAAND I

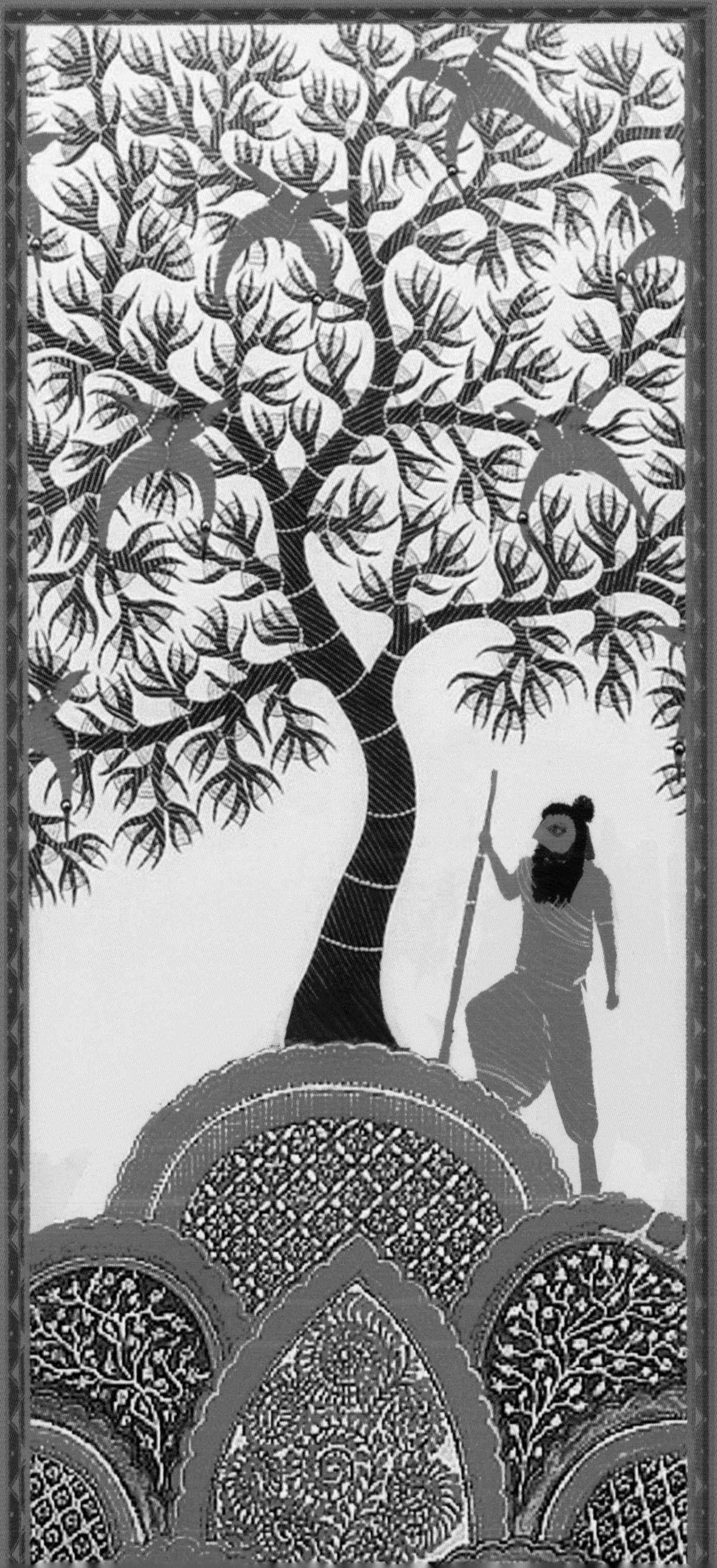

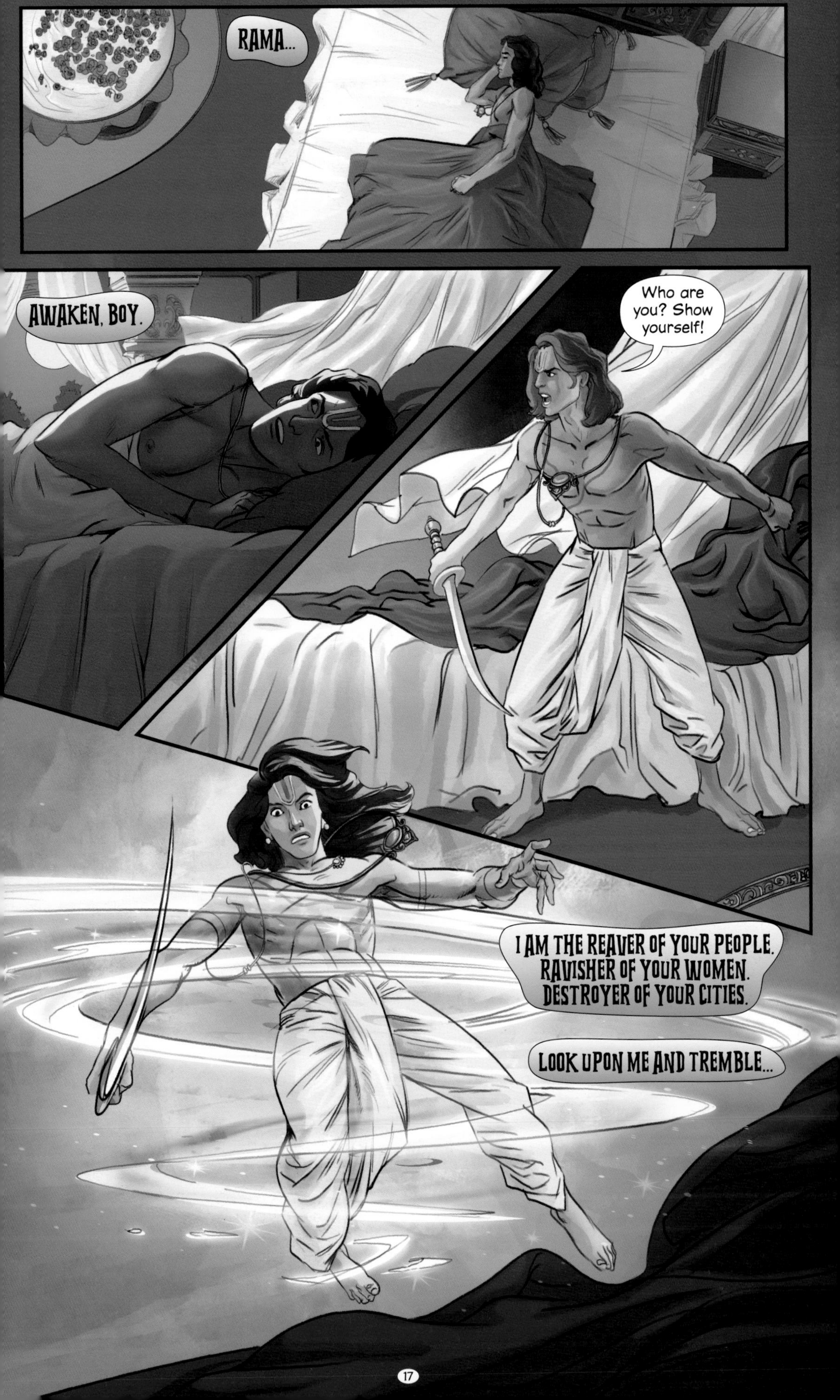
RAMA...
AWAKEN, BOY.
Who are you? Show yourself!
I AM THE REAVER OF YOUR PEOPLE. RAVISHER OF YOUR WOMEN. DESTROYER OF YOUR CITIES.
LOOK UPON ME AND TREMBLE...

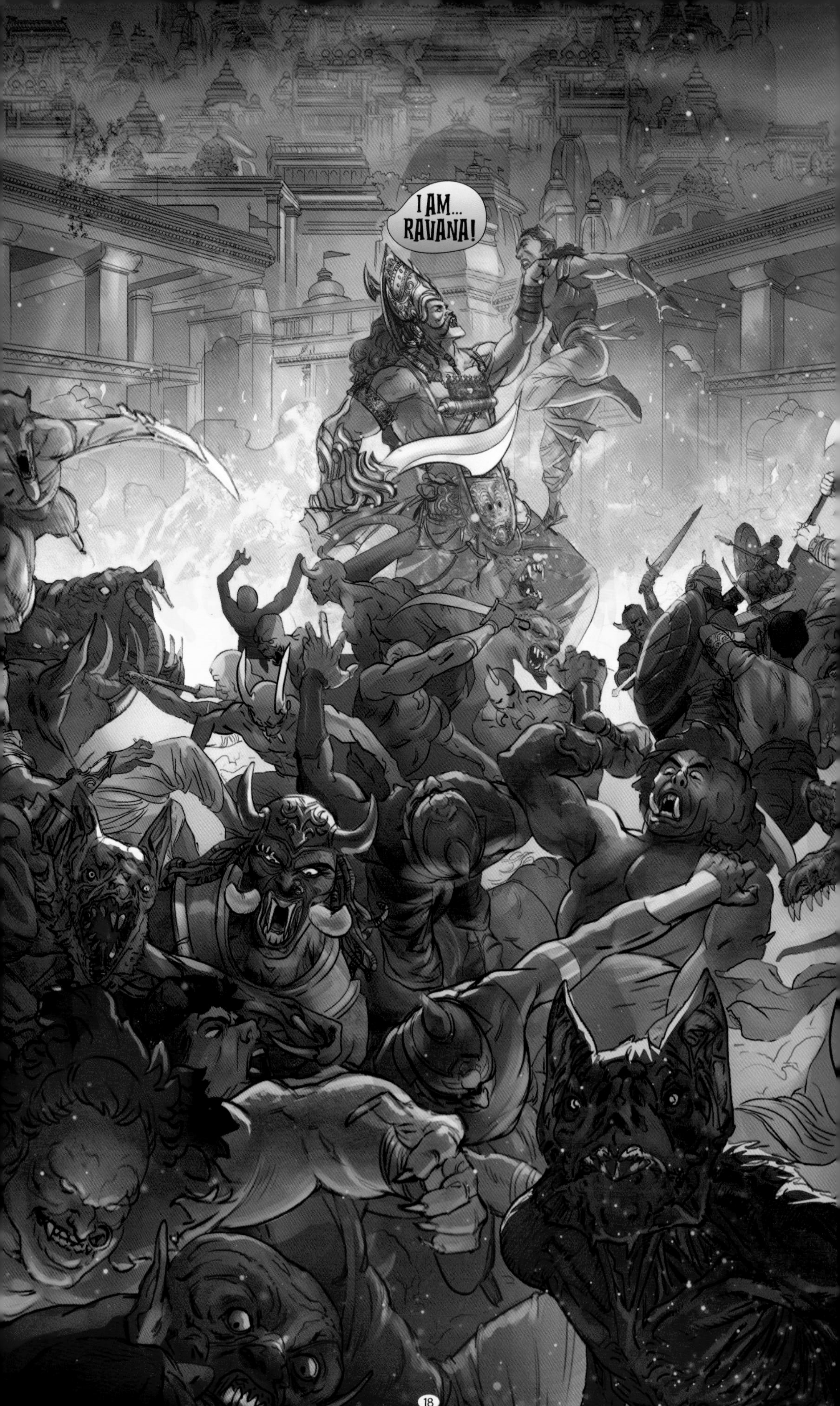
I AM... RAVANA!

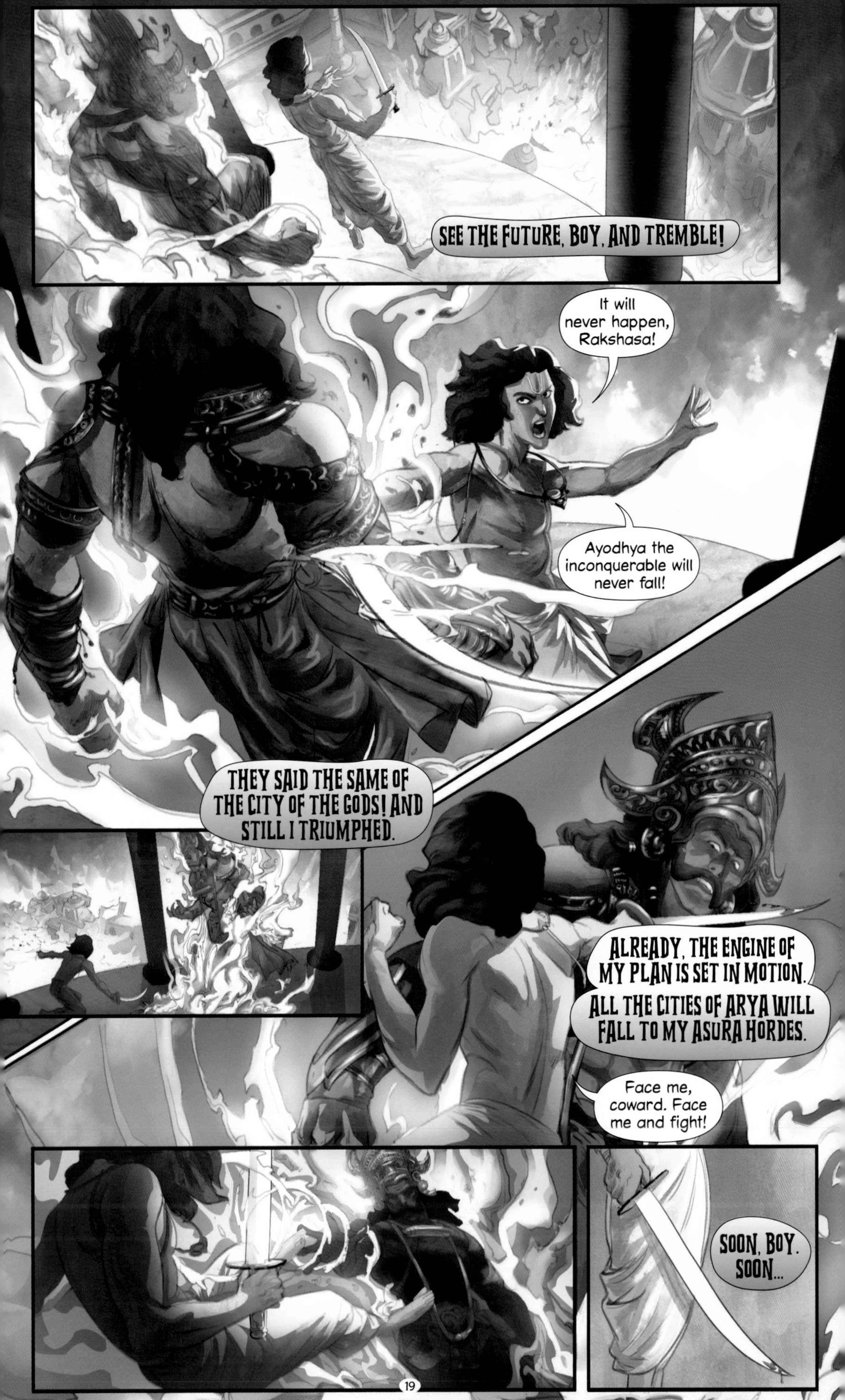
SEE THE FUTURE, BOY, AND TREMBLE!
It will never happen, Rakshasa!
Ayodhya the inconquerable will never fall!
THEY SAID THE SAME OF THE CITY OF THE GODS! AND STILL I TRIUMPHED.
ALREADY, THE ENGINE OF MY PLAN IS SET IN MOTION.
ALL THE CITIES OF ARYA WILL FALL TO MY ASURA HORDES.
Face me, coward. Face me and fight!
SOON, BOY. SOON...

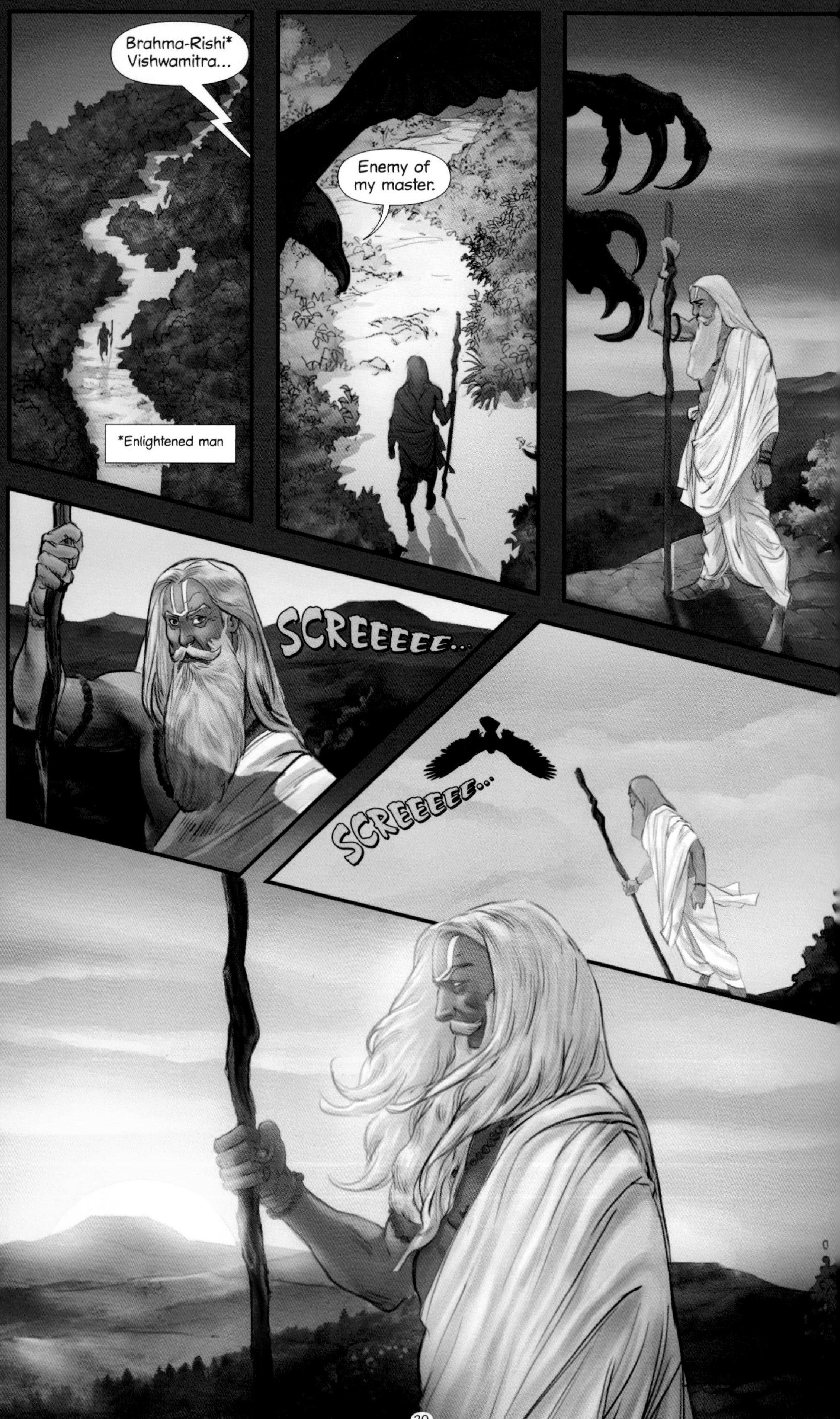

Brahma-Rishi* Vishwamitra...
*Enlightened man
Enemy of my master.
SCREEEEEE...
SCREEEEEE...

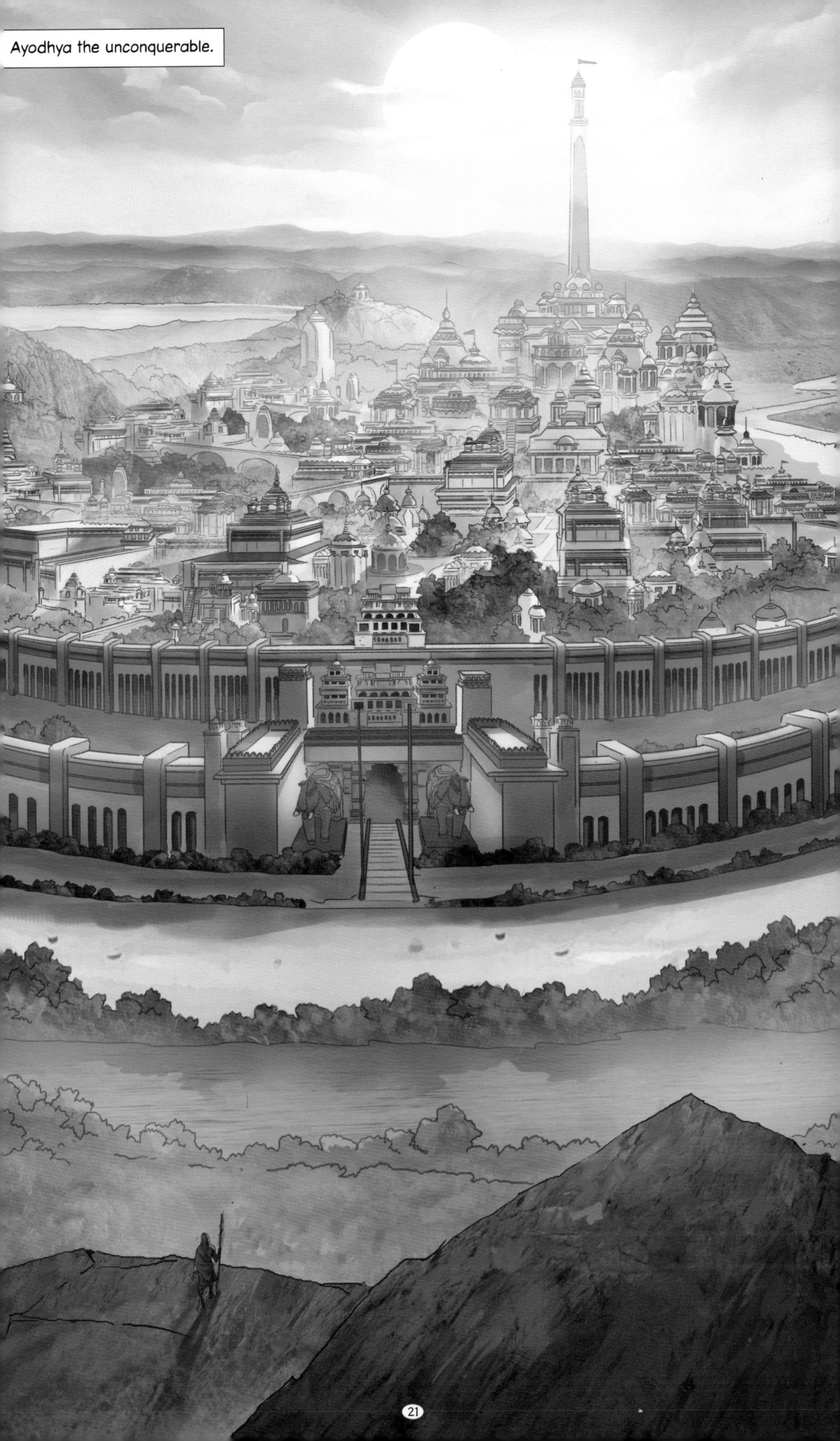
Ayodhya the unconquerable.

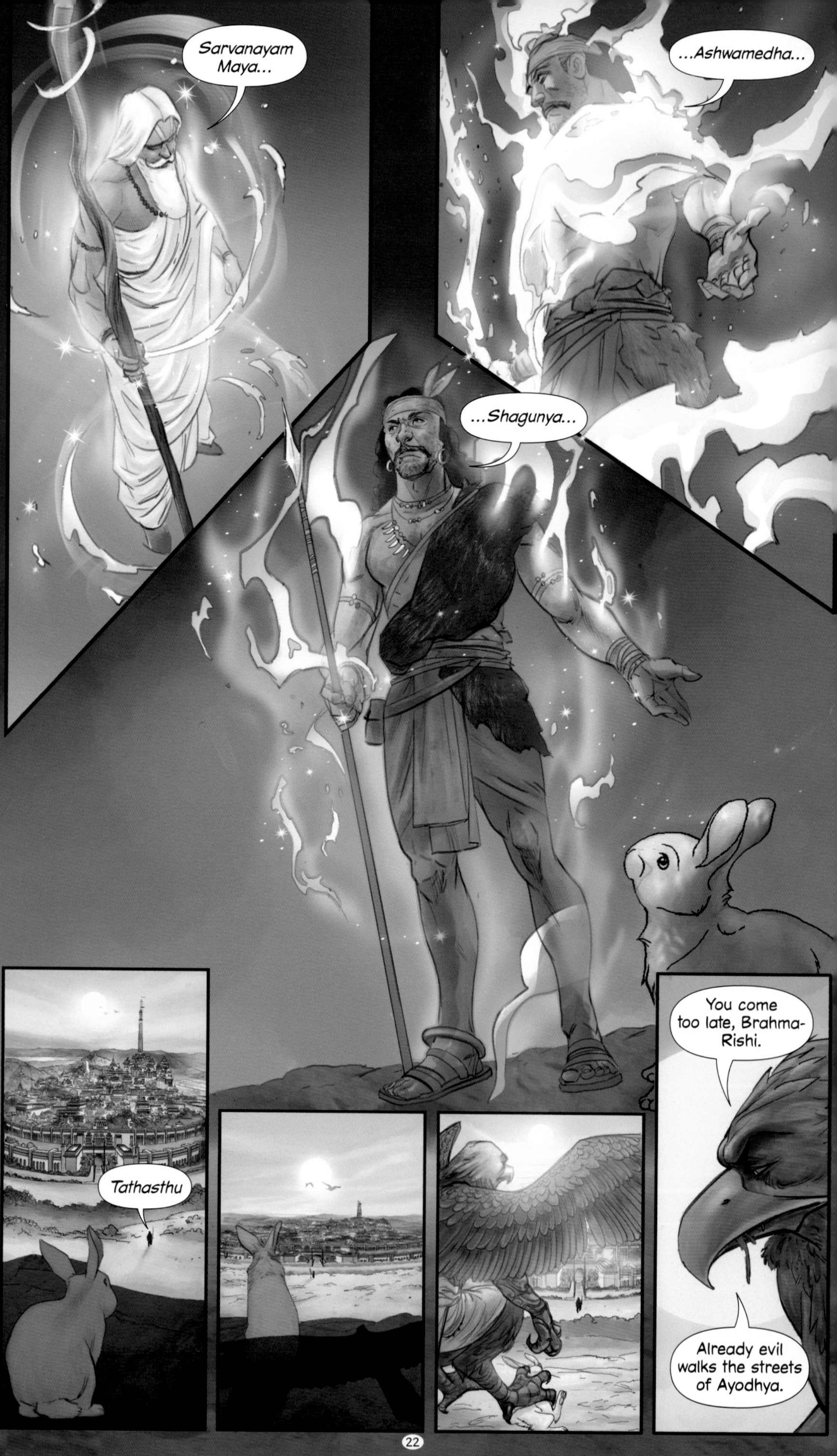
Sarvanayam Maya...
...Ashwamedha...
...Shagunya...
Tathasthu
You come too late, Brahma-Rishi.
Already evil walks the streets of Ayodhya.

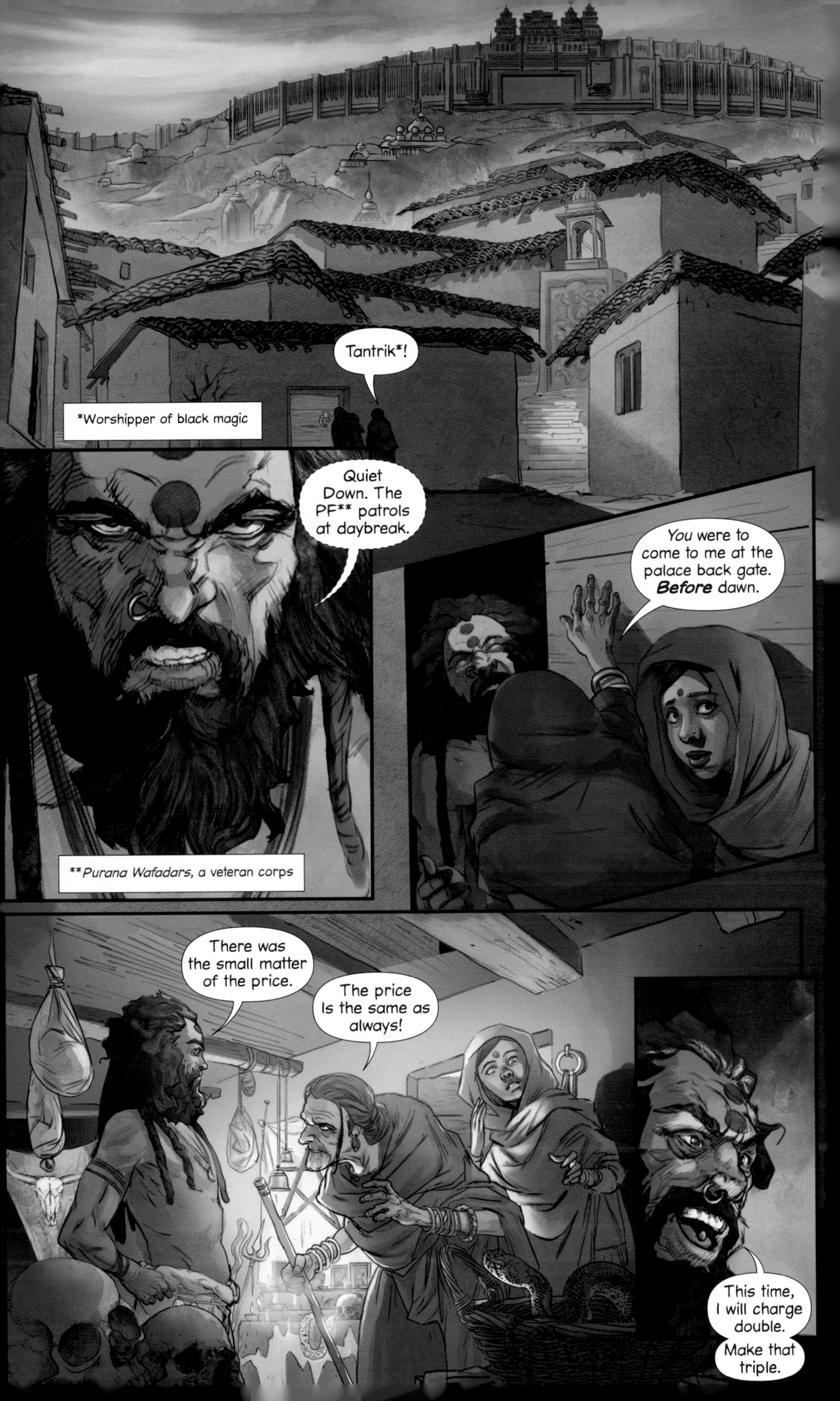
Tantrik*!
*Worshipper of black magic
Quiet Down. The PF** patrols at daybreak.
**Purana Wafadars, a veteran corps
You were to come to me at the palace back gate. Before dawn.
There was the small matter of the price.
The price Is the same as always!
This time, I will charge double.
Make that triple.

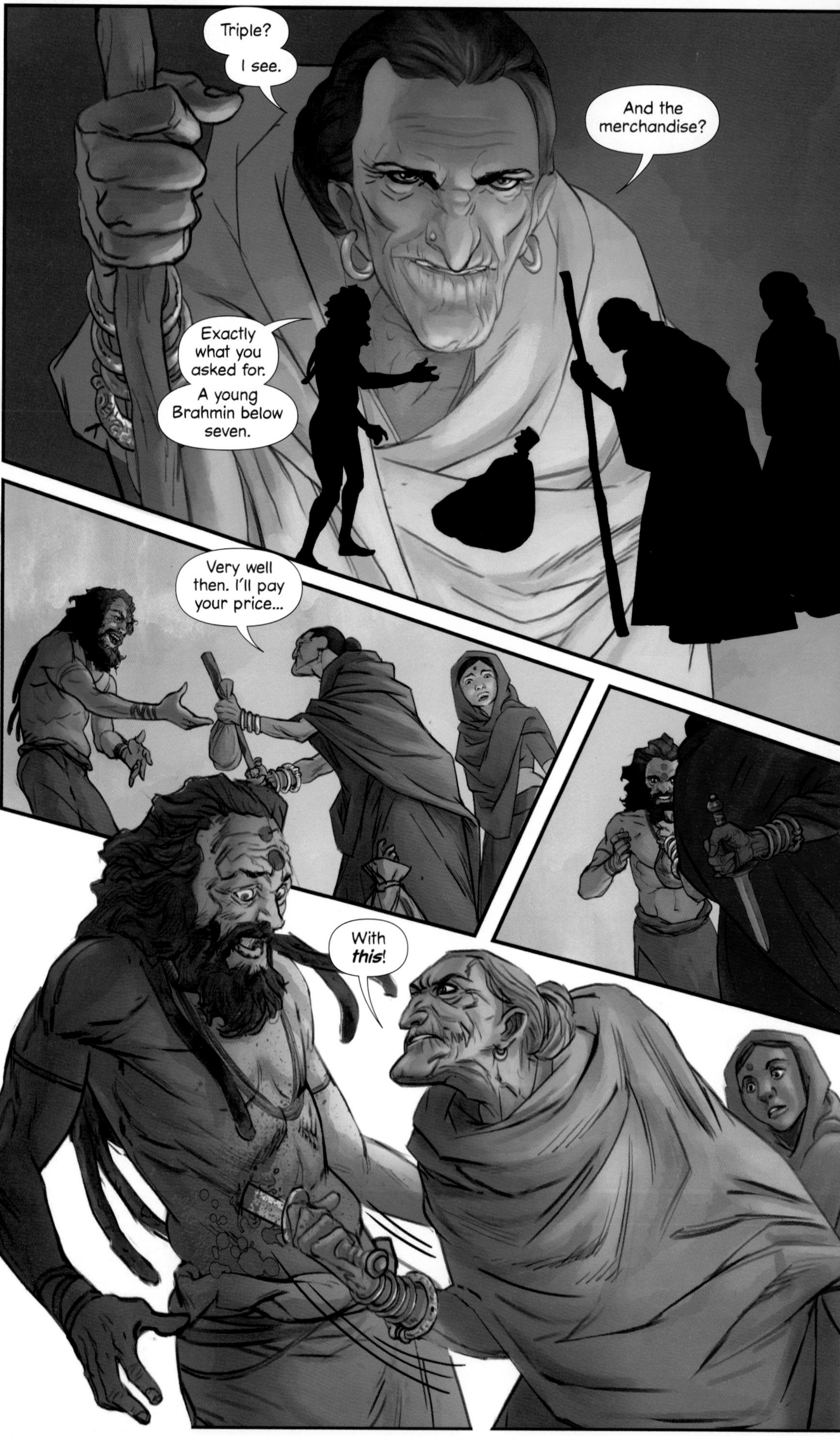
Triple?
I see.
And the merchandise?
Exactly what you asked for.
A young Brahmin below seven.
Very well then. I'll pay your price...
With *this*!

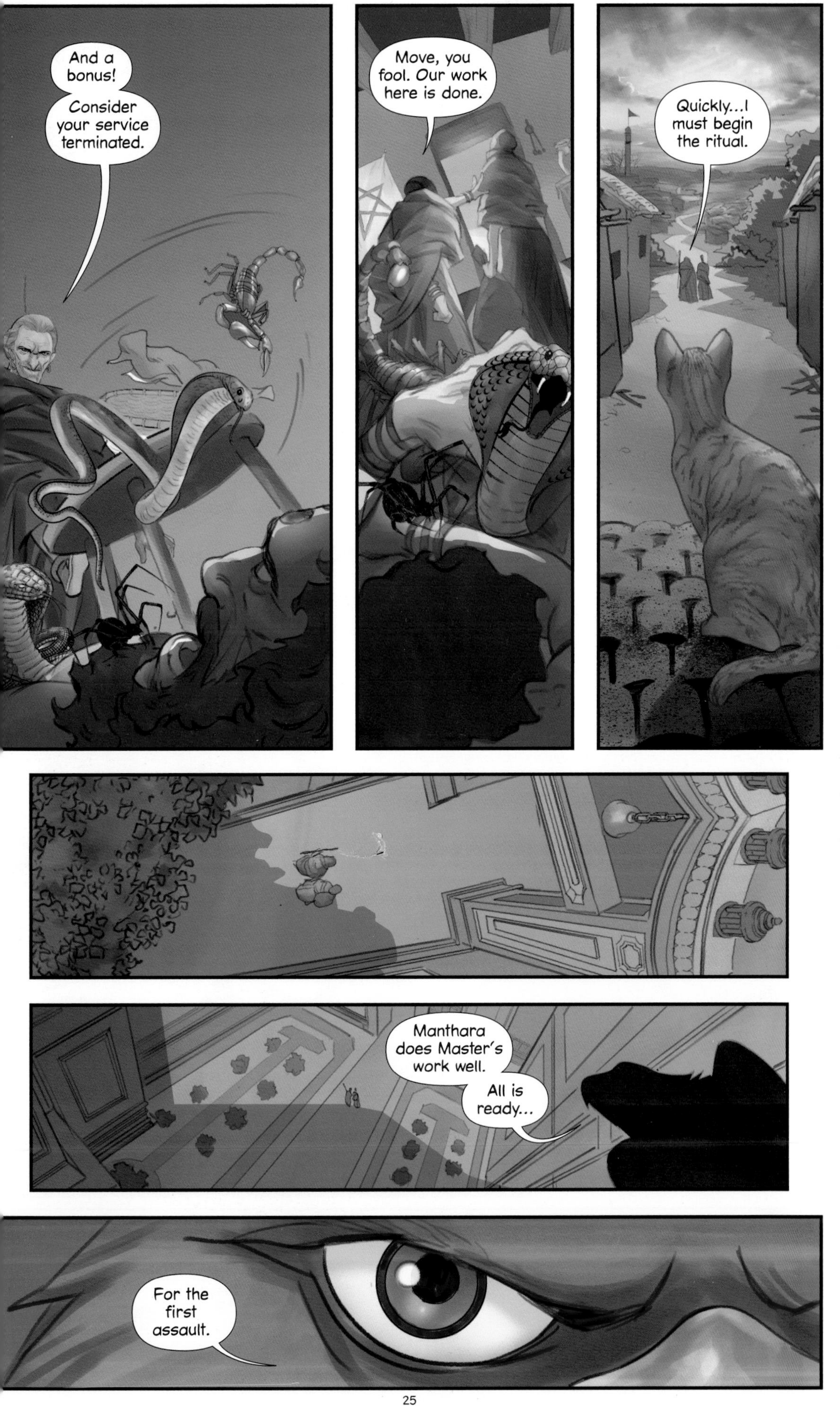
And a bonus!
Consider your service terminated.
Move, you fool. Our work here is done.
Quickly...I must begin the ritual.
Manthara does Master's work well.
All is ready...
For the first assault.

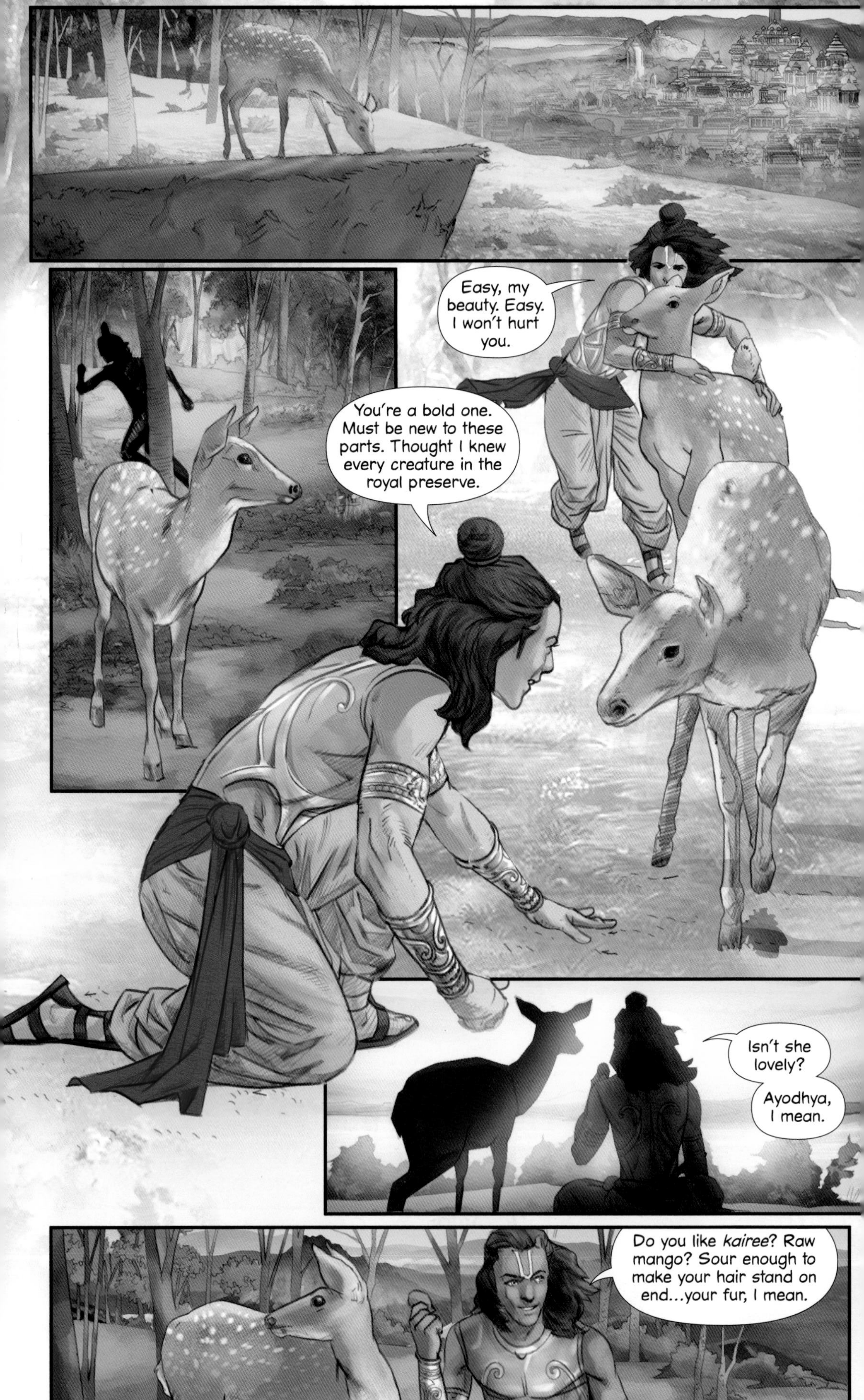
Easy, my beauty. Easy. I won't hurt you.
You're a bold one. Must be new to these parts. Thought I knew every creature in the royal preserve.
Isn't she lovely?
Ayodhya, I mean.
Do you like *kairee*? Raw mango? Sour enough to make your hair stand on end...your fur, I mean.

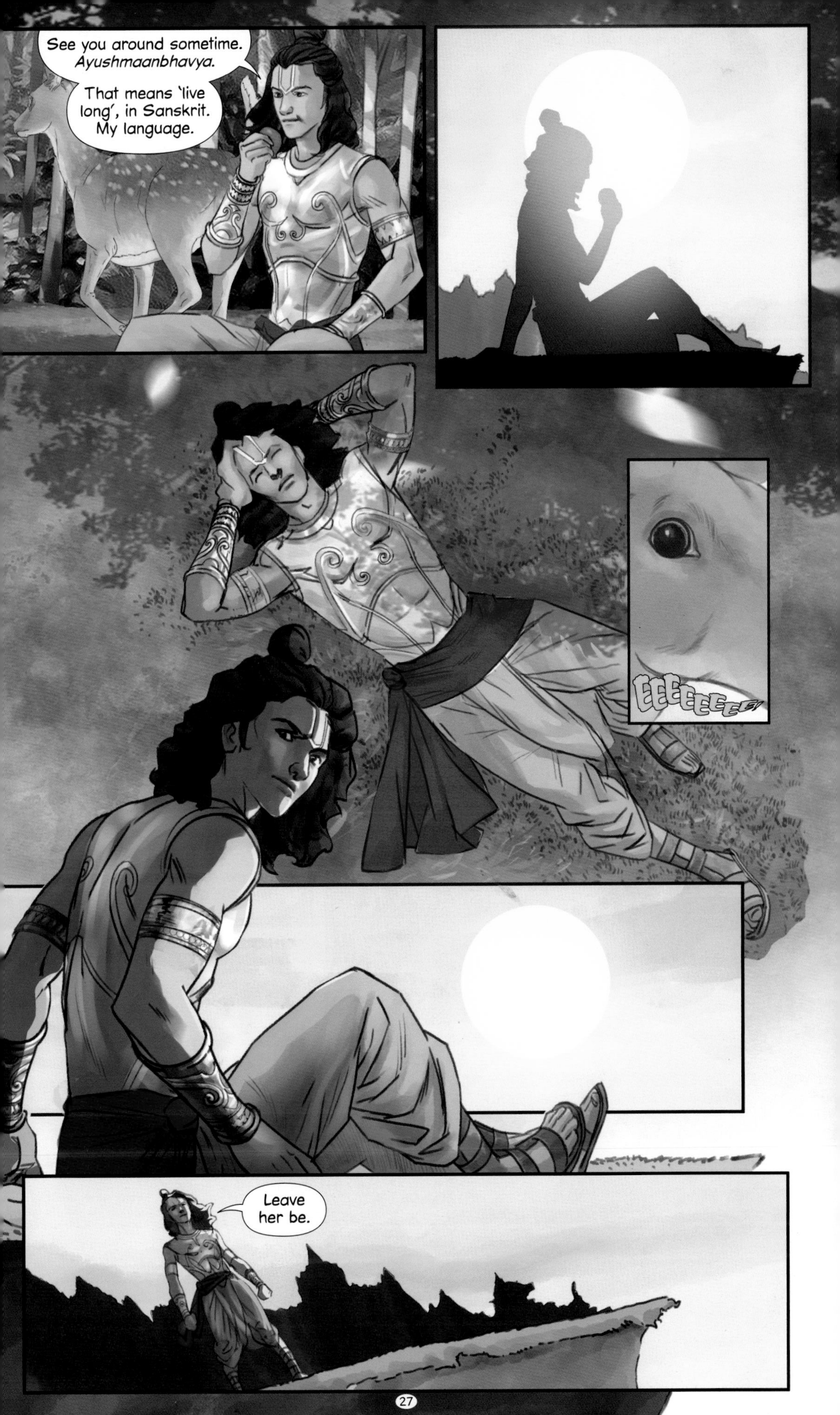

See you around sometime. *Ayushmaanbhavya.*
That means 'live long', in Sanskrit. My language.
EEEEEEEE!
Leave her be.

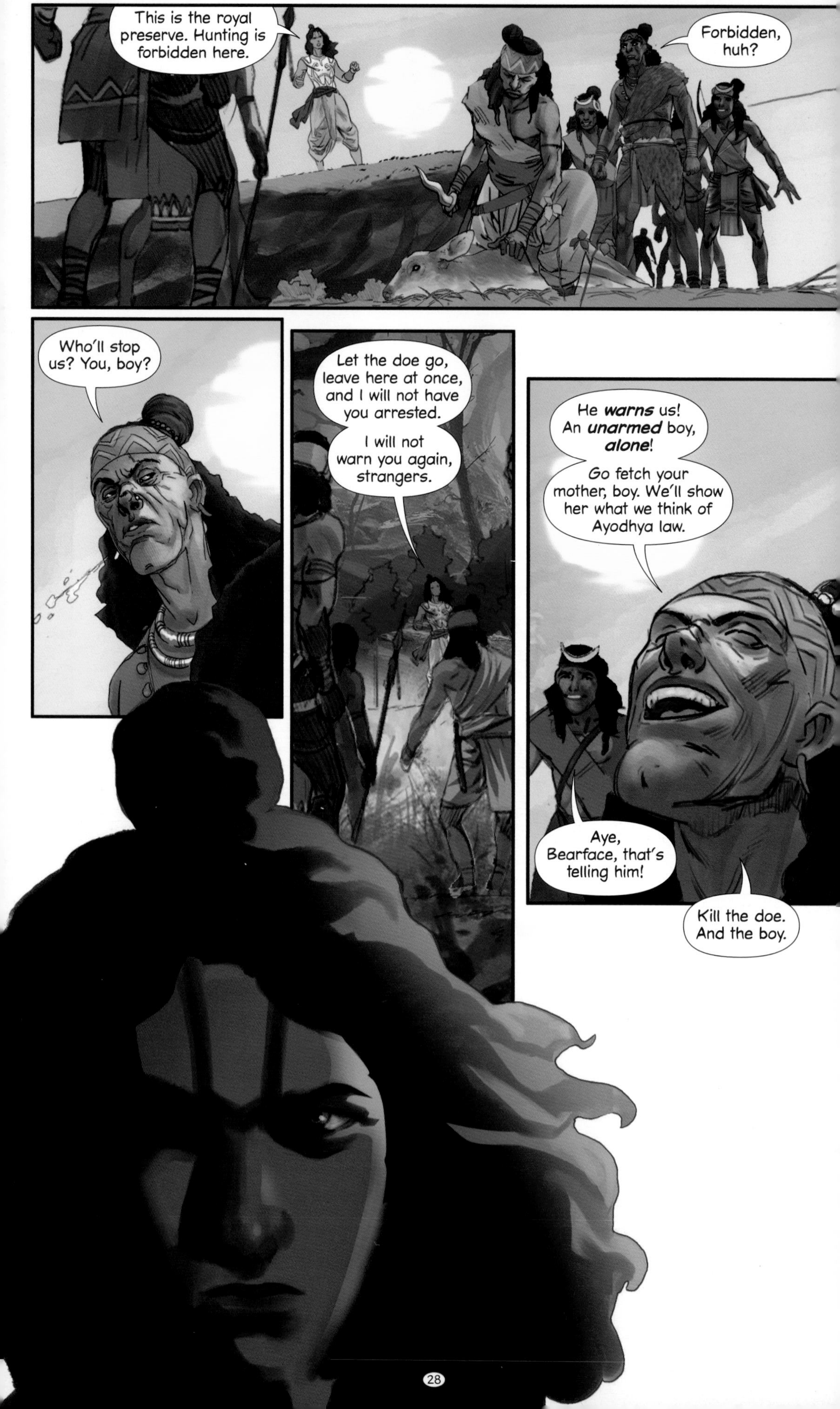
This is the royal preserve. Hunting is forbidden here.
Forbidden, huh?
Who'll stop us? You, boy?
Let the doe go, leave here at once, and I will not have you arrested.
I will not warn you again, strangers.
He **warns** us! An **unarmed** boy, **alone**!
Go fetch your mother, boy. We'll show her what we think of Ayodhya law.
Aye, Bearface, that's telling him!
Kill the doe. And the boy.

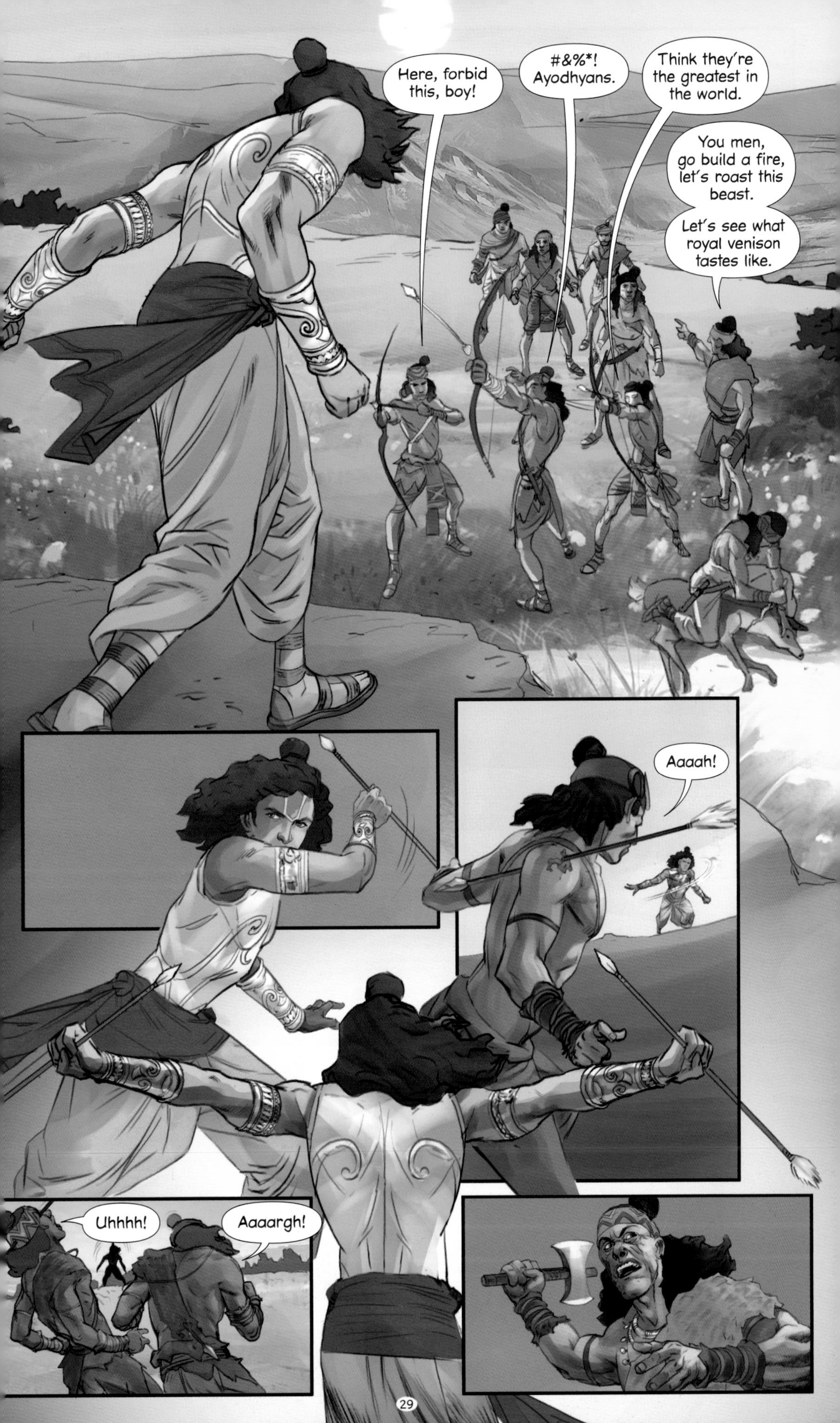
Here, forbid this, boy!
#&%*! Ayodhyans.
Think they're the greatest in the world.
You men, go build a fire, let's roast this beast.
Let's see what royal venison tastes like.
Aaaah!
Uhhhh!
Aaaargh!

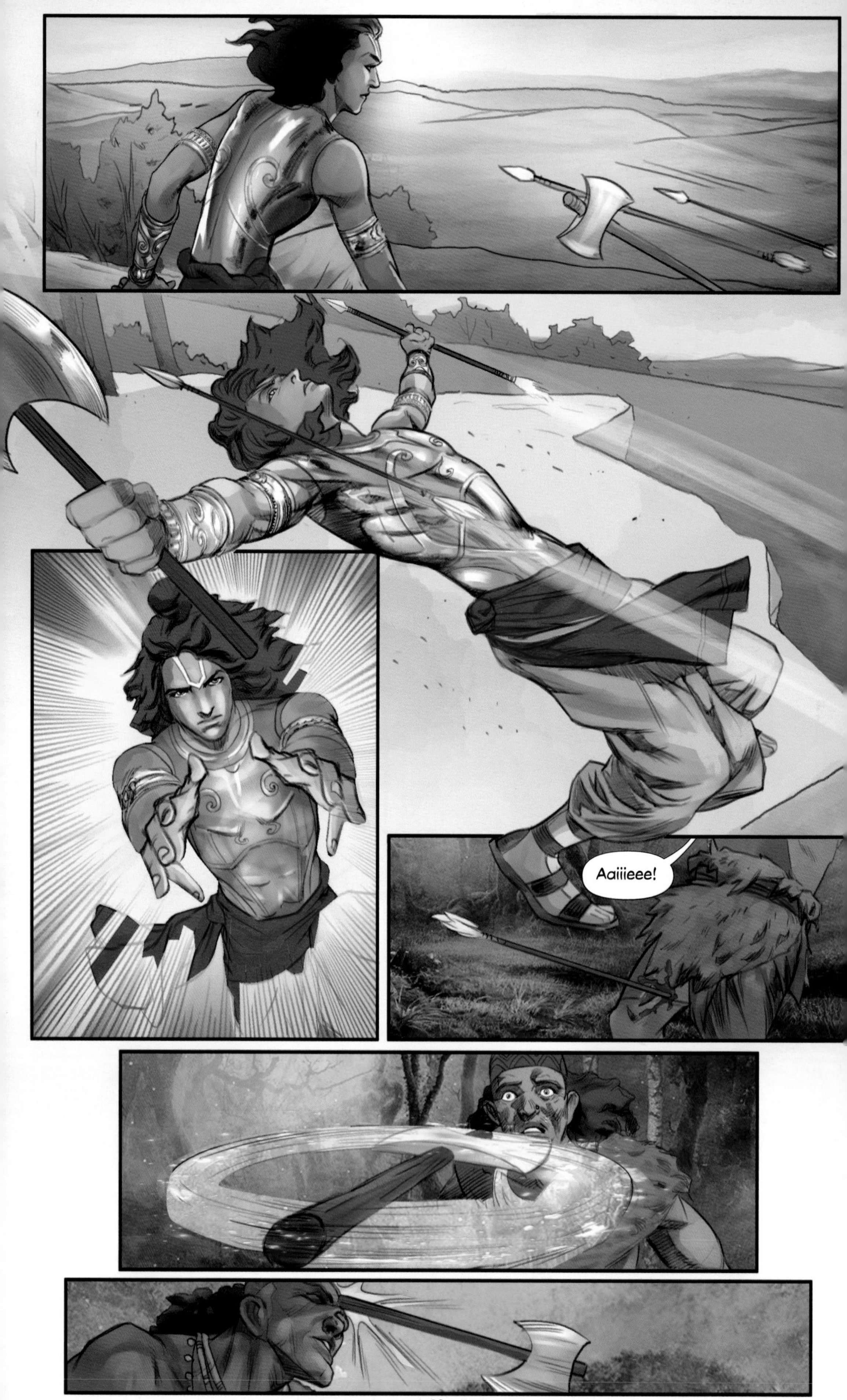
Aaiiieee!

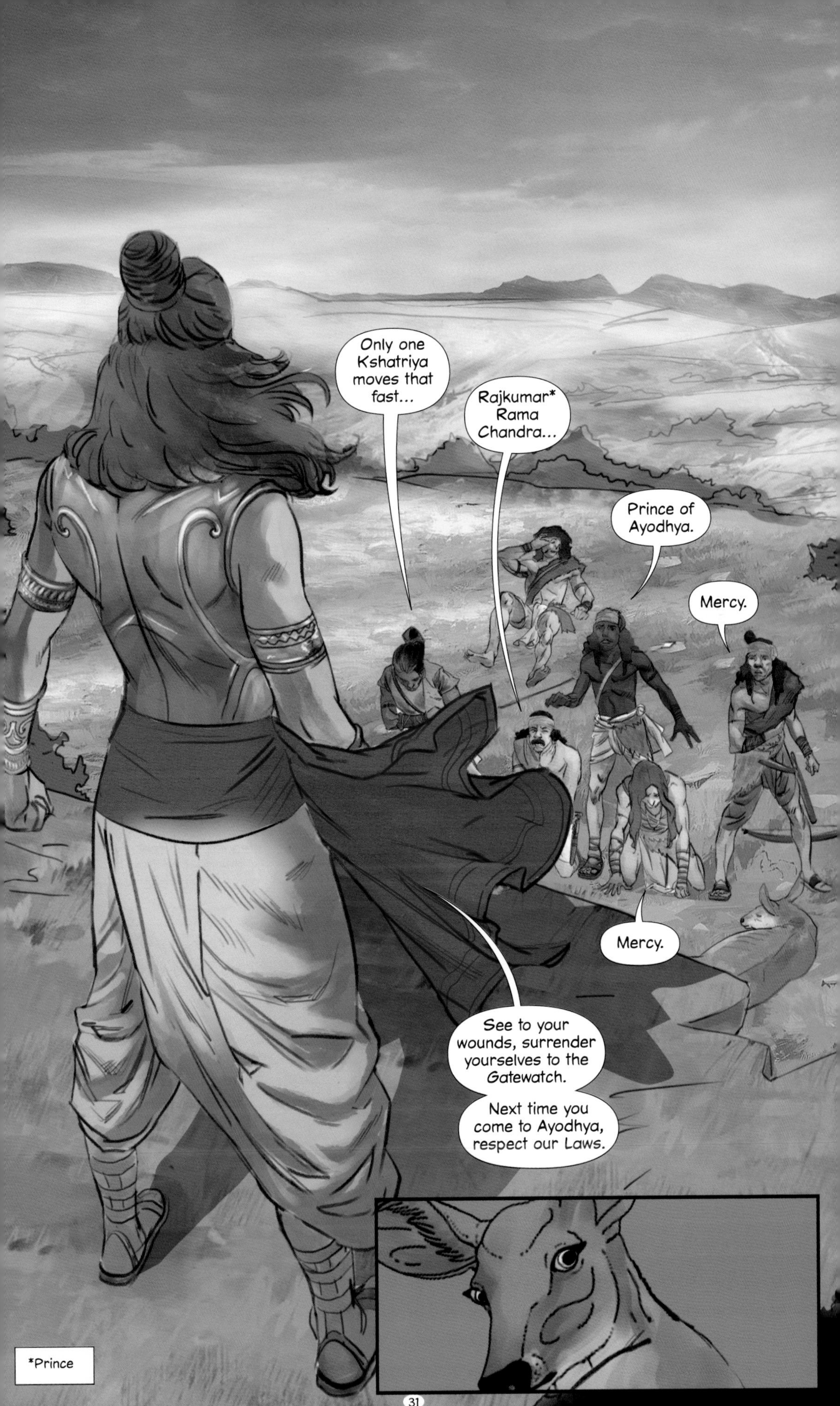
Only one Kshatriya moves that fast...
Rajkumar* Rama Chandra...
Prince of Ayodhya.
Mercy.
Mercy.
See to your wounds, surrender yourselves to the Gatewatch.
Next time you come to Ayodhya, respect our Laws.

*Prince

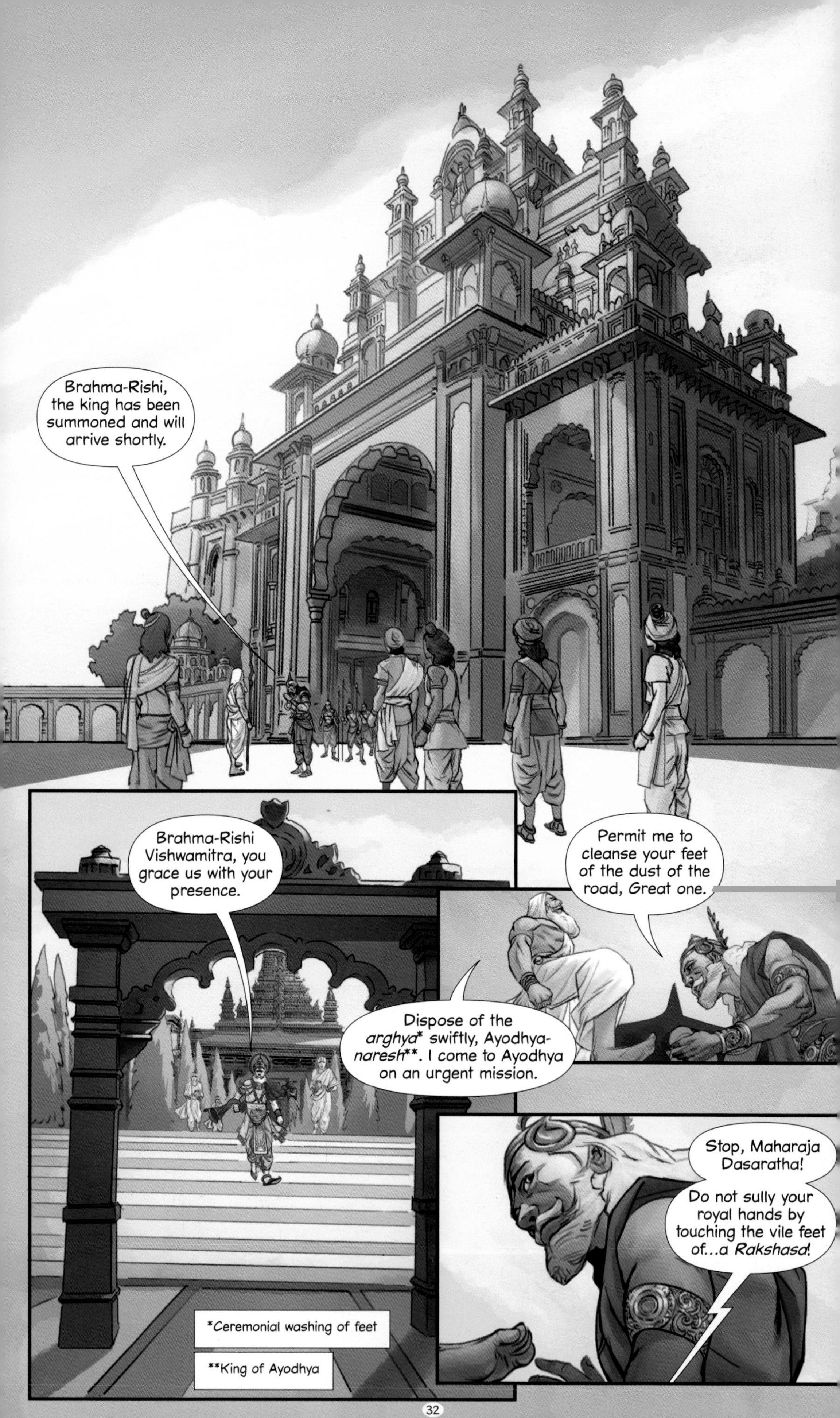
Brahma-Rishi, the king has been summoned and will arrive shortly.
Brahma-Rishi Vishwamitra, you grace us with your presence.
Dispose of the *arghya** swiftly, Ayodhya-*naresh***. I come to Ayodhya on an urgent mission.
Permit me to cleanse your feet of the dust of the road, Great one.
Stop, Maharaja Dasaratha!
Do not sully your royal hands by touching the vile feet of...a *Rakshasa*!
*Ceremonial washing of feet
**King of Ayodhya

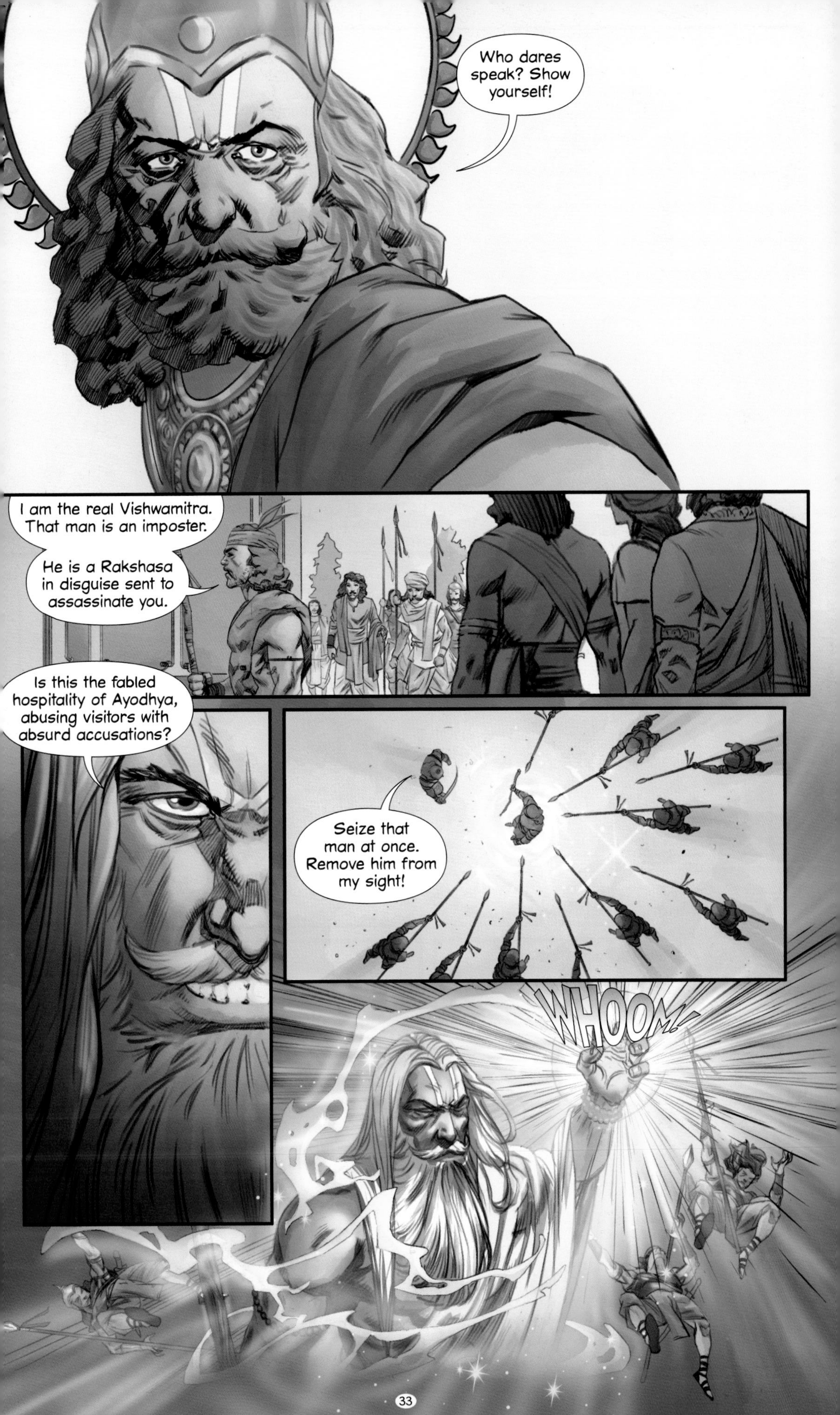

Who dares speak? Show yourself!
I am the real Vishwamitra. That man is an imposter.
He is a Rakshasa in disguise sent to assassinate you.
Is this the fabled hospitality of Ayodhya, abusing visitors with absurd accusations?
Seize that man at once. Remove him from my sight!
WHOOM!

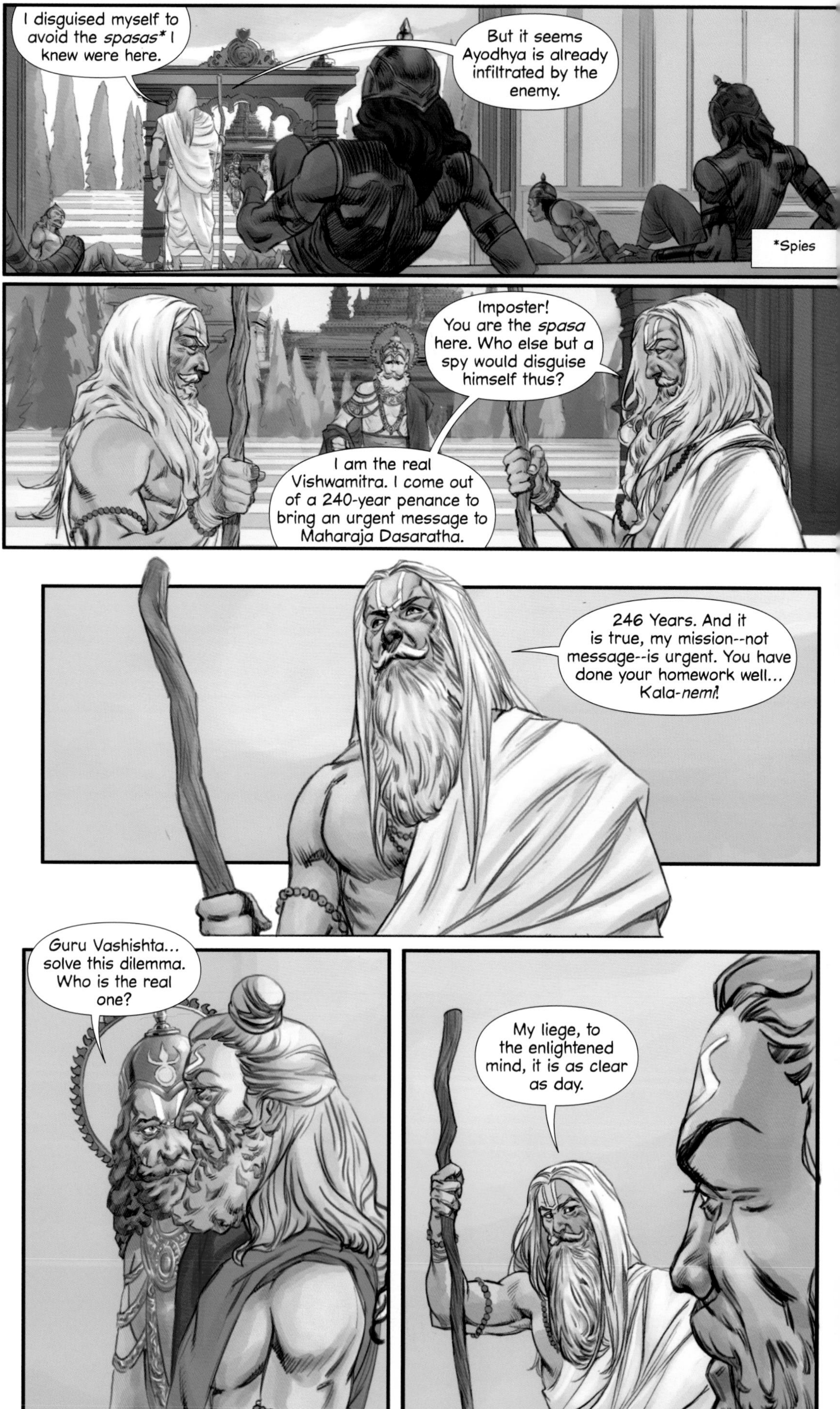
I disguised myself to avoid the spasas* I knew were here.
But it seems Ayodhya is already infiltrated by the enemy.
*Spies
Imposter! You are the spasa here. Who else but a spy would disguise himself thus?
I am the real Vishwamitra. I come out of a 240-year penance to bring an urgent message to Maharaja Dasaratha.
246 Years. And it is true, my mission--not message--is urgent. You have done your homework well... Kala-nemi!
Guru Vashishta... solve this dilemma. Who is the real one?
My liege, to the enlightened mind, it is as clear as day.

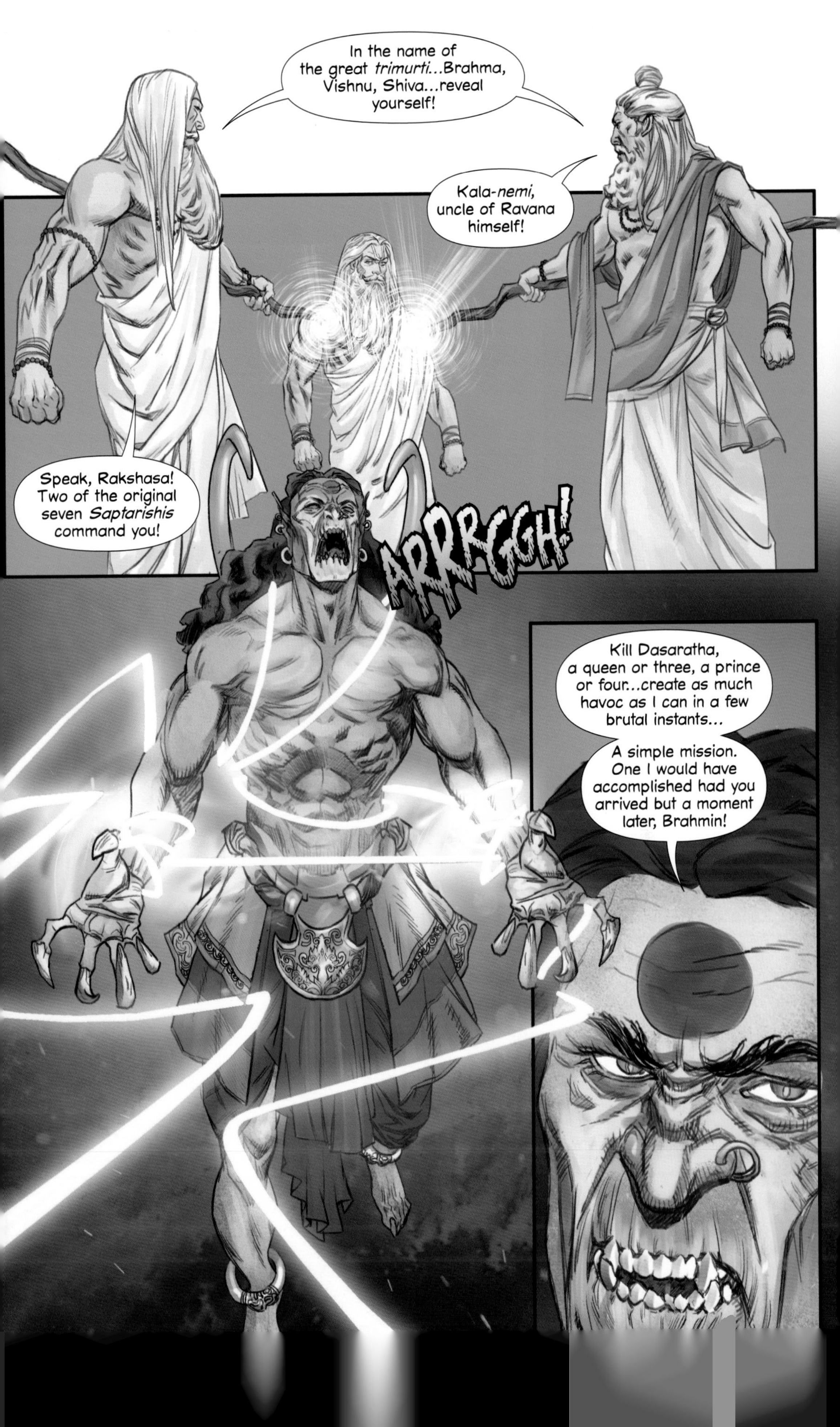
In the name of the great *trimurti*...Brahma, Vishnu, Shiva...reveal yourself!
Kala-*nemi*, uncle of Ravana himself!
Speak, Rakshasa! Two of the original seven *Saptarishis* command you!
ARRRGGH!
Kill Dasaratha, a queen or three, a prince or four...create as much havoc as I can in a few brutal instants...
A simple mission. One I would have accomplished had you arrived but a moment later, Brahmin!

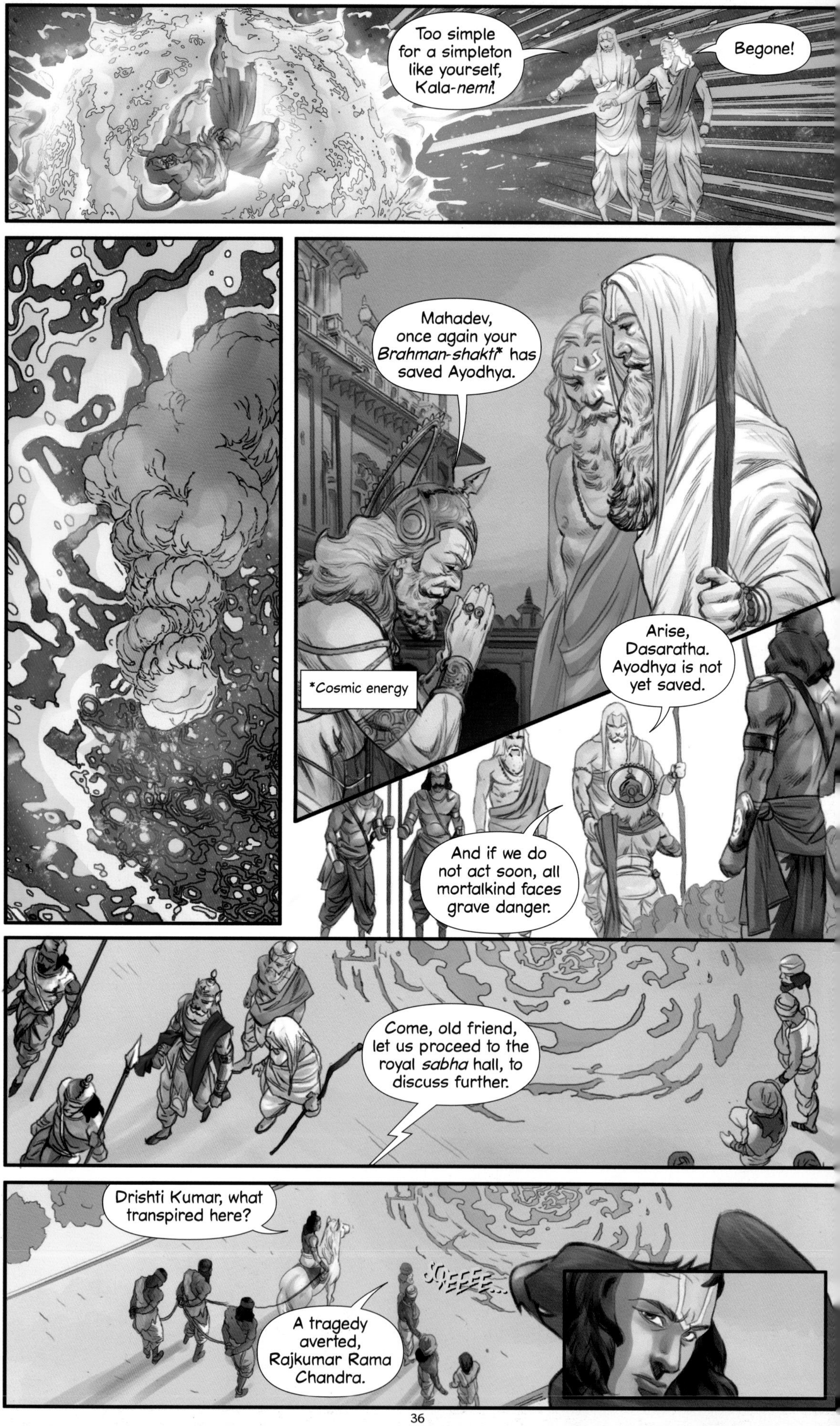
Too simple for a simpleton like yourself, Kala-*nemi*!
Begone!
Mahadev, once again your *Brahman-shakti** has saved Ayodhya.
*Cosmic energy
Arise, Dasaratha. Ayodhya is not yet saved.
And if we do not act soon, all mortalkind faces grave danger.
Come, old friend, let us proceed to the royal *sabha* hall, to discuss further.
Drishti Kumar, what transpired here?
SQEEEE...
A tragedy averted, Rajkumar Rama Chandra.

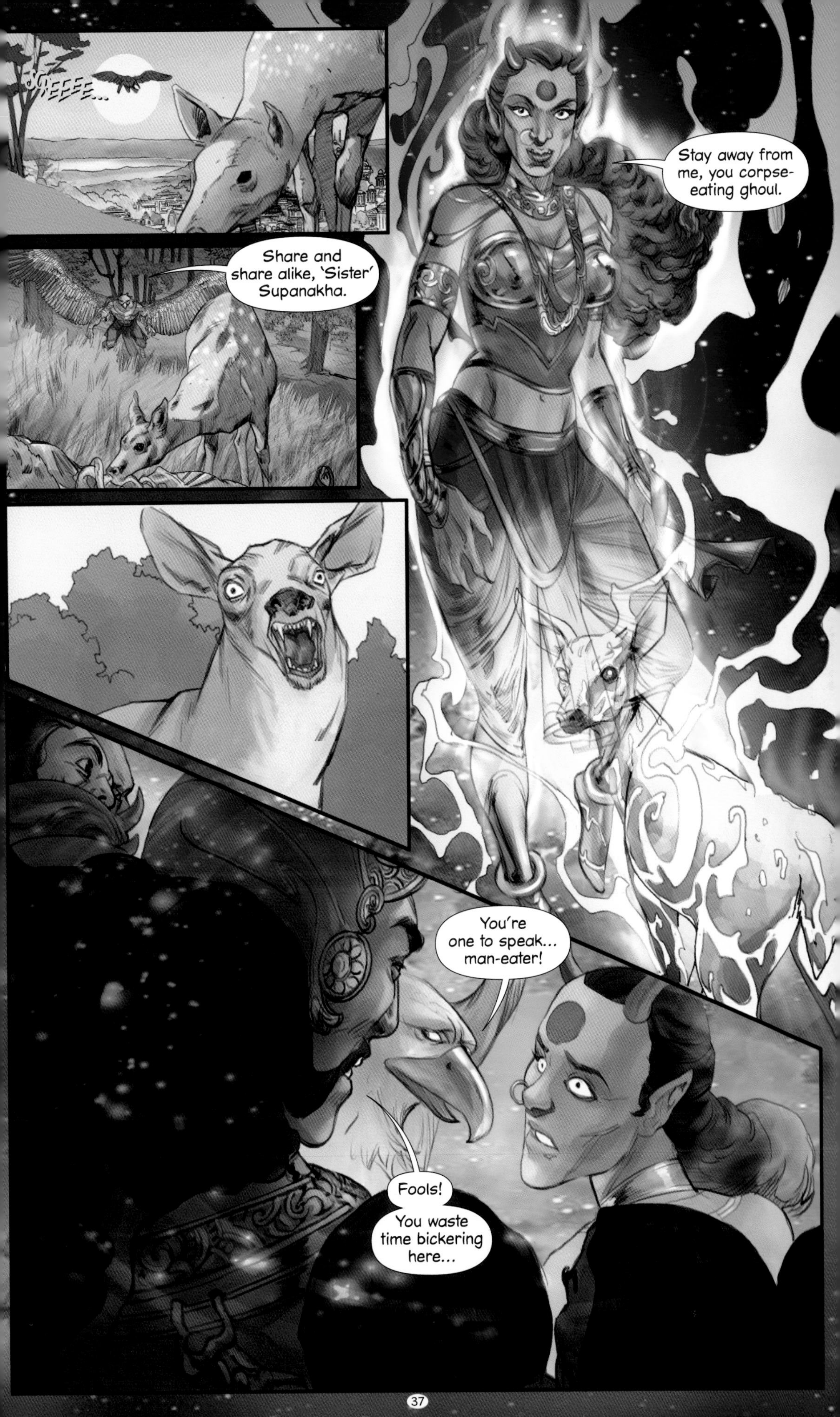
SCREEEE...
Share and share alike, 'Sister' Supanakha.
Stay away from me, you corpse-eating ghoul.
You're one to speak... man-eater!
Fools!
You waste time bickering here...

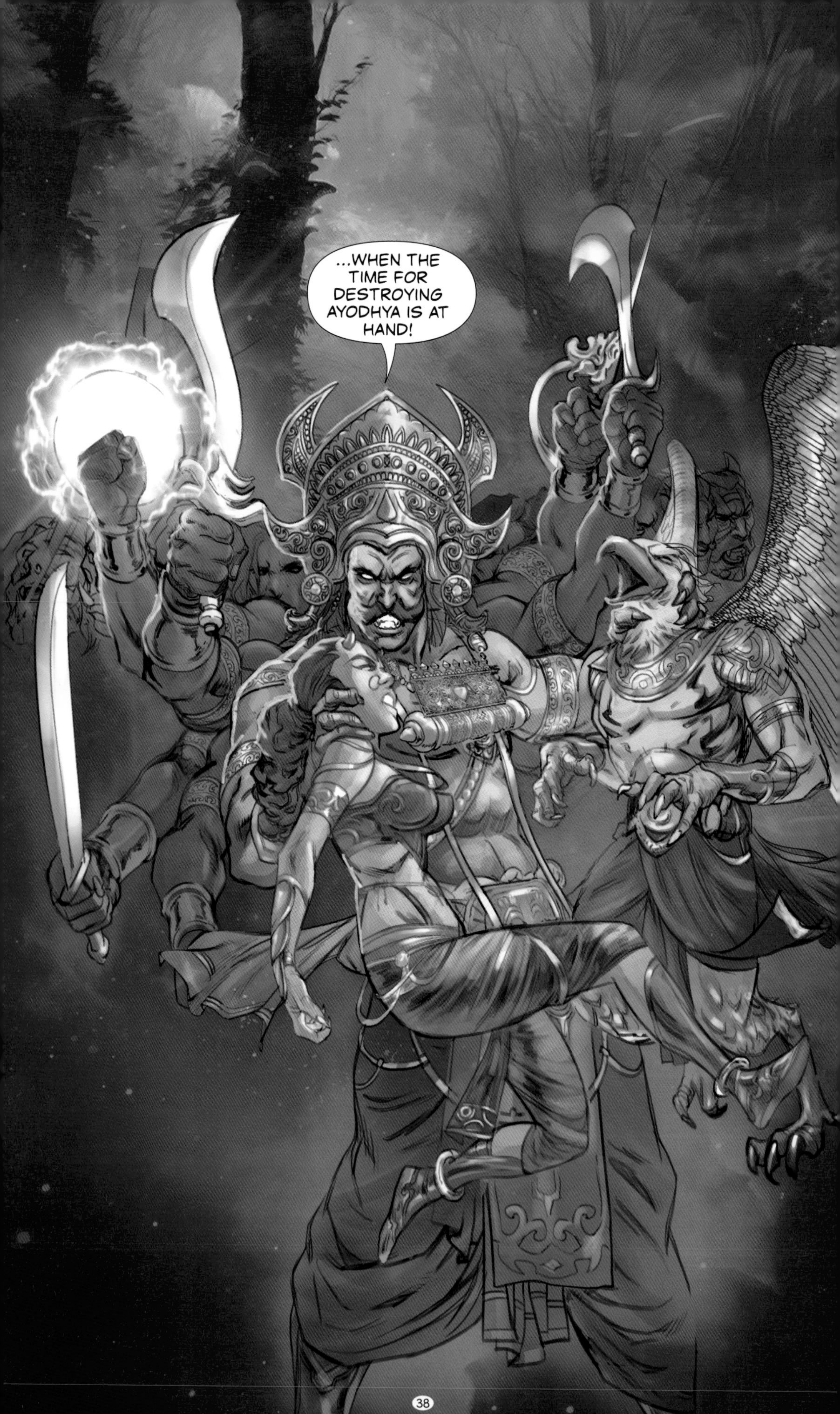
...WHEN THE TIME FOR DESTROYING AYODHYA IS AT HAND!

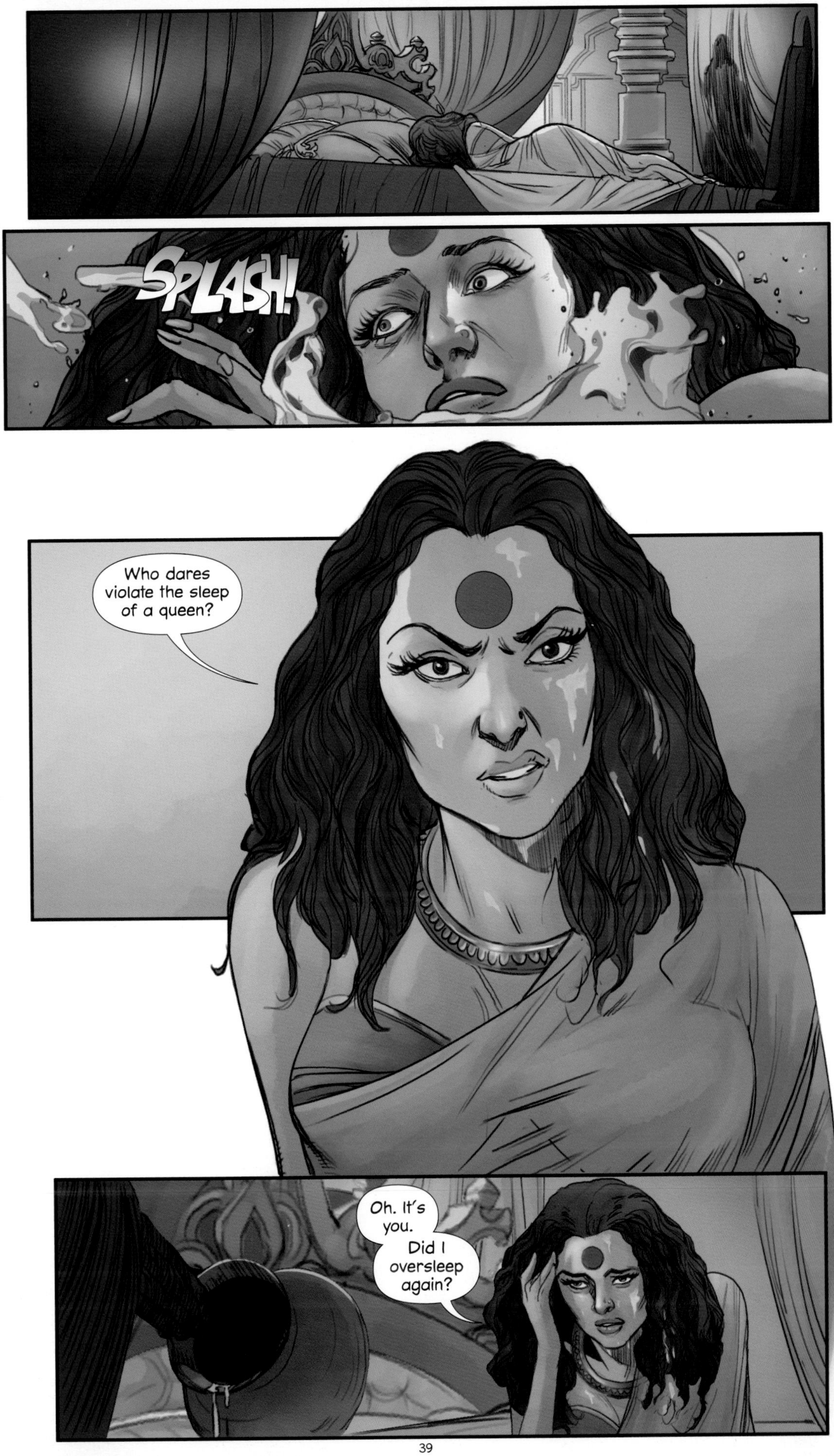
SPLASH!
Who dares violate the sleep of a queen?
Oh. It's you.
Did I oversleep again?

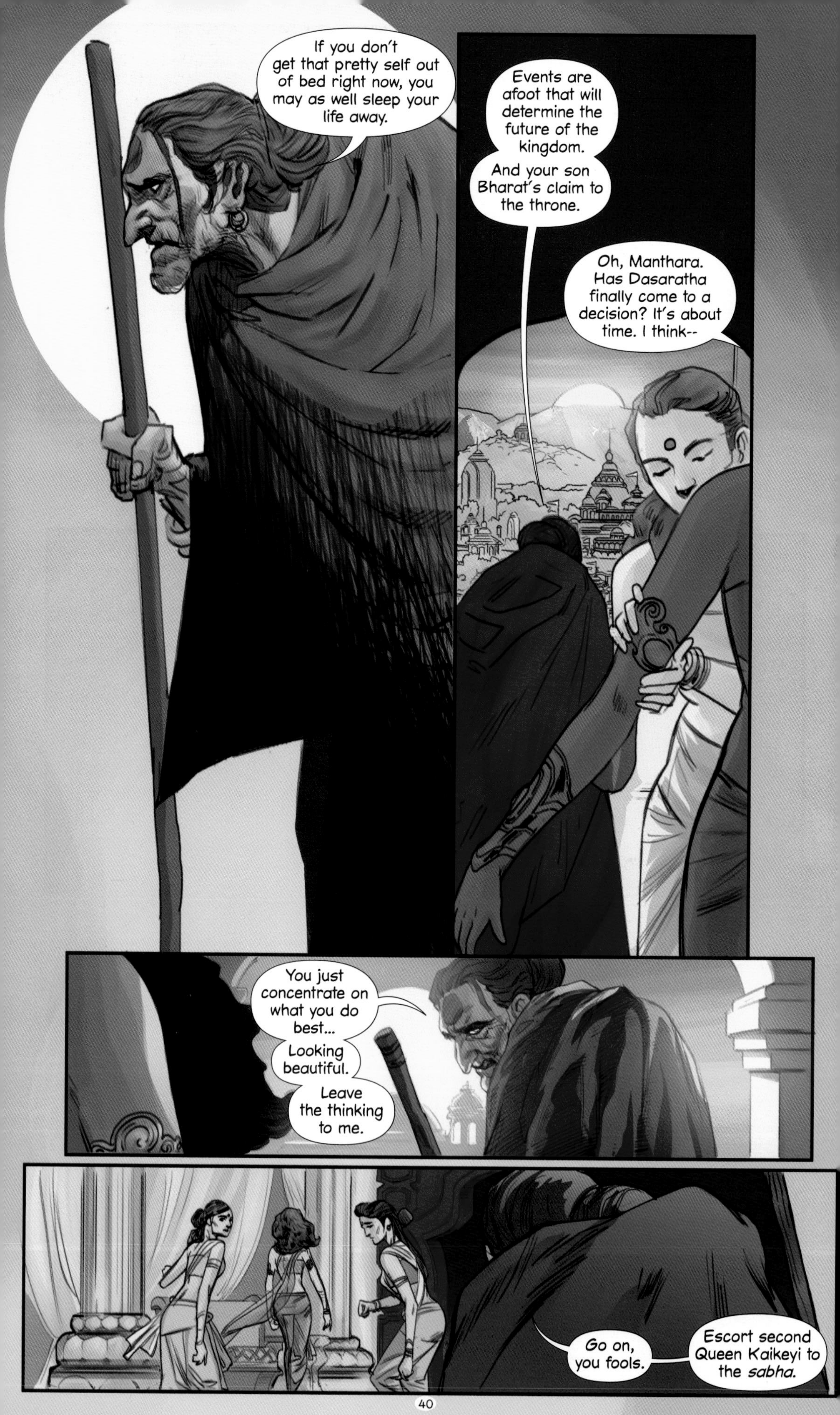

If you don't get that pretty self out of bed right now, you may as well sleep your life away.
Events are afoot that will determine the future of the kingdom.
And your son Bharat's claim to the throne.
Oh, Manthara. Has Dasaratha finally come to a decision? It's about time. I think--
You just concentrate on what you do best...
Looking beautiful.
Leave the thinking to me.
Escort second Queen Kaikeyi to the *sabha*.
Go on, you fools.

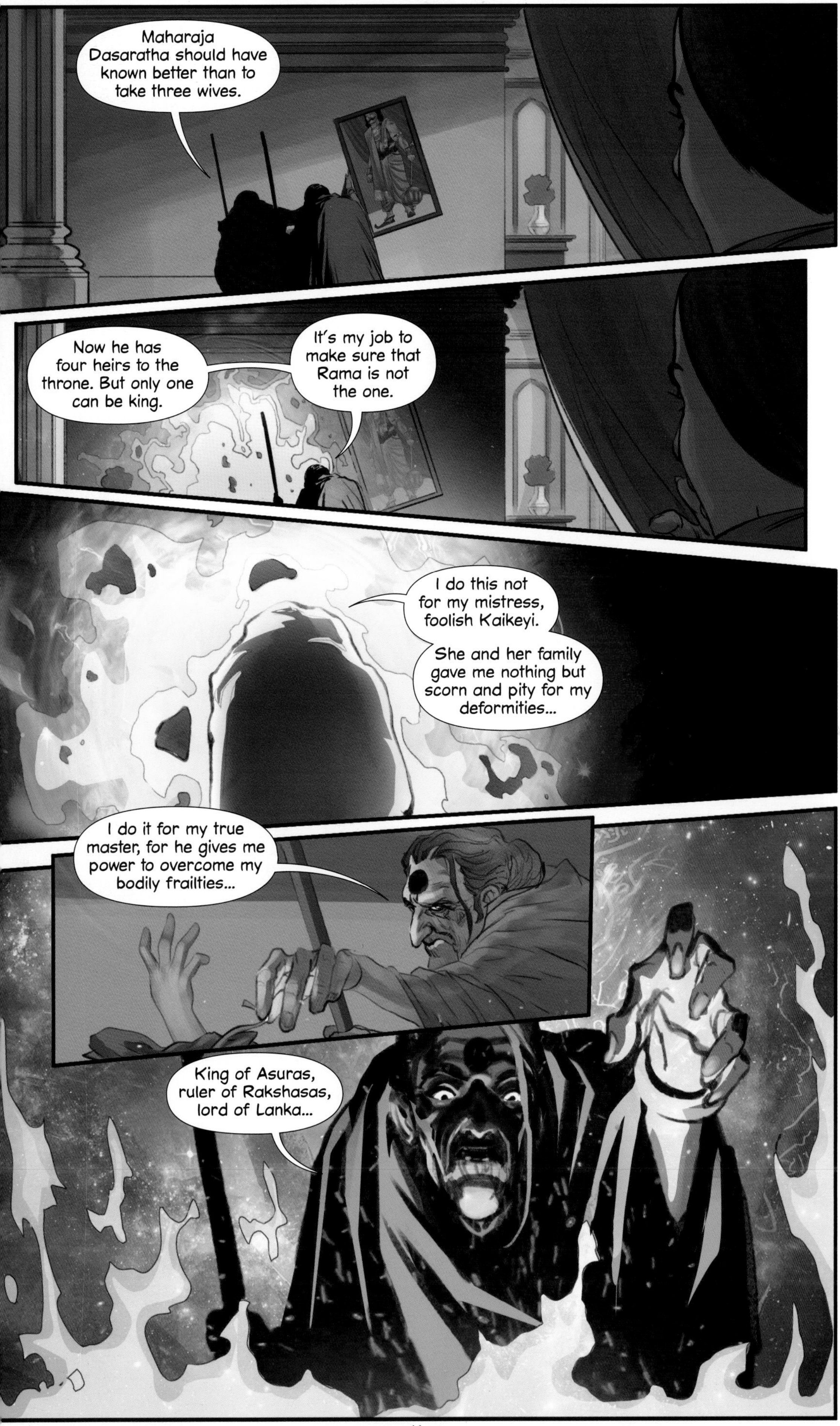
Maharaja Dasaratha should have known better than to take three wives.
Now he has four heirs to the throne. But only one can be king.
It's my job to make sure that Rama is not the one.
I do this not for my mistress, foolish Kaikeyi.
She and her family gave me nothing but scorn and pity for my deformities...
I do it for my true master, for he gives me power to overcome my bodily frailties...
King of Asuras, ruler of Rakshasas, lord of Lanka...

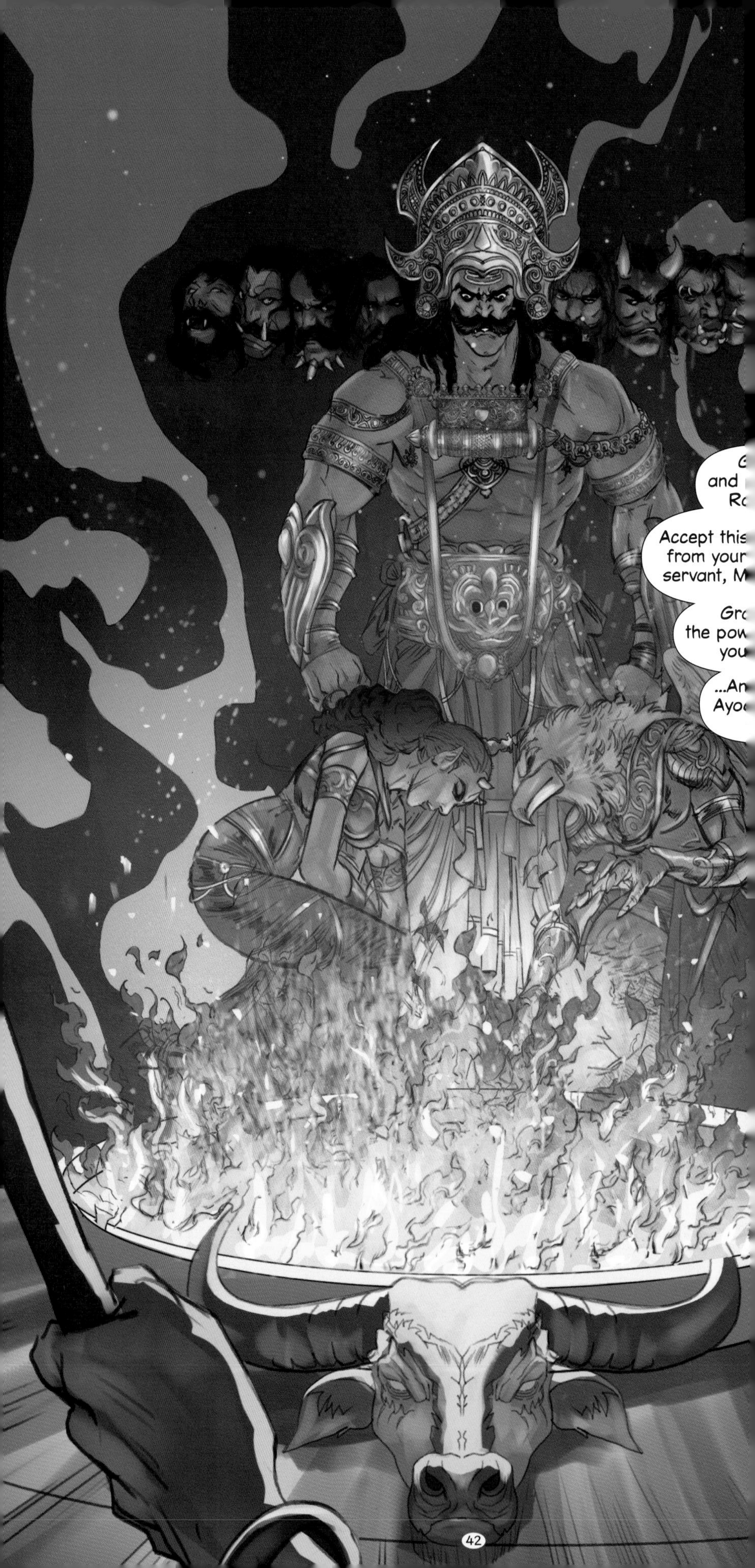
and
Accept this
from your
servant,

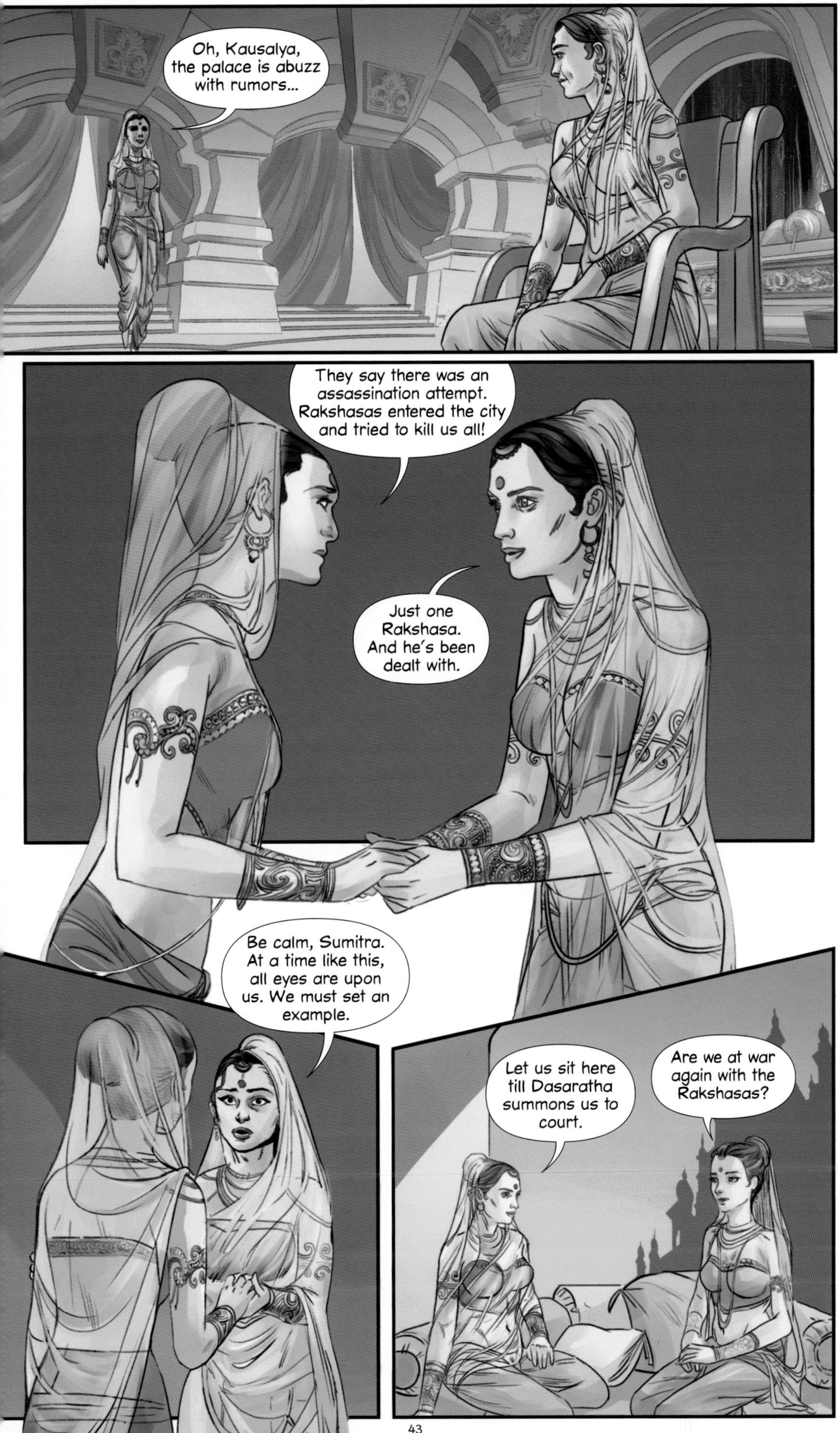
Oh, Kausalya, the palace is abuzz with rumors...
They say there was an assassination attempt. Rakshasas entered the city and tried to kill us all!
Just one Rakshasa. And he's been dealt with.
Be calm, Sumitra. At a time like this, all eyes are upon us. We must set an example.
Let us sit here till Dasaratha summons us to court.
Are we at war again with the Rakshasas?

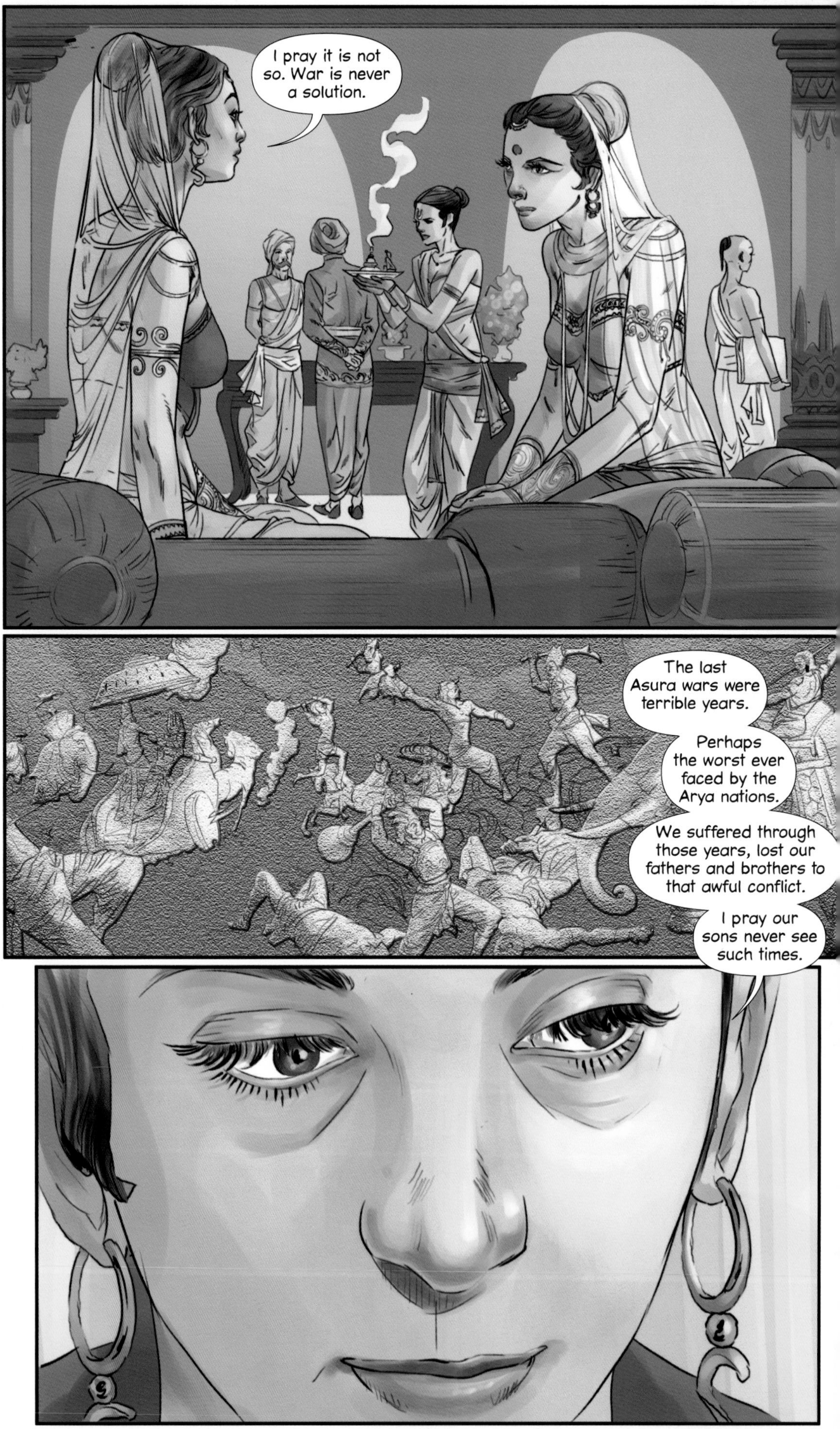
I pray it is not so. War is never a solution.
The last Asura wars were terrible years.
Perhaps the worst ever faced by the Arya nations.
We suffered through those years, lost our fathers and brothers to that awful conflict.
I pray our sons never see such times.

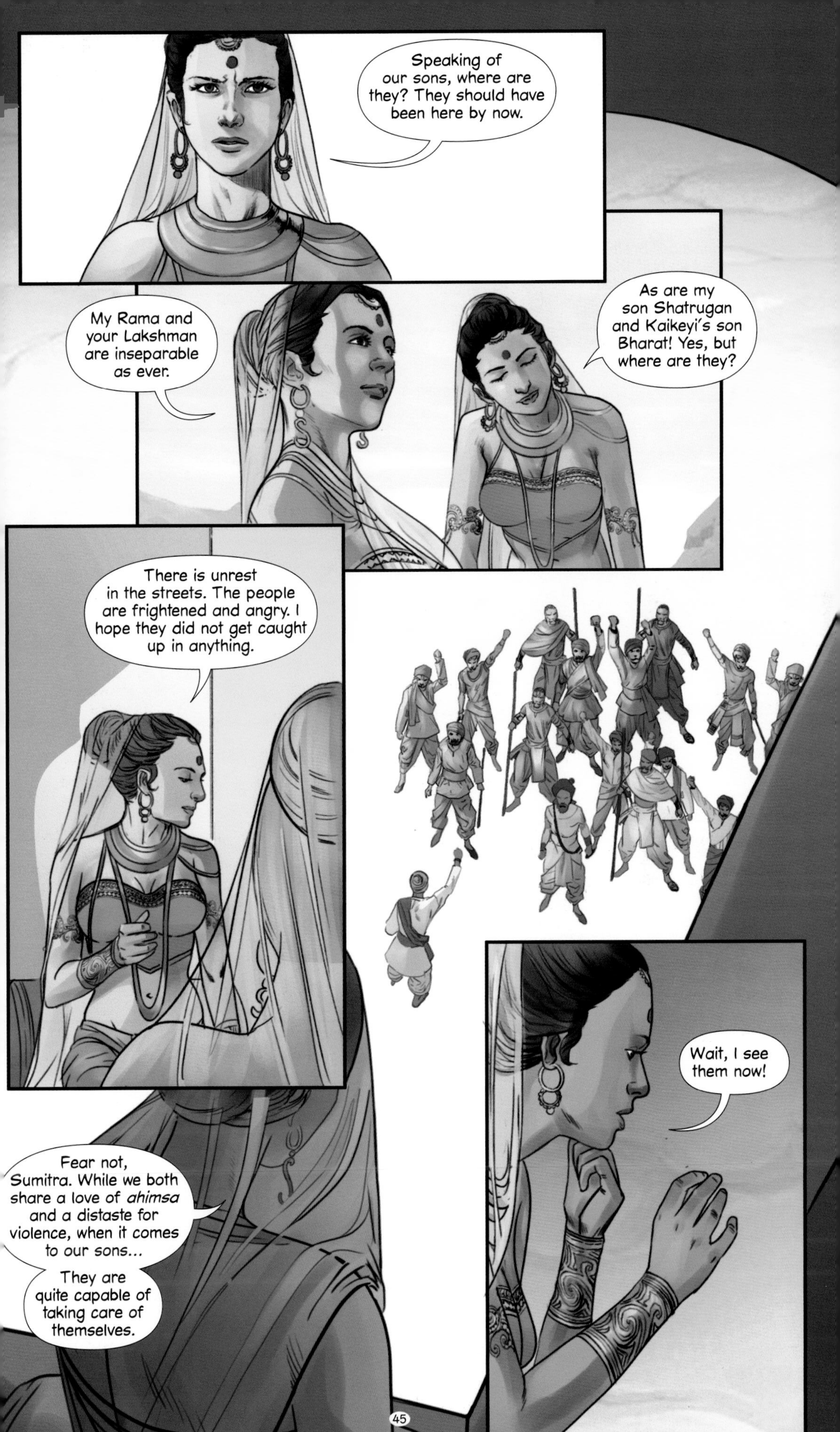
Speaking of our sons, where are they? They should have been here by now.
My Rama and your Lakshman are inseparable as ever.
As are my son Shatrugan and Kaikeyi's son Bharat! Yes, but where are they?
There is unrest in the streets. The people are frightened and angry. I hope they did not get caught up in anything.
Wait, I see them now!
Fear not, Sumitra. While we both share a love of *ahimsa* and a distaste for violence, when it comes to our sons...
They are quite capable of taking care of themselves.

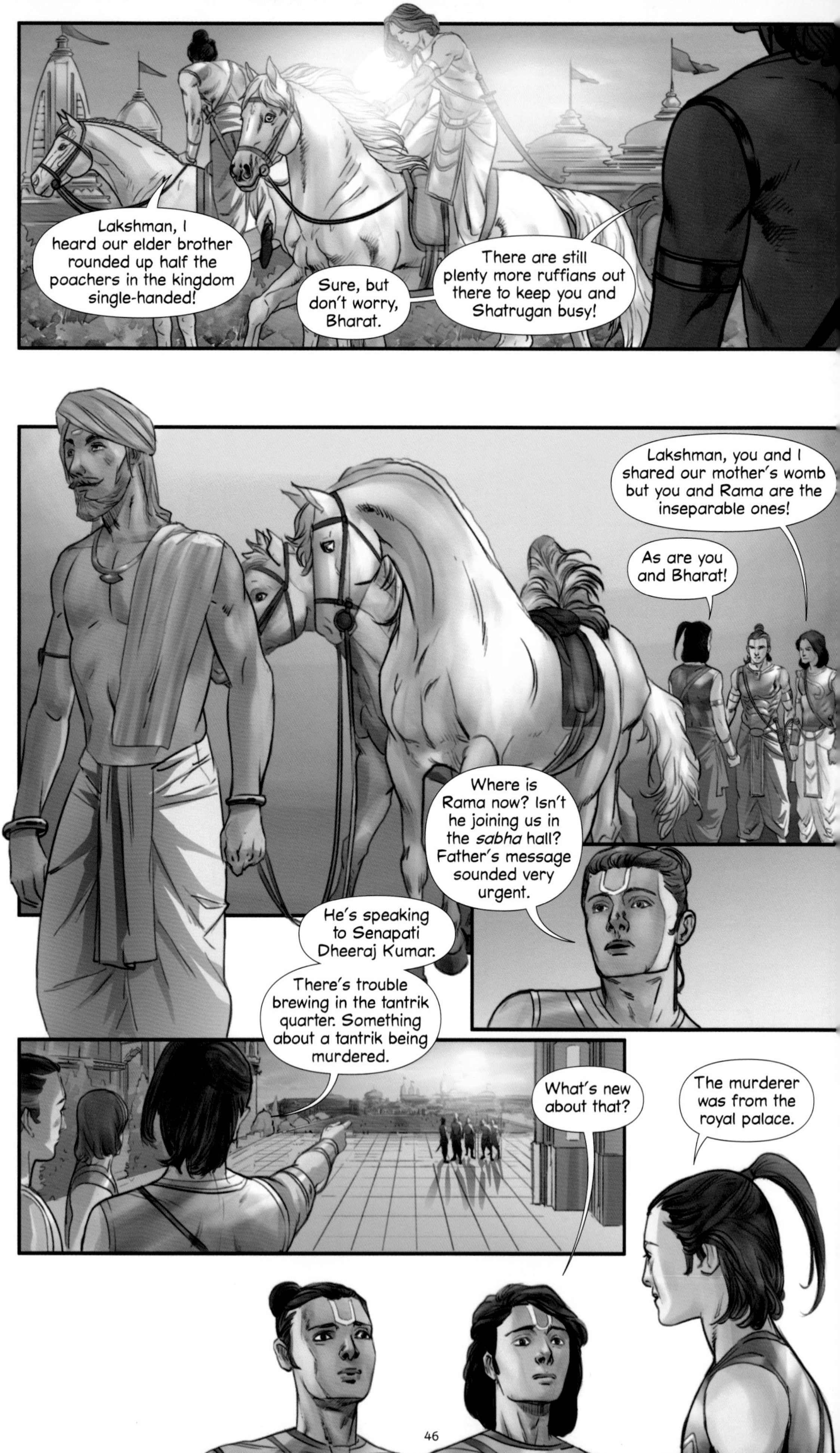

Lakshman, I heard our elder brother rounded up half the poachers in the kingdom single-handed!
Sure, but don't worry, Bharat.
There are still plenty more ruffians out there to keep you and Shatrugan busy!
Lakshman, you and I shared our mother's womb but you and Rama are the inseparable ones!
As are you and Bharat!
Where is Rama now? Isn't he joining us in the *sabha* hall? Father's message sounded very urgent.
He's speaking to Senapati Dheeraj Kumar.
There's trouble brewing in the tantrik quarter. Something about a tantrik being murdered.
What's new about that?
The murderer was from the royal palace.

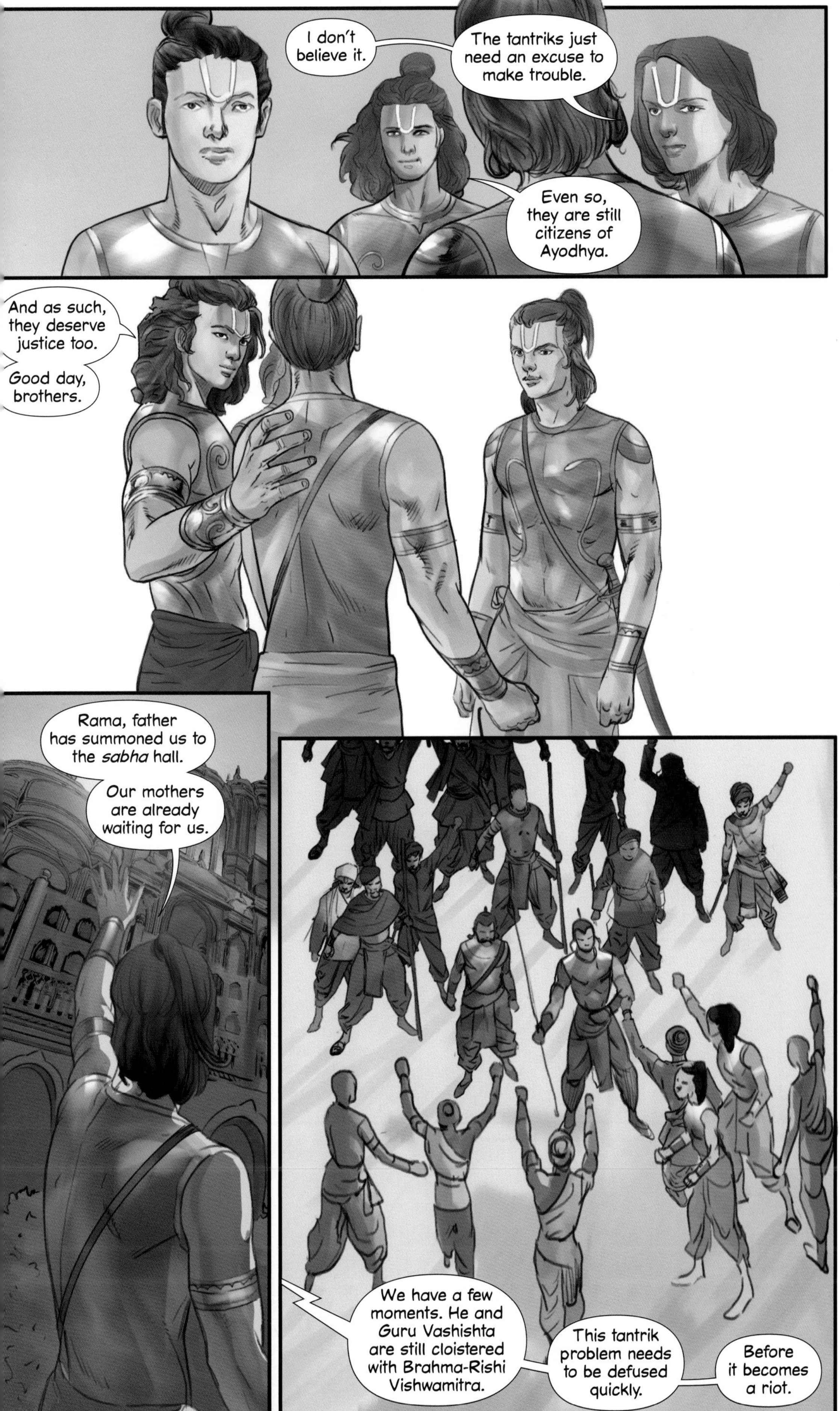

I don't believe it.
The tantriks just need an excuse to make trouble.
Even so, they are still citizens of Ayodhya.
And as such, they deserve justice too.
Good day, brothers.
Rama, father has summoned us to the *sabha* hall.
Our mothers are already waiting for us.
We have a few moments. He and Guru Vashishta are still cloistered with Brahma-Rishi Vishwamitra.
This tantrik problem needs to be defused quickly.
Before it becomes a riot.

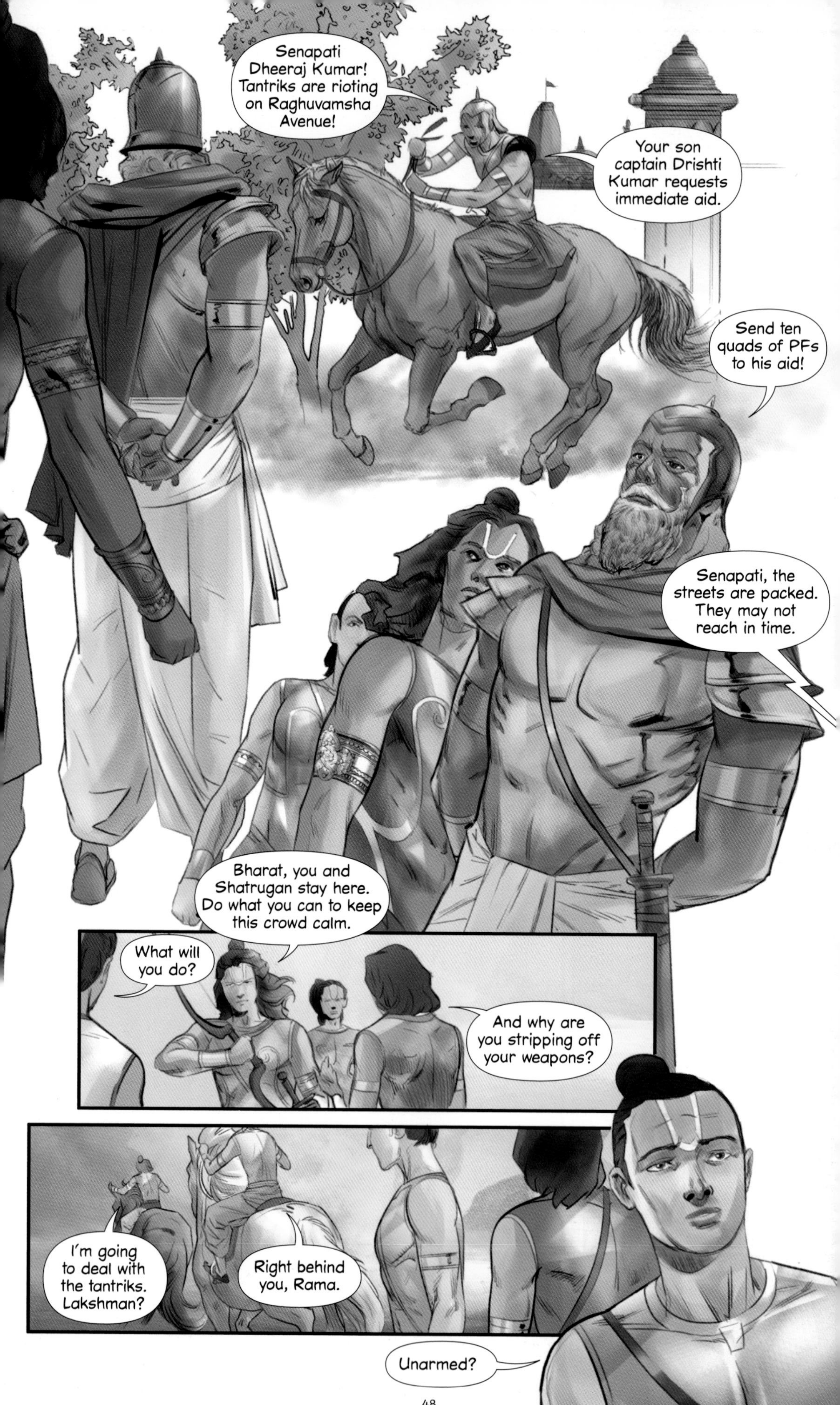
Senapati Dheeraj Kumar! Tantriks are rioting on Raghuvamsha Avenue!
Your son captain Drishti Kumar requests immediate aid.
Send ten quads of PFs to his aid!
Senapati, the streets are packed. They may not reach in time.
Bharat, you and Shatrugan stay here. Do what you can to keep this crowd calm.
What will you do?
And why are you stripping off your weapons?
I'm going to deal with the tantriks. Lakshman?
Right behind you, Rama.
Unarmed?

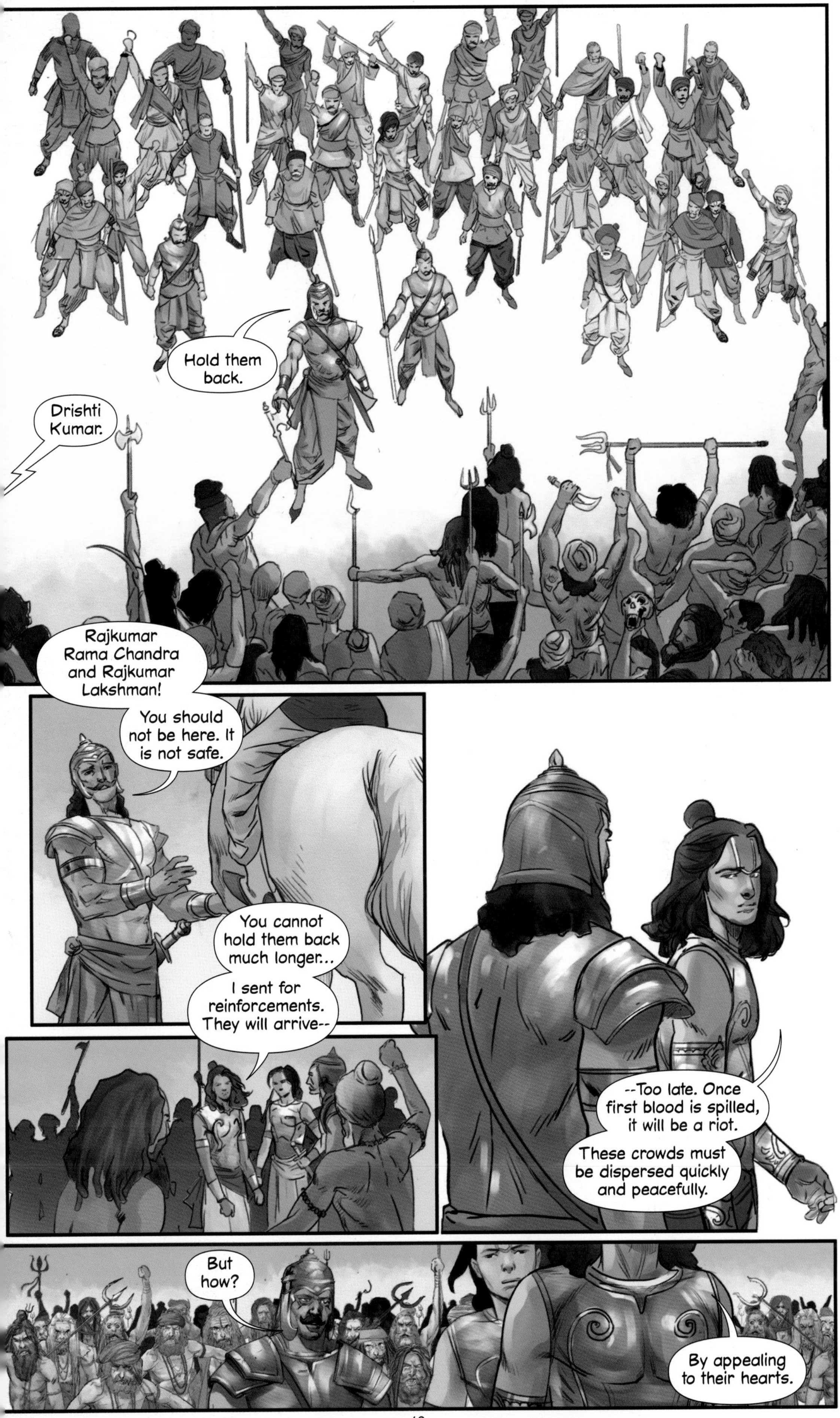
Hold them back.
Drishti Kumar.
Rajkumar Rama Chandra and Rajkumar Lakshman!
You should not be here. It is not safe.
You cannot hold them back much longer...
I sent for reinforcements. They will arrive--
--Too late. Once first blood is spilled, it will be a riot.
These crowds must be dispersed quickly and peacefully.
But how?
By appealing to their hearts.

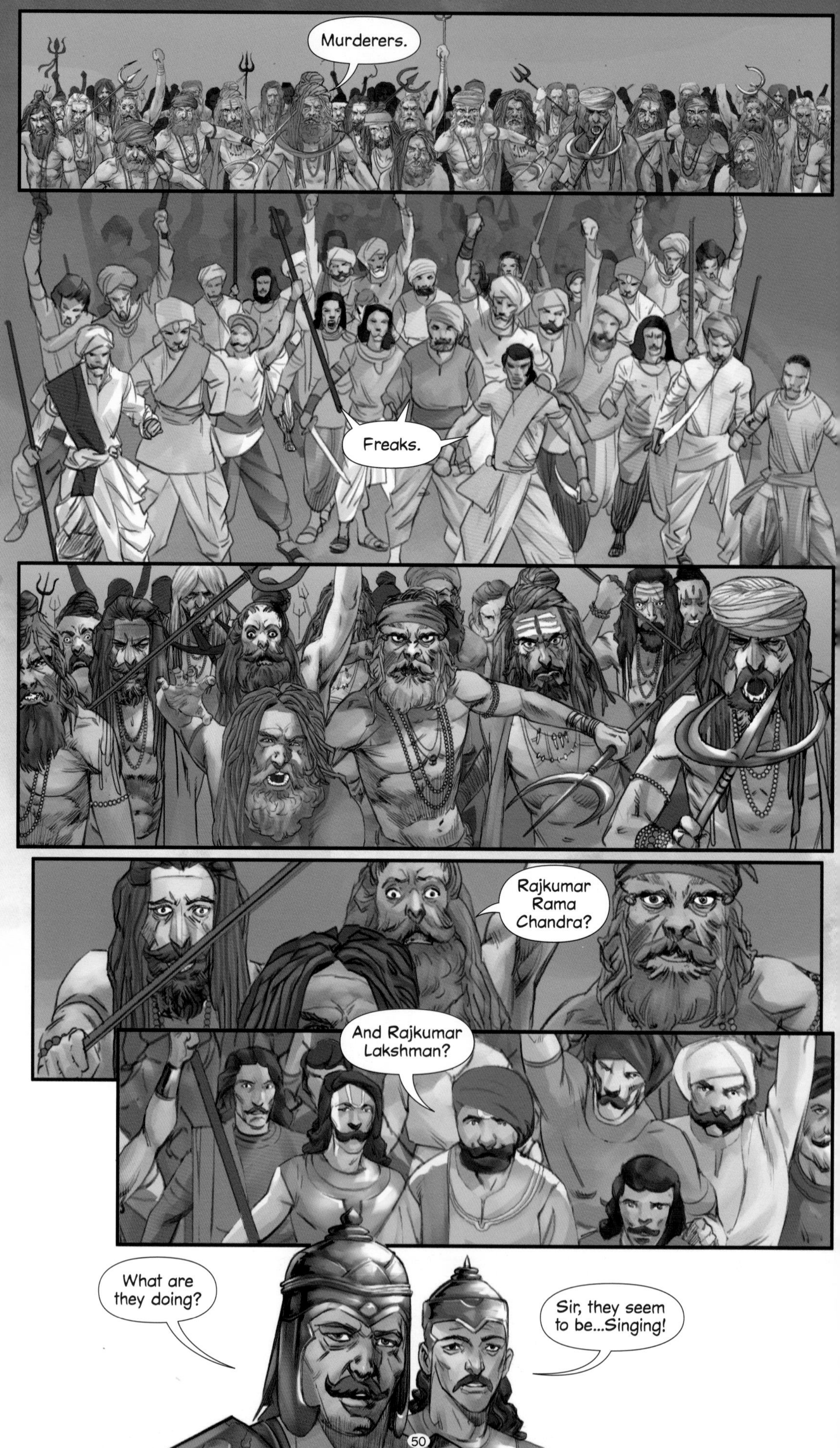
Murderers.
Freaks.
Rajkumar Rama Chandra?
And Rajkumar Lakshman?
What are they doing?
Sir, they seem to be...Singing!

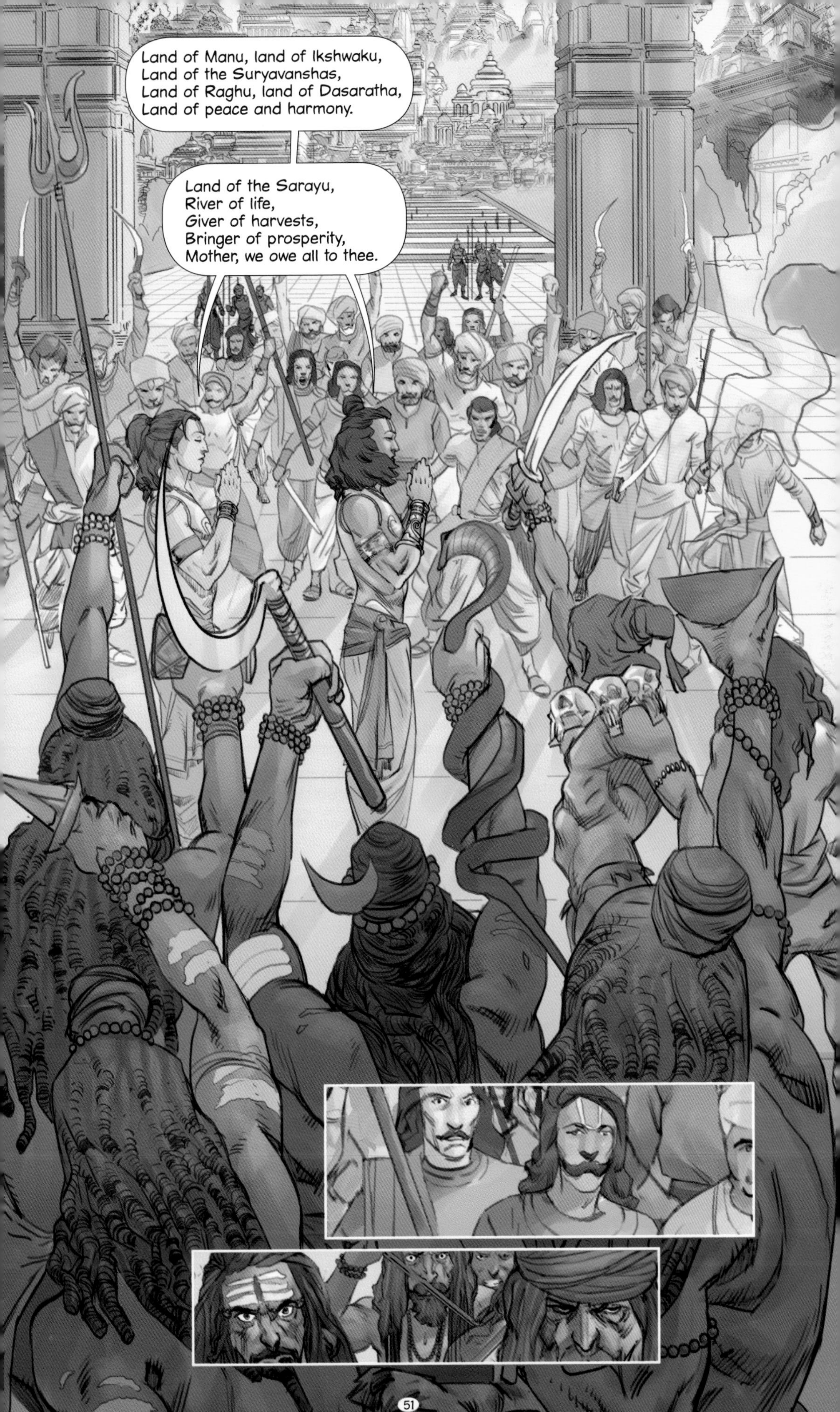
Land of Manu, land of Ikshwaku,
Land of the Suryavanshas,
Land of Raghu, land of Dasaratha,
Land of peace and harmony.
Land of the Sarayu,
River of life,
Giver of harvests,
Bringer of prosperity,
Mother, we owe all to thee.

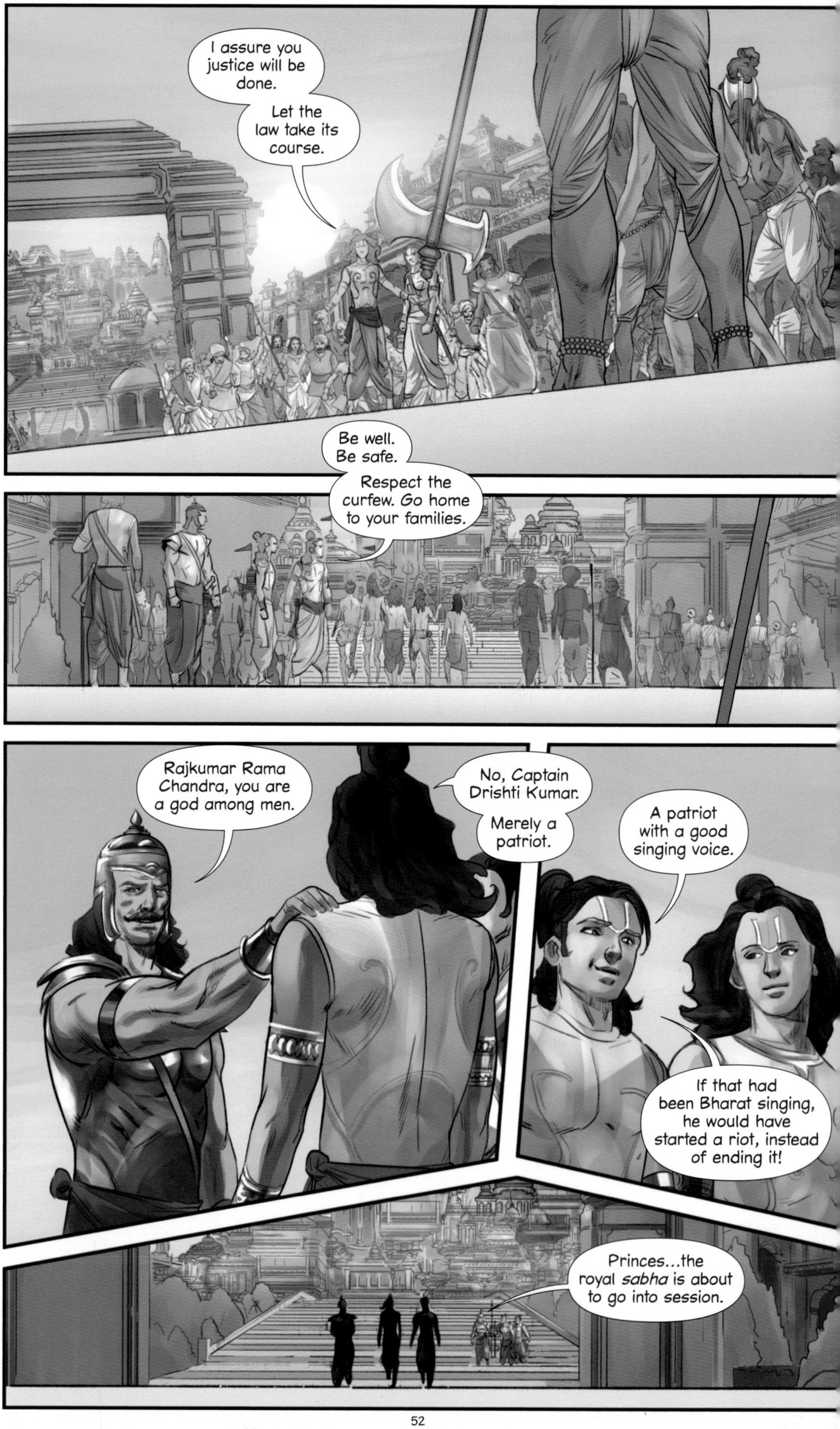

I assure you justice will be done.
Let the law take its course.
Be well. Be safe.
Respect the curfew. Go home to your families.
Rajkumar Rama Chandra, you are a god among men.
No, Captain Drishti Kumar.
Merely a patriot.
A patriot with a good singing voice.
If that had been Bharat singing, he would have started a riot, instead of ending it!
Princes...the royal *sabha* is about to go into session.

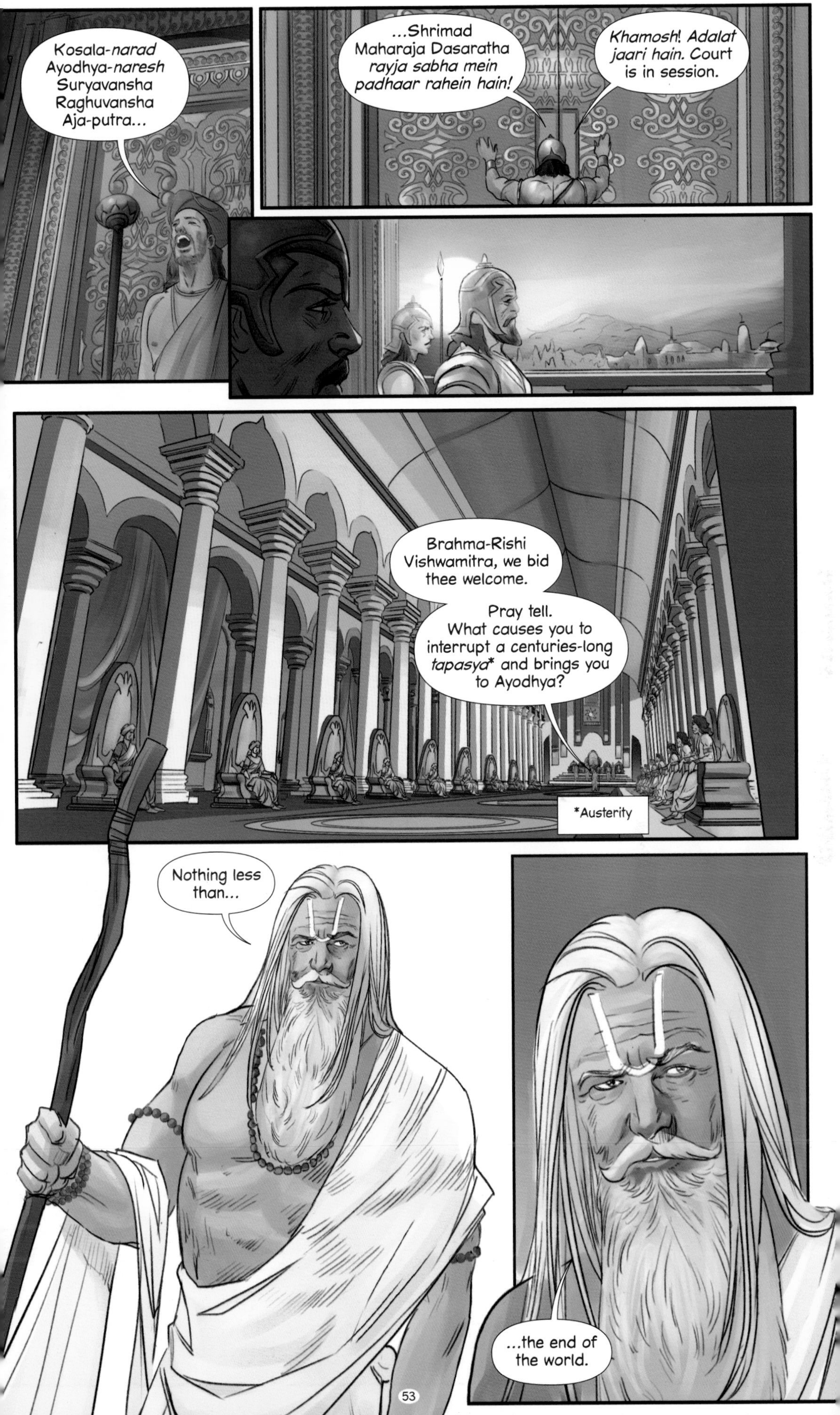
Kosala-narad Ayodhya-naresh Suryavansha Raghuvansha Aja-putra...
...Shrimad Maharaja Dasaratha rayja sabha mein padhaar rahein hain!
Khamosh! Adalat jaari hain. Court is in session.
Brahma-Rishi Vishwamitra, we bid thee welcome.
Pray tell. What causes you to interrupt a centuries-long tapasya* and brings you to Ayodhya?
*Austerity
Nothing less than...
...the end of the world.

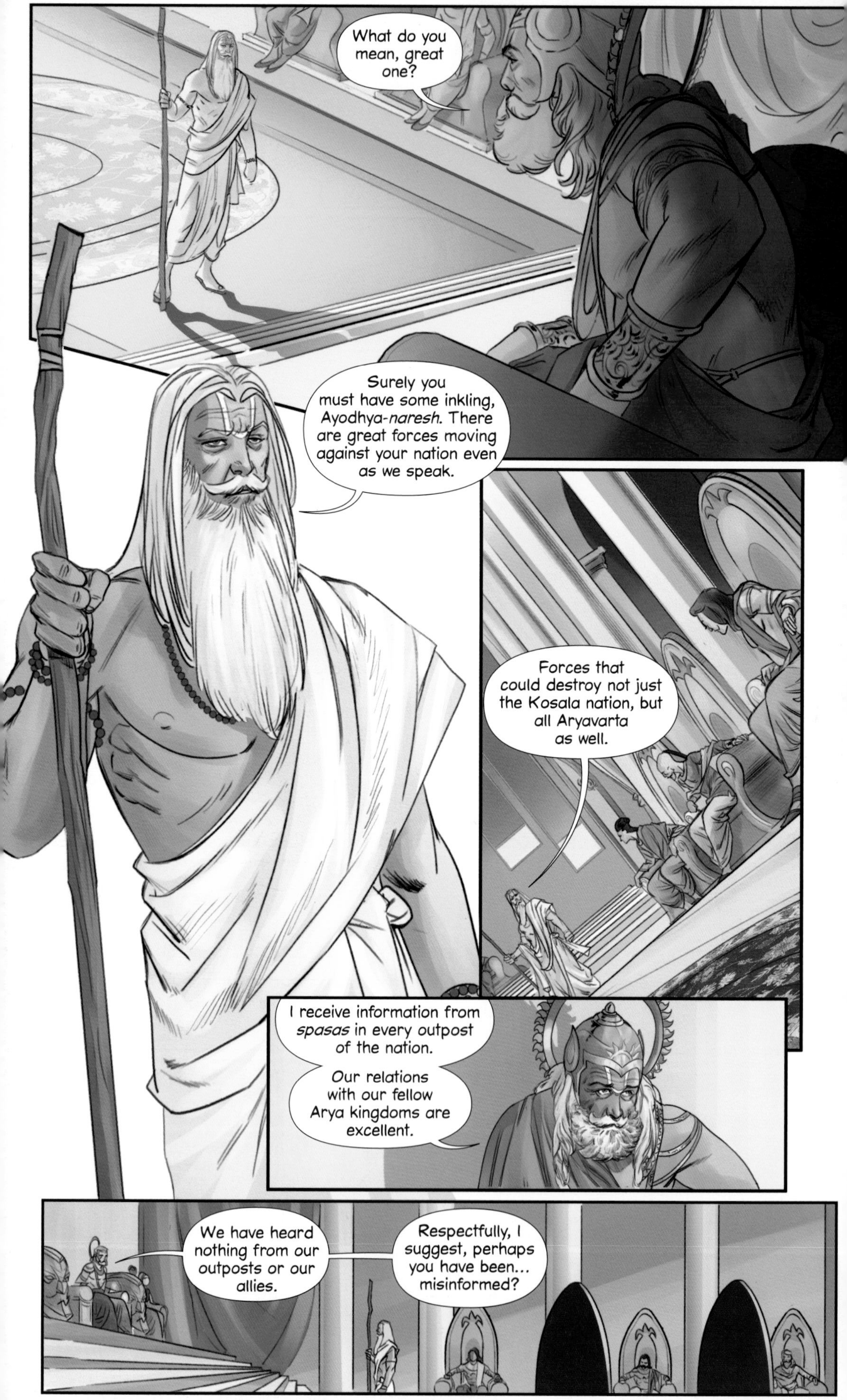
What do you mean, great one?
Surely you must have some inkling, Ayodhya-*naresh*. There are great forces moving against your nation even as we speak.
Forces that could destroy not just the Kosala nation, but all Aryavarta as well.
I receive information from *spasas* in every outpost of the nation.
Our relations with our fellow Arya kingdoms are excellent.
We have heard nothing from our outposts or our allies.
Respectfully, I suggest, perhaps you have been... misinformed?

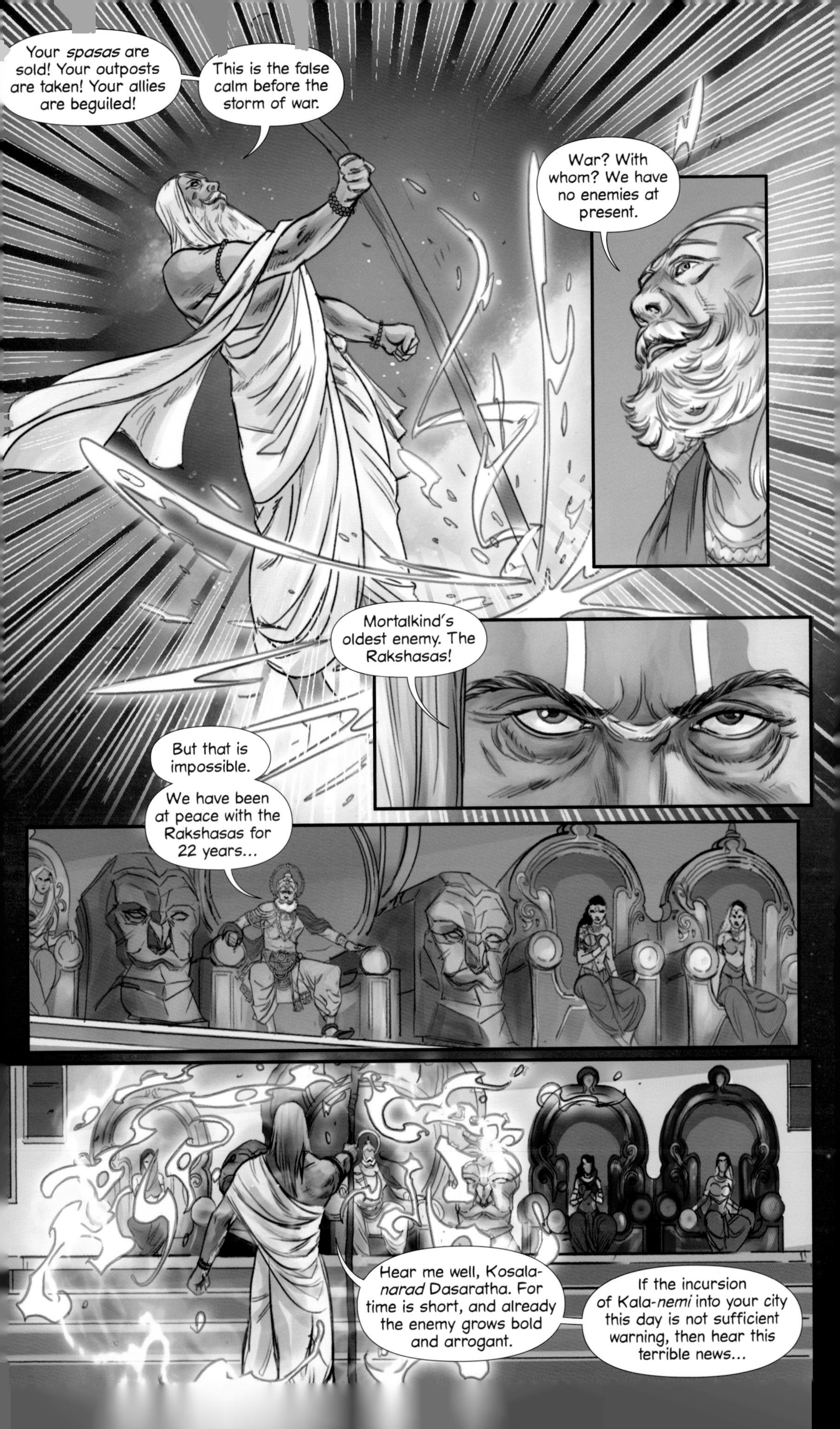
Your *spasas* are sold! Your outposts are taken! Your allies are beguiled!
This is the false calm before the storm of war.
War? With whom? We have no enemies at present.
Mortalkind's oldest enemy. The Rakshasas!
But that is impossible.
We have been at peace with the Rakshasas for 22 years...
Hear me well, Kosala-*narad* Dasaratha. For time is short, and already the enemy grows bold and arrogant.
If the incursion of Kala-*nemi* into your city this day is not sufficient warning, then hear this terrible news...

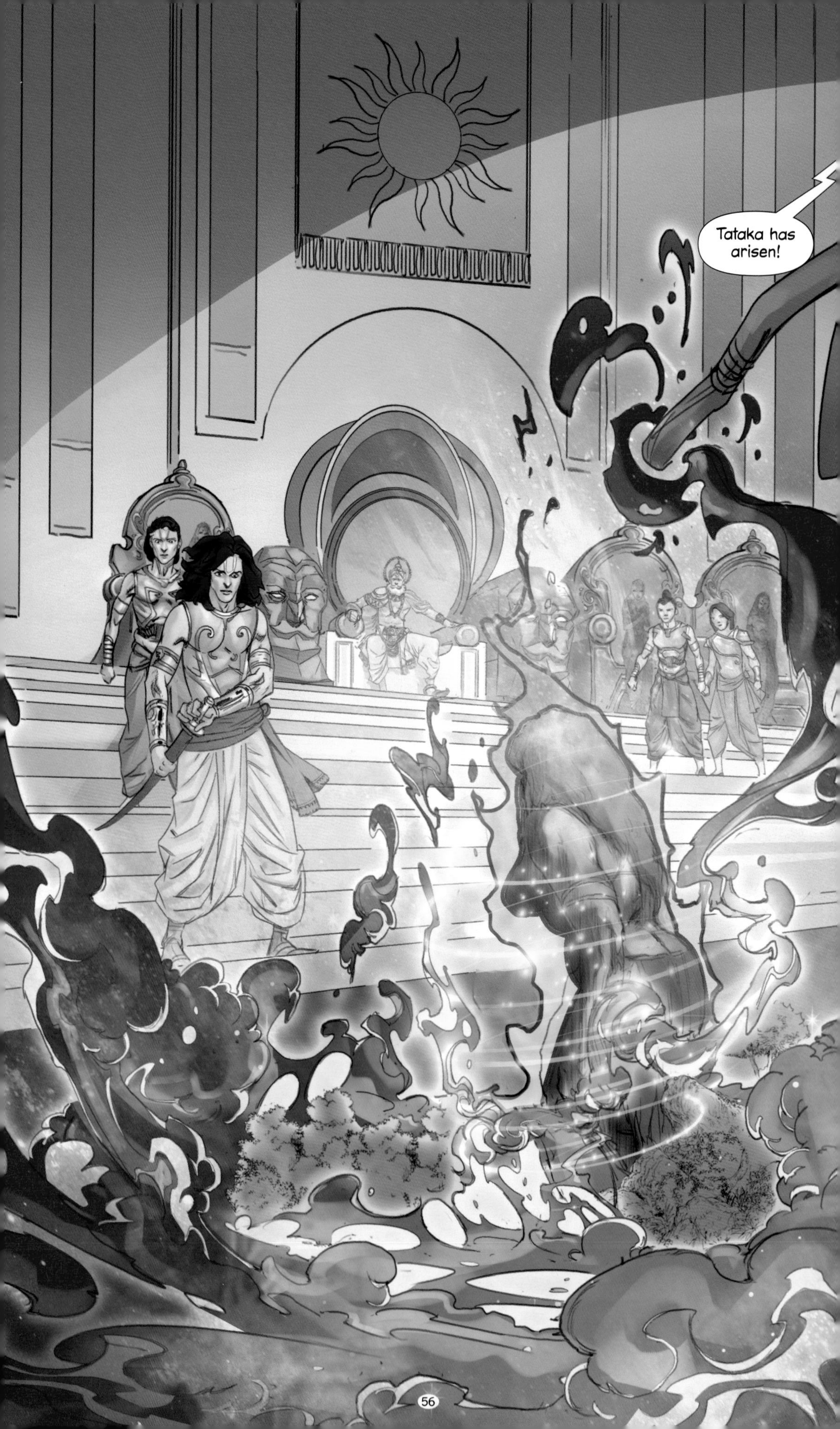
Tataka has arisen!

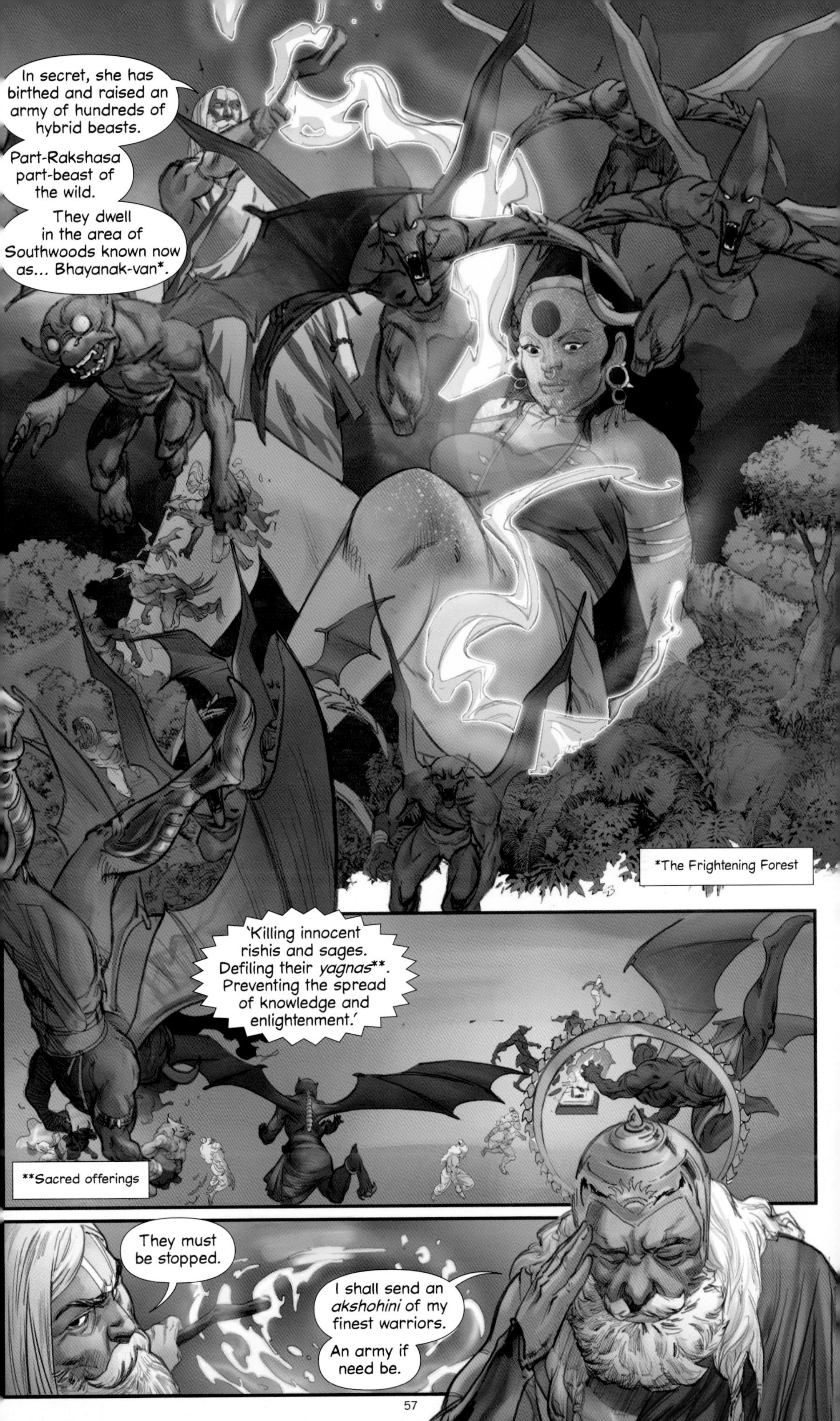

In secret, she has birthed and raised an army of hundreds of hybrid beasts.
Part-Rakshasa part-beast of the wild.
They dwell in the area of Southwoods known now as... Bhayanak-van*.
*The Frightening Forest
'Killing innocent rishis and sages. Defiling their *yagnas***. Preventing the spread of knowledge and enlightenment.'
**Sacred offerings
They must be stopped.
I shall send an *akshohini* of my finest warriors.
An army if need be.

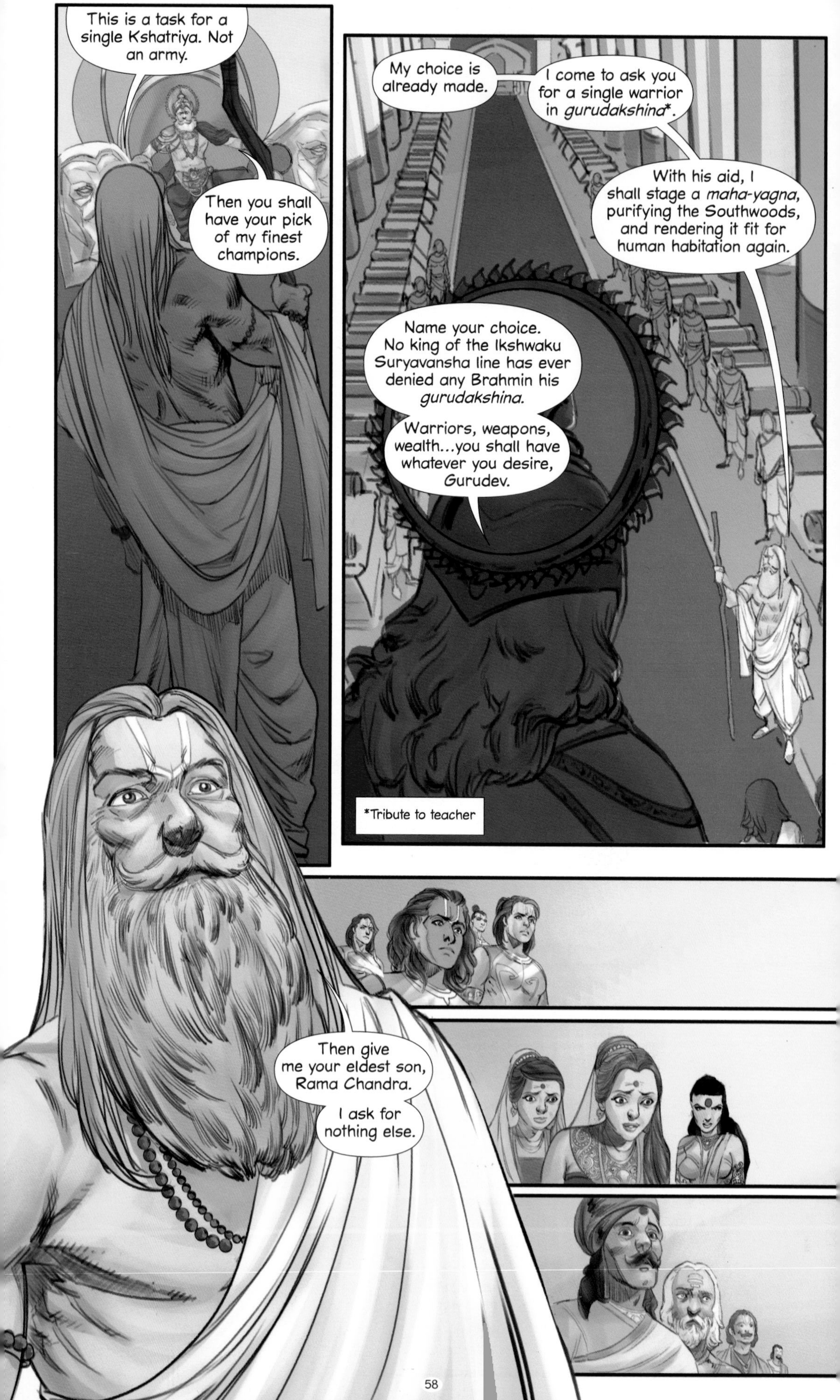
This is a task for a single Kshatriya. Not an army.
Then you shall have your pick of my finest champions.
My choice is already made.
I come to ask you for a single warrior in *gurudakshina**.
With his aid, I shall stage a *maha-yagna*, purifying the Southwoods, and rendering it fit for human habitation again.
Name your choice. No king of the Ikshwaku Suryavansha line has ever denied any Brahmin his *gurudakshina*.
Warriors, weapons, wealth...you shall have whatever you desire, Gurudev.
*Tribute to teacher
Then give me your eldest son, Rama Chandra.
I ask for nothing else.

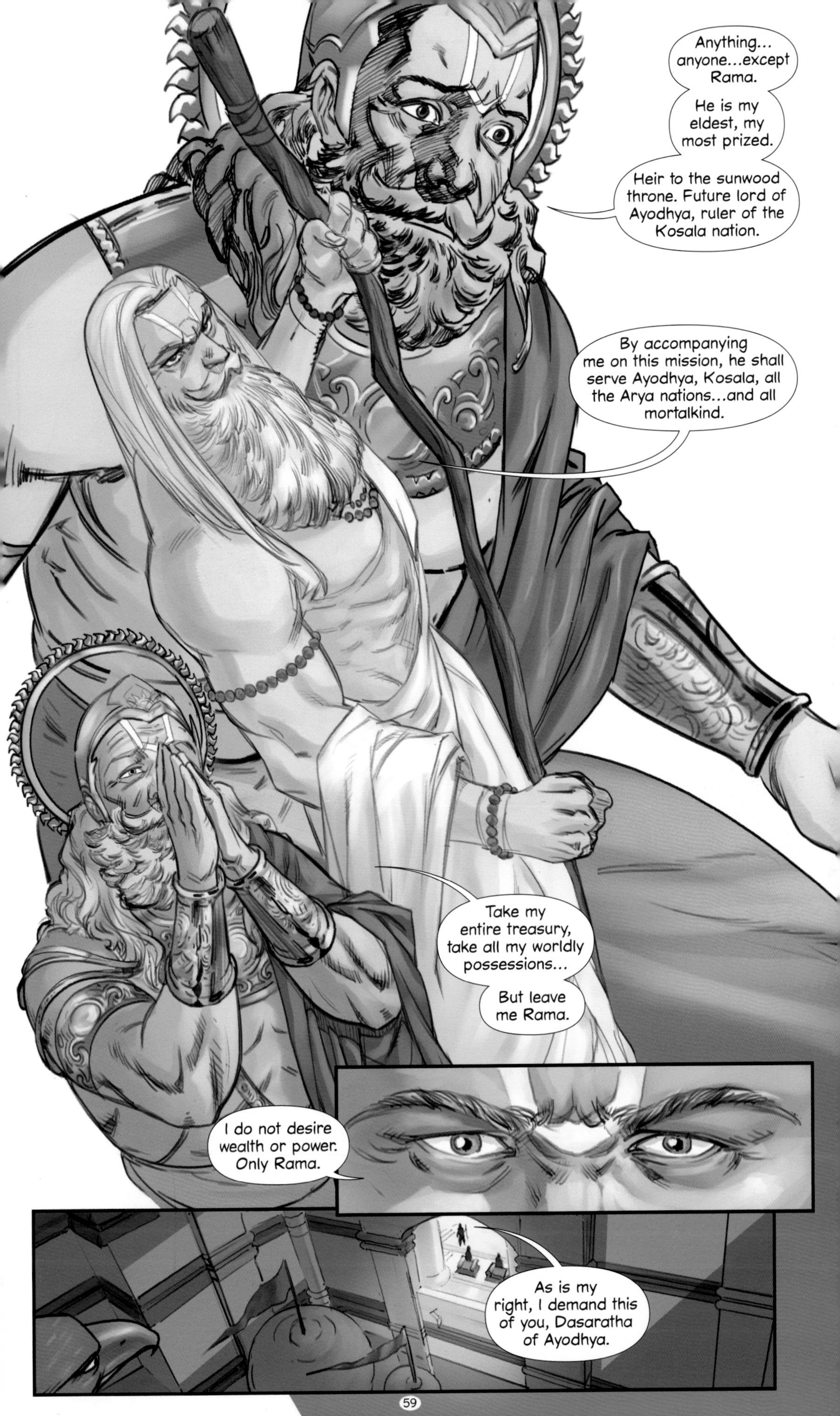

Anything... anyone...except Rama.
He is my eldest, my most prized.
Heir to the sunwood throne. Future lord of Ayodhya, ruler of the Kosala nation.
By accompanying me on this mission, he shall serve Ayodhya, Kosala, all the Arya nations...and all mortalkind.
Take my entire treasury, take all my worldly possessions...
But leave me Rama.
I do not desire wealth or power. Only Rama.
As is my right, I demand this of you, Dasaratha of Ayodhya.

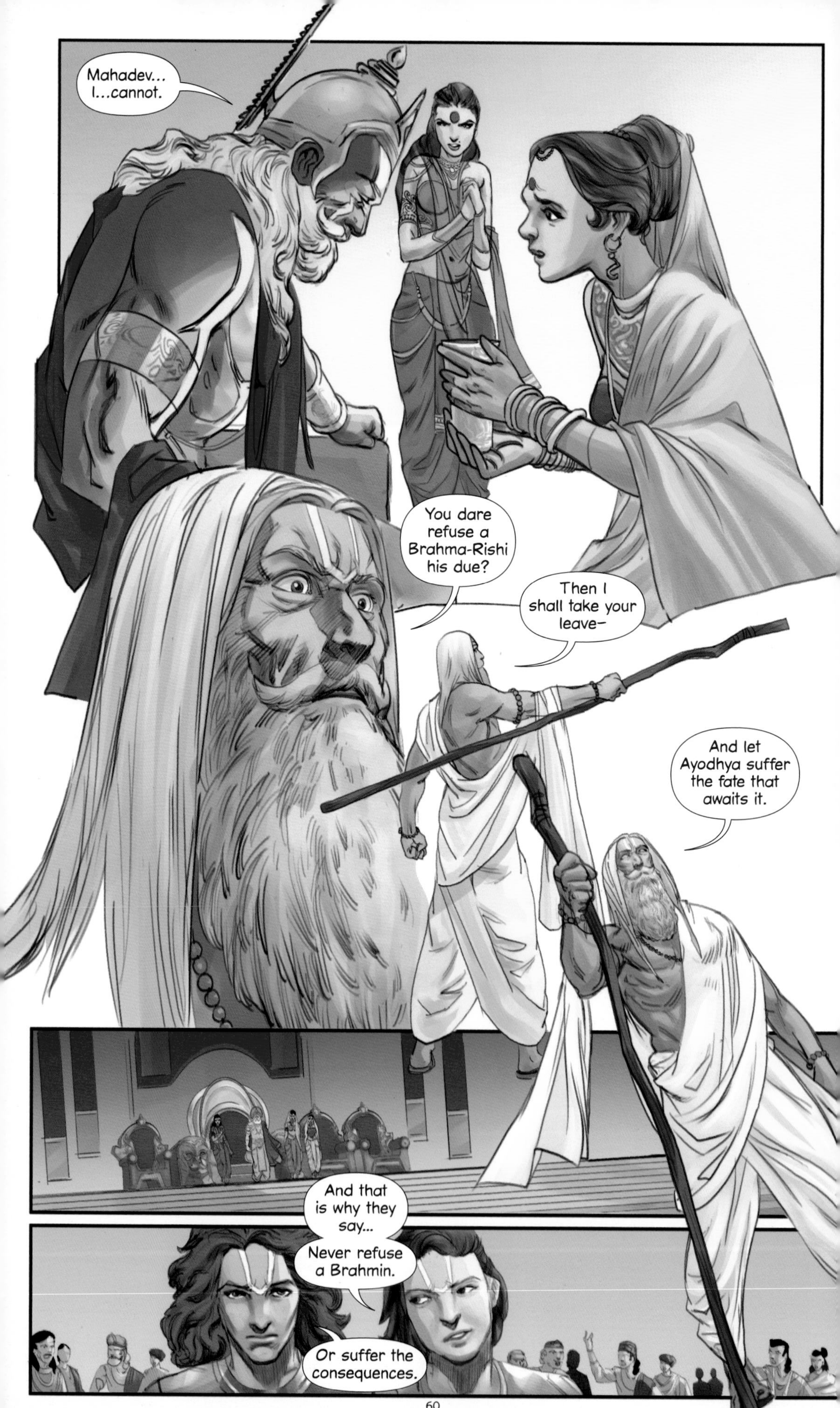
Mahadev...
I...cannot.
You dare refuse a Brahma-Rishi his due?
Then I shall take your leave–
And let Ayodhya suffer the fate that awaits it.
And that is why they say...
Never refuse a Brahmin.
Or suffer the consequences.

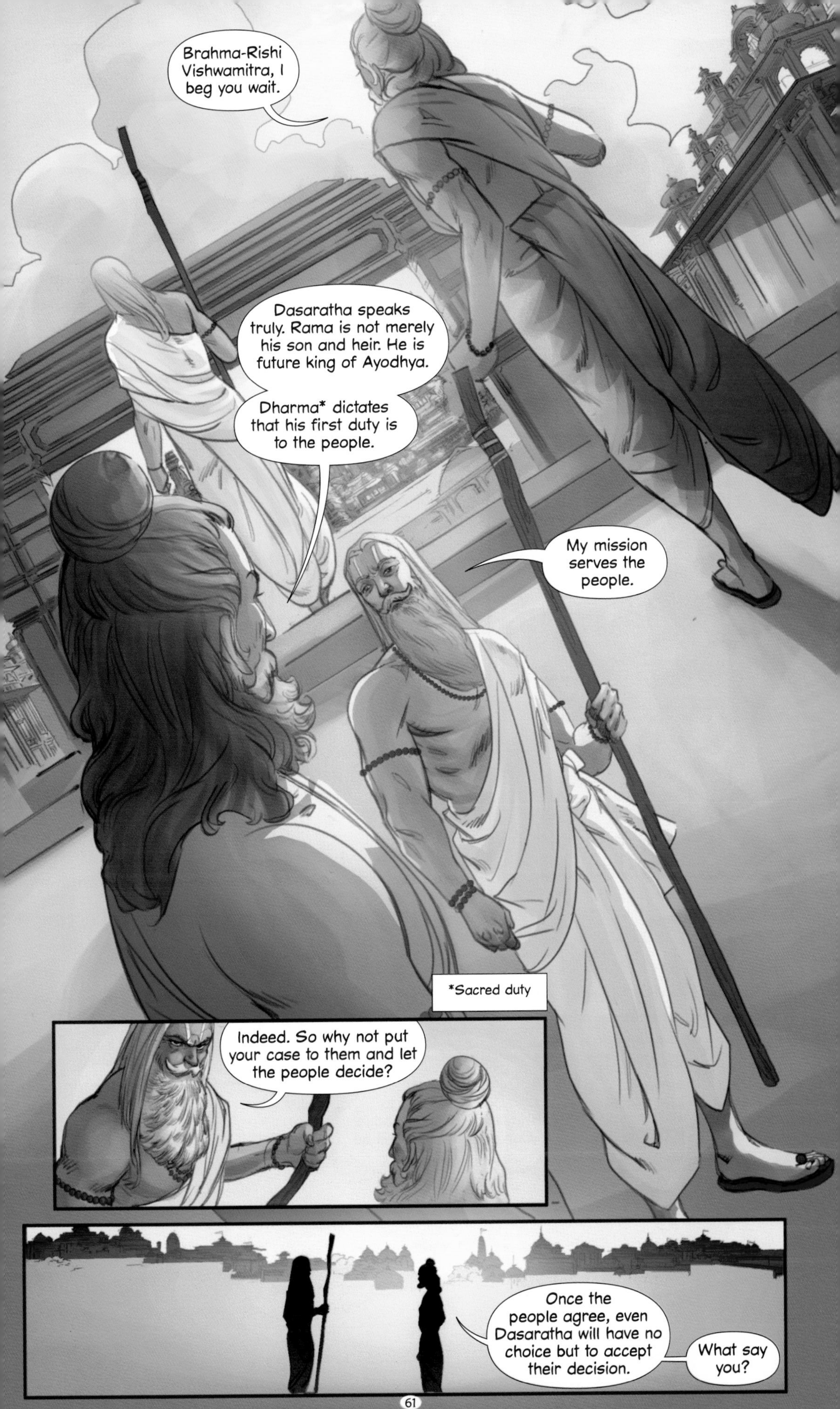
Brahma-Rishi Vishwamitra, I beg you wait.
Dasaratha speaks truly. Rama is not merely his son and heir. He is future king of Ayodhya.
Dharma* dictates that his first duty is to the people.
My mission serves the people.
*Sacred duty
Indeed. So why not put your case to them and let the people decide?
Once the people agree, even Dasaratha will have no choice but to accept their decision.
What say you?

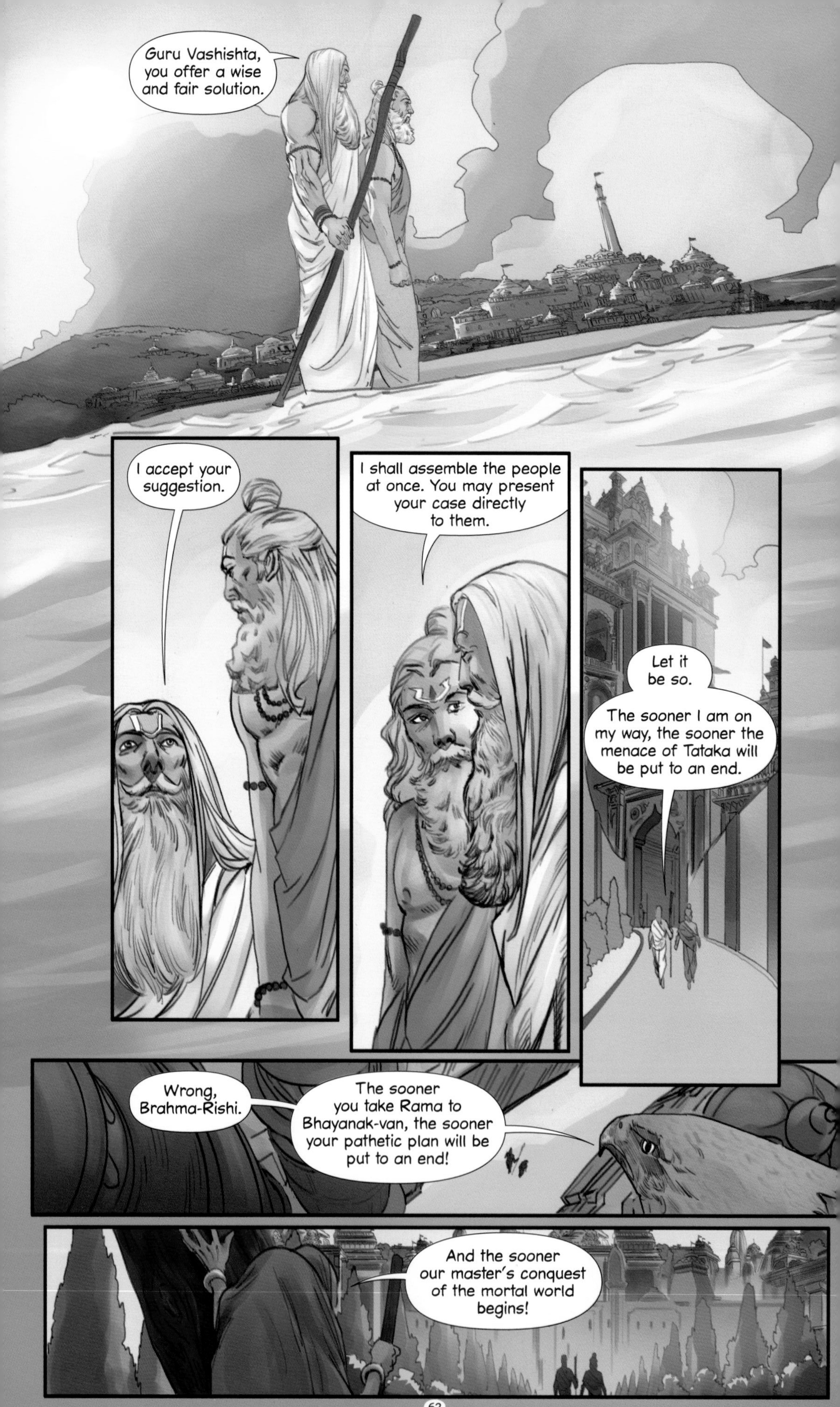
Guru Vashishta, you offer a wise and fair solution.
I accept your suggestion.
I shall assemble the people at once. You may present your case directly to them.
Let it be so.
The sooner I am on my way, the sooner the menace of Tataka will be put to an end.
Wrong, Brahma-Rishi.
The sooner you take Rama to Bhayanak-van, the sooner your pathetic plan will be put to an end!
And the sooner our master's conquest of the mortal world begins!

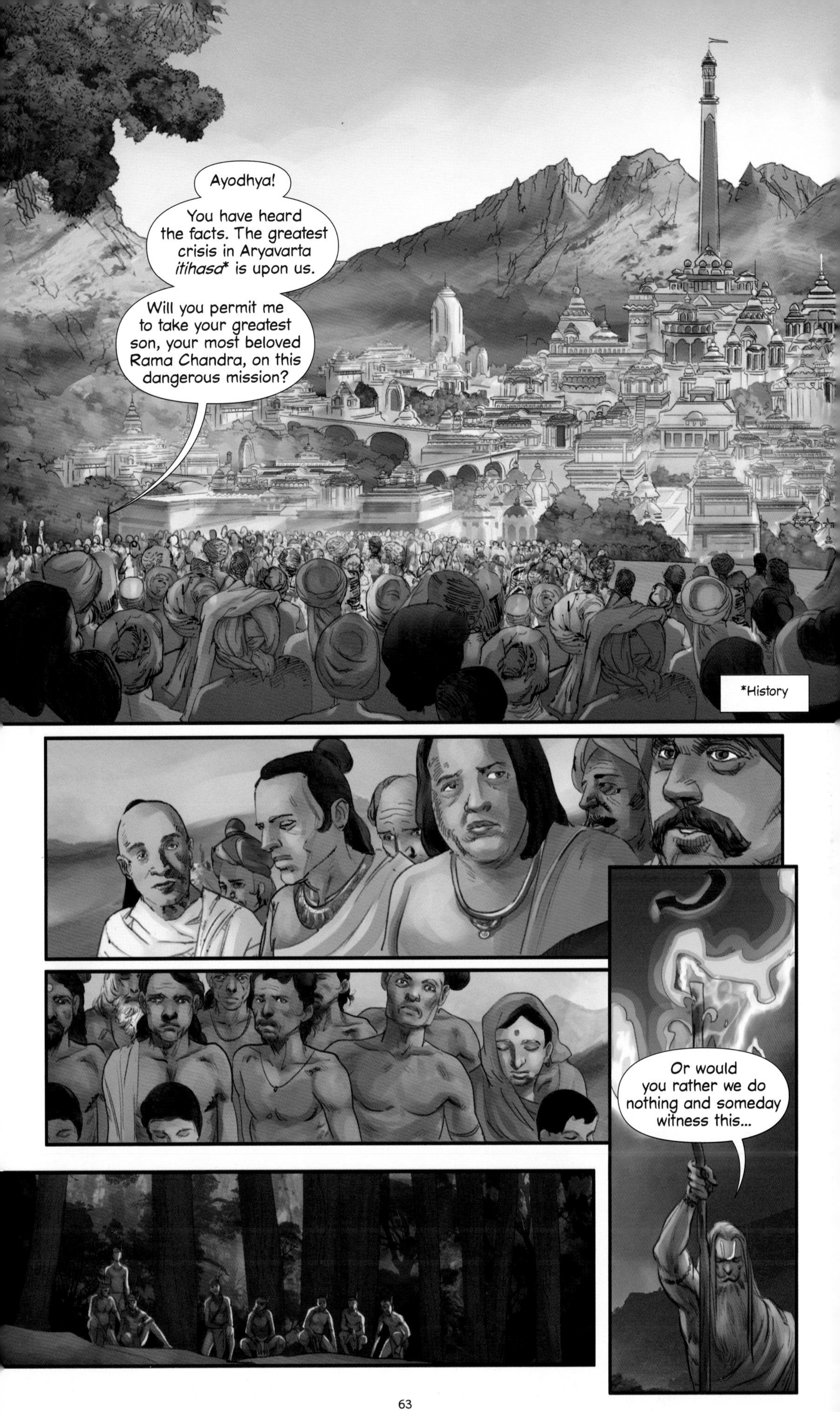
Ayodhya!
You have heard the facts. The greatest crisis in Aryavarta *itihasa** is upon us.
Will you permit me to take your greatest son, your most beloved Rama Chandra, on this dangerous mission?
*History
Or would you rather we do nothing and someday witness this...

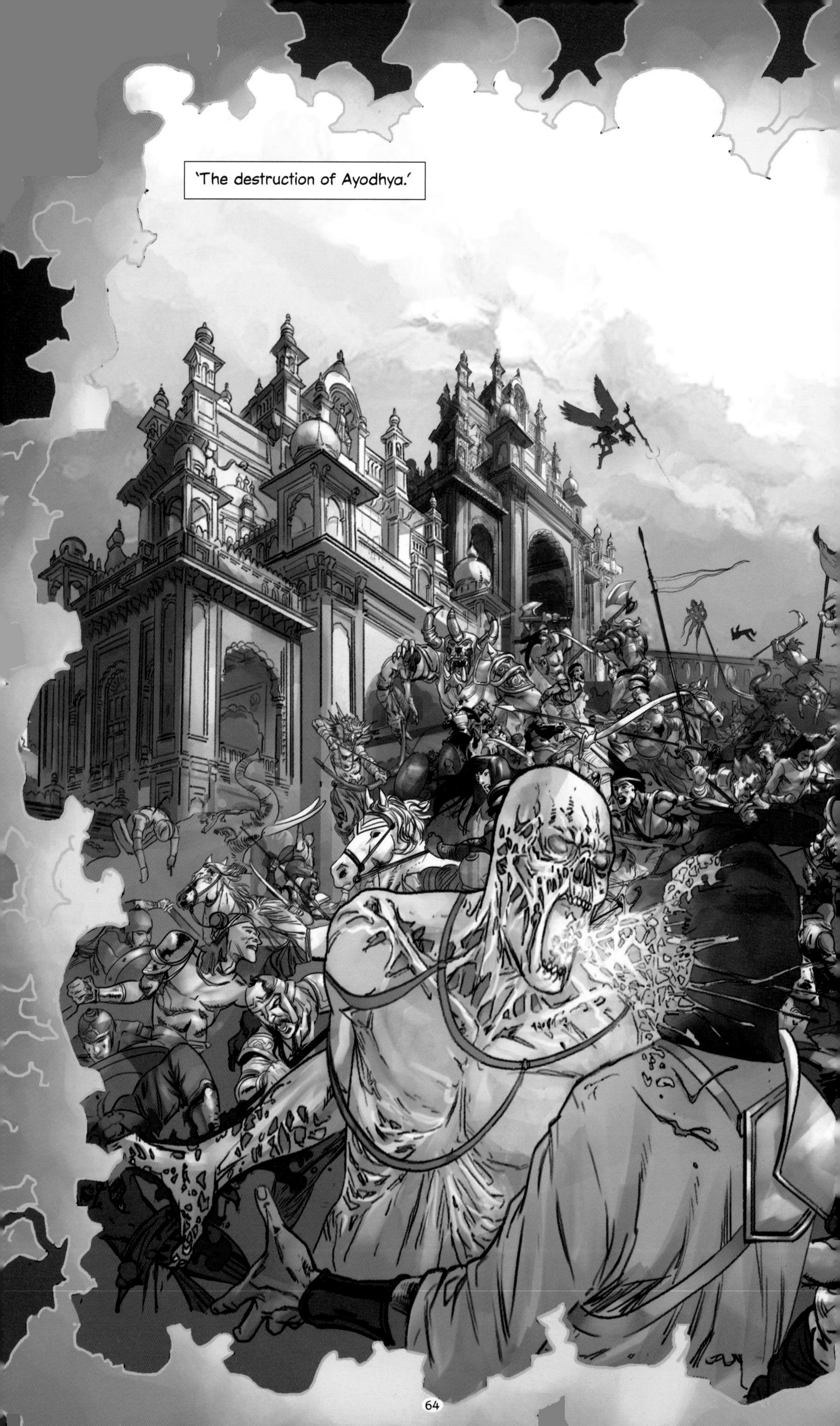
'The destruction of Ayodhya.'

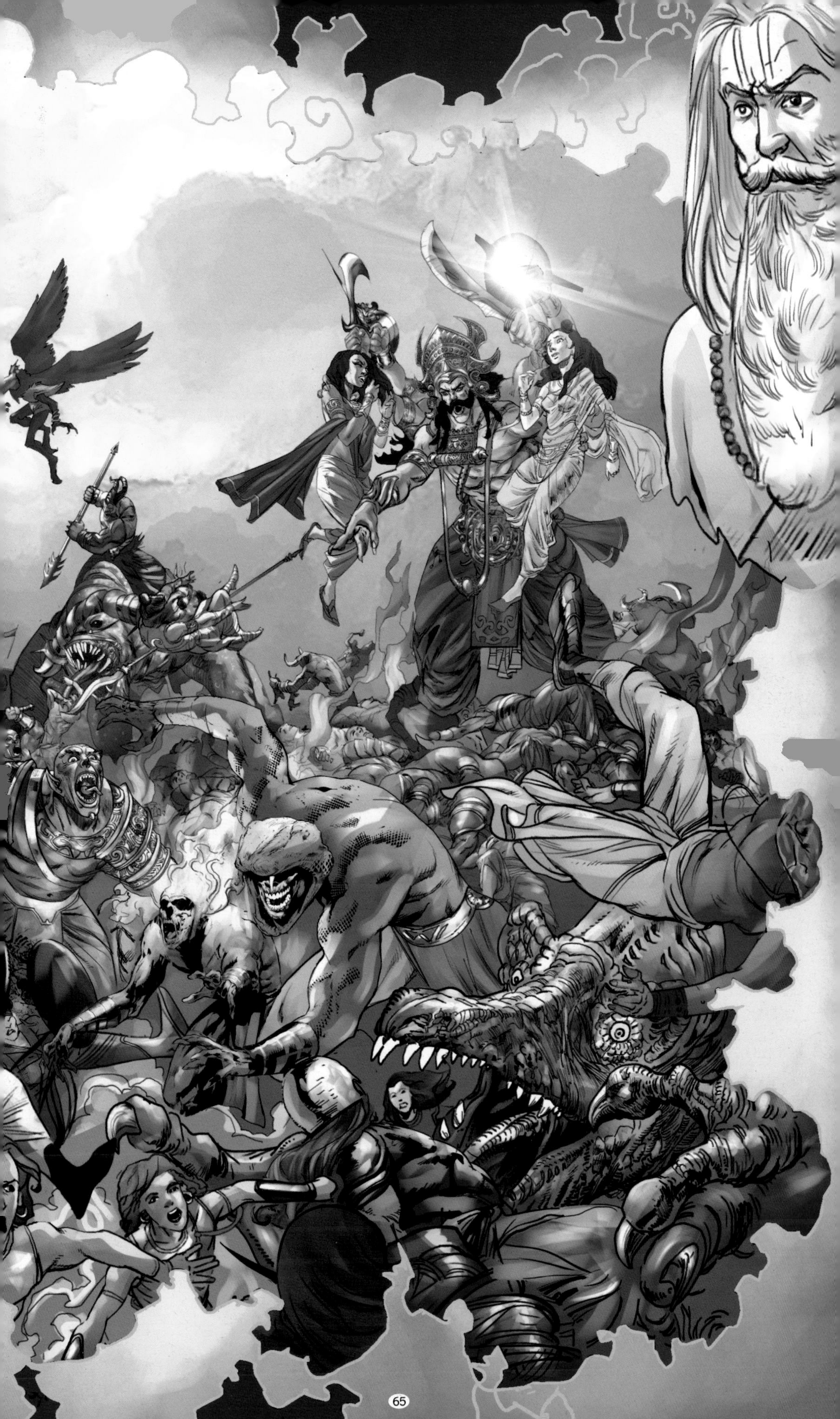

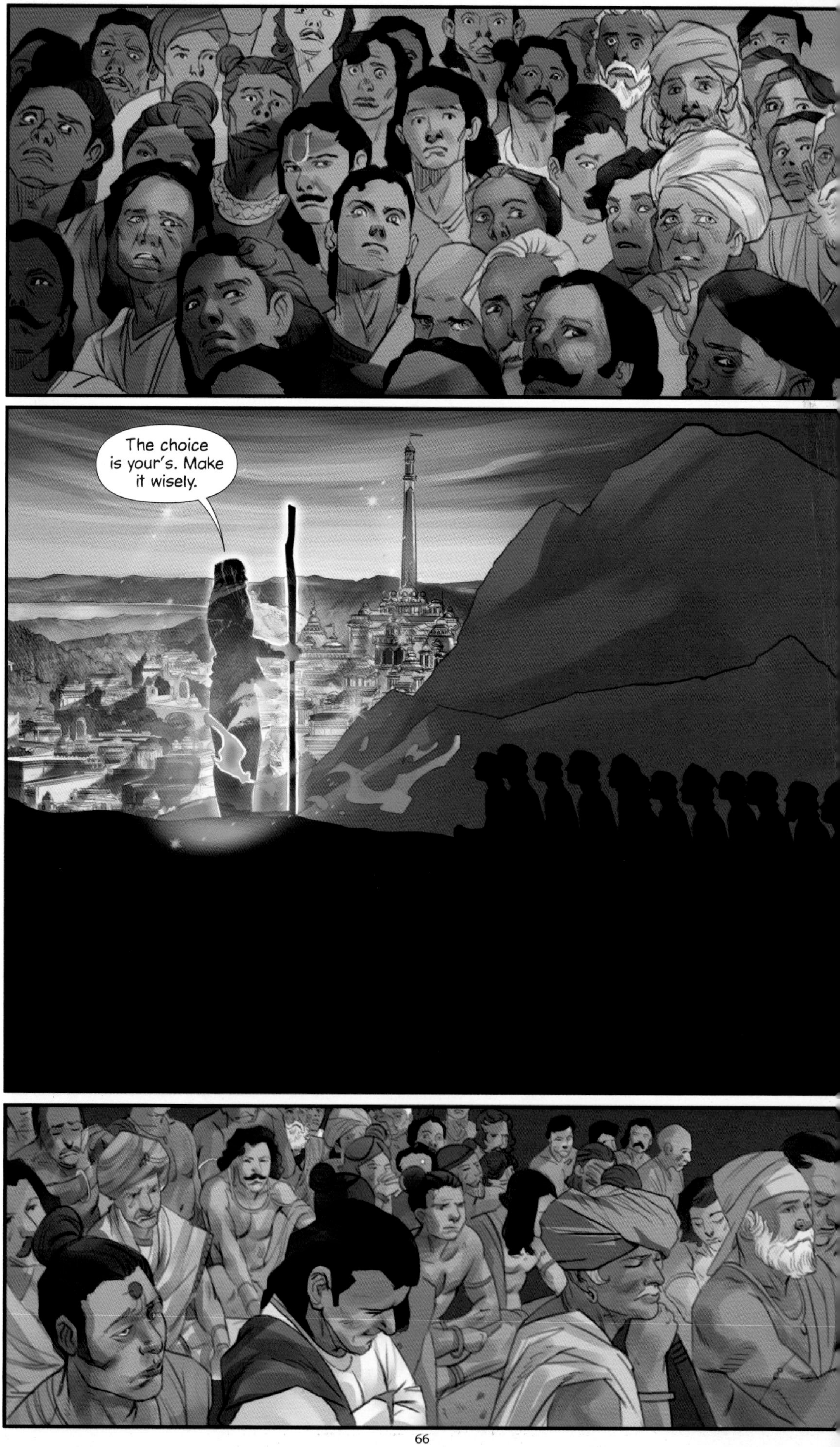
The choice is your's. Make it wisely.

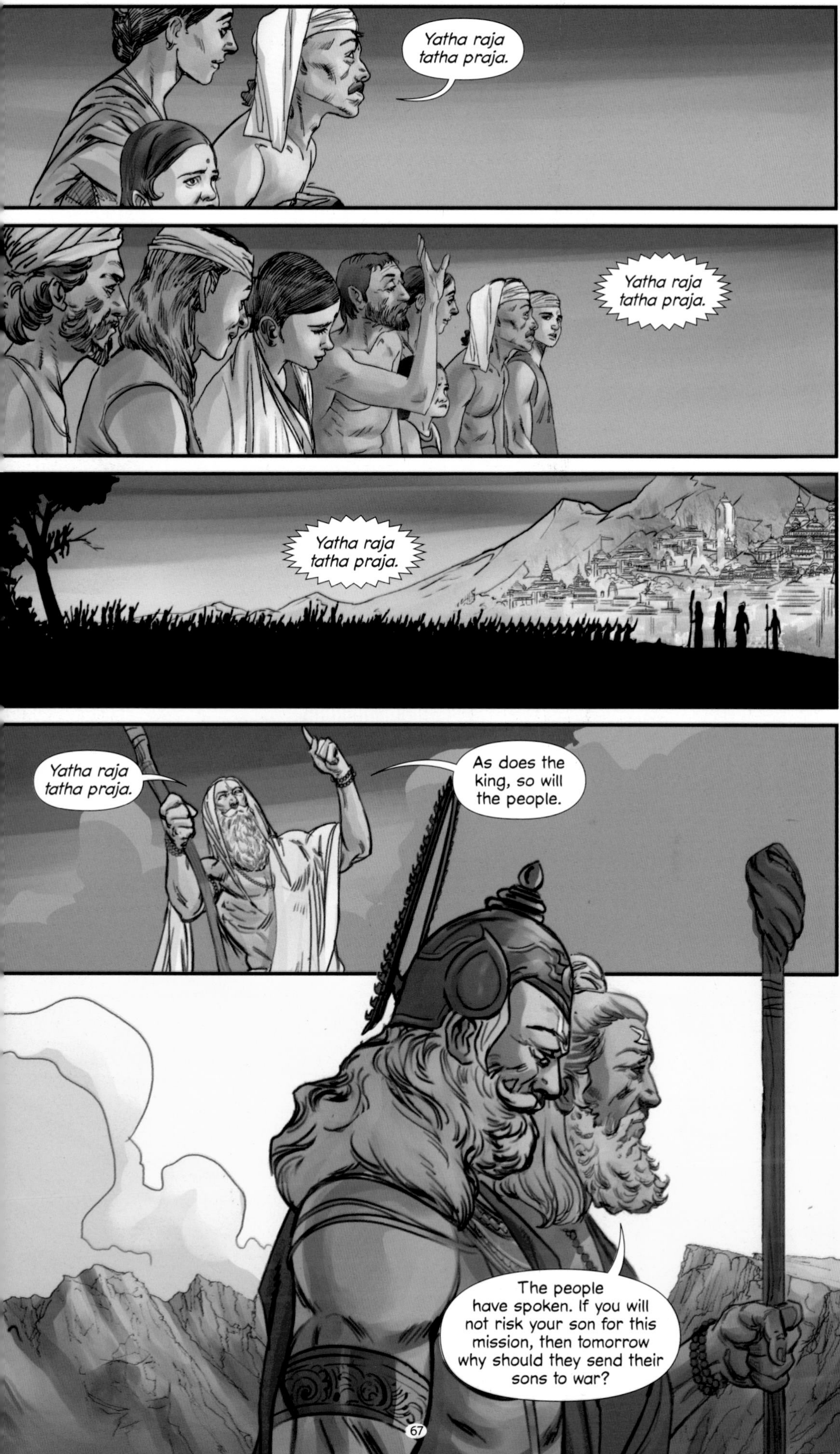
Yatha raja tatha praja.
Yatha raja tatha praja.
Yatha raja tatha praja.
Yatha raja tatha praja.
As does the king, so will the people.
The people have spoken. If you will not risk your son for this mission, then tomorrow why should they send their sons to war?

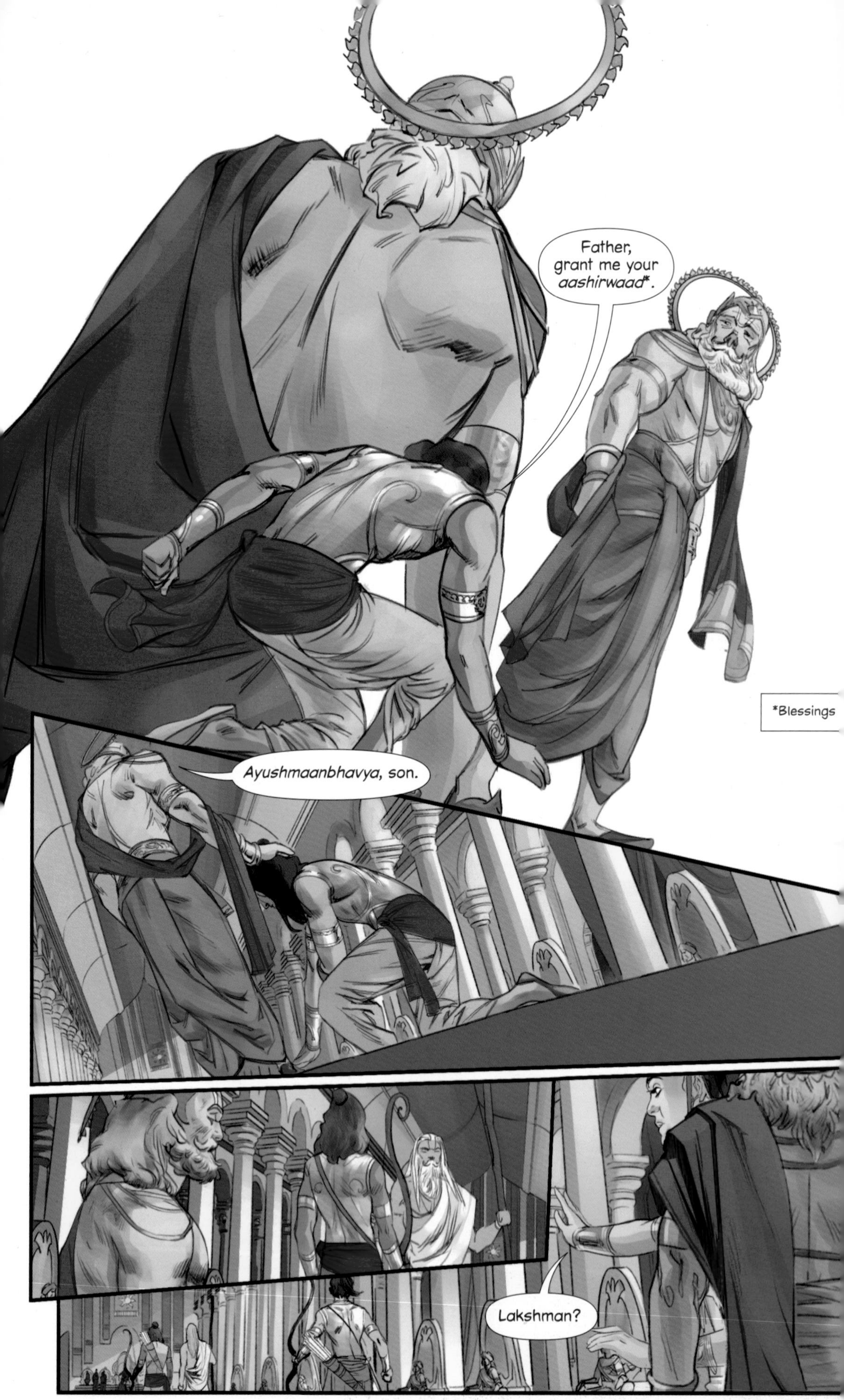
Father,
grant me your
*aashirwaad**.
*Blessings
Ayushmaanbhavya, son.
Lakshman?

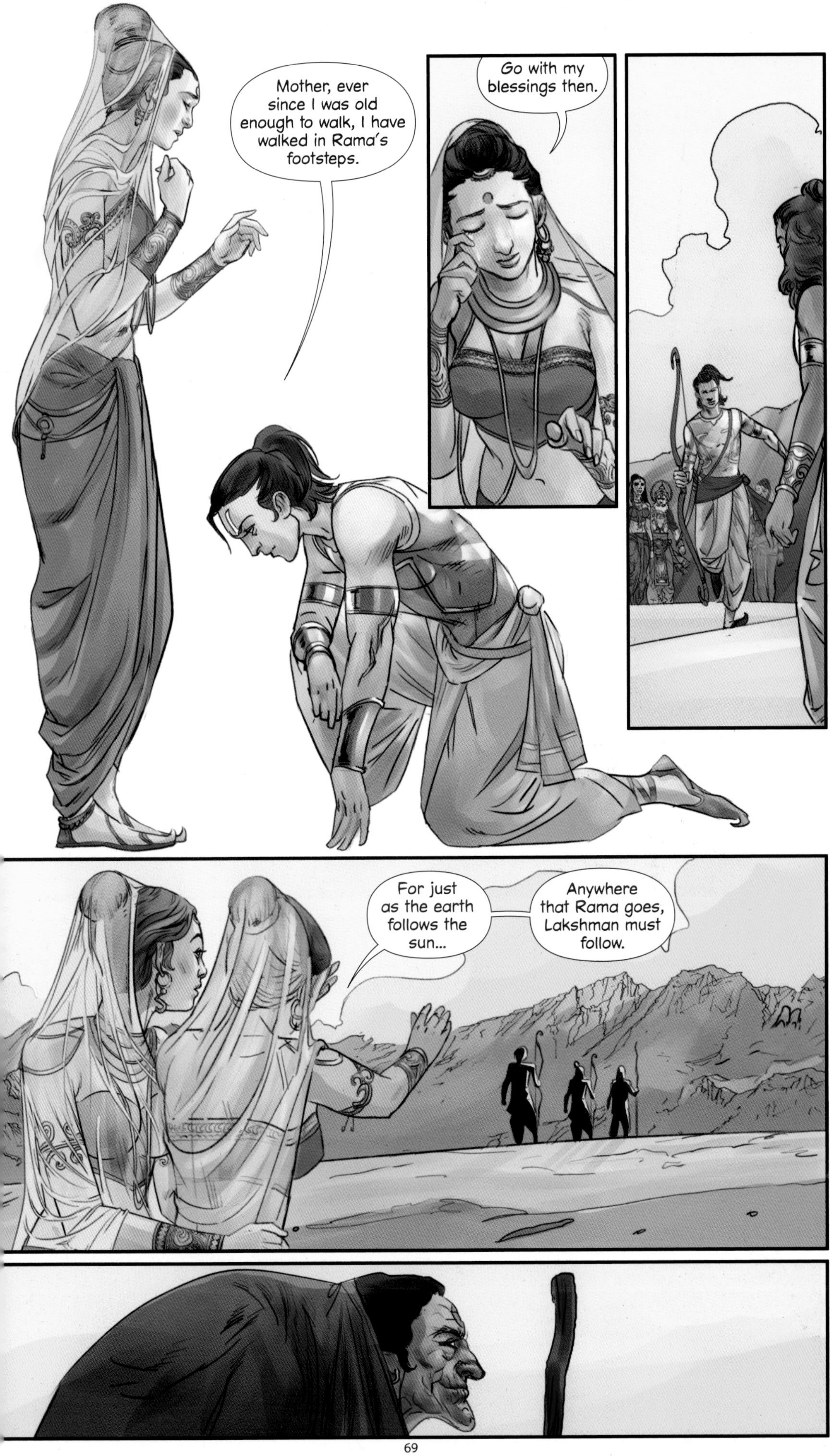
Mother, ever since I was old enough to walk, I have walked in Rama's footsteps.
Go with my blessings then.
For just as the earth follows the sun...
Anywhere that Rama goes, Lakshman must follow.

In my long lifetime, I have seen many Ayodhyans bid their sons goodbye as they go to war.

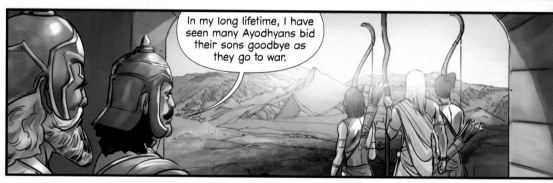

But today, Ayodhya makes her greatest sacrifice of all time.

Her two greatest sons.

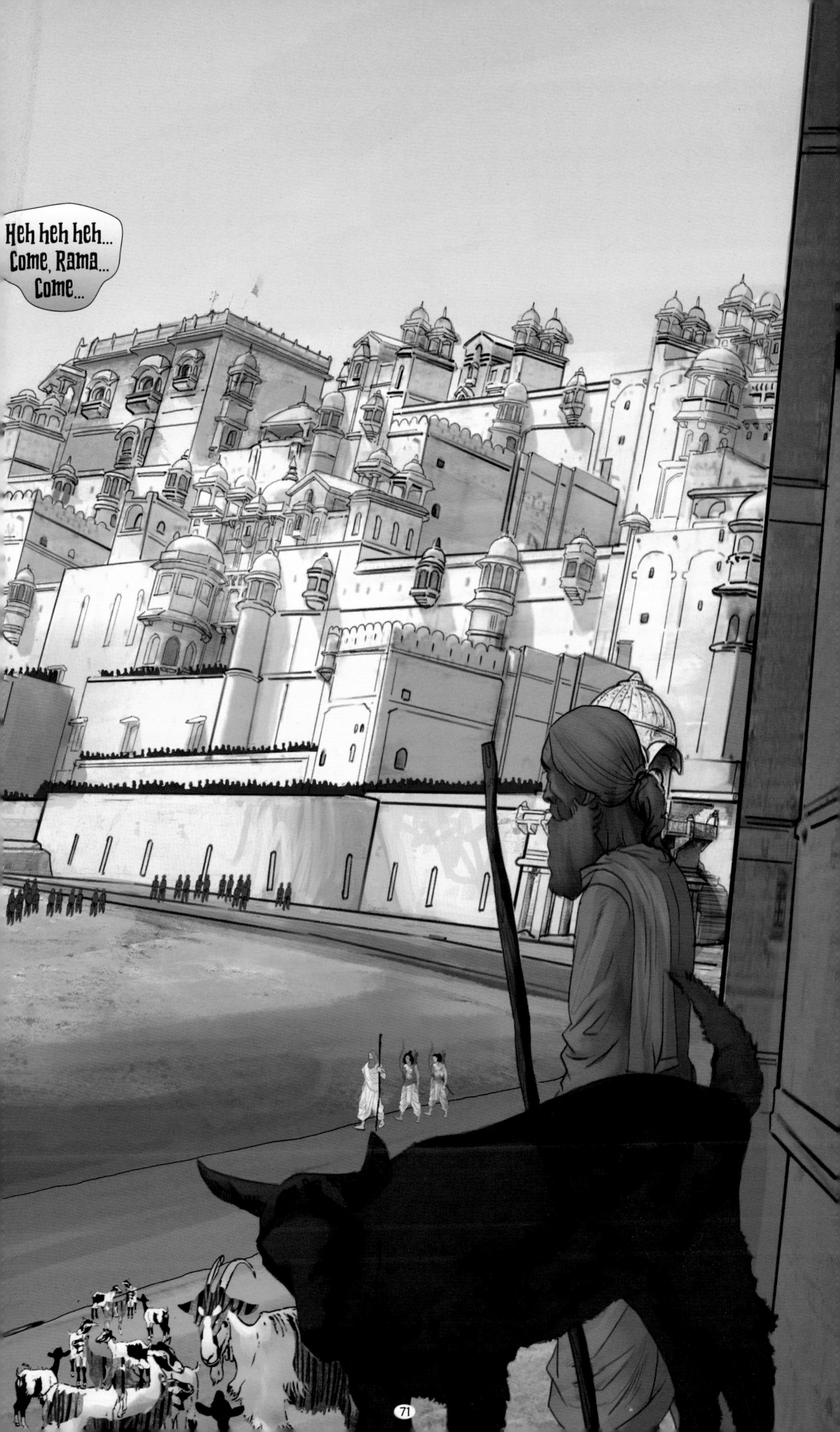
Heh heh heh... Come, Rama... Come...

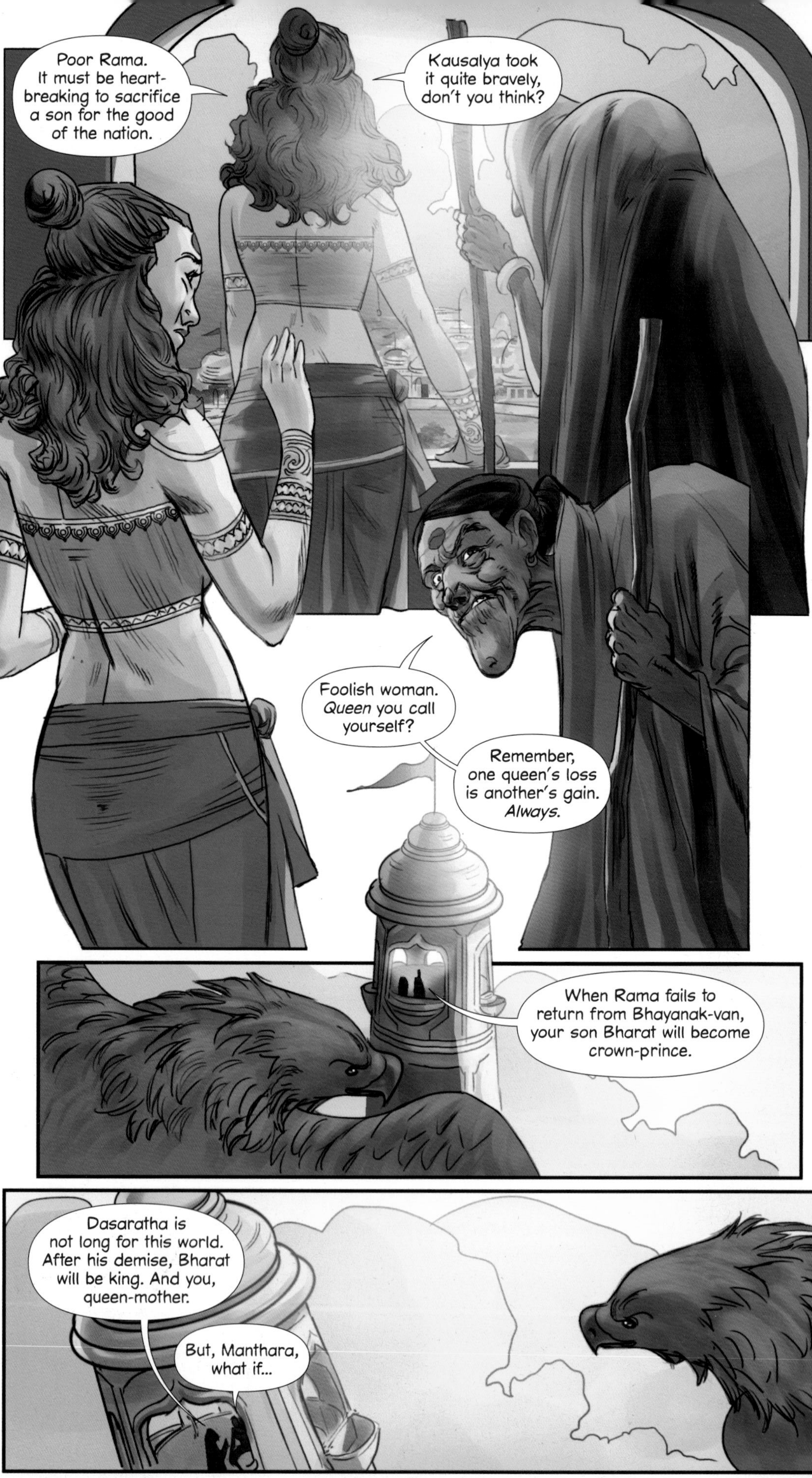
Poor Rama. It must be heart-breaking to sacrifice a son for the good of the nation.
Kausalya took it quite bravely, don't you think?
Foolish woman. *Queen* you call yourself?
Remember, one queen's loss is another's gain. *Always.*
When Rama fails to return from Bhayanak-van, your son Bharat will become crown-prince.
Dasaratha is not long for this world. After his demise, Bharat will be king. And you, queen-mother.
But, Manthara, what if...

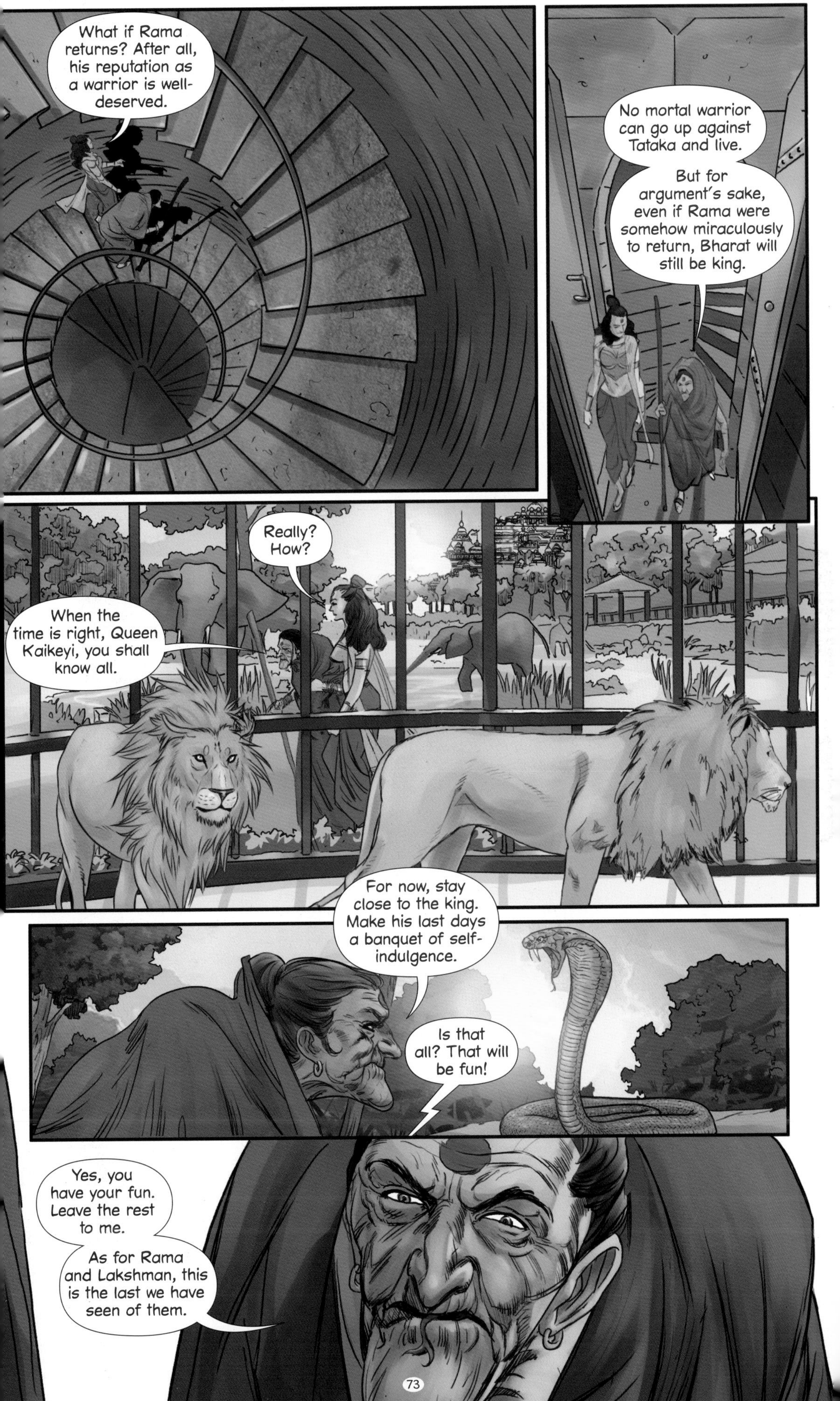
What if Rama returns? After all, his reputation as a warrior is well-deserved.
No mortal warrior can go up against Tataka and live.
But for argument's sake, even if Rama were somehow miraculously to return, Bharat will still be king.
Really? How?
When the time is right, Queen Kaikeyi, you shall know all.
For now, stay close to the king. Make his last days a banquet of self-indulgence.
Is that all? That will be fun!
Yes, you have your fun. Leave the rest to me.
As for Rama and Lakshman, this is the last we have seen of them.

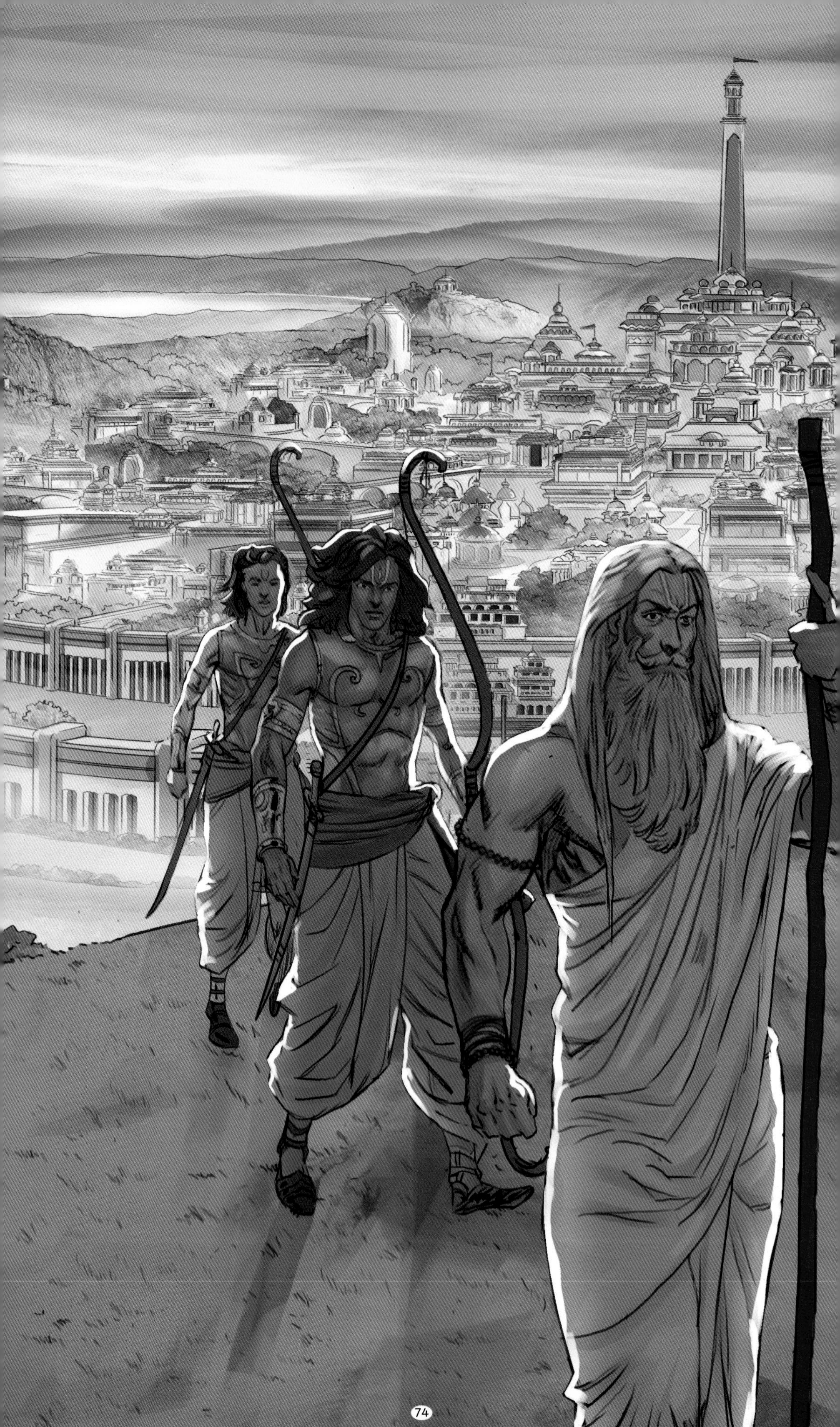

KAAND II

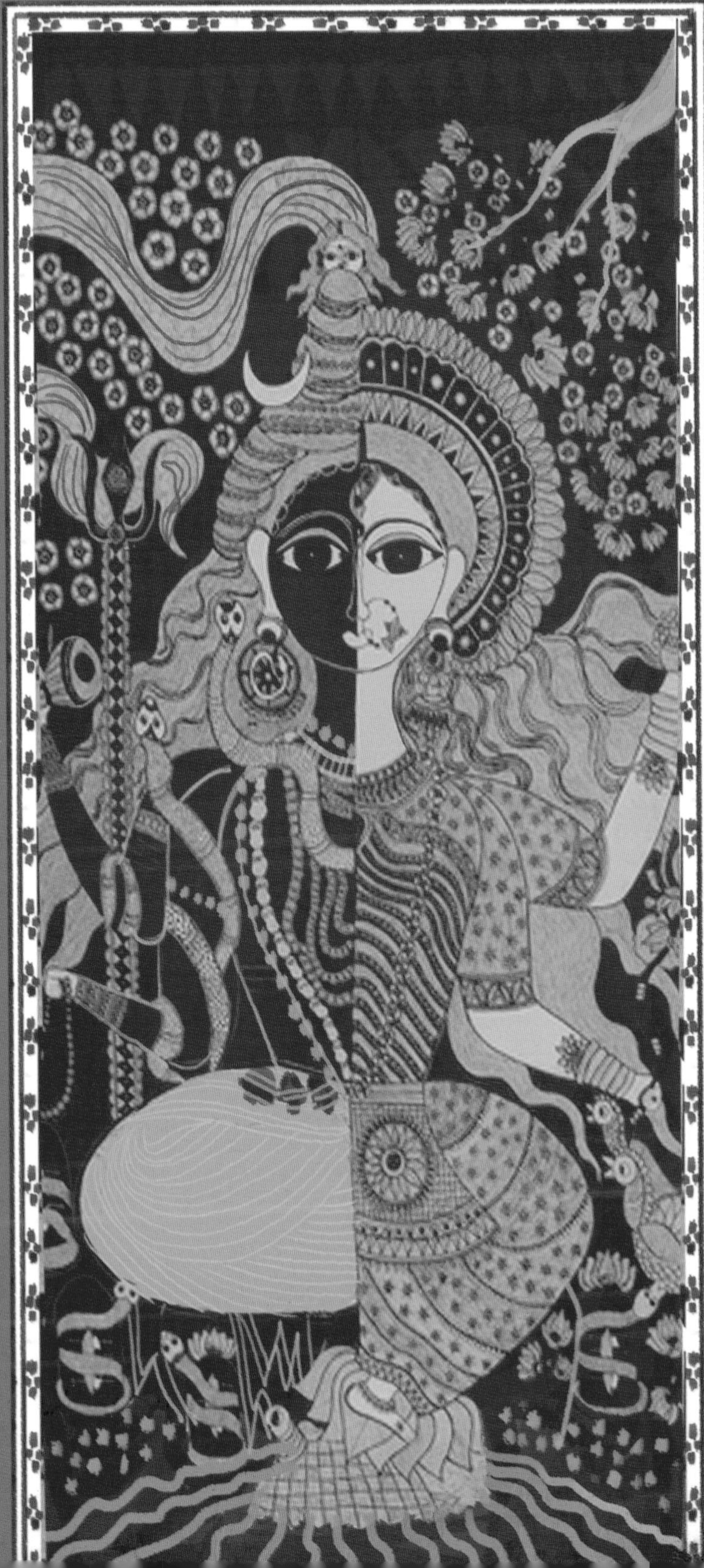

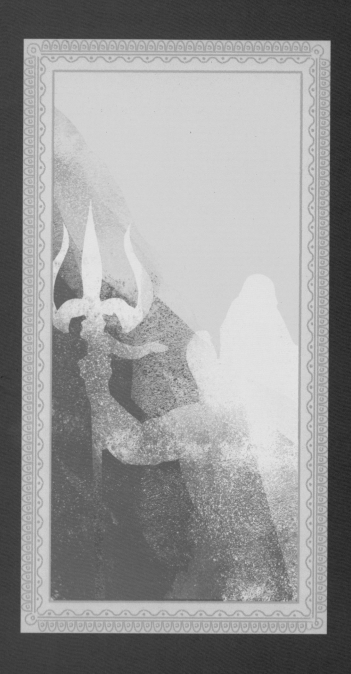

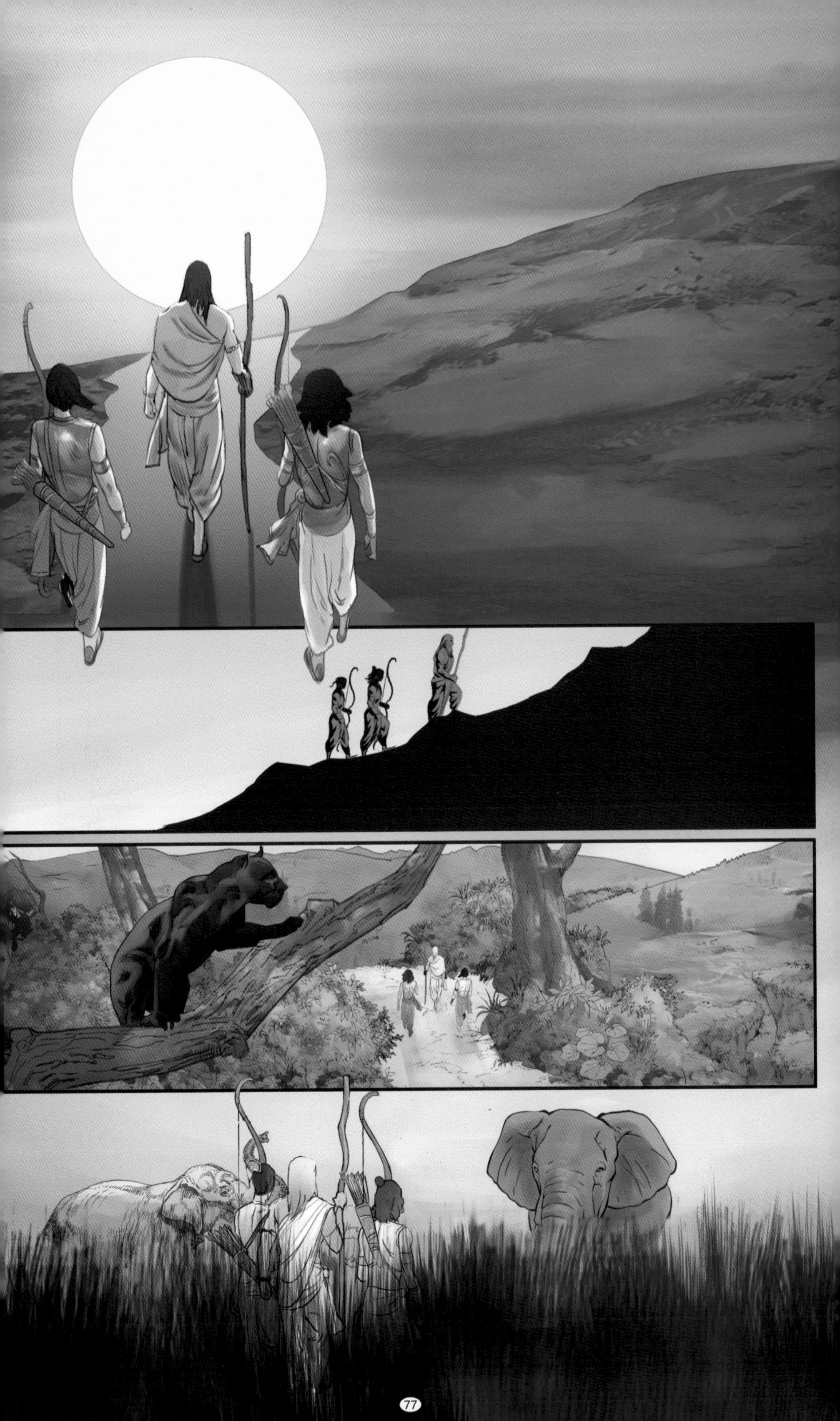

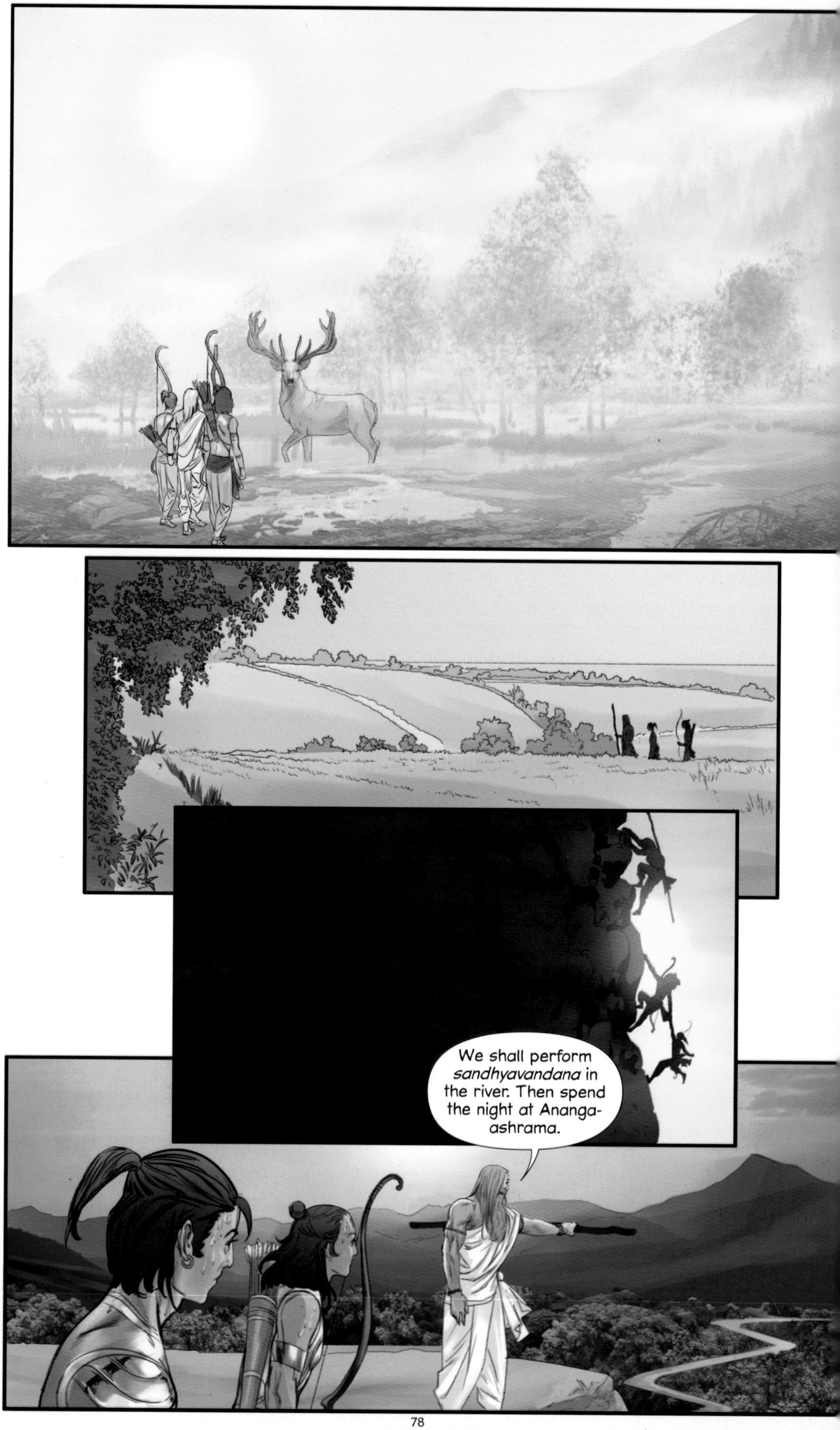
We shall perform *sandhyavandana* in the river. Then spend the night at Ananga-ashrama.

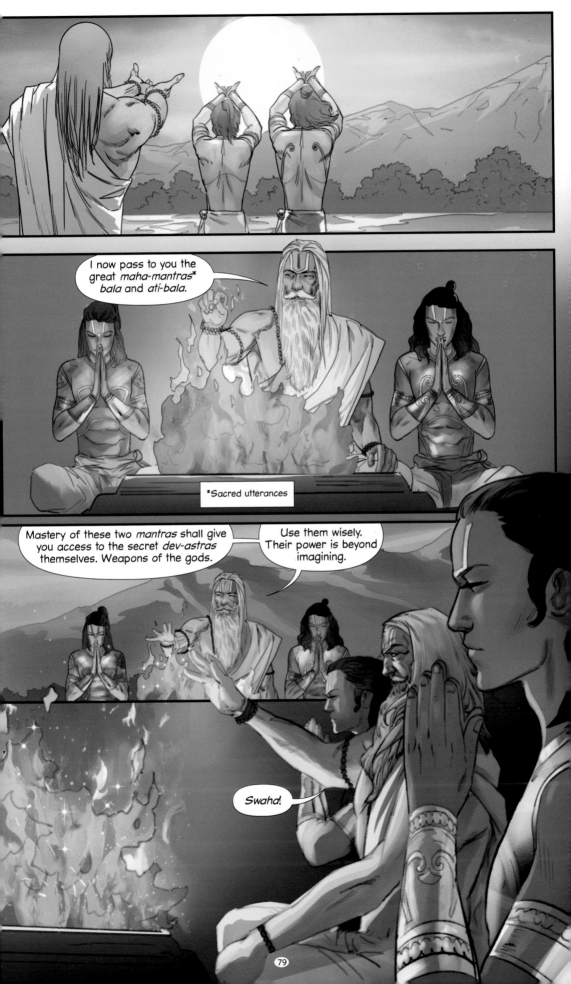

I now pass to you the great *maha-mantras** *bala* and *ati-bala*.

*Sacred utterances

Mastery of these two *mantras* shall give you access to the secret *dev-astras* themselves. Weapons of the gods.

Use them wisely. Their power is beyond imagining.

Swaha!

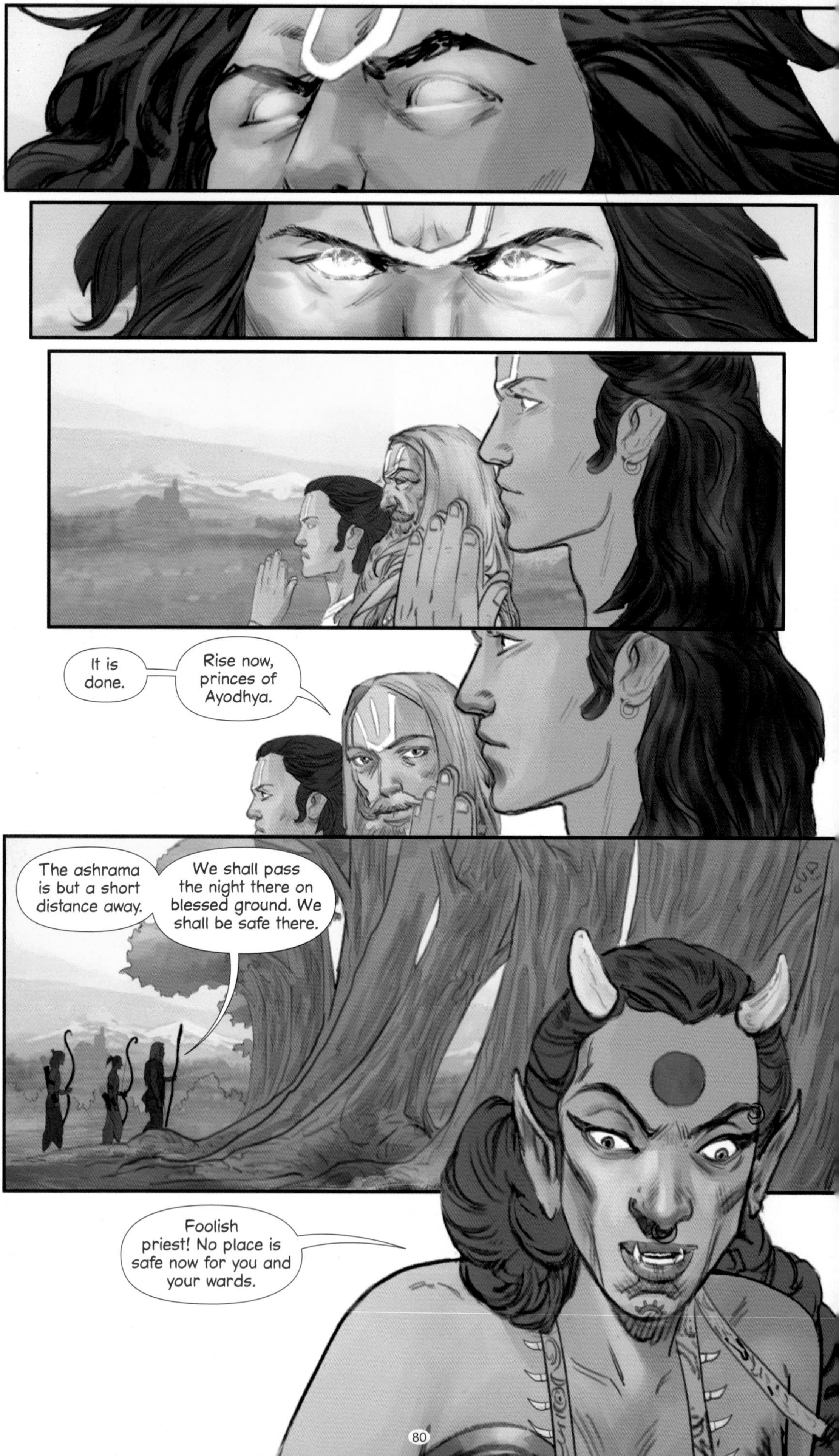

It is done.
Rise now, princes of Ayodhya.
The ashrama is but a short distance away.
We shall pass the night there on blessed ground. We shall be safe there.
Foolish priest! No place is safe now for you and your wards.

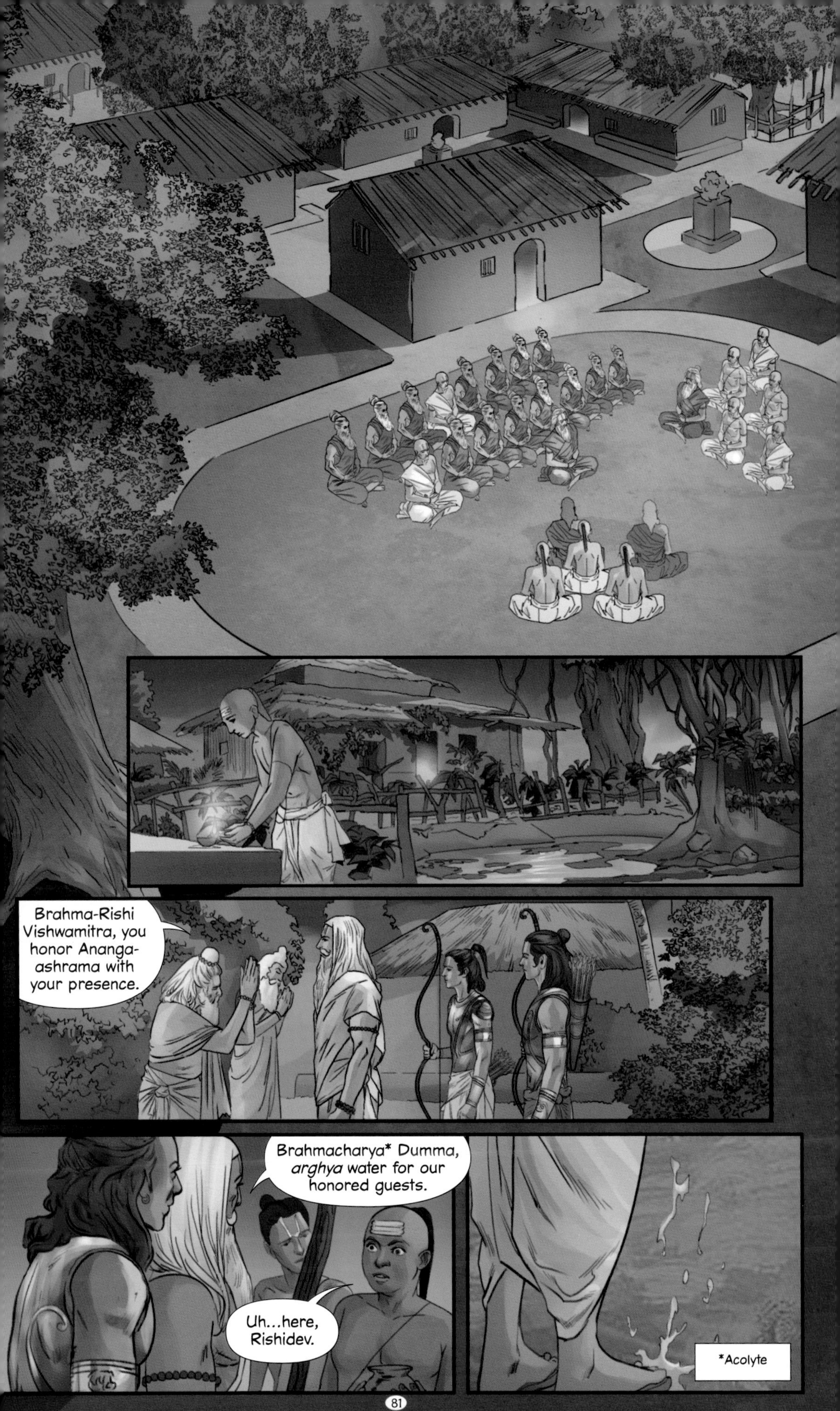
Brahma-Rishi Vishwamitra, you honor Ananga-ashrama with your presence.
Brahmacharya* Dumma, *arghya* water for our honored guests.
Uh...here, Rishidev.
*Acolyte

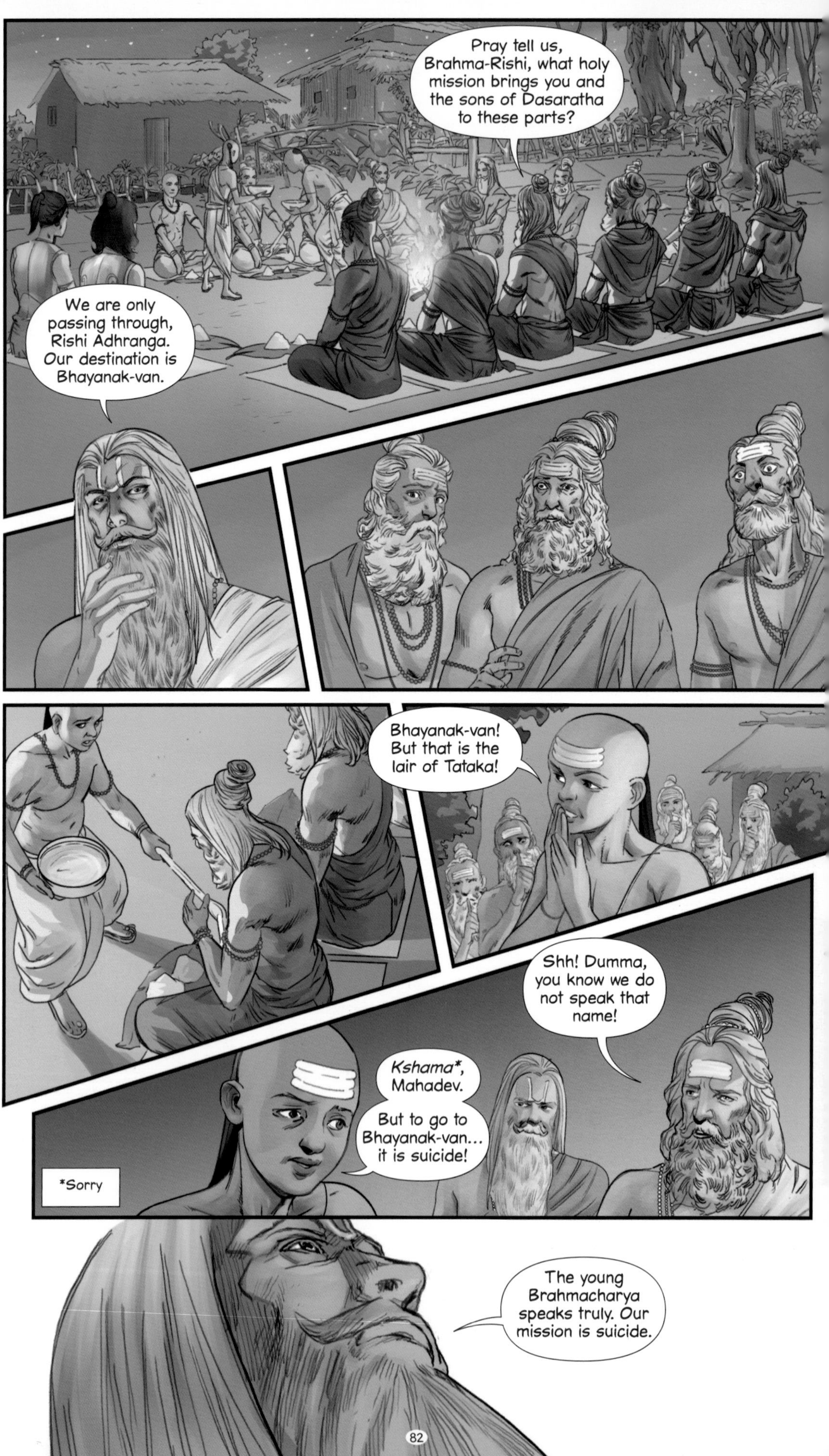
Pray tell us, Brahma-Rishi, what holy mission brings you and the sons of Dasaratha to these parts?
We are only passing through, Rishi Adhranga. Our destination is Bhayanak-van.
Bhayanak-van! But that is the lair of Tataka!
Shh! Dumma, you know we do not speak that name!
*Kshama**, Mahadev.
But to go to Bhayanak-van... it is suicide!
*Sorry
The young Brahmacharya speaks truly. Our mission is suicide.

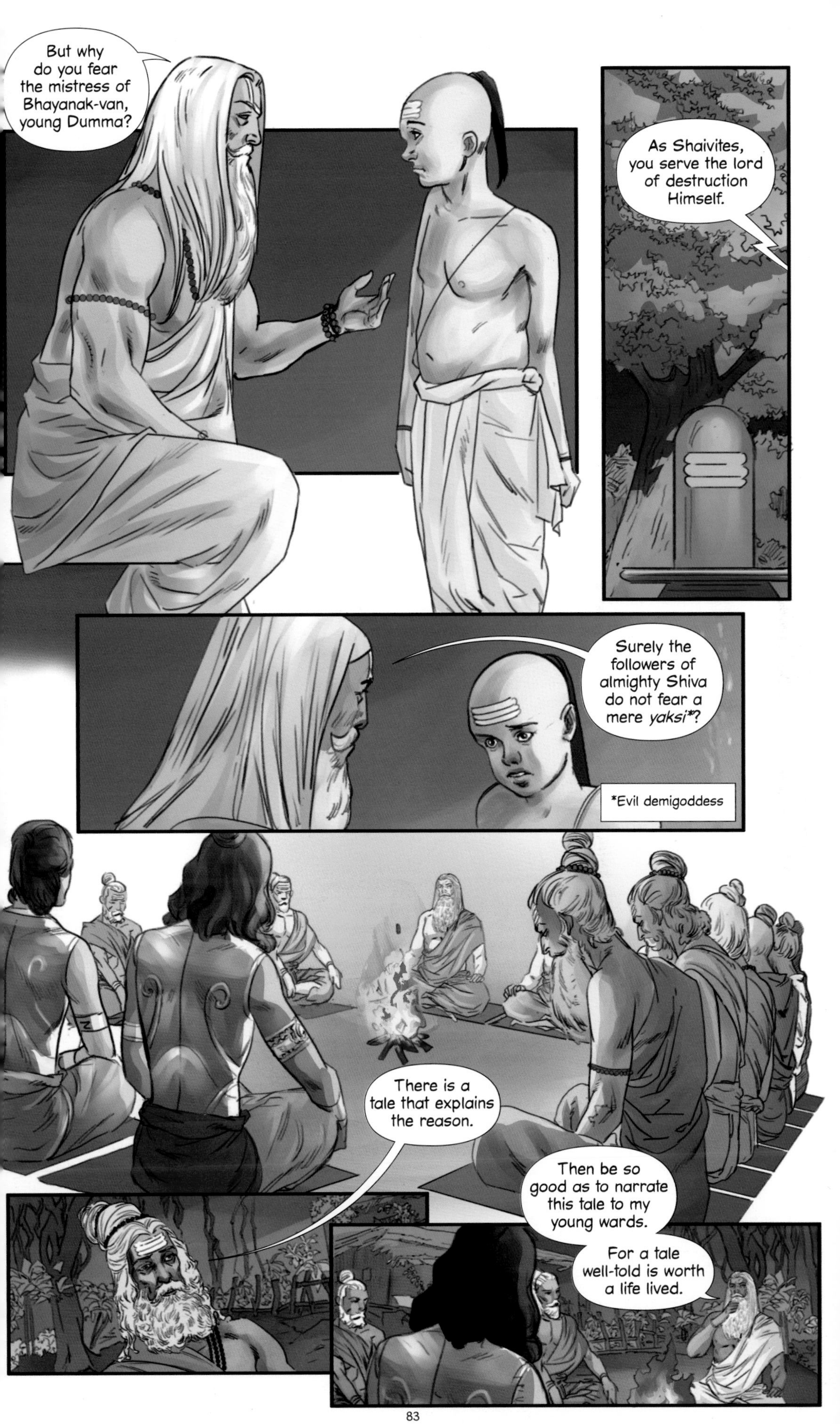

But why do you fear the mistress of Bhayanak-van, young Dumma?
As Shaivites, you serve the lord of destruction Himself.
Surely the followers of almighty Shiva do not fear a mere *yaksi**?
*Evil demigoddess
There is a tale that explains the reason.
Then be so good as to narrate this tale to my young wards.
For a tale well-told is worth a life lived.

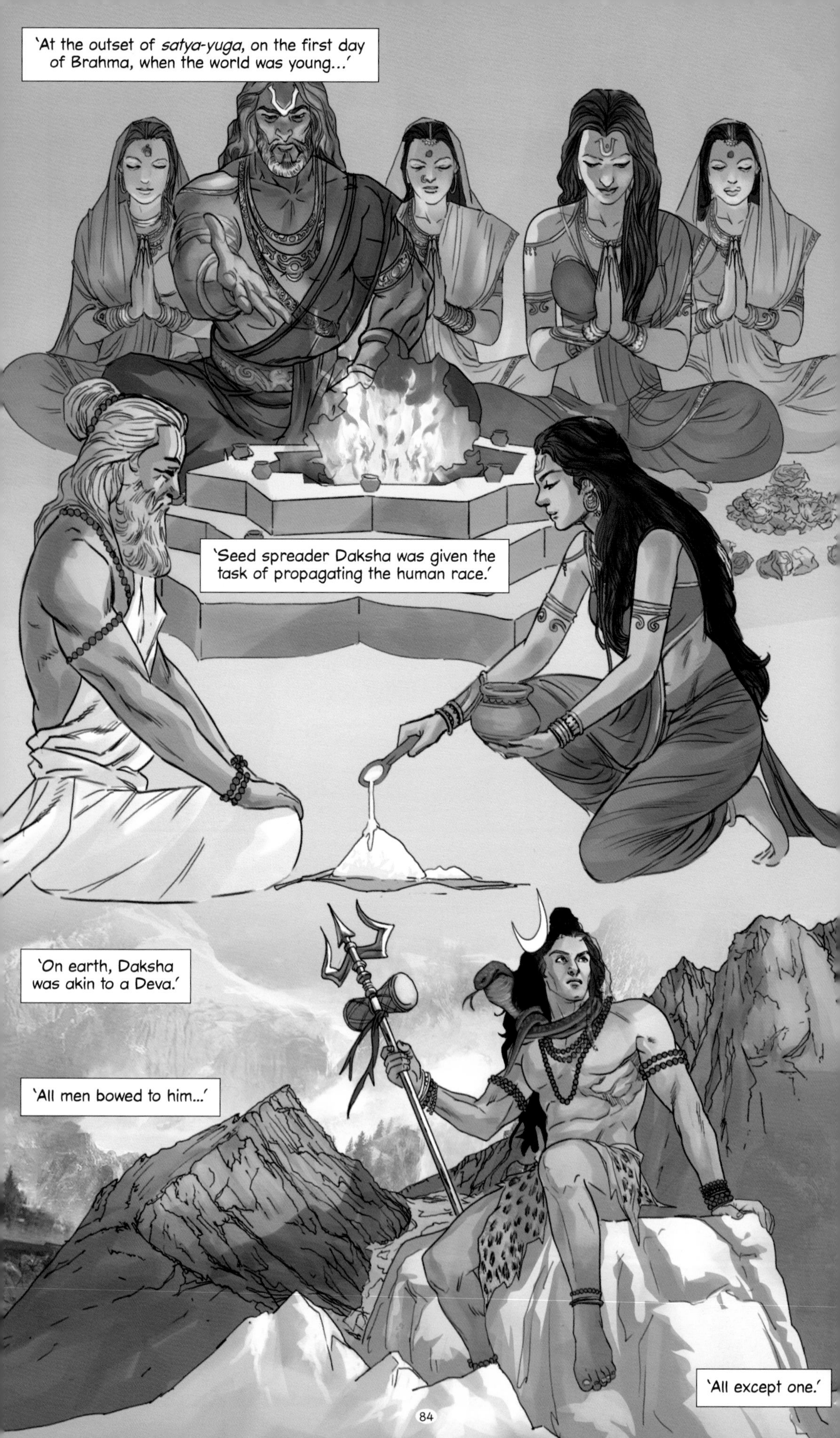
'At the outset of *satya-yuga*, on the first day of Brahma, when the world was young...'
'Seed spreader Daksha was given the task of propagating the human race.'
'On earth, Daksha was akin to a Deva.'
'All men bowed to him...'
'All except one.'

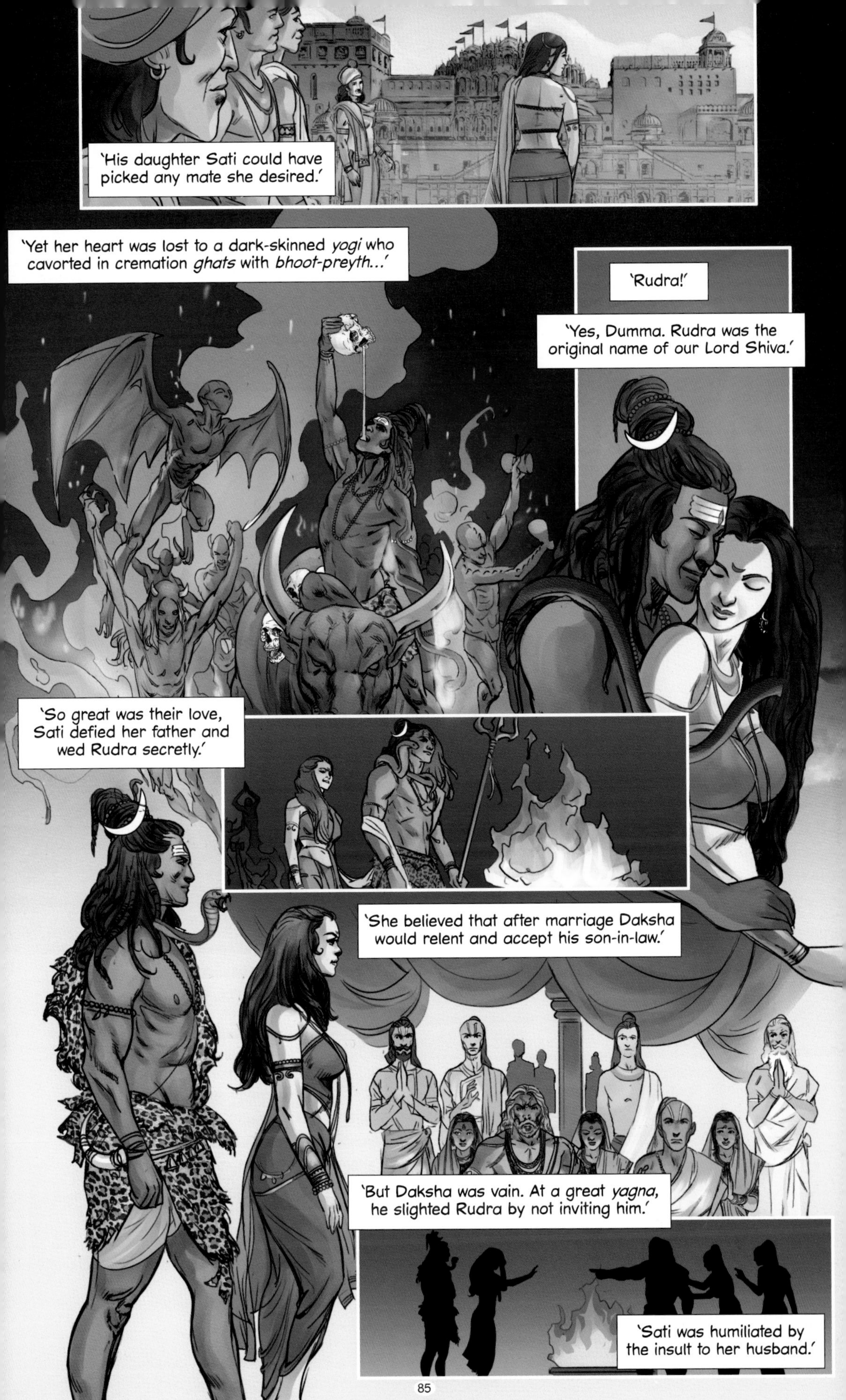
'His daughter Sati could have picked any mate she desired.'
'Yet her heart was lost to a dark-skinned *yogi* who cavorted in cremation *ghats* with *bhoot-preyth...*'
'Rudra!'
'Yes, Dumma. Rudra was the original name of our Lord Shiva.'
'So great was their love, Sati defied her father and wed Rudra secretly.'
'She believed that after marriage Daksha would relent and accept his son-in-law.'
'But Daksha was vain. At a great *yagna*, he slighted Rudra by not inviting him.'
'Sati was humiliated by the insult to her husband.'

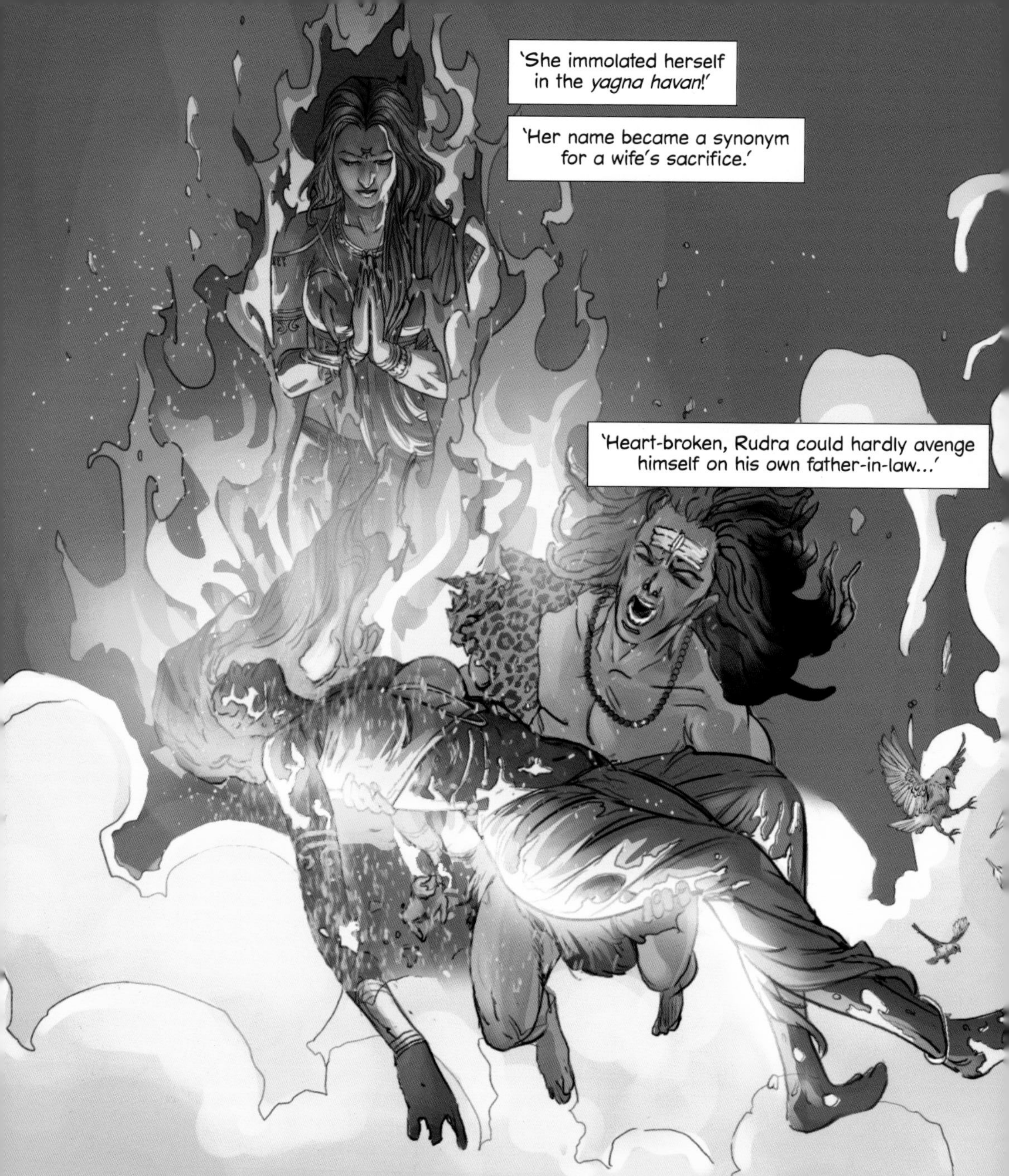
'She immolated herself in the *yagna havan*!'
'Her name became a synonym for a wife's sacrifice.'
'Heart-broken, Rudra could hardly avenge himself on his own father-in-law...'

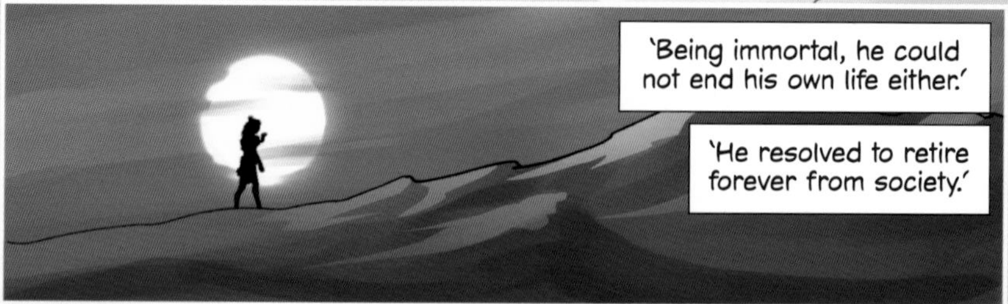
'Being immortal, he could not end his own life either.'
'He resolved to retire forever from society.'

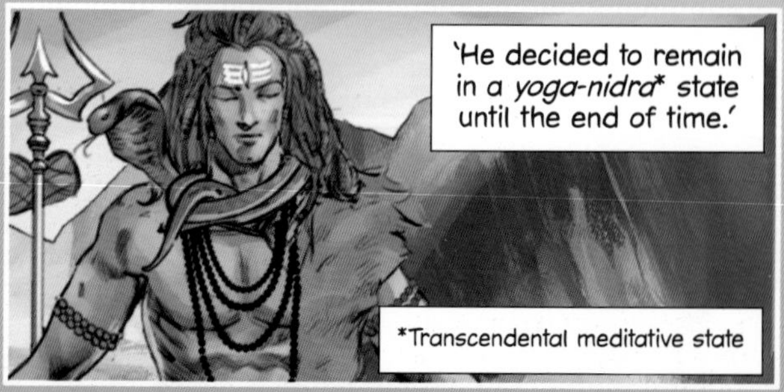
'He decided to remain in a *yoga-nidra** state until the end of time.'
*Transcendental meditative state

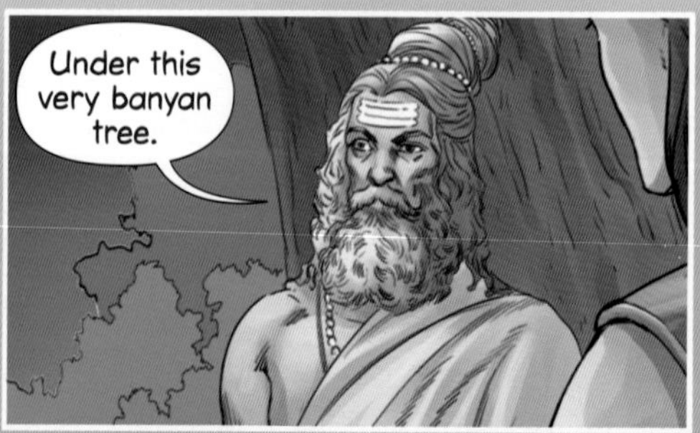
Under this very banyan tree.

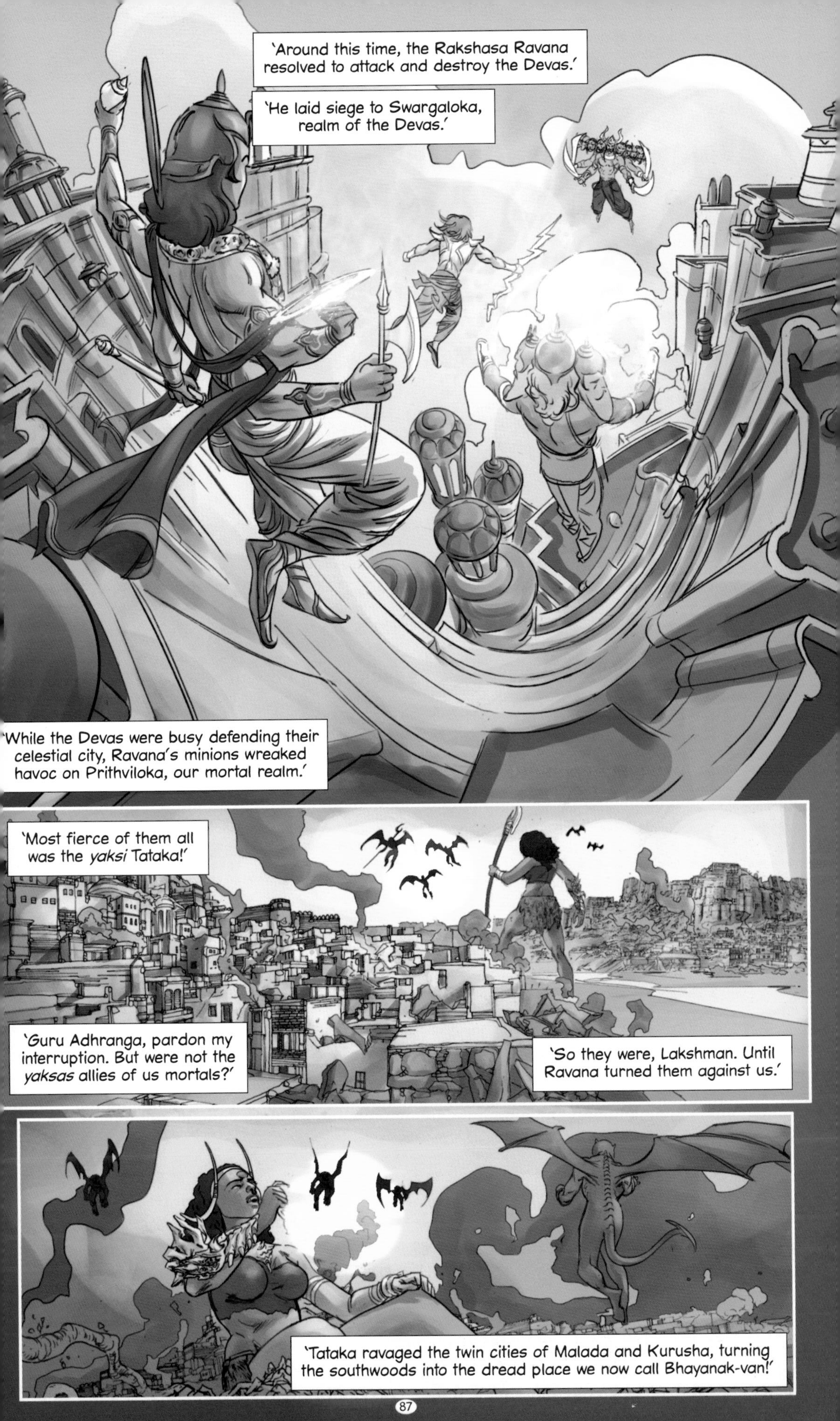
'Around this time, the Rakshasa Ravana resolved to attack and destroy the Devas.'
'He laid siege to Swargaloka, realm of the Devas.'
'While the Devas were busy defending their celestial city, Ravana's minions wreaked havoc on Prithviloka, our mortal realm.'
'Most fierce of them all was the *yaksi* Tataka!'
'Guru Adhranga, pardon my interruption. But were not the *yaksas* allies of us mortals?'
'So they were, Lakshman. Until Ravana turned them against us.'
'Tataka ravaged the twin cities of Malada and Kurusha, turning the southwoods into the dread place we now call Bhayanak-van!'

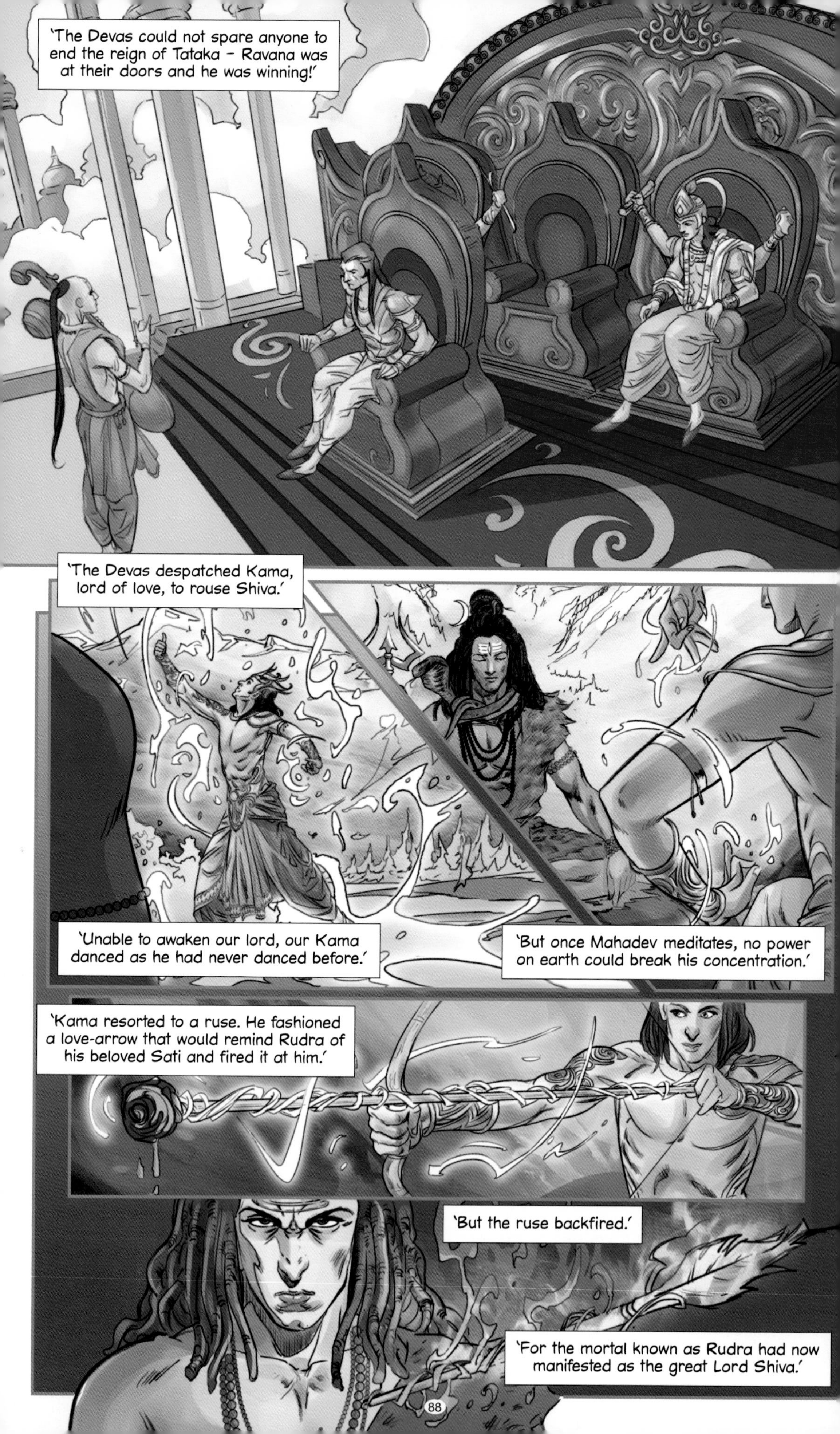
'The Devas could not spare anyone to end the reign of Tataka – Ravana was at their doors and he was winning!'
'The Devas despatched Kama, lord of love, to rouse Shiva.'
'Unable to awaken our lord, our Kama danced as he had never danced before.'
'But once Mahadev meditates, no power on earth could break his concentration.'
'Kama resorted to a ruse. He fashioned a love-arrow that would remind Rudra of his beloved Sati and fired it at him.'
'But the ruse backfired.'
'For the mortal known as Rudra had now manifested as the great Lord Shiva.'

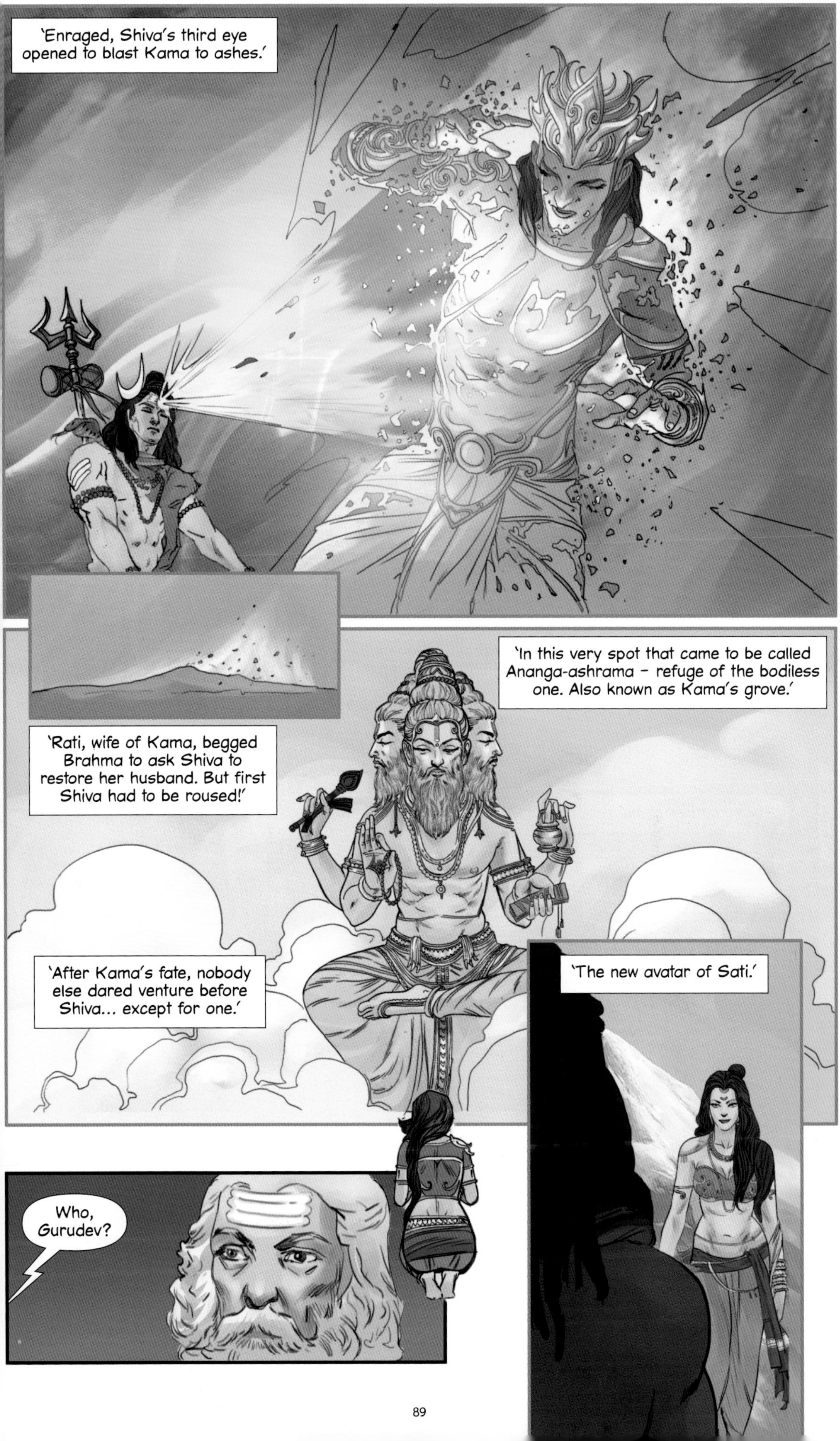
'Enraged, Shiva's third eye opened to blast Kama to ashes.'
'In this very spot that came to be called Ananga-ashrama – refuge of the bodiless one. Also known as Kama's grove.'
'Rati, wife of Kama, begged Brahma to ask Shiva to restore her husband. But first Shiva had to be roused!'
'After Kama's fate, nobody else dared venture before Shiva... except for one.'
'The new avatar of Sati.'
Who, Gurudev?

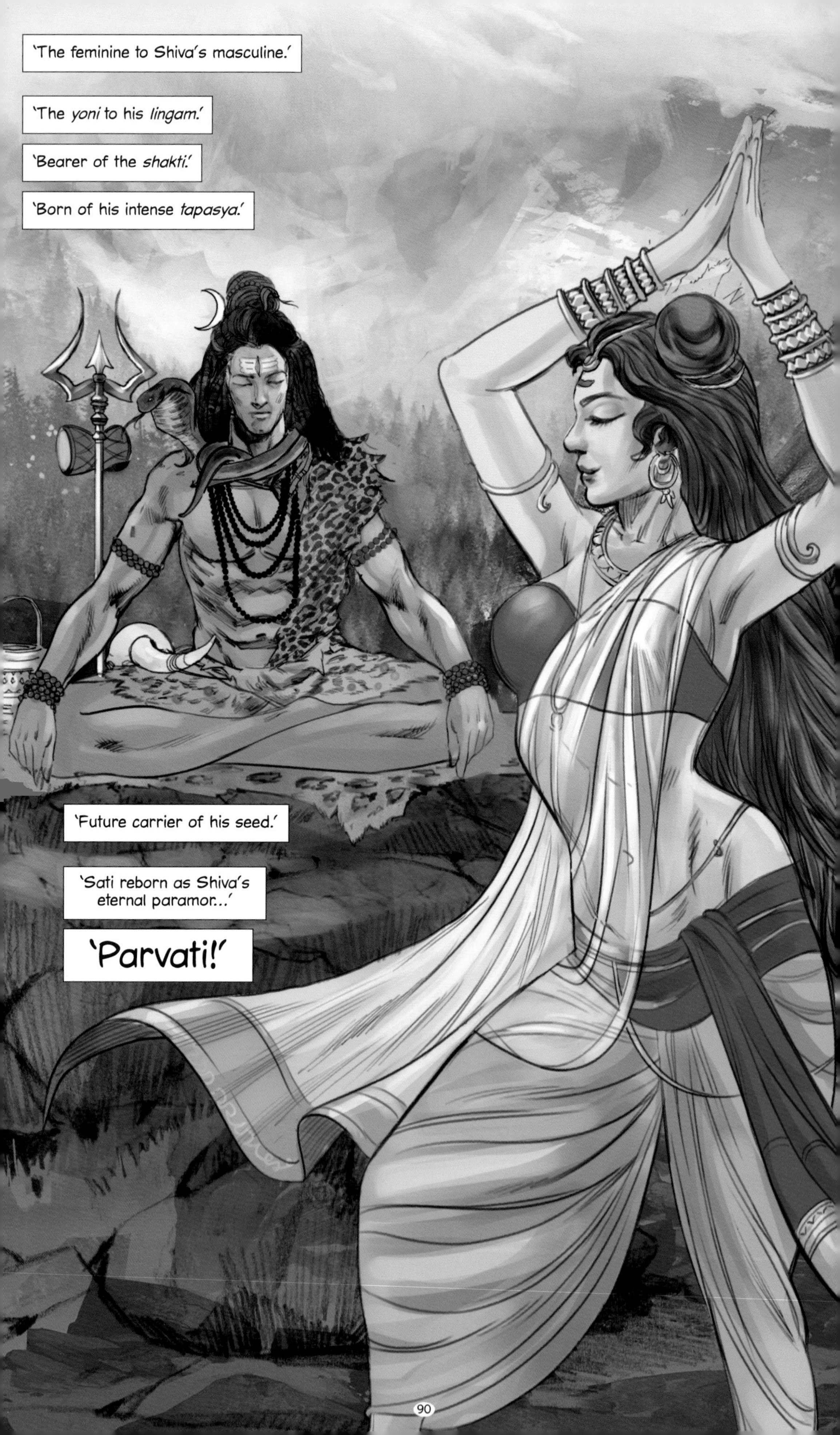
'The feminine to Shiva's masculine.'
'The *yoni* to his *lingam*.'
'Bearer of the *shakti*.'
'Born of his intense *tapasya*.'
'Future carrier of his seed.'
'Sati reborn as Shiva's eternal paramor...'
'Parvati!'

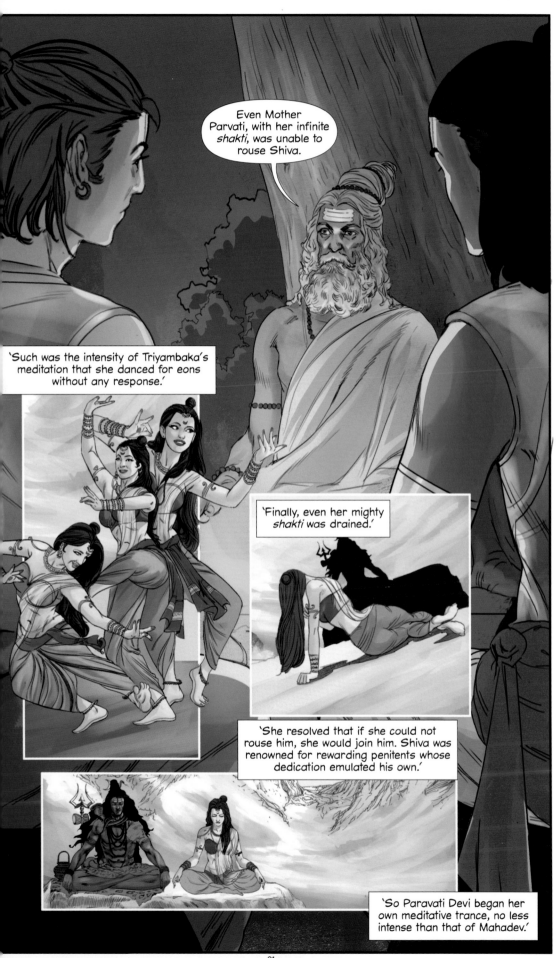

Even Mother Parvati, with her infinite *shakti*, was unable to rouse Shiva.

'Such was the intensity of Triyambaka's meditation that she danced for eons without any response.'

'Finally, even her mighty *shakti* was drained.'

'She resolved that if she could not rouse him, she would join him. Shiva was renowned for rewarding penitents whose dedication emulated his own.'

'So Paravati Devi began her own meditative trance, no less intense than that of Mahadev.'

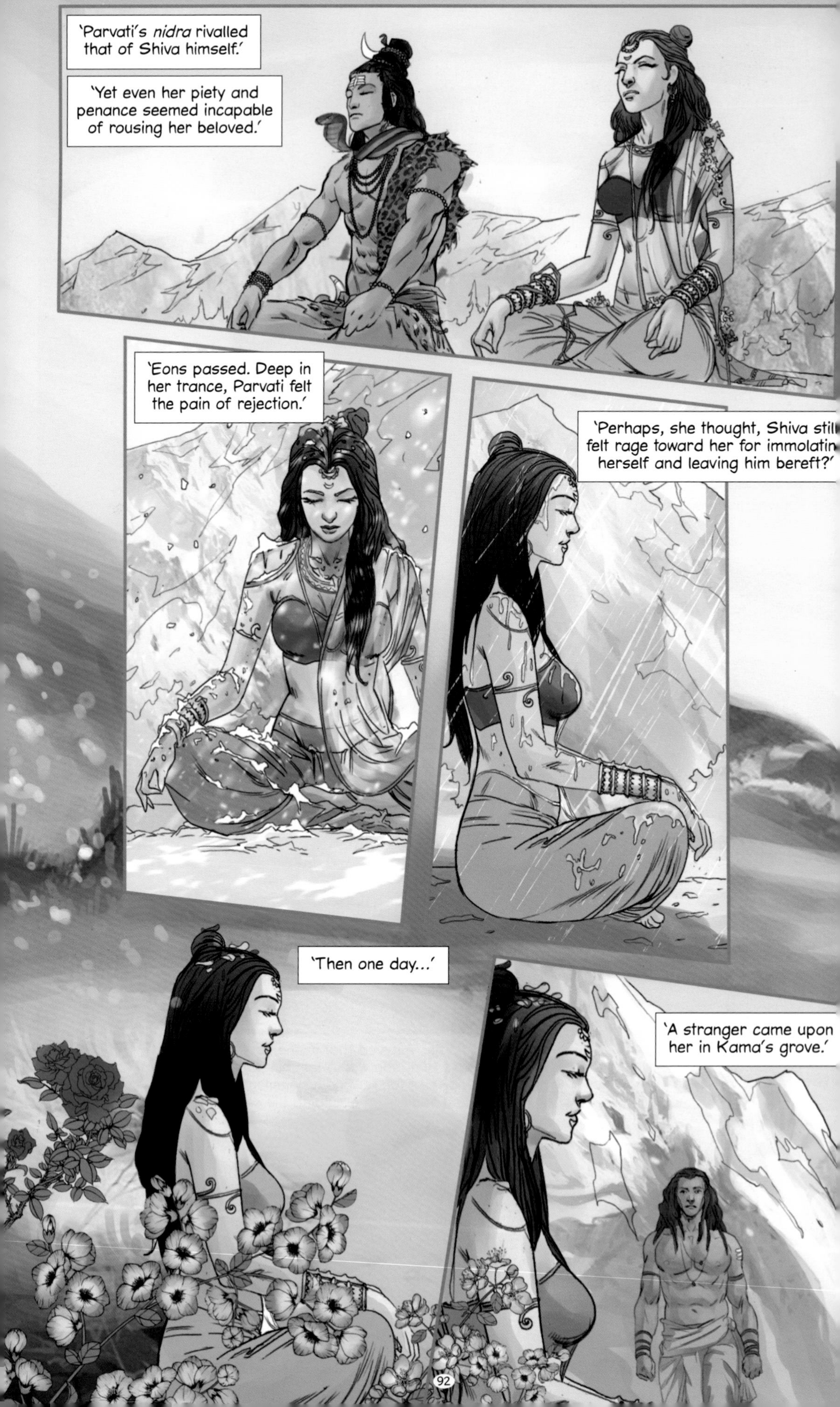
'Parvati's *nidra* rivalled that of Shiva himself.'
'Yet even her piety and penance seemed incapable of rousing her beloved.'
'Eons passed. Deep in her trance, Parvati felt the pain of rejection.'
'Perhaps, she thought, Shiva still felt rage toward her for immolatin herself and leaving him bereft?'
'Then one day...'
'A stranger came upon her in Kama's grove.'

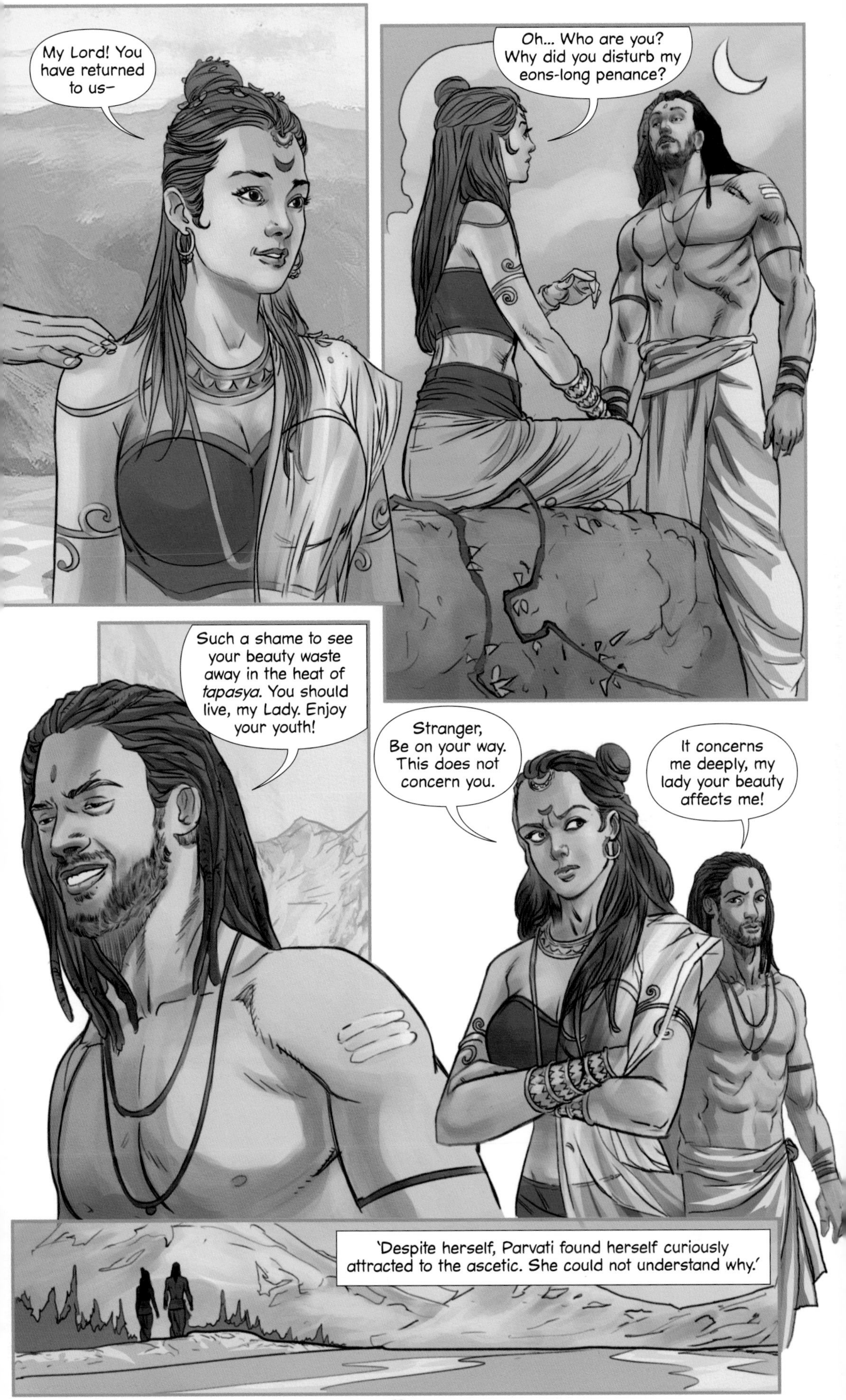

My Lord! You have returned to us–
Oh... Who are you? Why did you disturb my eons-long penance?
Such a shame to see your beauty waste away in the heat of *tapasya*. You should live, my Lady. Enjoy your youth!
Stranger, Be on your way. This does not concern you.
It concerns me deeply, my lady your beauty affects me!
'Despite herself, Parvati found herself curiously attracted to the ascetic. She could not understand why.'

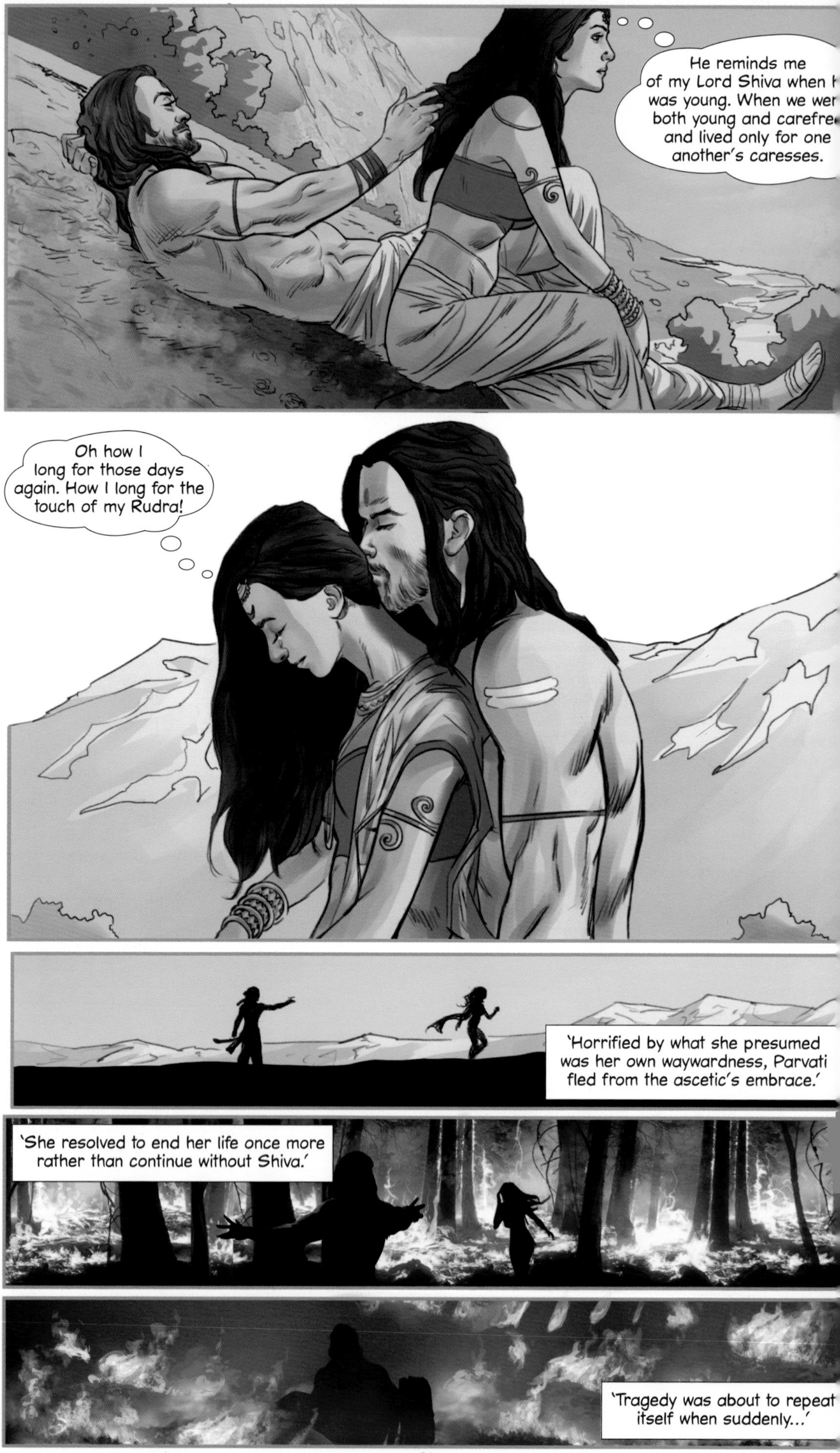
He reminds me of my Lord Shiva when
was young. When we wer both young and carefre and lived only for one another's caresses.
Oh how I long for those days again. How I long for the touch of my Rudra!
'Horrified by what she presumed was her own waywardness, Parvati fled from the ascetic's embrace.'
'She resolved to end her life once more rather than continue without Shiva.'
'Tragedy was about to repeat itself when suddenly...'

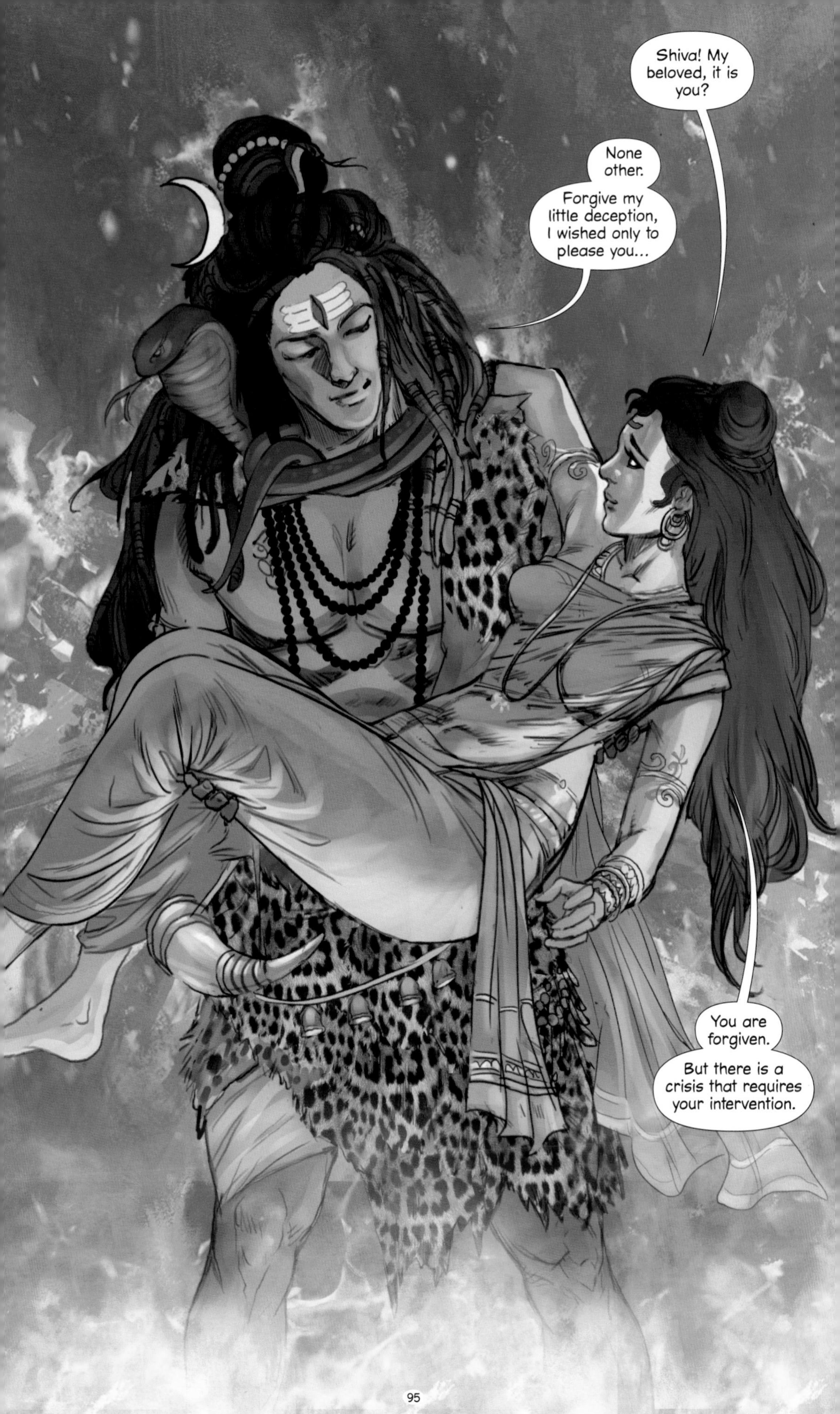
Shiva! My beloved, it is you?
None other.
Forgive my little deception, I wished only to please you...
You are forgiven.
But there is a crisis that requires your intervention.

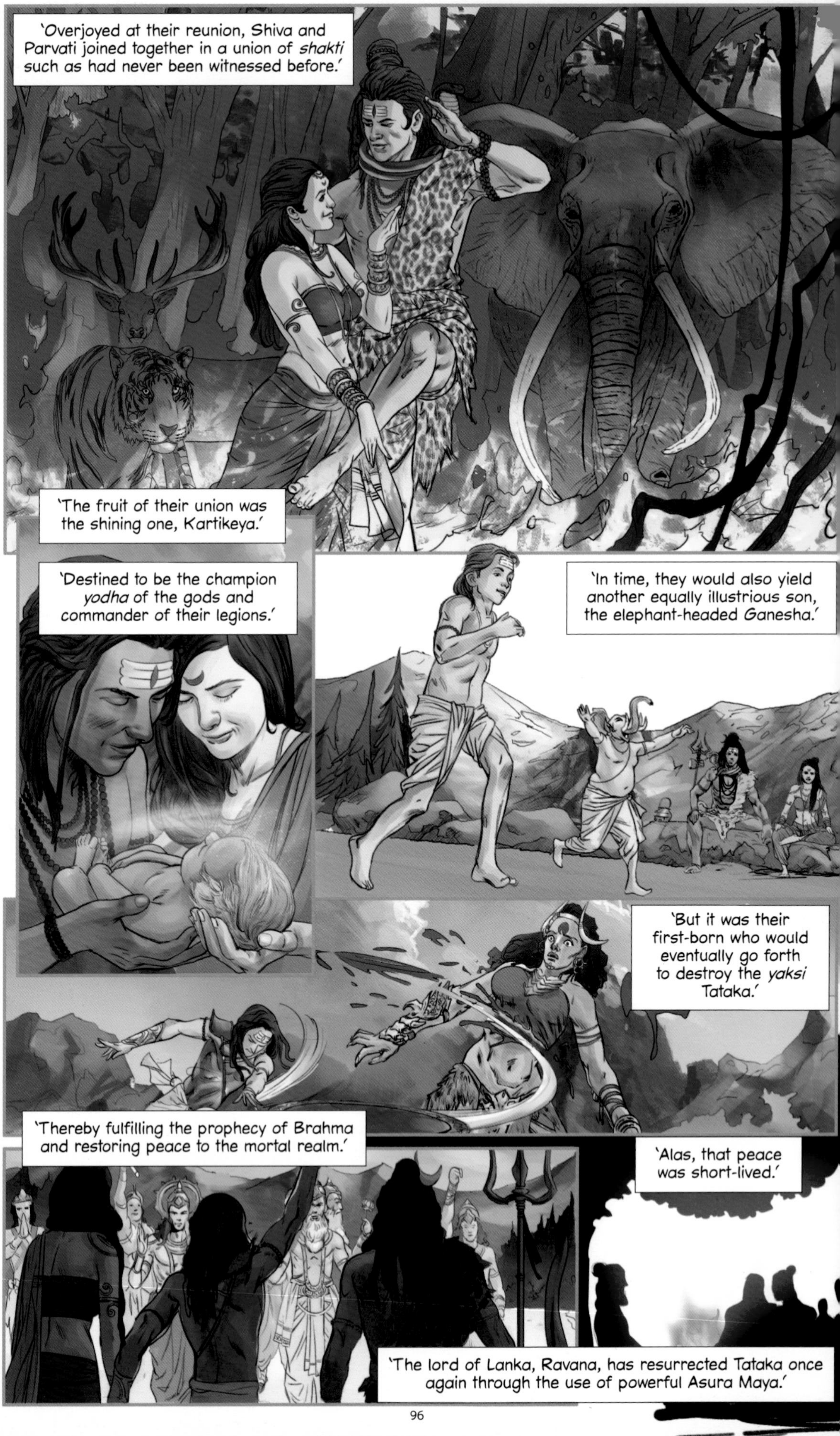
'Overjoyed at their reunion, Shiva and Parvati joined together in a union of *shakti* such as had never been witnessed before.'
'The fruit of their union was the shining one, Kartikeya.'
'Destined to be the champion *yodha* of the gods and commander of their legions.'
'In time, they would also yield another equally illustrious son, the elephant-headed Ganesha.'
'But it was their first-born who would eventually go forth to destroy the *yaksi* Tataka.'
'Thereby fulfilling the prophecy of Brahma and restoring peace to the mortal realm.'
'Alas, that peace was short-lived.'
'The lord of Lanka, Ravana, has resurrected Tataka once again through the use of powerful Asura Maya.'

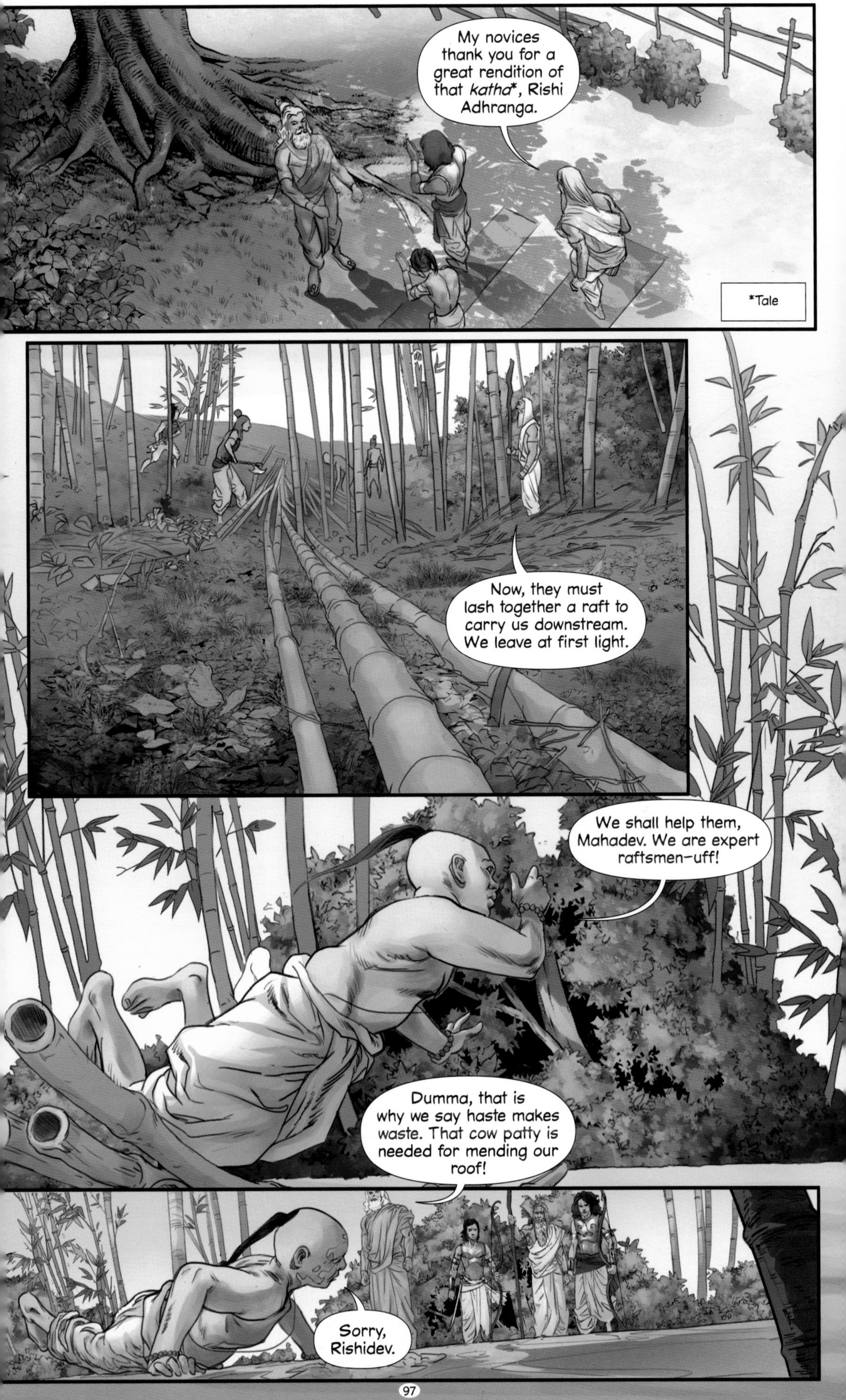
My novices thank you for a great rendition of that *katha**, Rishi Adhranga.
*Tale
Now, they must lash together a raft to carry us downstream. We leave at first light.
We shall help them, Mahadev. We are expert raftsmen–uff!
Dumma, that is why we say haste makes waste. That cow patty is needed for mending our roof!
Sorry, Rishidev.

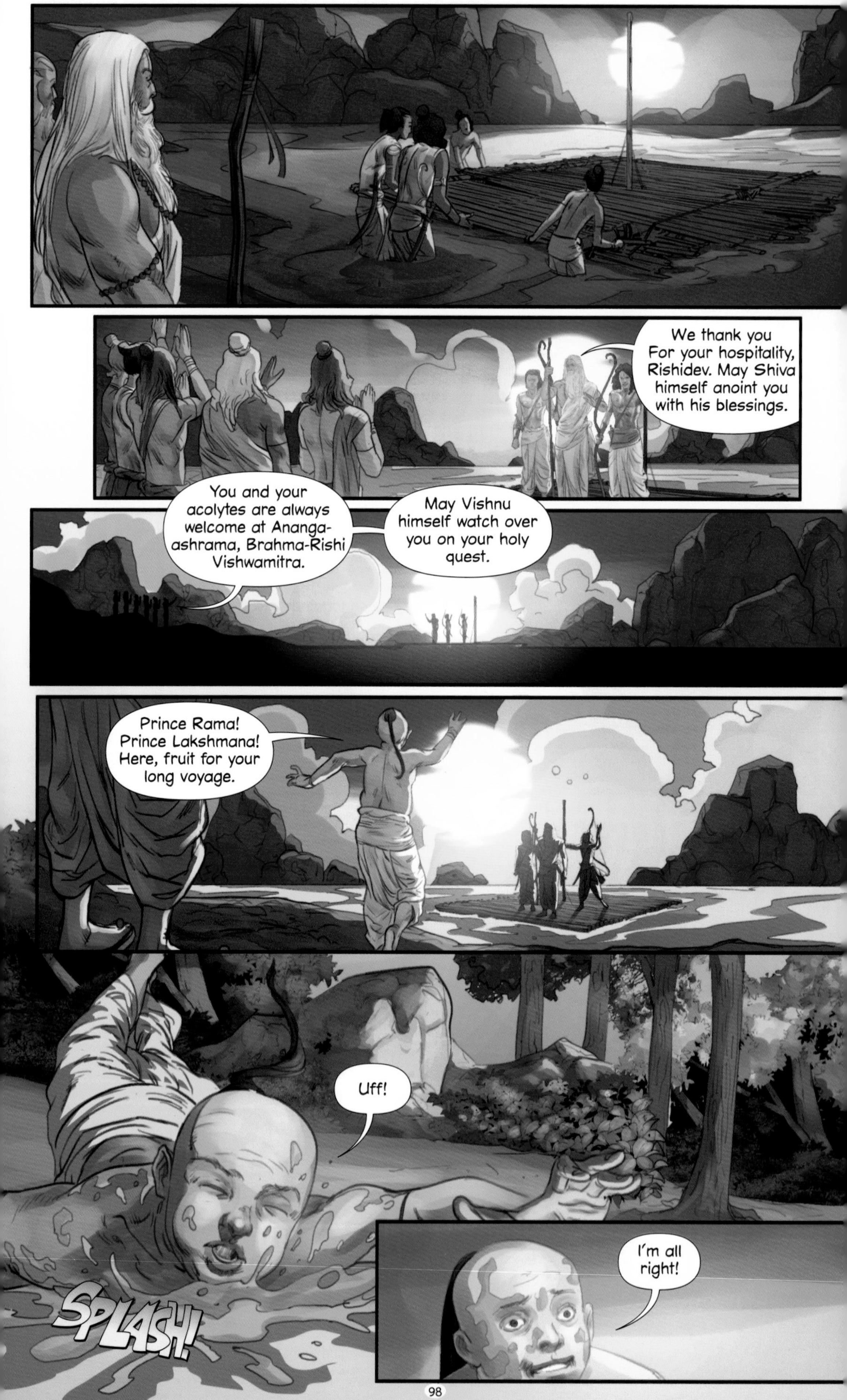
We thank you
For your hospitality,
Rishidev. May Shiva
himself anoint you
with his blessings.
You and your acolytes are always welcome at Ananga-ashrama, Brahma-Rishi Vishwamitra.
May Vishnu himself watch over you on your holy quest.
Prince Rama! Prince Lakshmana! Here, fruit for your long voyage.
Uff!
SPLASH!
I'm all right!

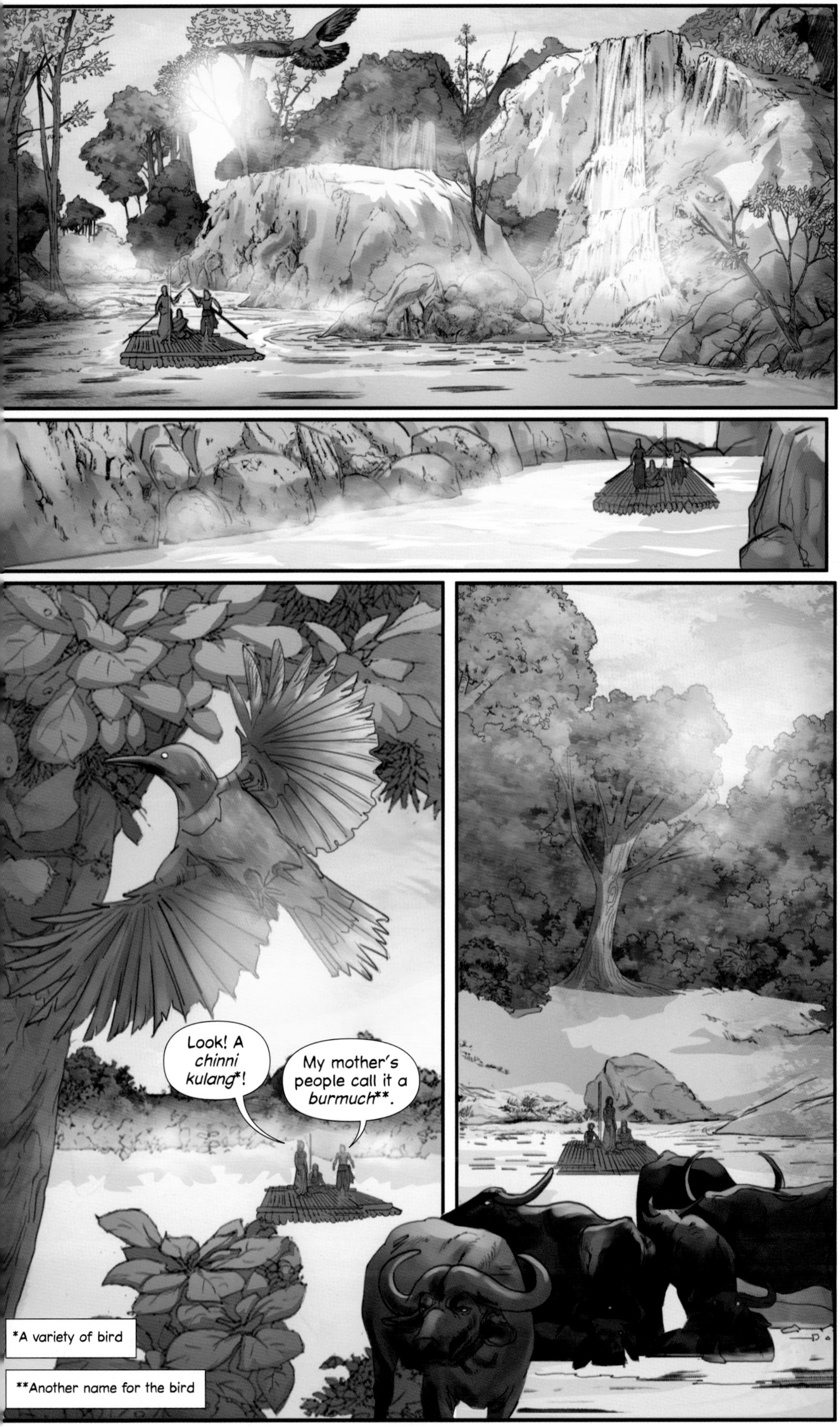
Look! A *chinni kulang**!
My mother's people call it a *burmuch***.
*A variety of bird
**Another name for the bird

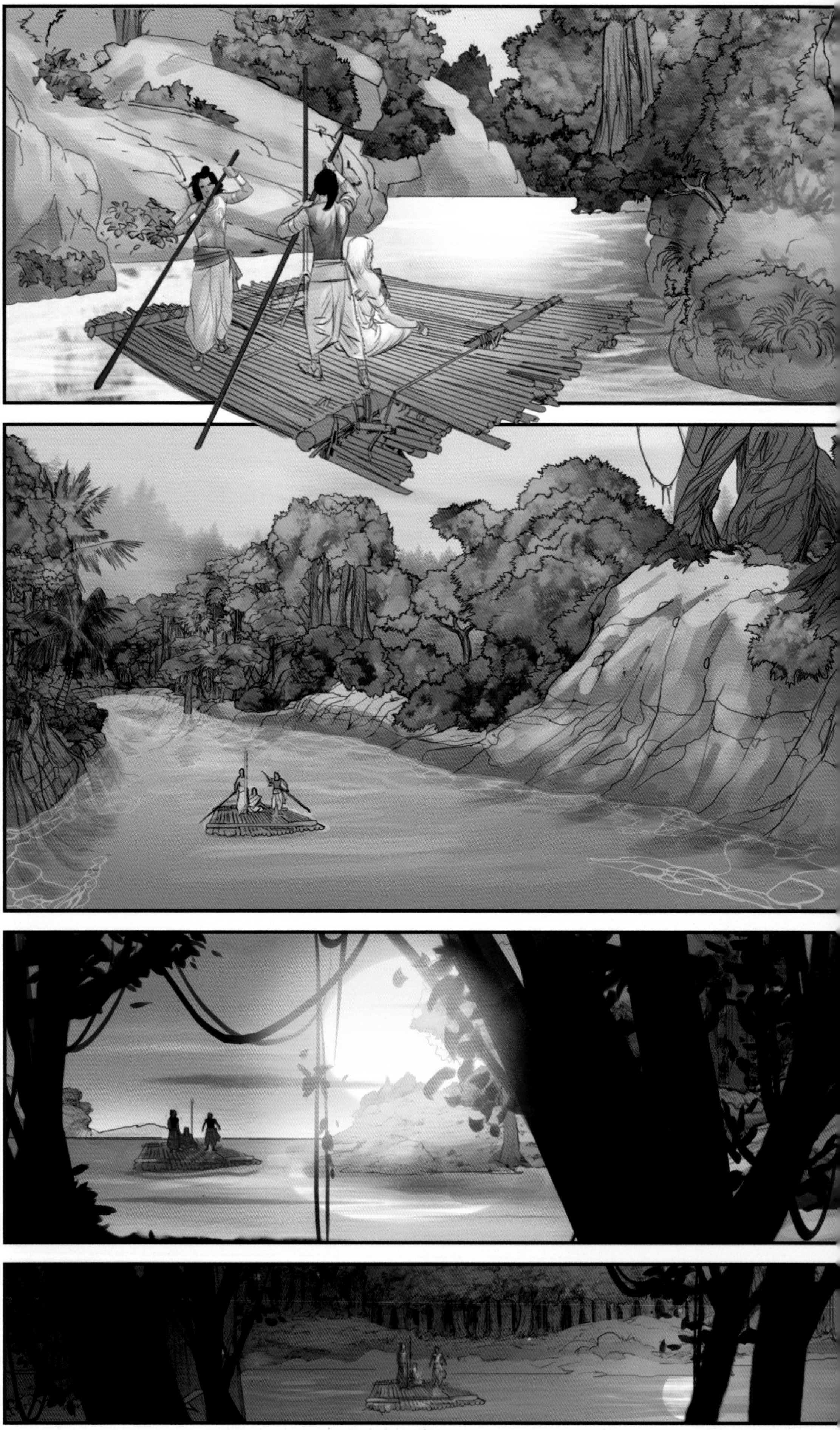

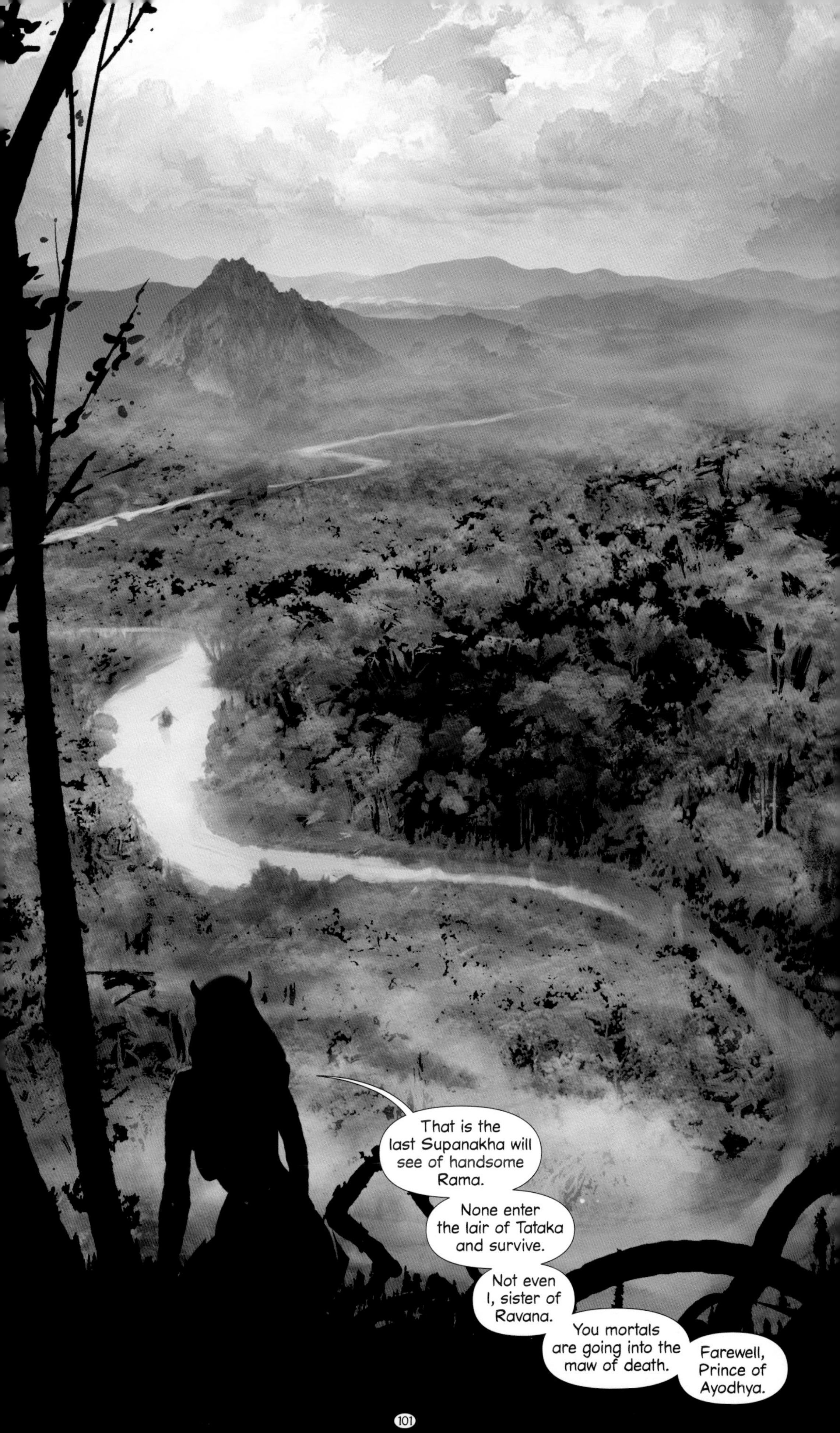
That is the last Supanakha will see of handsome Rama.
None enter the lair of Tataka and survive.
Not even I, sister of Ravana.
You mortals are going into the maw of death.
Farewell, Prince of Ayodhya.

KAAND III

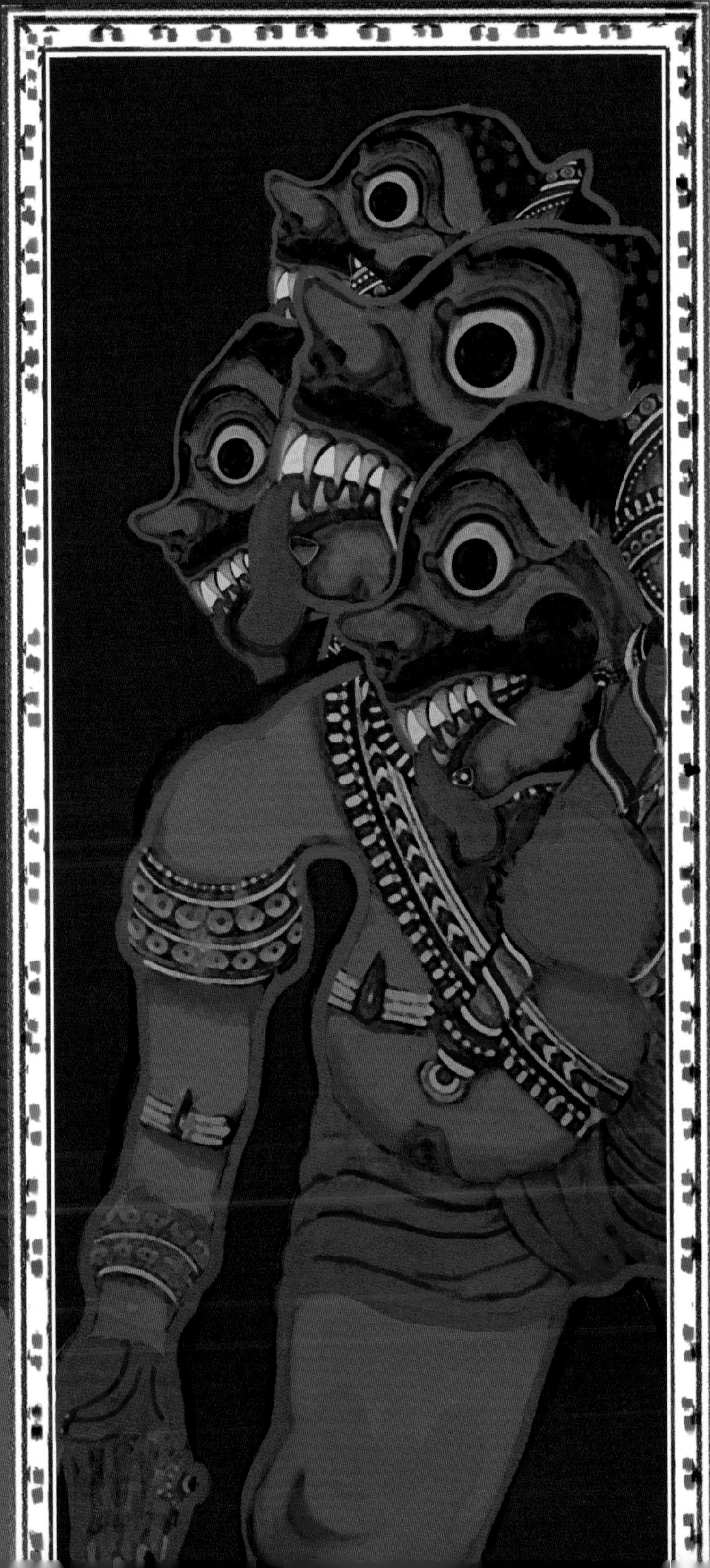

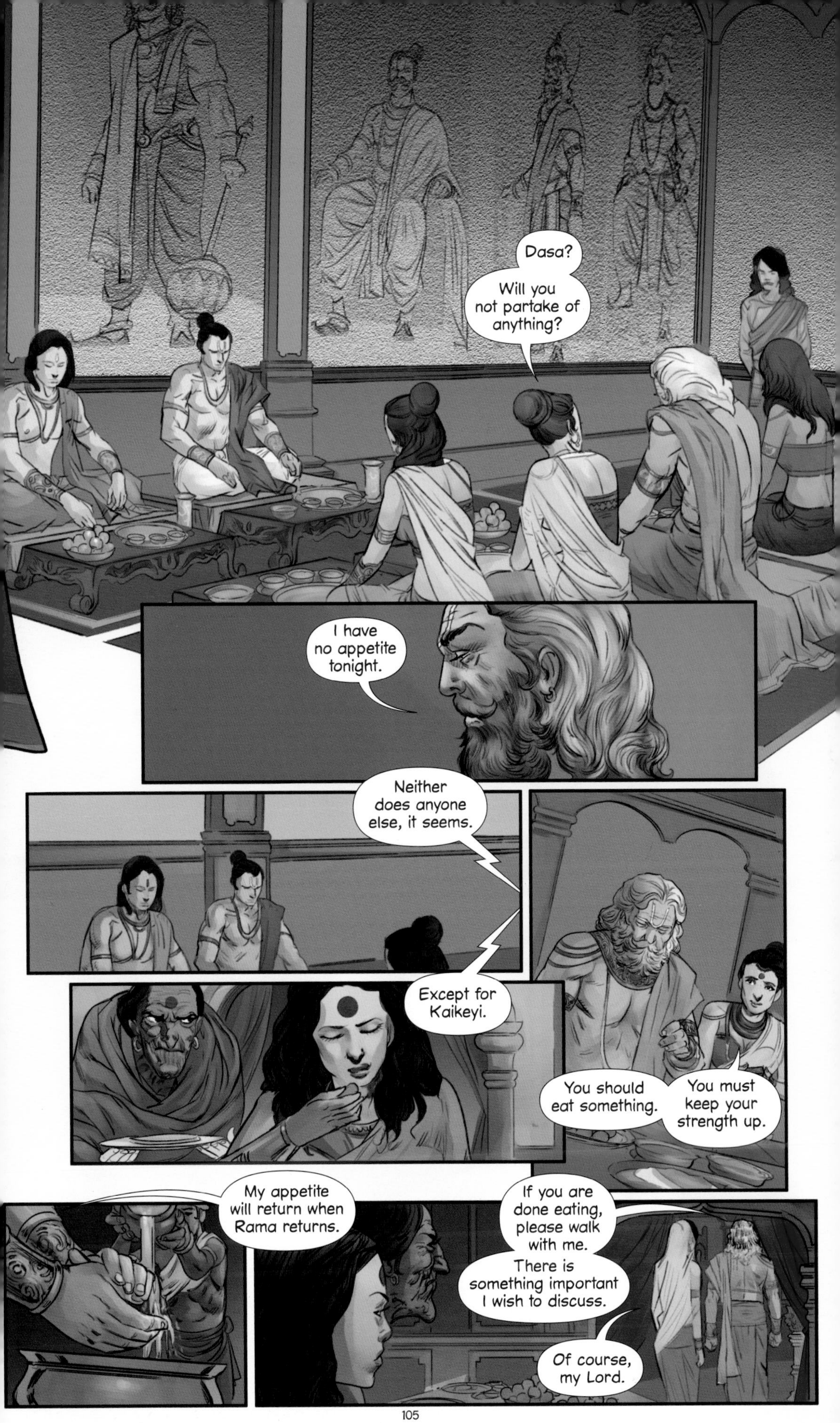
Dasa?
Will you not partake of anything?
I have no appetite tonight.
Neither does anyone else, it seems.
Except for Kaikeyi.
You should eat something.
You must keep your strength up.
My appetite will return when Rama returns.
If you are done eating, please walk with me.
There is something important I wish to discuss.
Of course, my Lord.

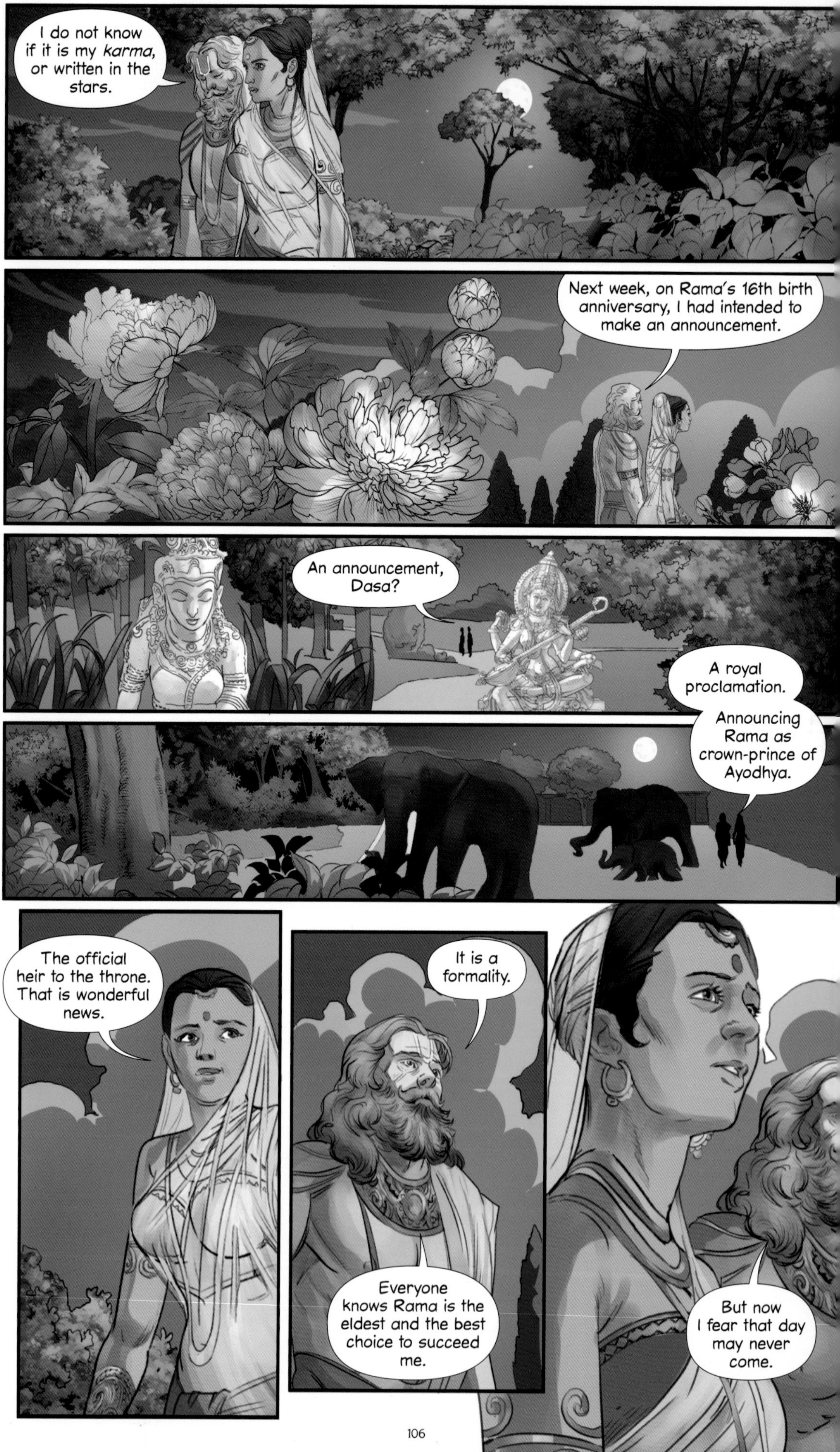
I do not know if it is my *karma*, or written in the stars.
Next week, on Rama's 16th birth anniversary, I had intended to make an announcement.
An announcement, Dasa?
A royal proclamation.
Announcing Rama as crown-prince of Ayodhya.
The official heir to the throne. That is wonderful news.
It is a formality.
Everyone knows Rama is the eldest and the best choice to succeed me.
But now I fear that day may never come.

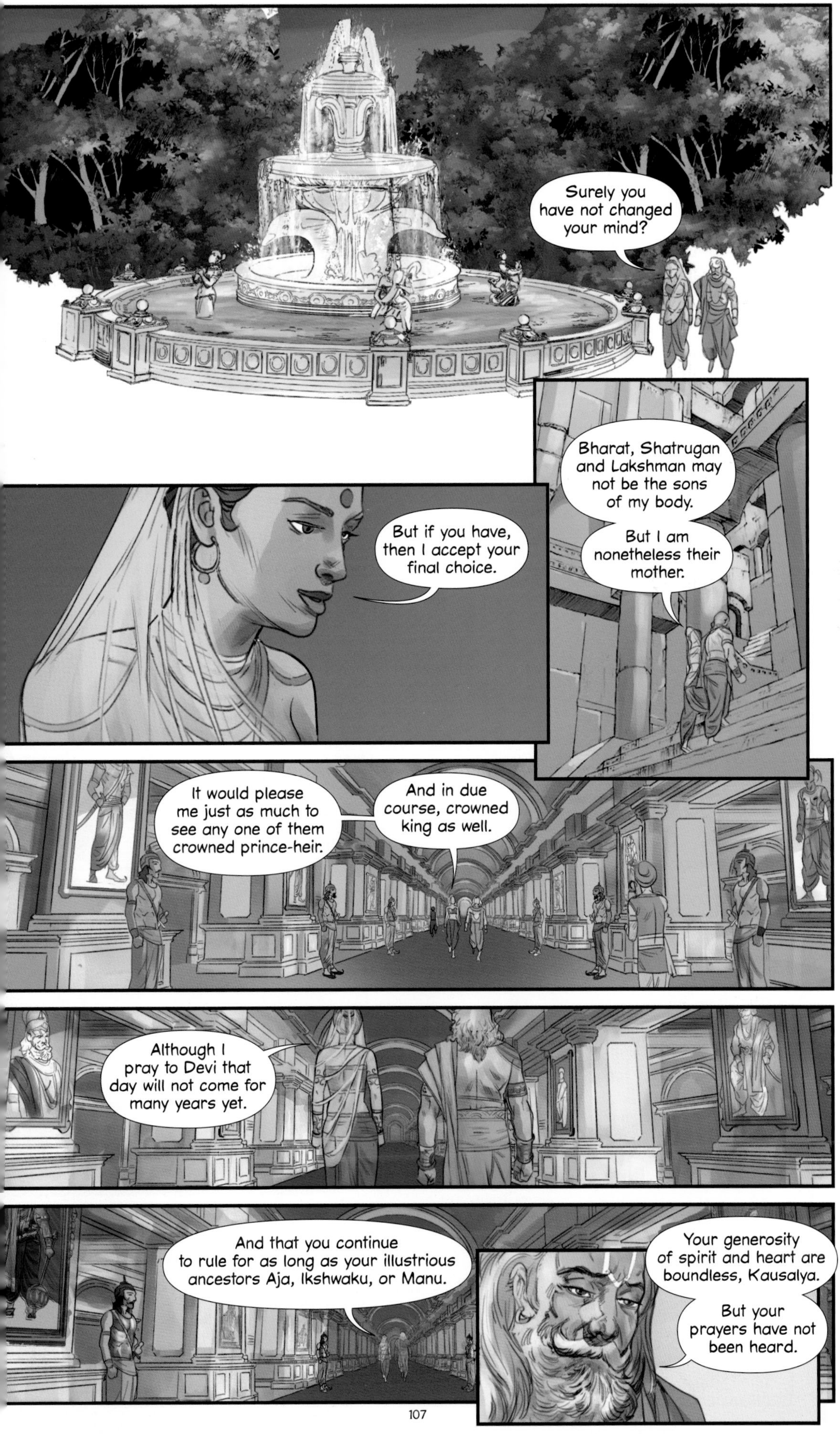
Surely you have not changed your mind?
Bharat, Shatrugan and Lakshman may not be the sons of my body.
But I am nonetheless their mother.
But if you have, then I accept your final choice.
It would please me just as much to see any one of them crowned prince-heir.
And in due course, crowned king as well.
Although I pray to Devi that day will not come for many years yet.
And that you continue to rule for as long as your illustrious ancestors Aja, Ikshwaku, or Manu.
Your generosity of spirit and heart are boundless, Kausalya.
But your prayers have not been heard.

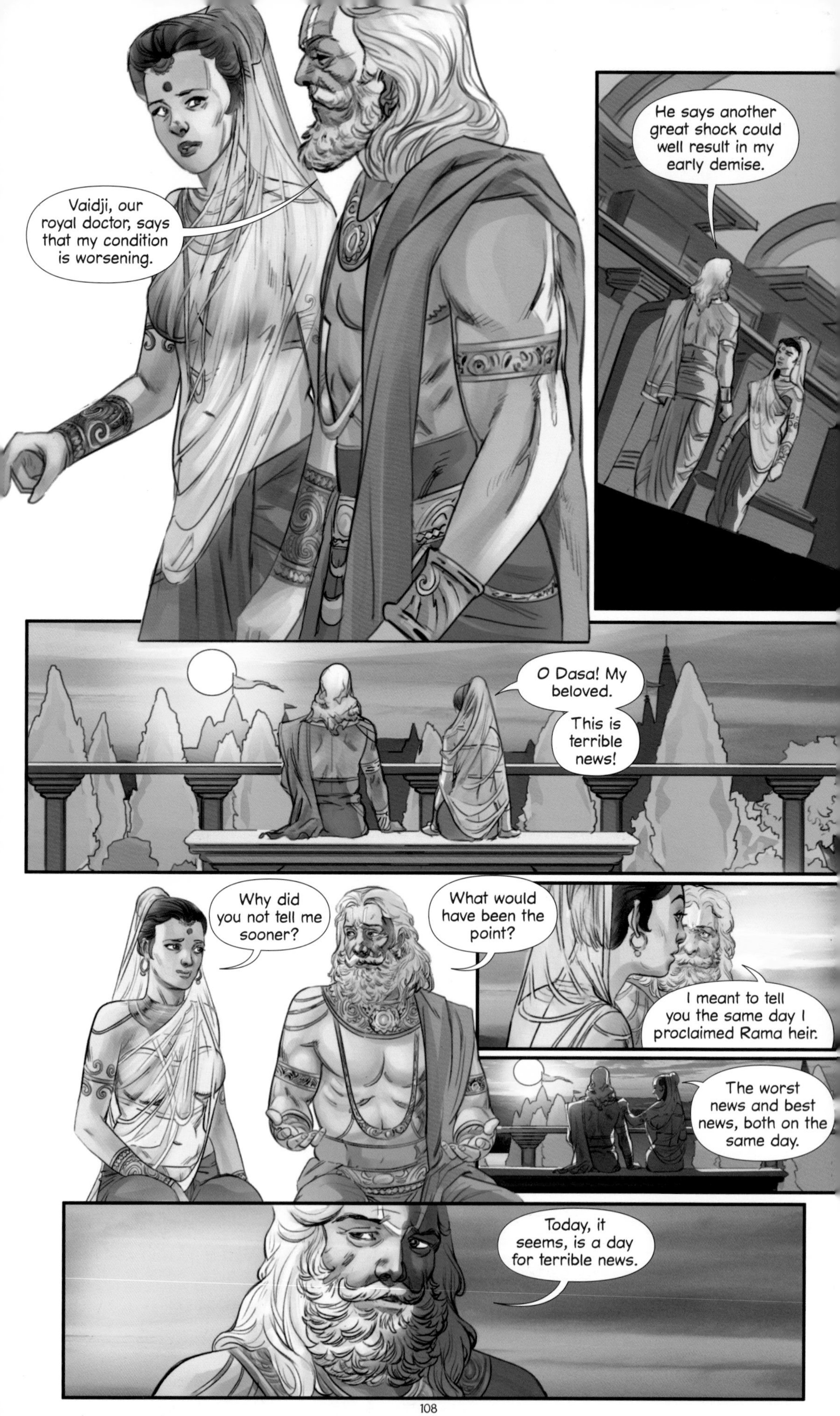

Vaidji, our royal doctor, says that my condition is worsening.
He says another great shock could well result in my early demise.
O Dasa! My beloved.
This is terrible news!
Why did you not tell me sooner?
What would have been the point?
I meant to tell you the same day I proclaimed Rama heir.
The worst news and best news, both on the same day.
Today, it seems, is a day for terrible news.

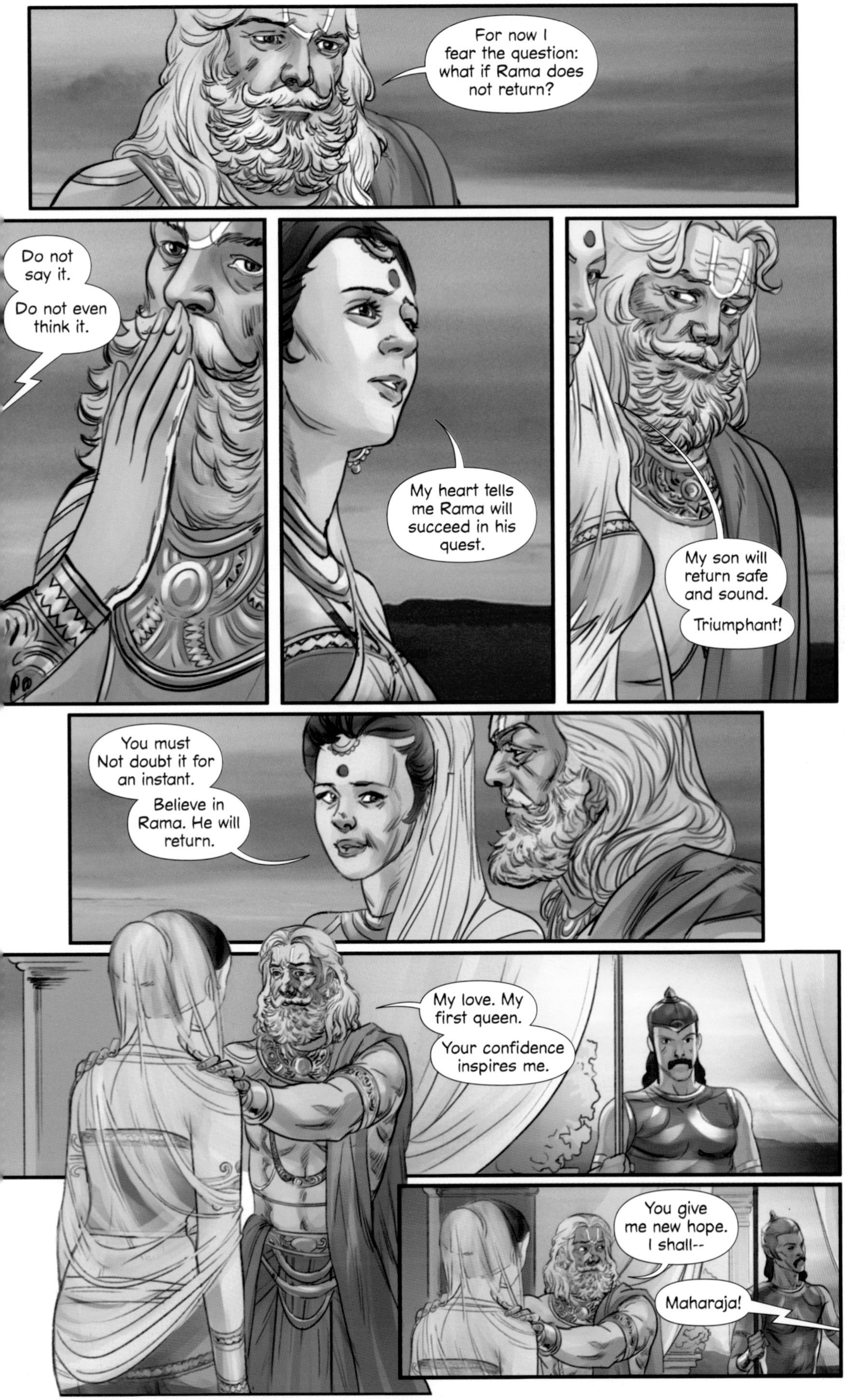

For now I fear the question: what if Rama does not return?
Do not say it.
Do not even think it.
My heart tells me Rama will succeed in his quest.
My son will return safe and sound.
Triumphant!
You must Not doubt it for an instant.
Believe in Rama. He will return.
My love. My first queen.
Your confidence inspires me.
You give me new hope. I shall--
Maharaja!

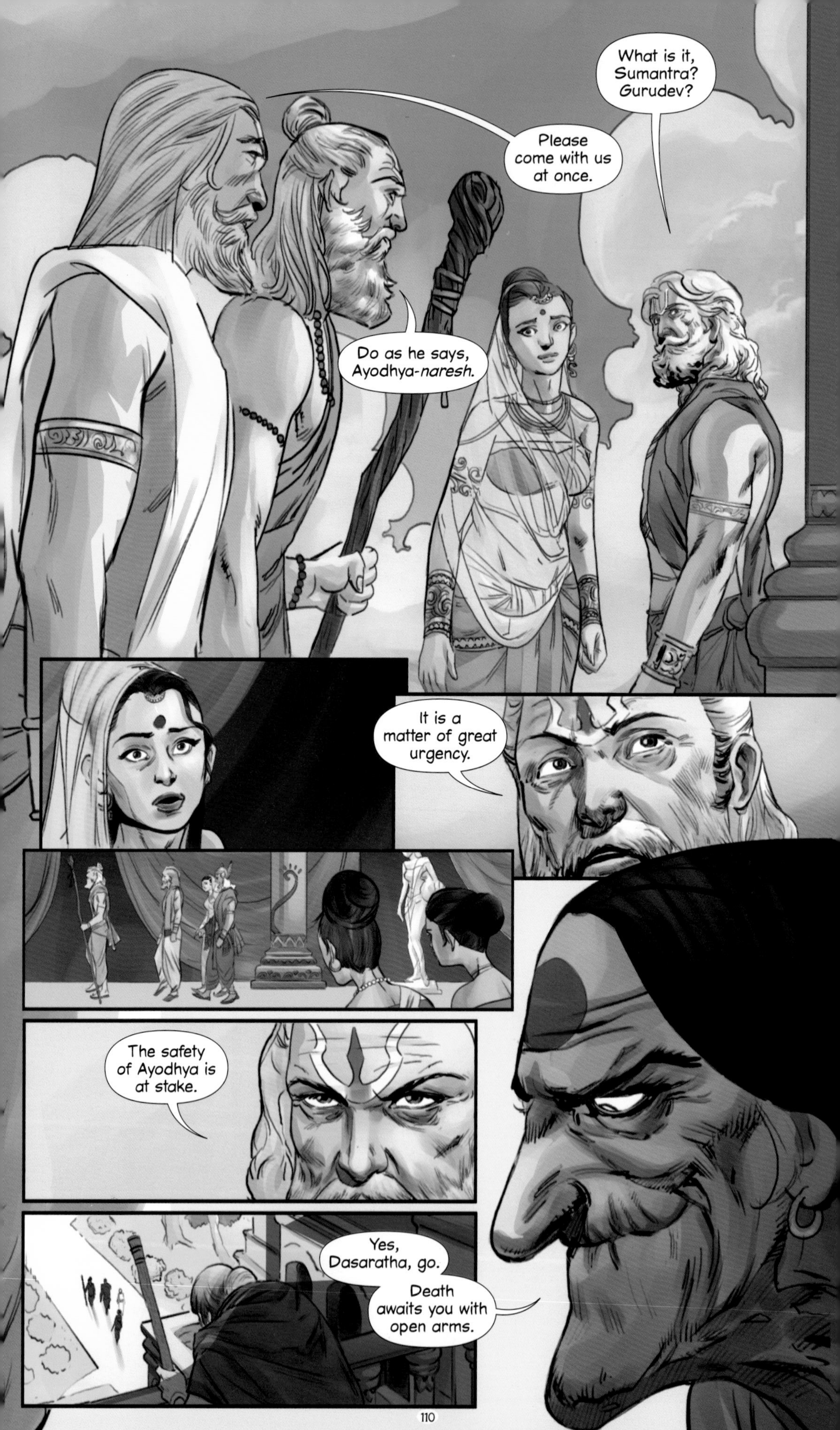
What is it, Sumantra? Gurudev?
Please come with us at once.
Do as he says, Ayodhya-*naresh*.
It is a matter of great urgency.
The safety of Ayodhya is at stake.
Yes, Dasaratha, go.
Death awaits you with open arms.

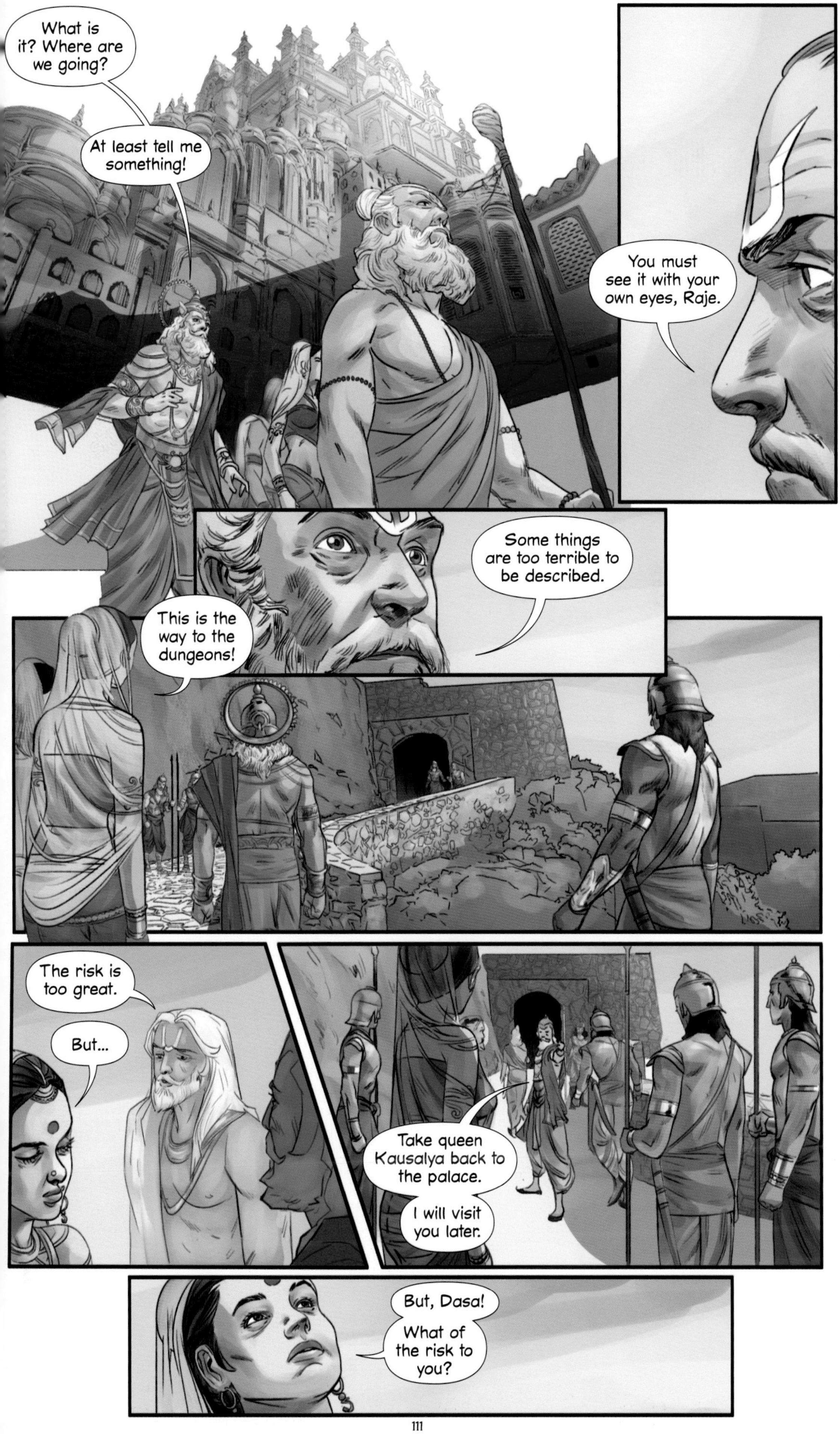
What is it? Where are we going?
At least tell me something!
You must see it with your own eyes, Raje.
Some things are too terrible to be described.
This is the way to the dungeons!
The risk is too great.
But...
Take queen Kausalya back to the palace.
I will visit you later.
But, Dasa!
What of the risk to you?

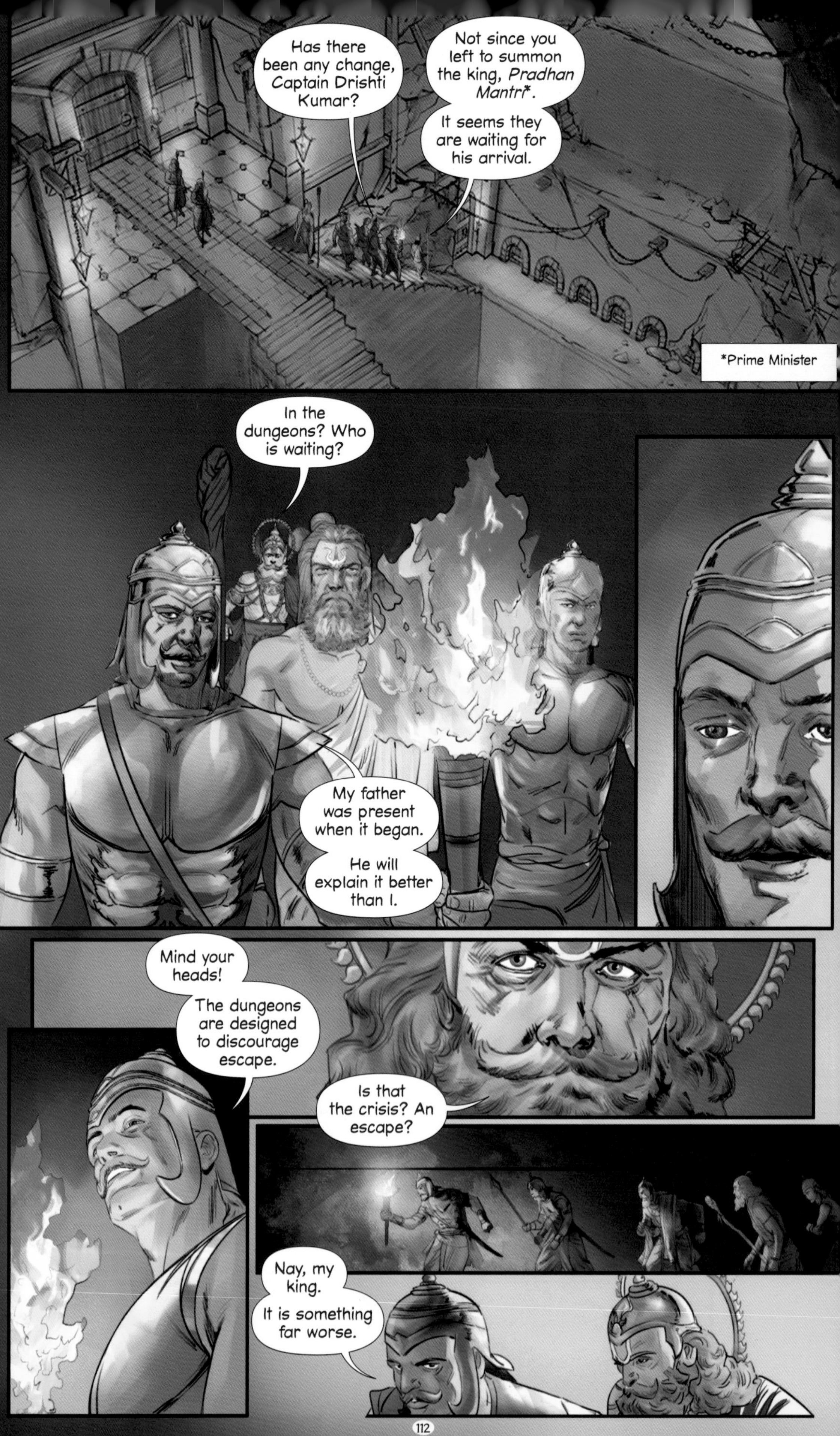
Has there been any change, Captain Drishti Kumar?
Not since you left to summon the king, *Pradhan Mantri**.
It seems they are waiting for his arrival.
*Prime Minister
In the dungeons? Who is waiting?
My father was present when it began.
He will explain it better than I.
Mind your heads!
The dungeons are designed to discourage escape.
Is that the crisis? An escape?
Nay, my king.
It is something far worse.

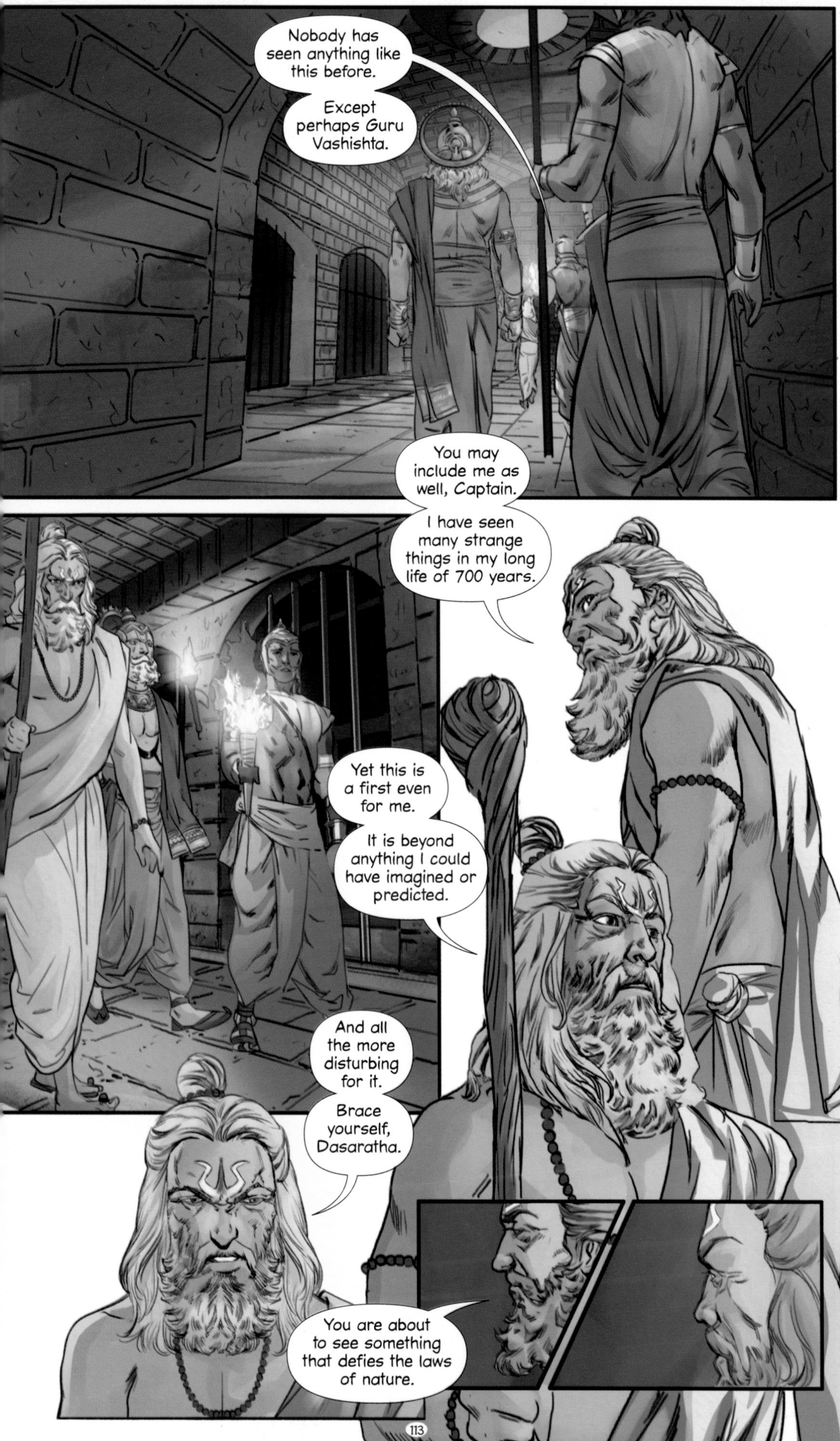
Nobody has seen anything like this before.
Except perhaps Guru Vashishta.
You may include me as well, Captain.
I have seen many strange things in my long life of 700 years.
Yet this is a first even for me.
It is beyond anything I could have imagined or predicted.
And all the more disturbing for it.
Brace yourself, Dasaratha.
You are about to see something that defies the laws of nature.

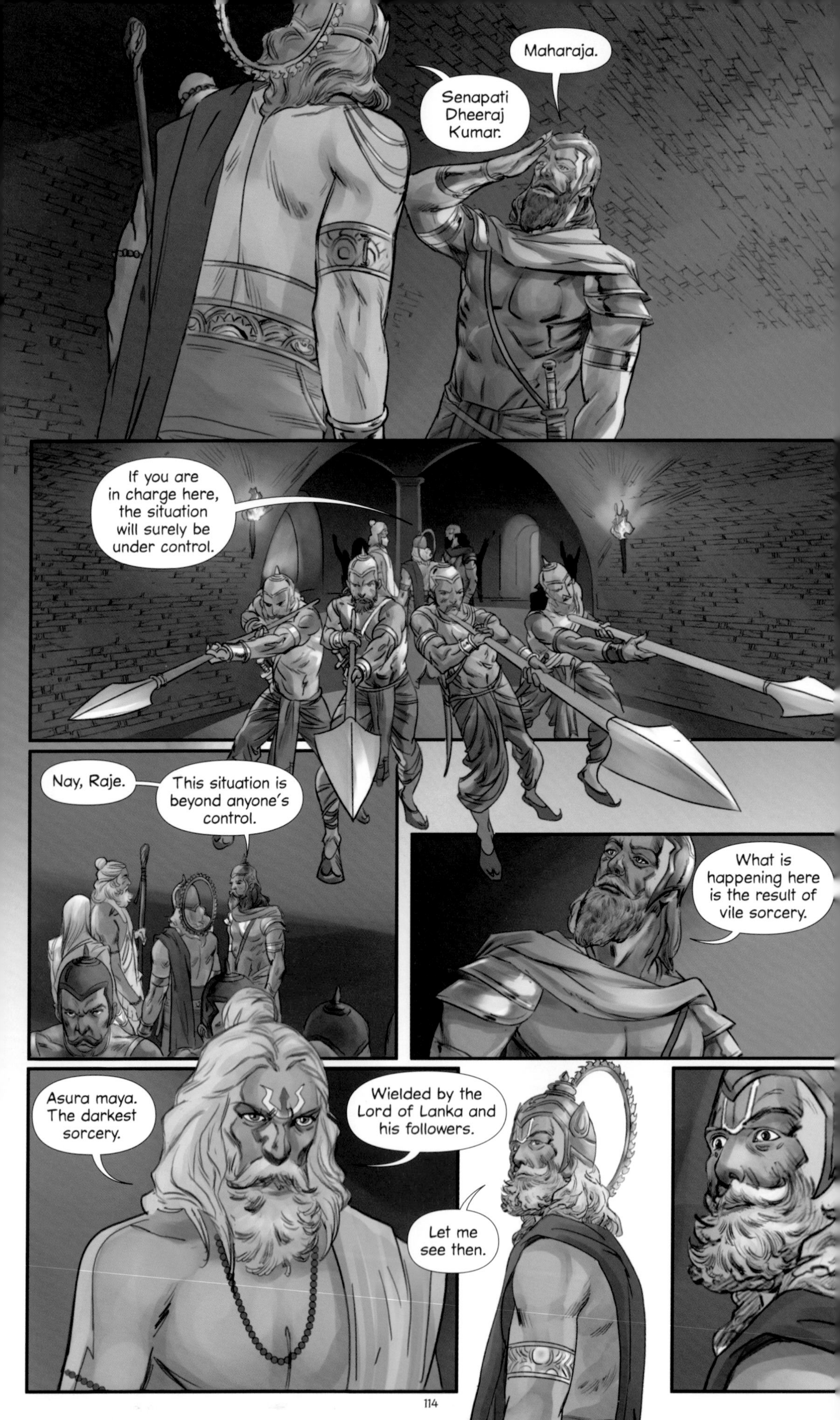
Maharaja.
Senapati Dheeraj Kumar.
If you are in charge here, the situation will surely be under control.
Nay, Raje.
This situation is beyond anyone's control.
What is happening here is the result of vile sorcery.
Asura maya. The darkest sorcery.
Wielded by the Lord of Lanka and his followers.
Let me see then.

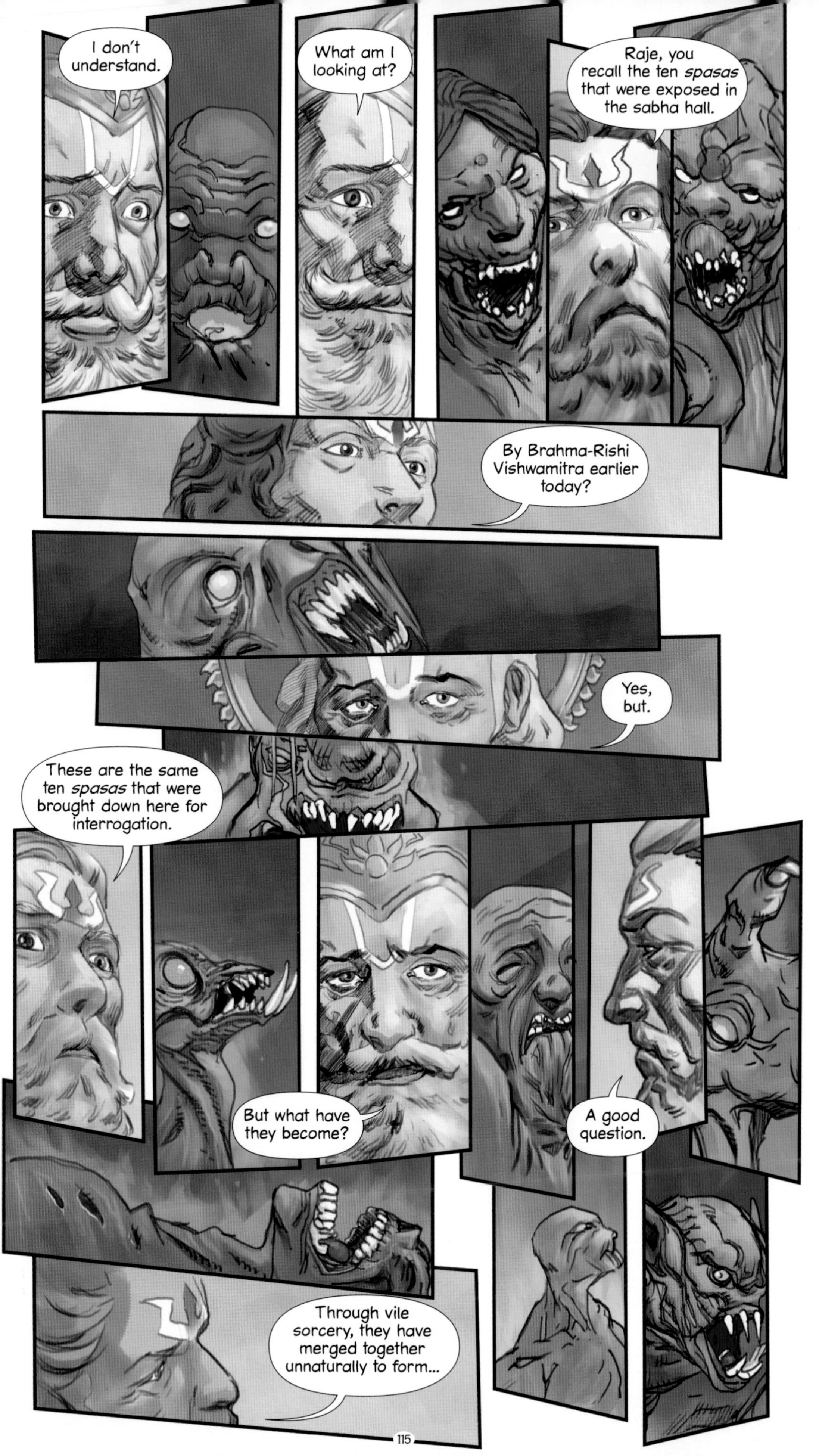
I don't understand.
What am I looking at?
Raje, you recall the ten *spasas* that were exposed in the sabha hall.
By Brahma-Rishi Vishwamitra earlier today?
Yes, but.
These are the same ten *spasas* that were brought down here for interrogation.
But what have they become?
A good question.
Through vile sorcery, they have merged together unnaturally to form...

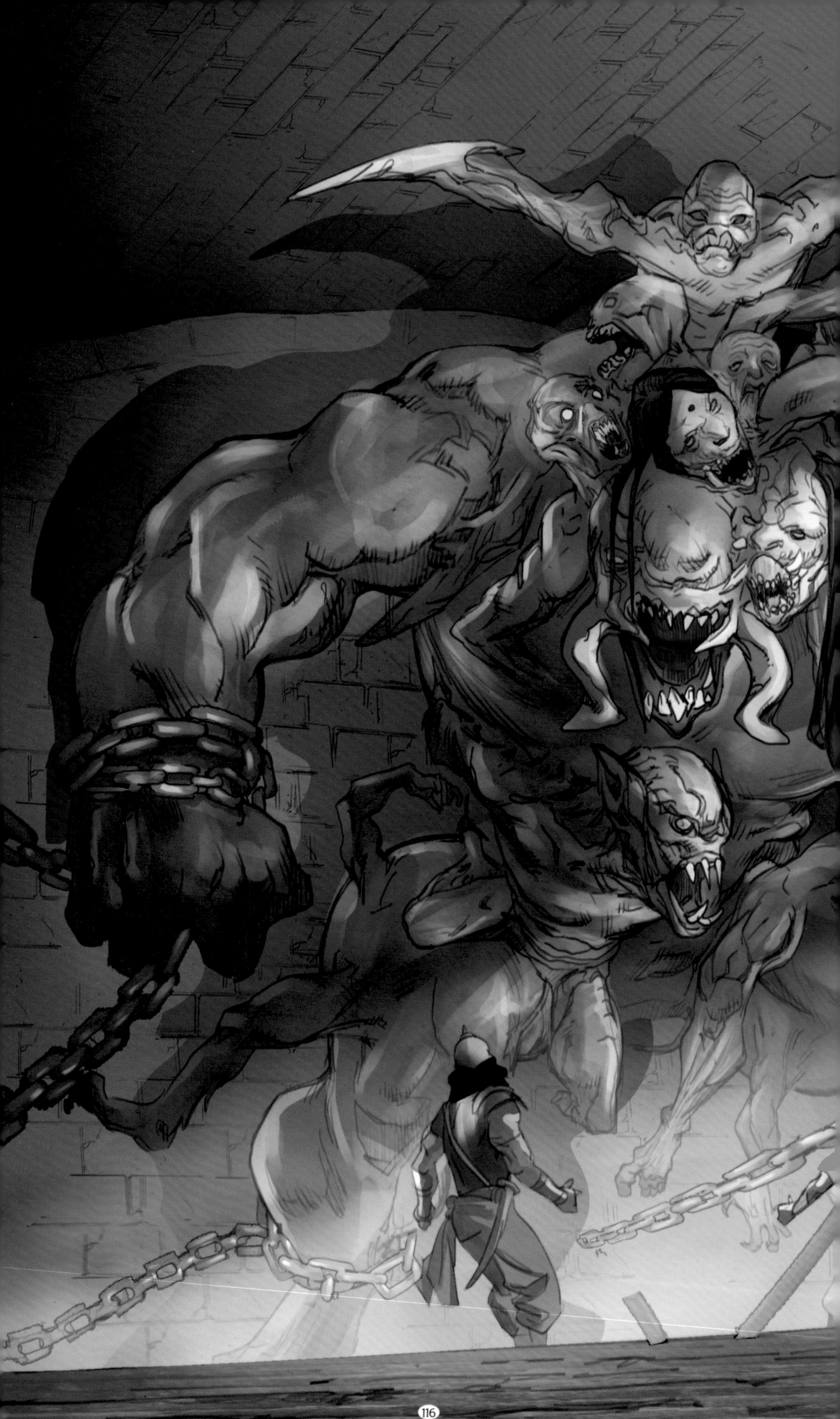

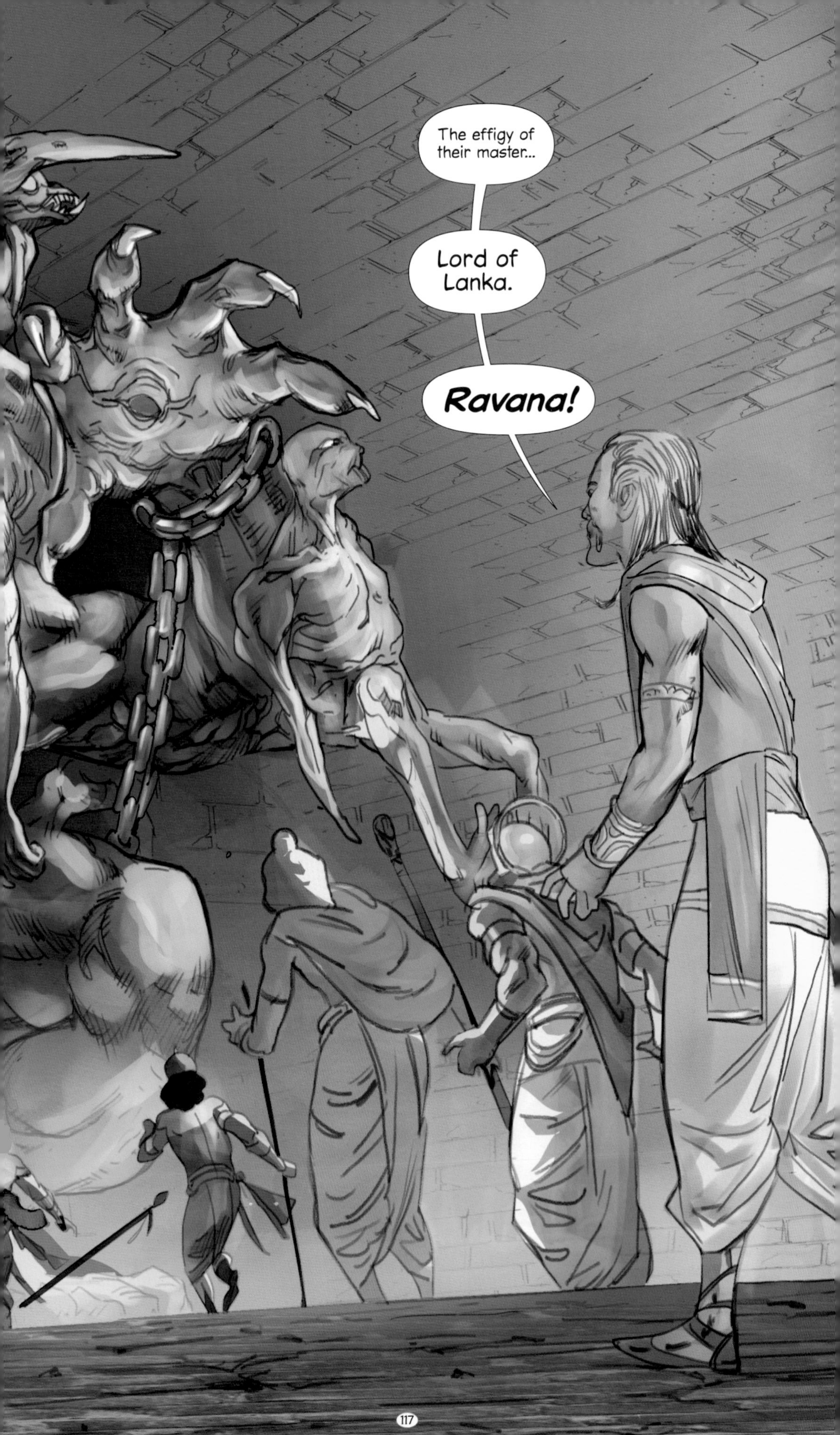
The effigy of their master...
Lord of Lanka.
Ravana!

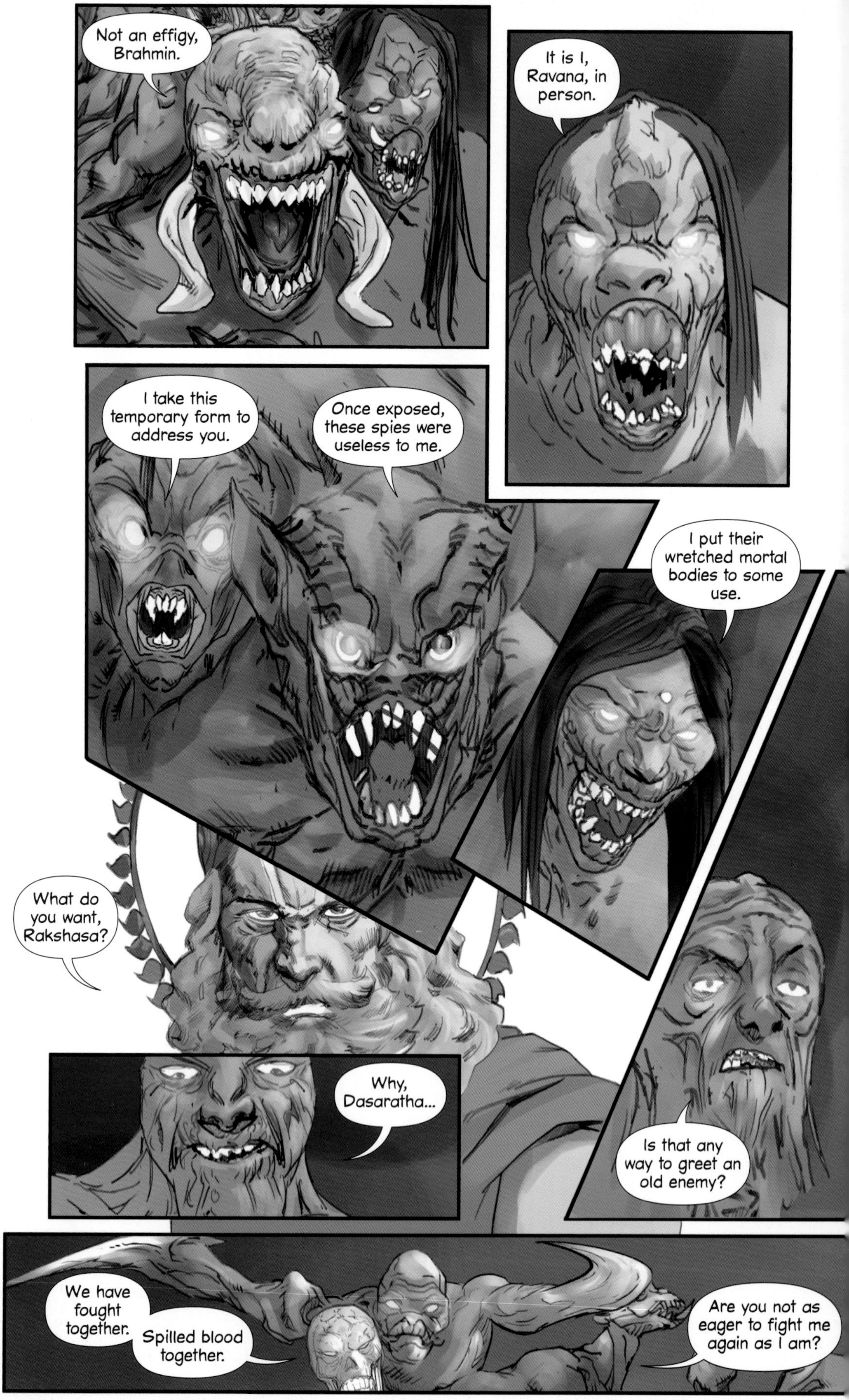
Not an effigy, Brahmin.
It is I, Ravana, in person.
I take this temporary form to address you.
Once exposed, these spies were useless to me.
I put their wretched mortal bodies to some use.
What do you want, Rakshasa?
Why, Dasaratha...
Is that any way to greet an old enemy?
We have fought together.
Spilled blood together.
Are you not as eager to fight me again as I am?

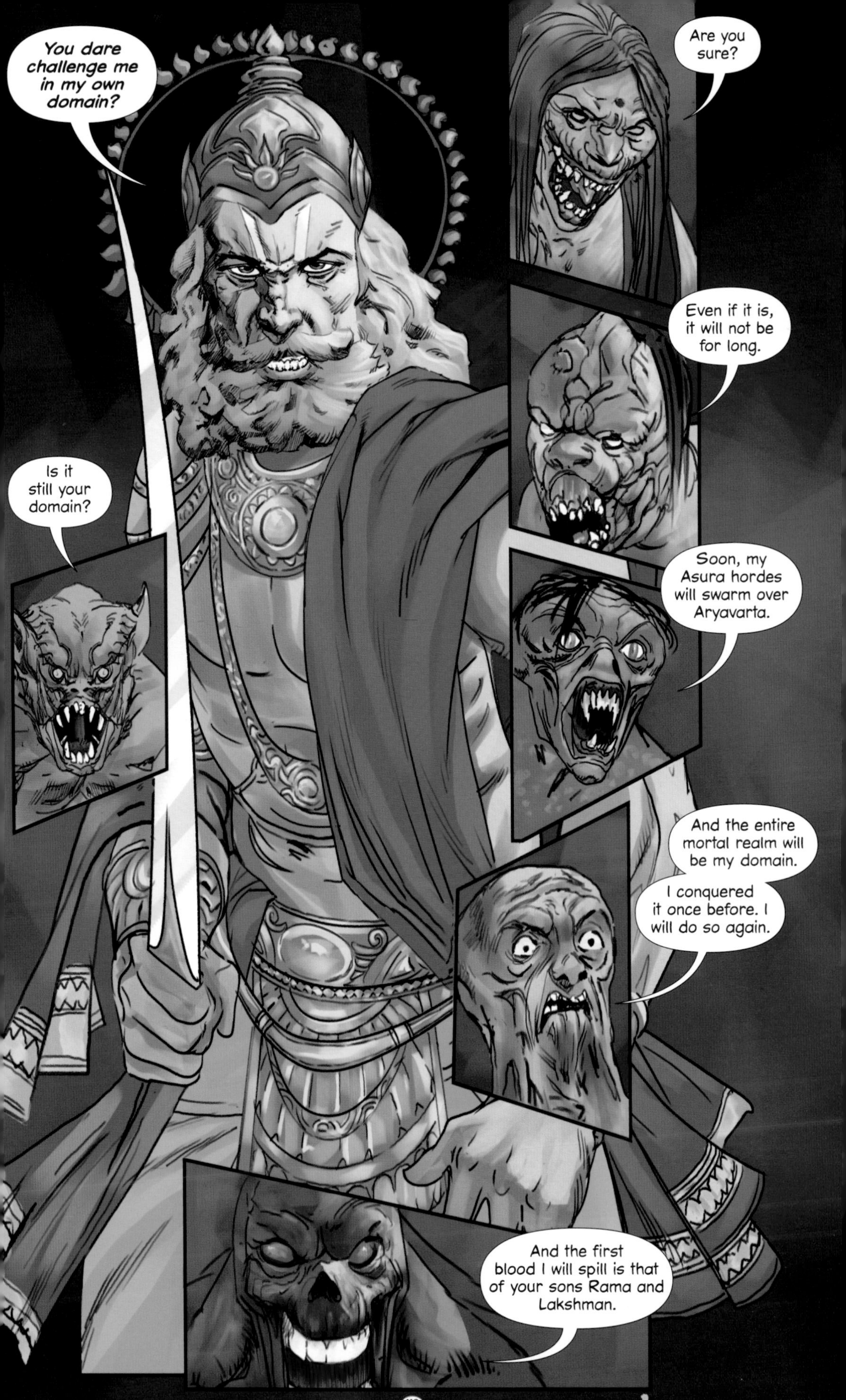

You dare challenge me in my own domain?
Are you sure?
Even if it is, it will not be for long.
Is it still your domain?
Soon, my Asura hordes will swarm over Aryavarta.
And the entire mortal realm will be my domain.
I conquered it once before. I will do so again.
And the first blood I will spill is that of your sons Rama and Lakshman.

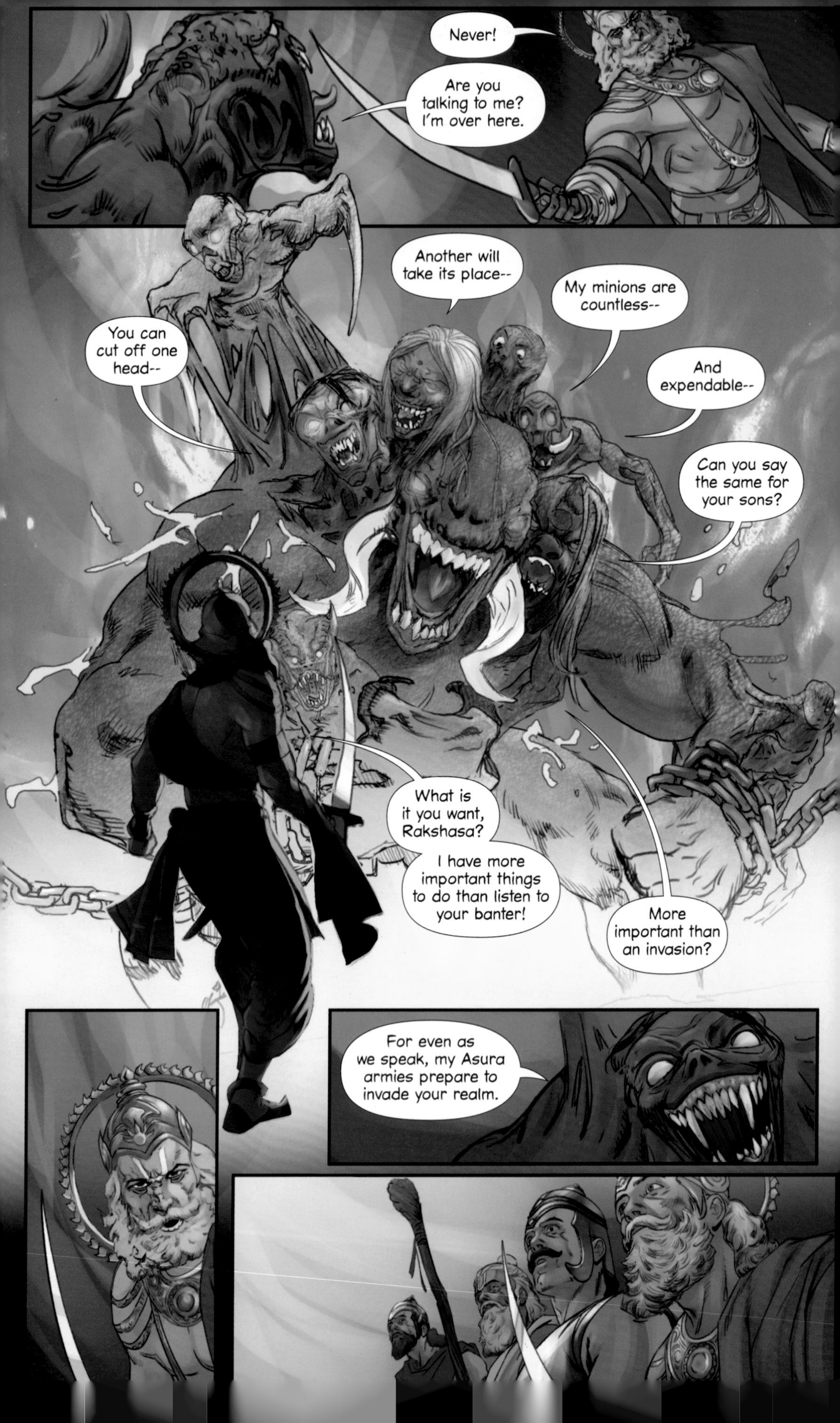
Never!
Are you talking to me? I'm over here.
You can cut off one head--
Another will take its place--
My minions are countless--
And expendable--
Can you say the same for your sons?
What is it you want, Rakshasa?
I have more important things to do than listen to your banter!
More important than an invasion?
For even as we speak, my Asura armies prepare to invade your realm.

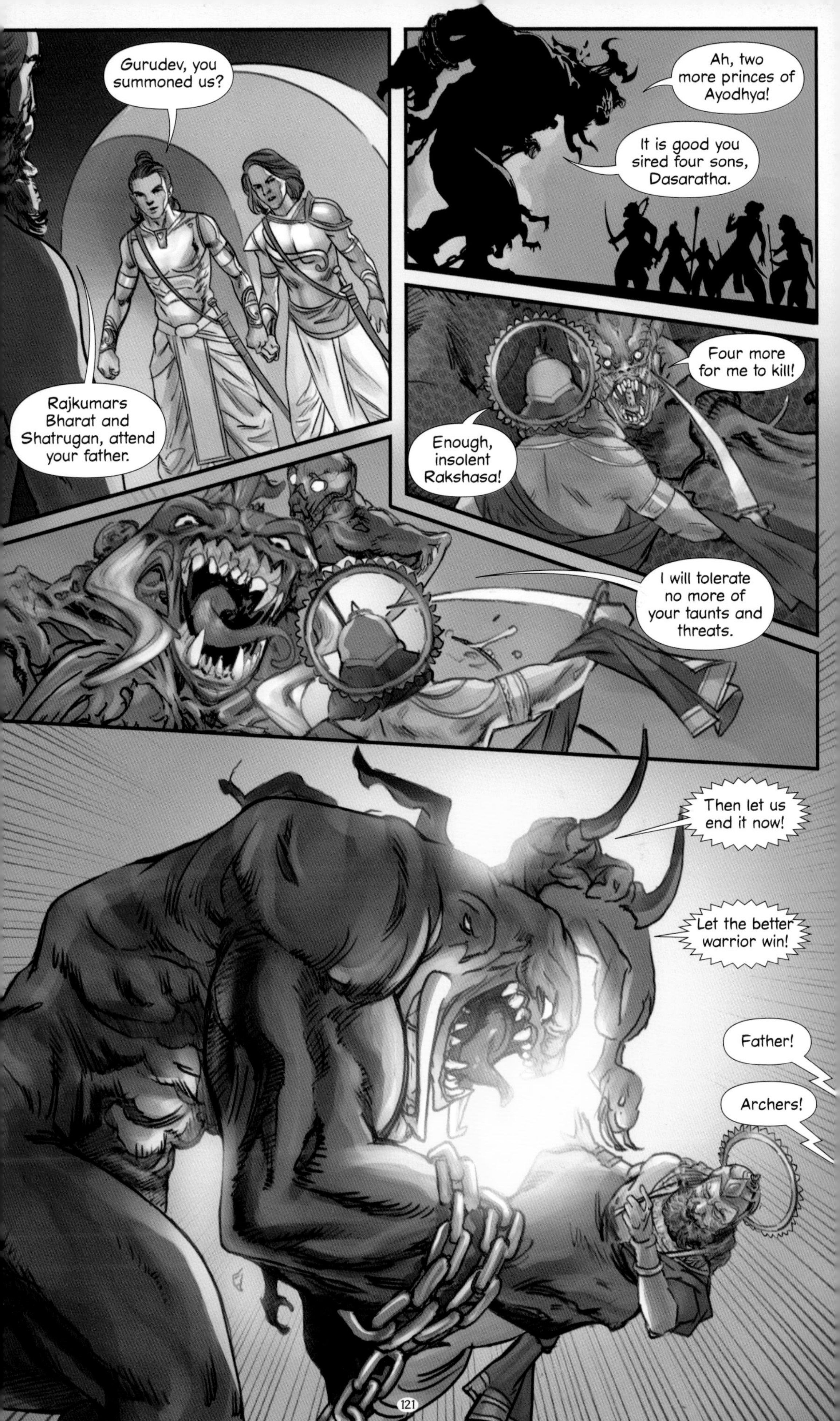
Gurudev, you summoned us?
Rajkumars Bharat and Shatrugan, attend your father.
Ah, two more princes of Ayodhya!
It is good you sired four sons, Dasaratha.
Four more for me to kill!
Enough, insolent Rakshasa!
I will tolerate no more of your taunts and threats.
Then let us end it now!
Let the better warrior win!
Father!
Archers!

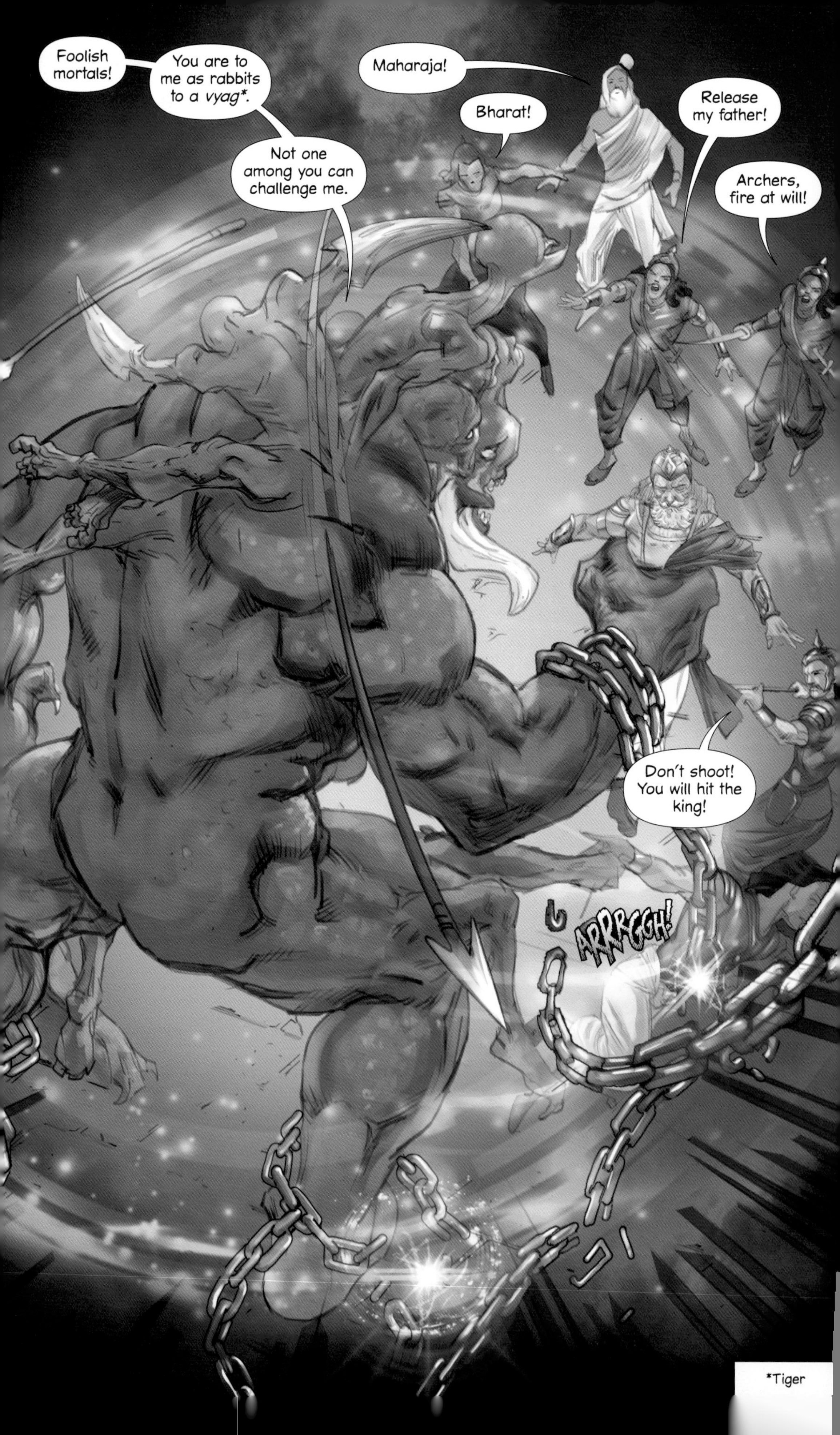

Foolish mortals!
You are to me as rabbits to a *vyag**.
Not one among you can challenge me.
Maharaja!
Bharat!
Release my father!
Archers, fire at will!
Don't shoot! You will hit the king!
ARRRGGH!

*Tiger

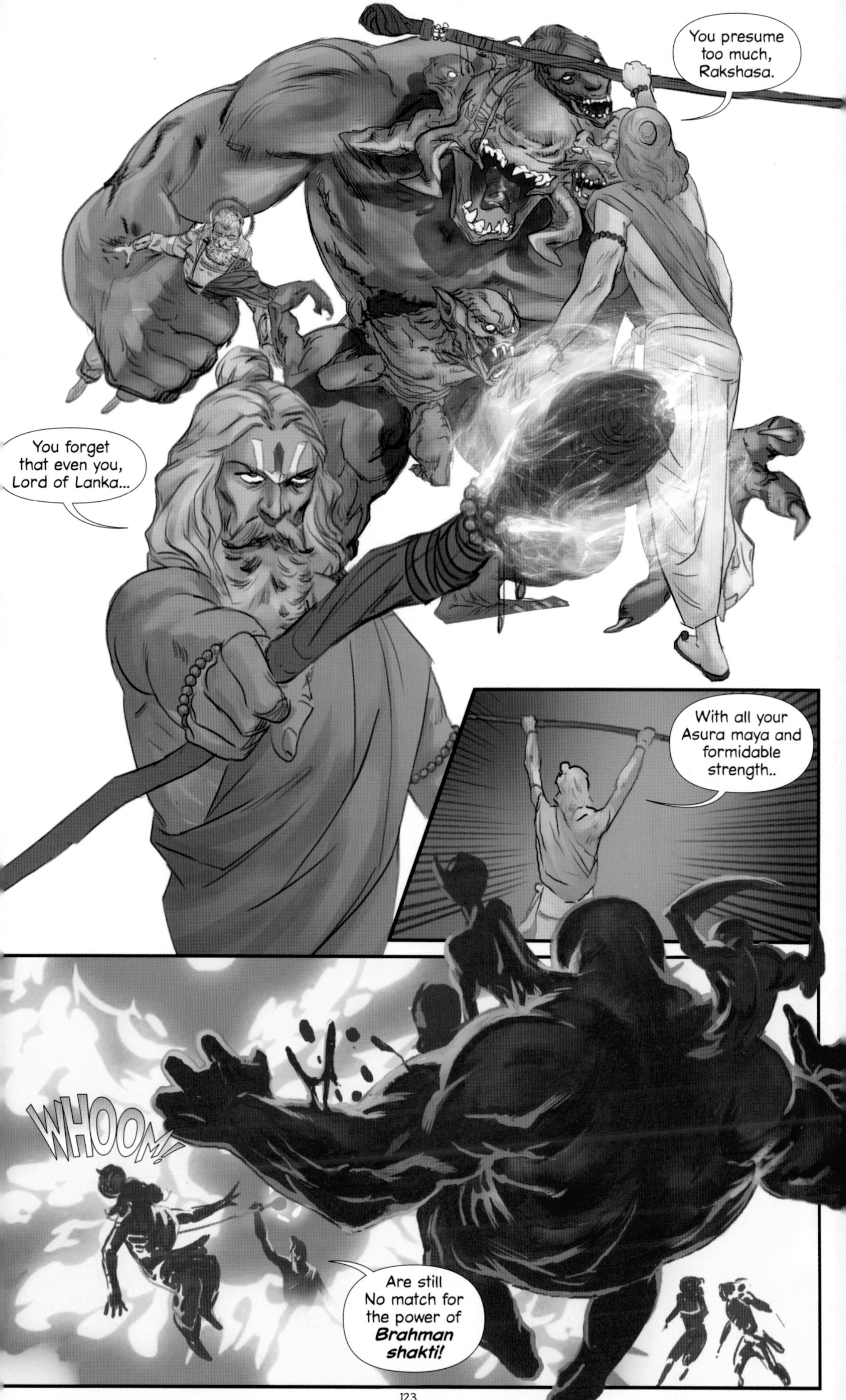
You presume too much, Rakshasa.
You forget that even you, Lord of Lanka...
With all your Asura maya and formidable strength..
WHOOM!
Are still No match for the power of ***Brahman shakti!***

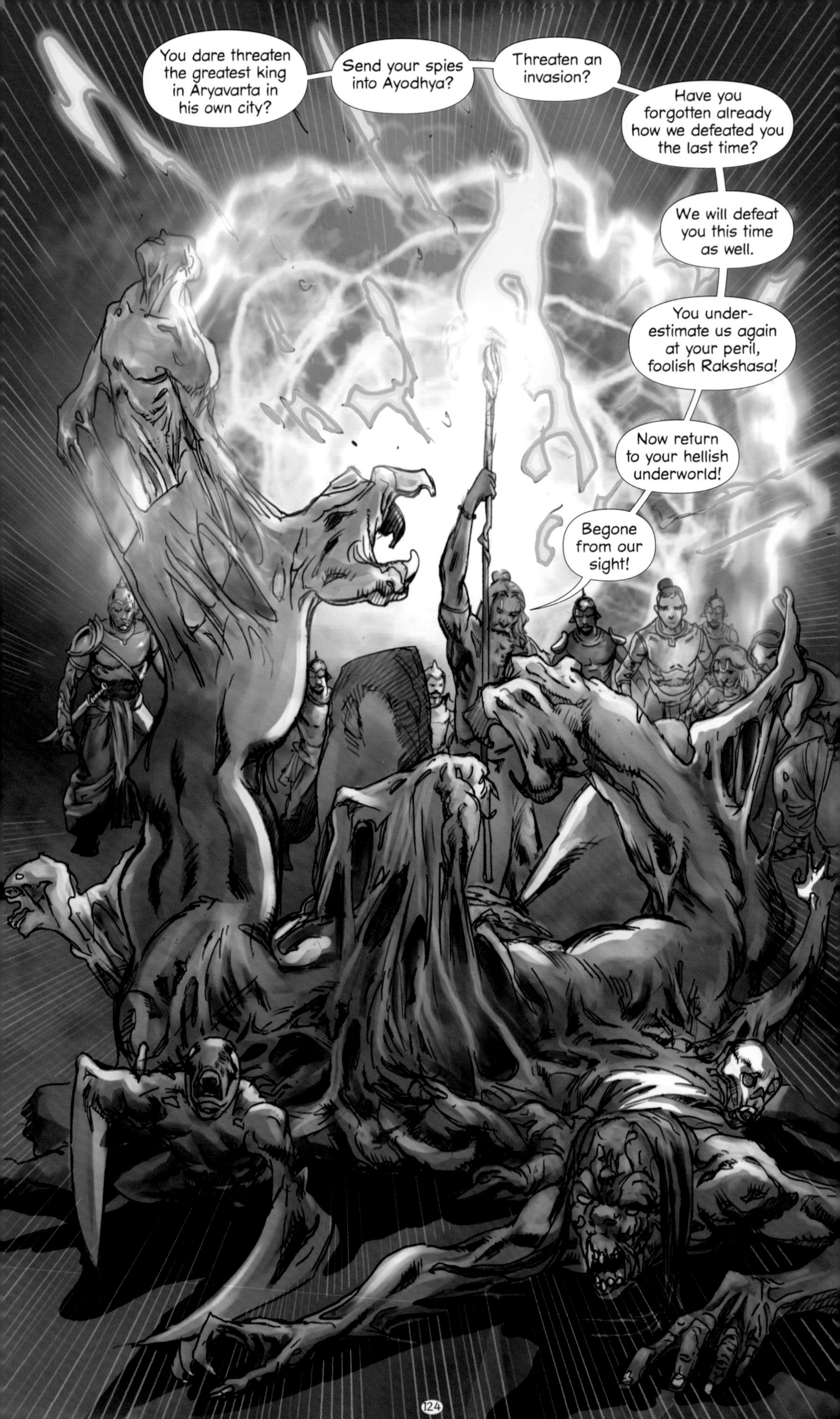
You dare threaten the greatest king in Aryavarta in his own city?
Send your spies into Ayodhya?
Threaten an invasion?
Have you forgotten already how we defeated you the last time?
We will defeat you this time as well.
You under-estimate us again at your peril, foolish Rakshasa!
Now return to your hellish underworld!
Begone from our sight!

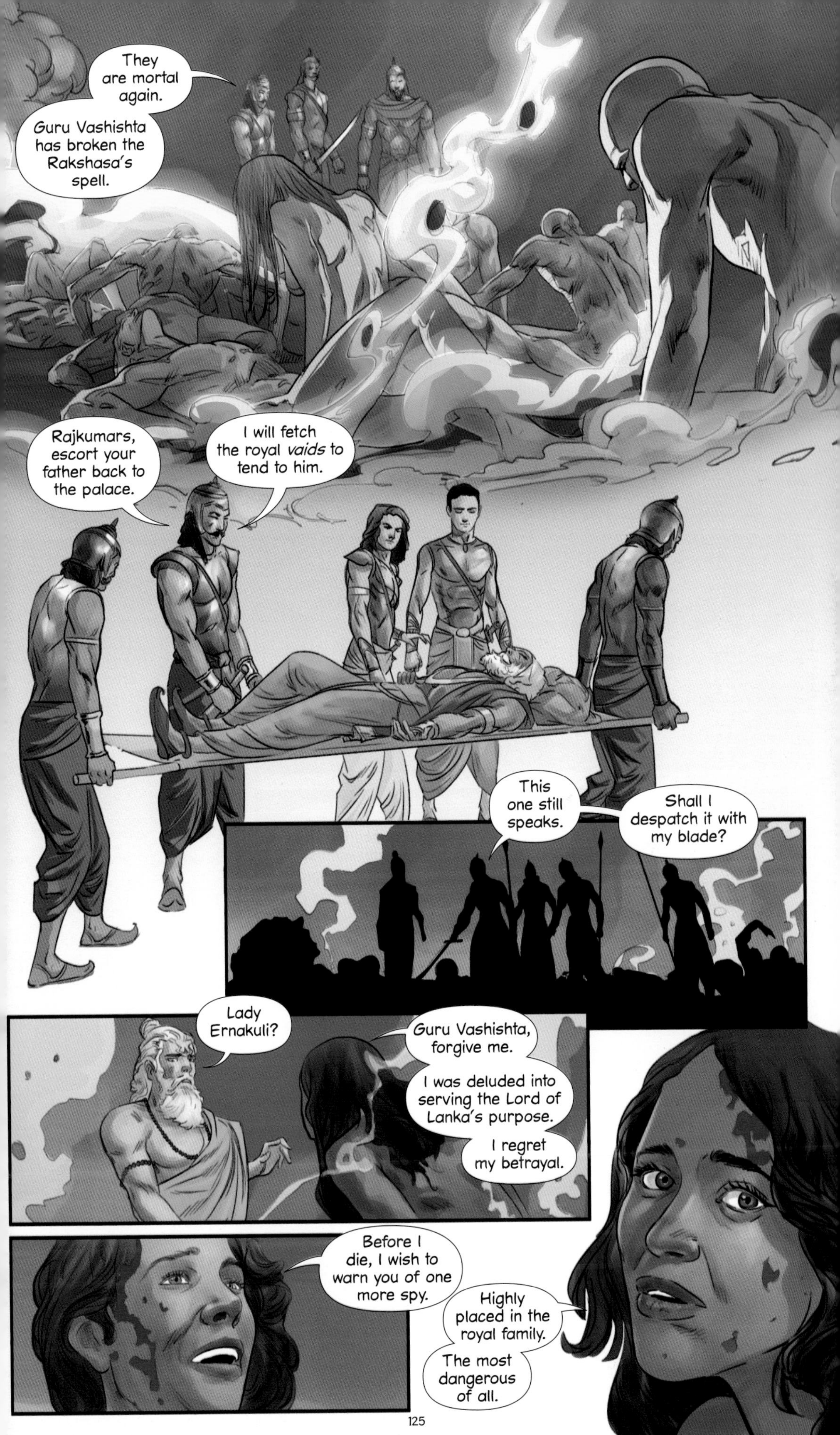
They are mortal again.
Guru Vashishta has broken the Rakshasa's spell.
Rajkumars, escort your father back to the palace.
I will fetch the royal *vaids* to tend to him.
This one still speaks.
Shall I despatch it with my blade?
Lady Ernakuli?
Guru Vashishta, forgive me.
I was deluded into serving the Lord of Lanka's purpose.
I regret my betrayal.
Before I die, I wish to warn you of one more spy.
Highly placed in the royal family.
The most dangerous of all.

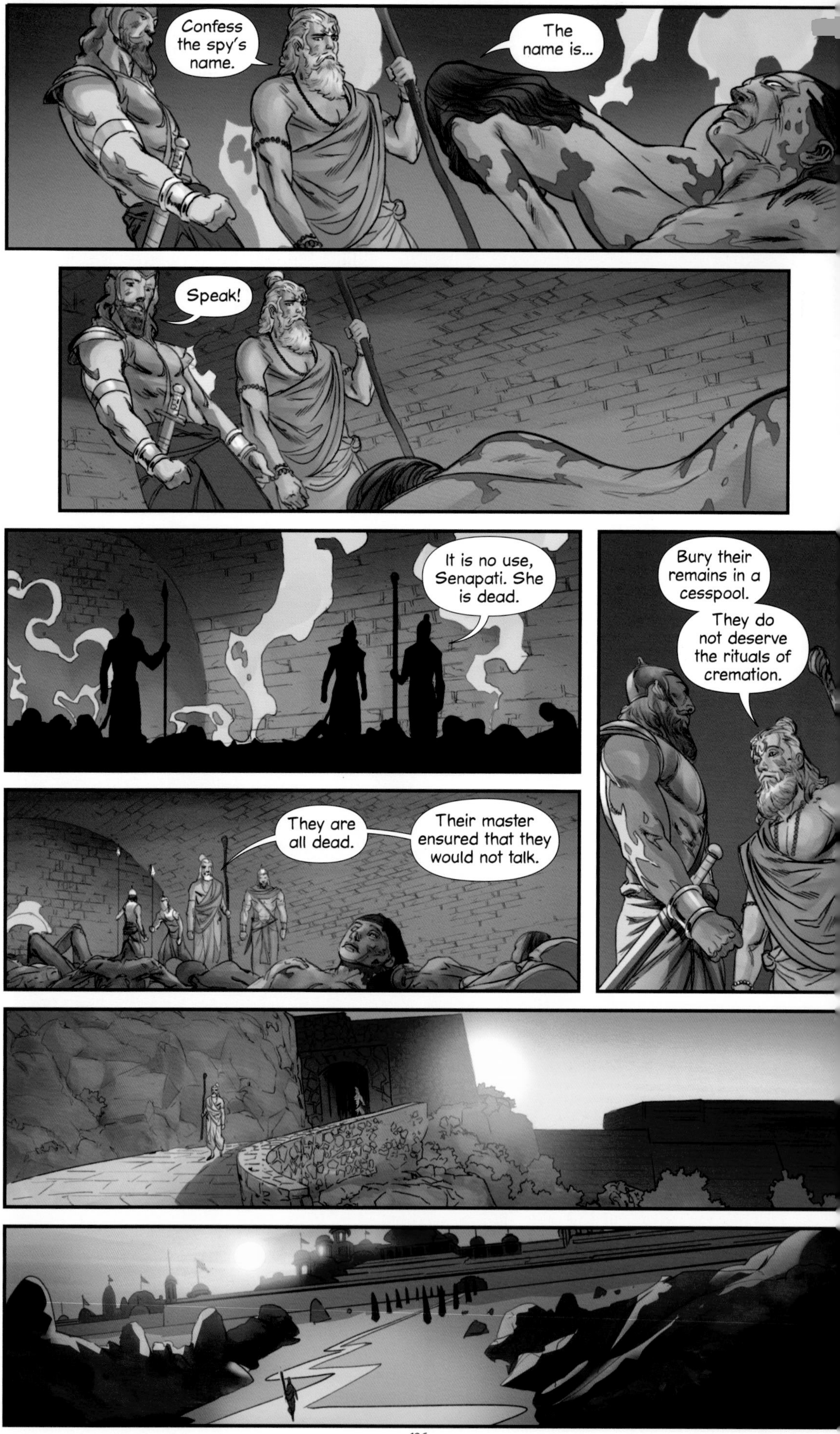
Confess the spy's name.
The name is...
Speak!
It is no use, Senapati. She is dead.
Bury their remains in a cesspool.
They do not deserve the rituals of cremation.
They are all dead.
Their master ensured that they would not talk.

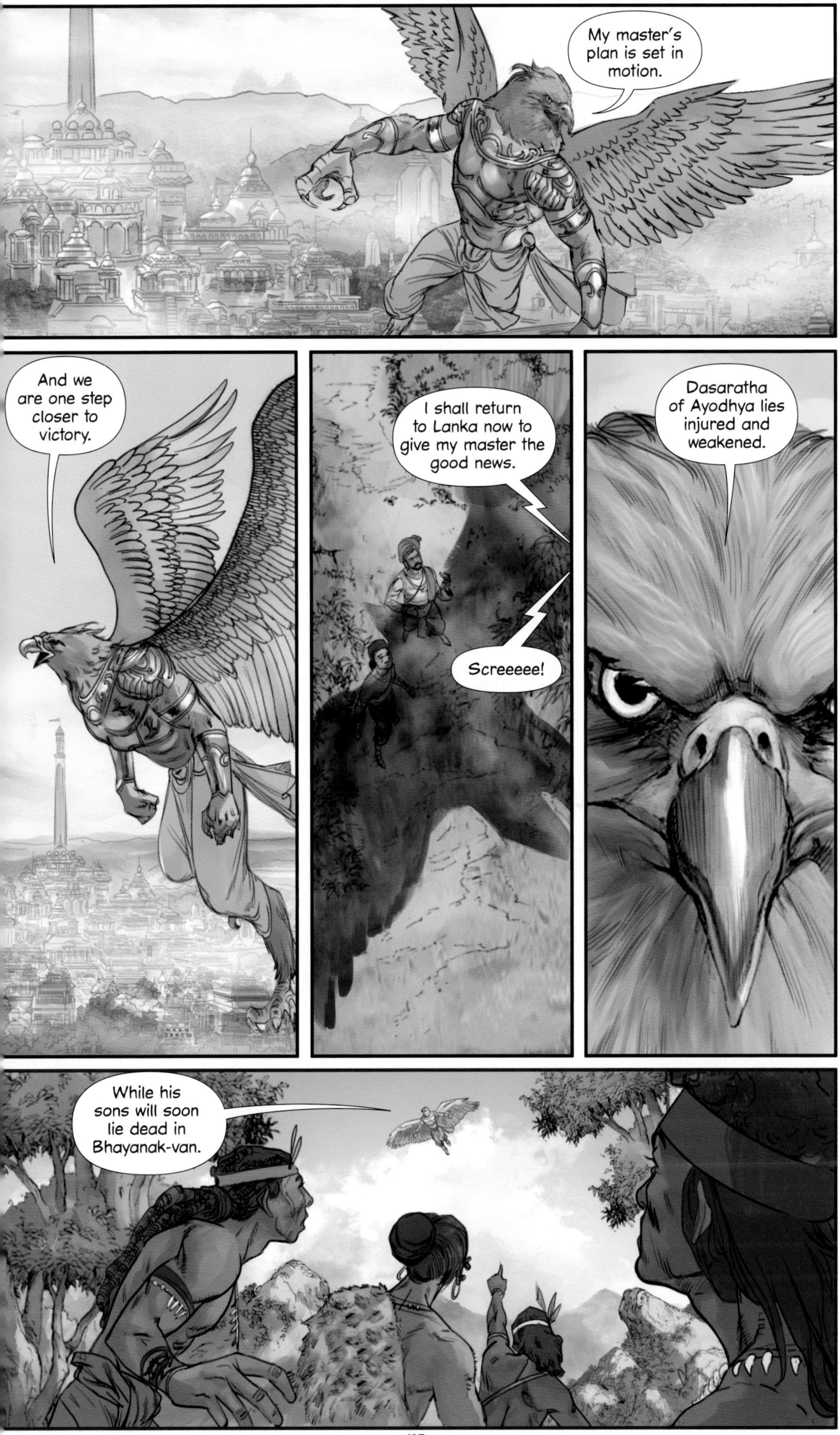
My master's plan is set in motion.
And we are one step closer to victory.
I shall return to Lanka now to give my master the good news.
Screeeee!
Dasaratha of Ayodhya lies injured and weakened.
While his sons will soon lie dead in Bhayanak-van.

KAAND IV

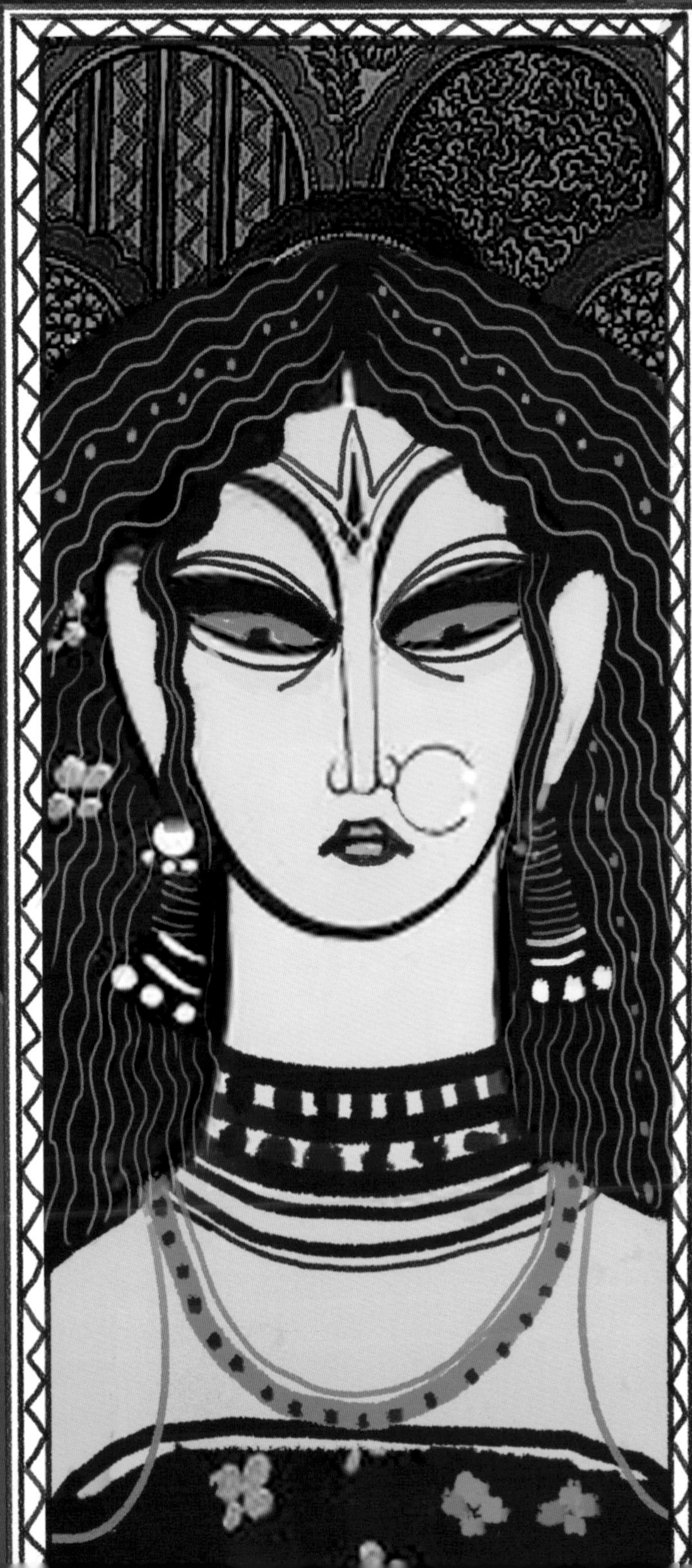

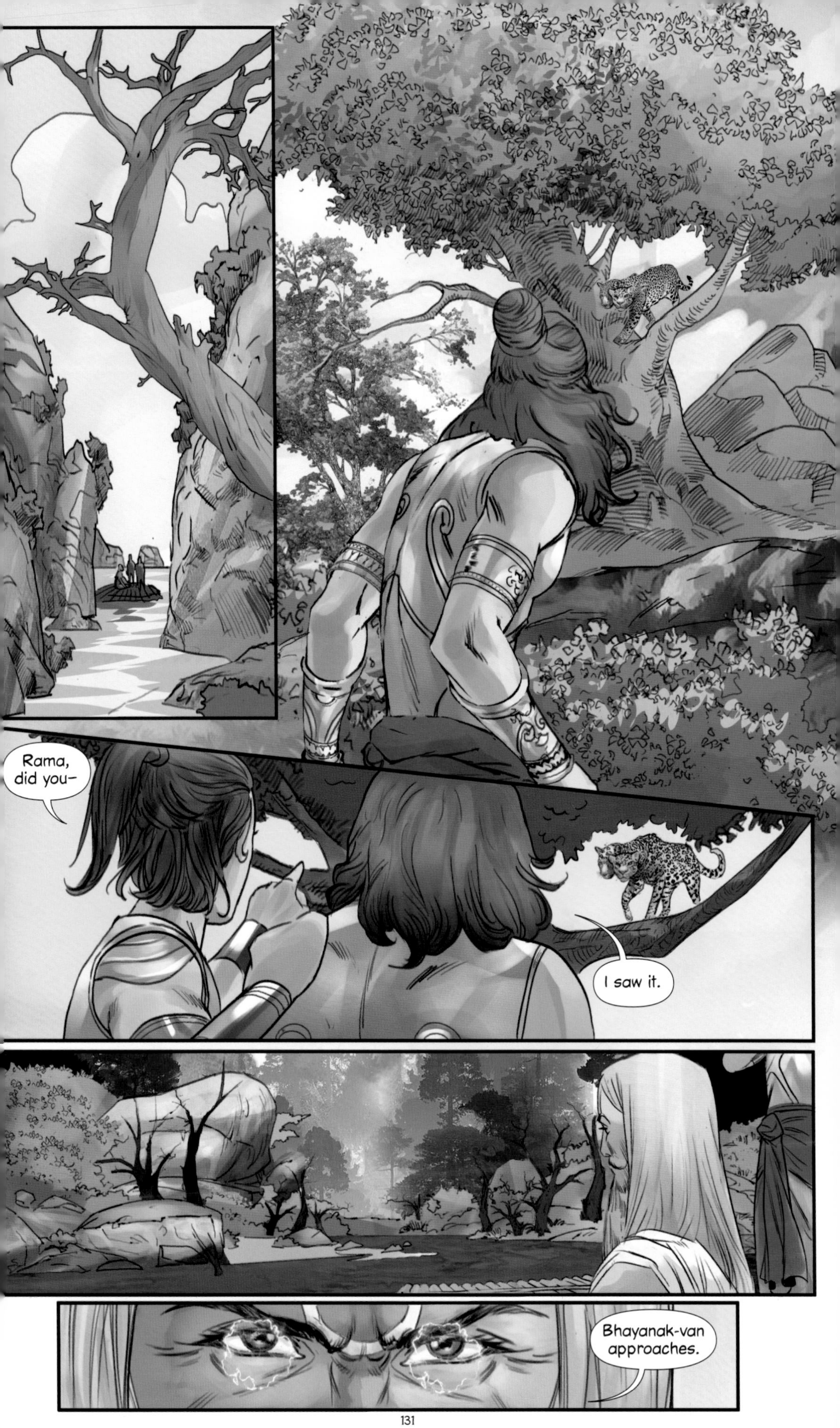

Rama, did you-
I saw it.
Bhayanak-van approaches.

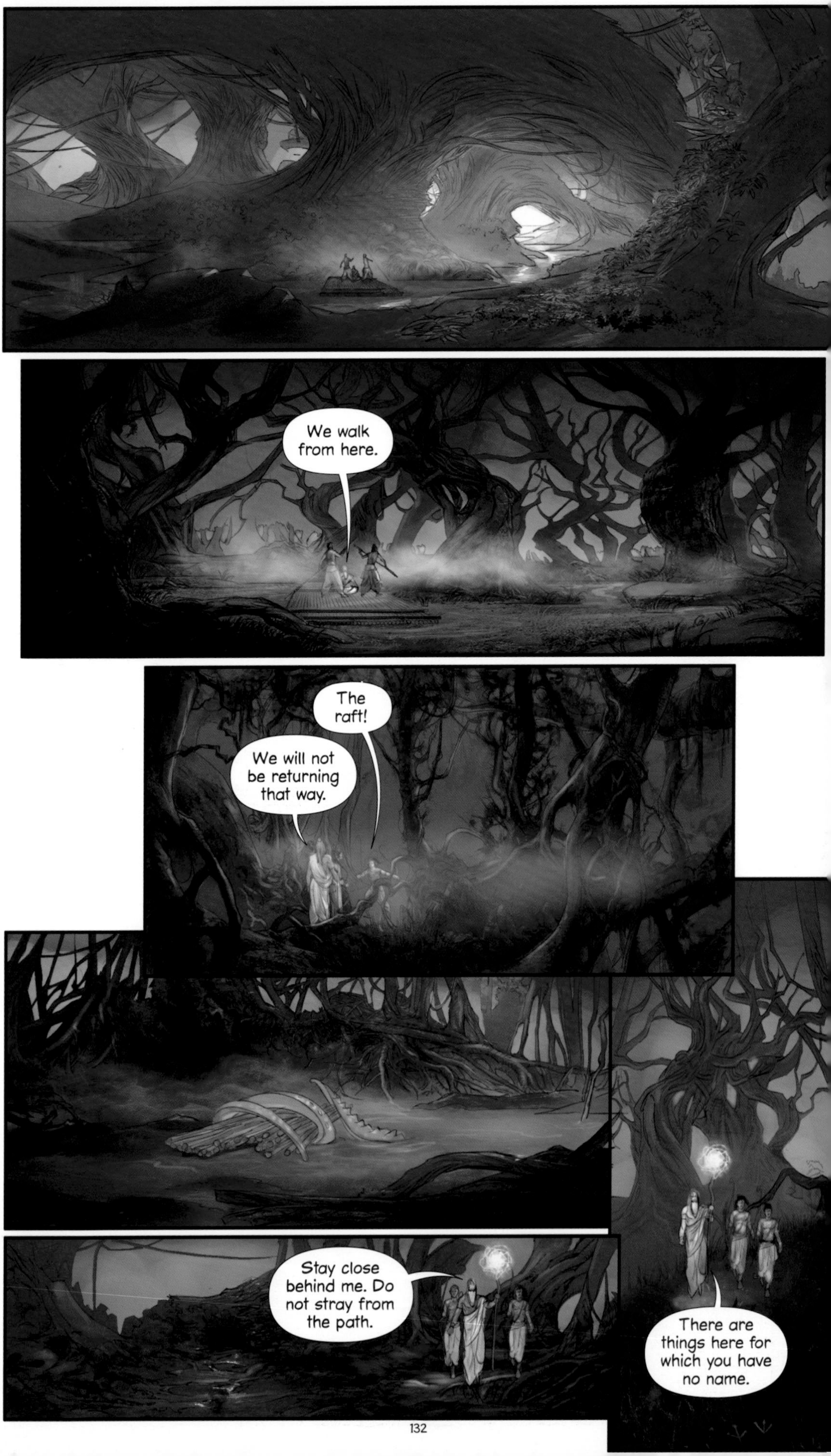

We walk from here.
The raft!
We will not be returning that way.
Stay close behind me. Do not stray from the path.
There are things here for which you have no name.

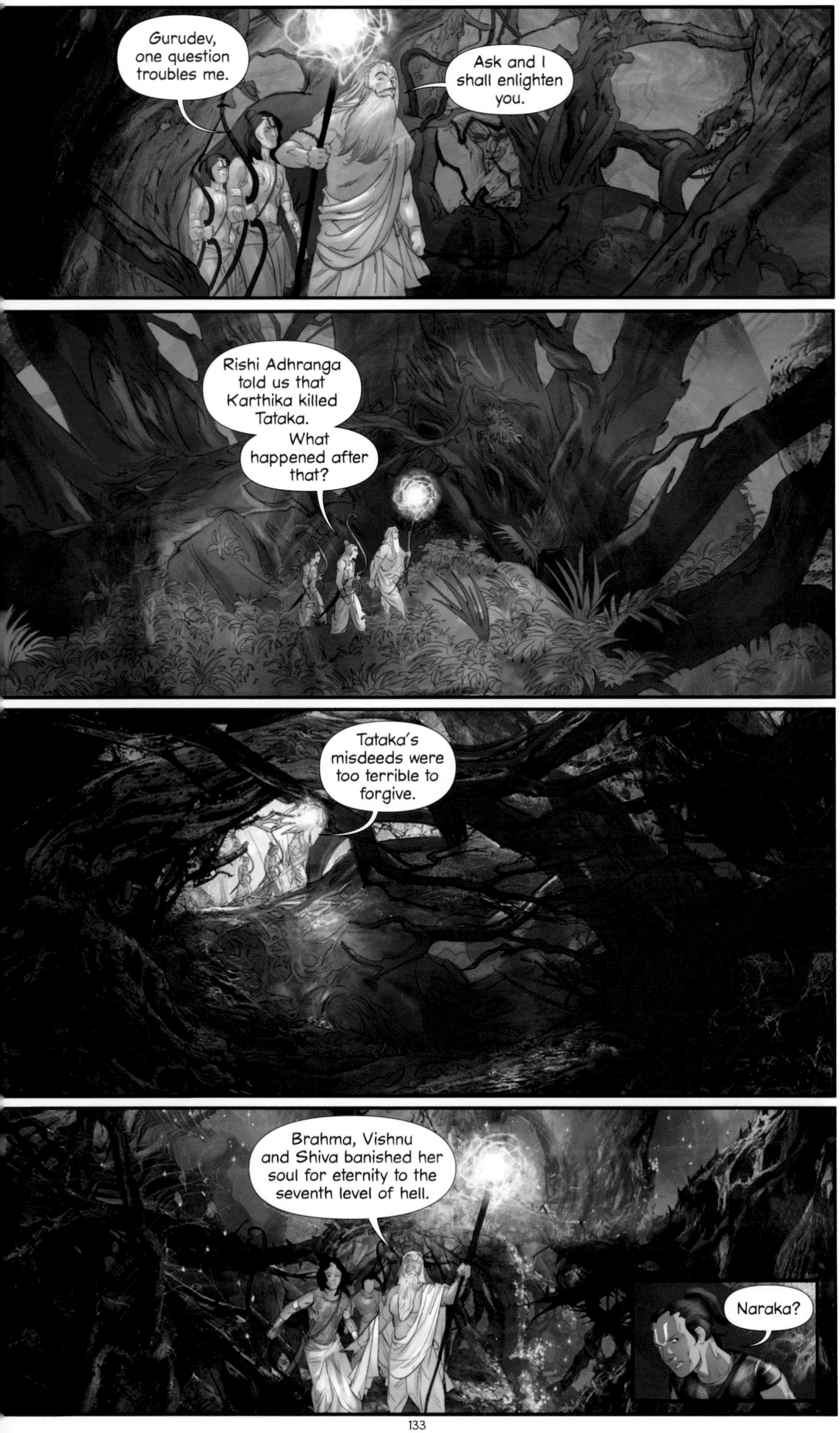
Gurudev, one question troubles me.
Ask and I shall enlighten you.
Rishi Adhranga told us that Karthika killed Tataka.
What happened after that?
Tataka's misdeeds were too terrible to forgive.
Brahma, Vishnu and Shiva banished her soul for eternity to the seventh level of hell.
Naraka?

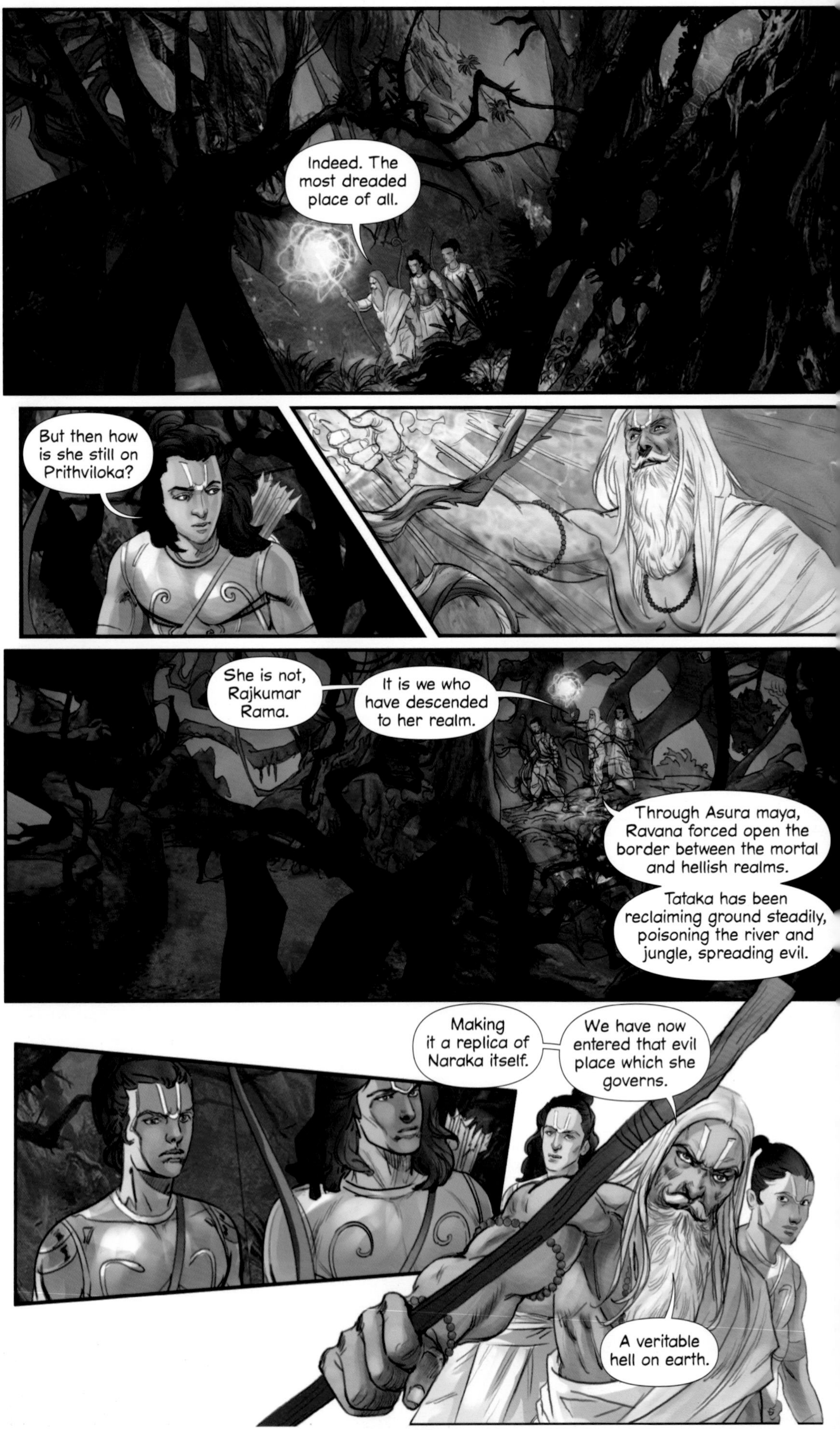
Indeed. The most dreaded place of all.
But then how is she still on Prithviloka?
She is not, Rajkumar Rama.
It is we who have descended to her realm.
Through Asura maya, Ravana forced open the border between the mortal and hellish realms.
Tataka has been reclaiming ground steadily, poisoning the river and jungle, spreading evil.
Making it a replica of Naraka itself.
We have now entered that evil place which she governs.
A veritable hell on earth.

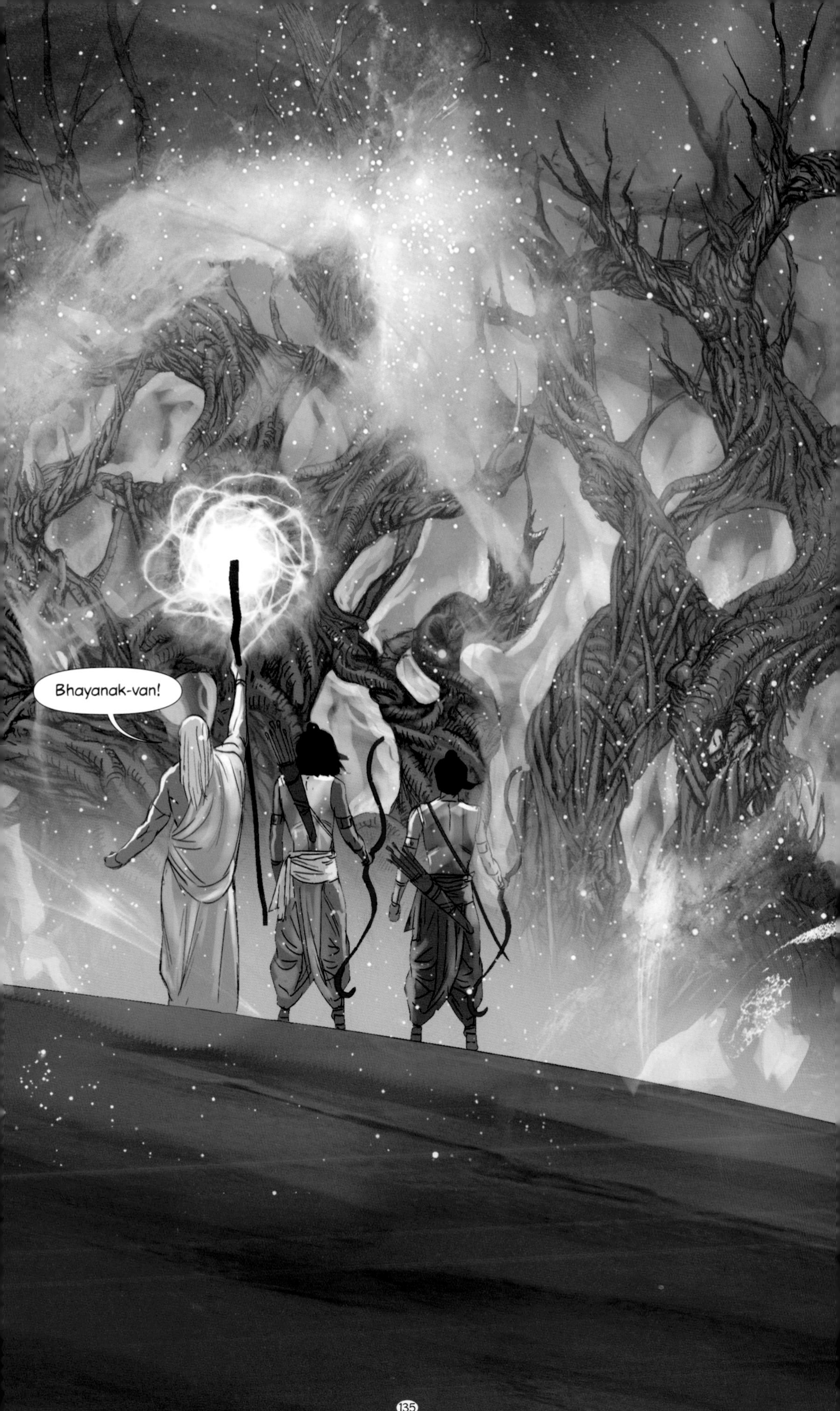
Bhayanak-van!

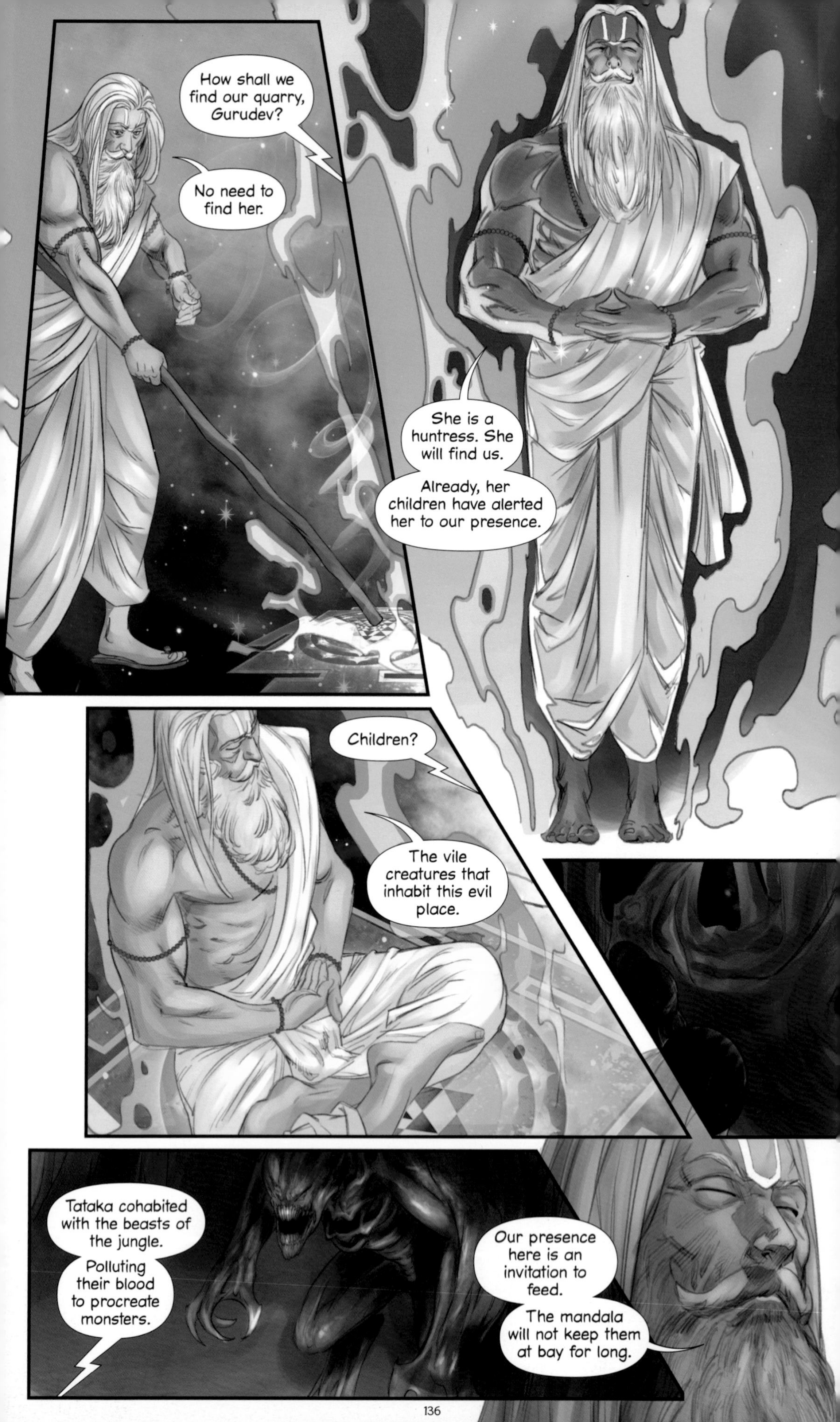
How shall we find our quarry, Gurudev?
No need to find her.
She is a huntress. She will find us.
Already, her children have alerted her to our presence.
Children?
The vile creatures that inhabit this evil place.
Tataka cohabited with the beasts of the jungle.
Polluting their blood to procreate monsters.
Our presence here is an invitation to feed.
The mandala will not keep them at bay for long.

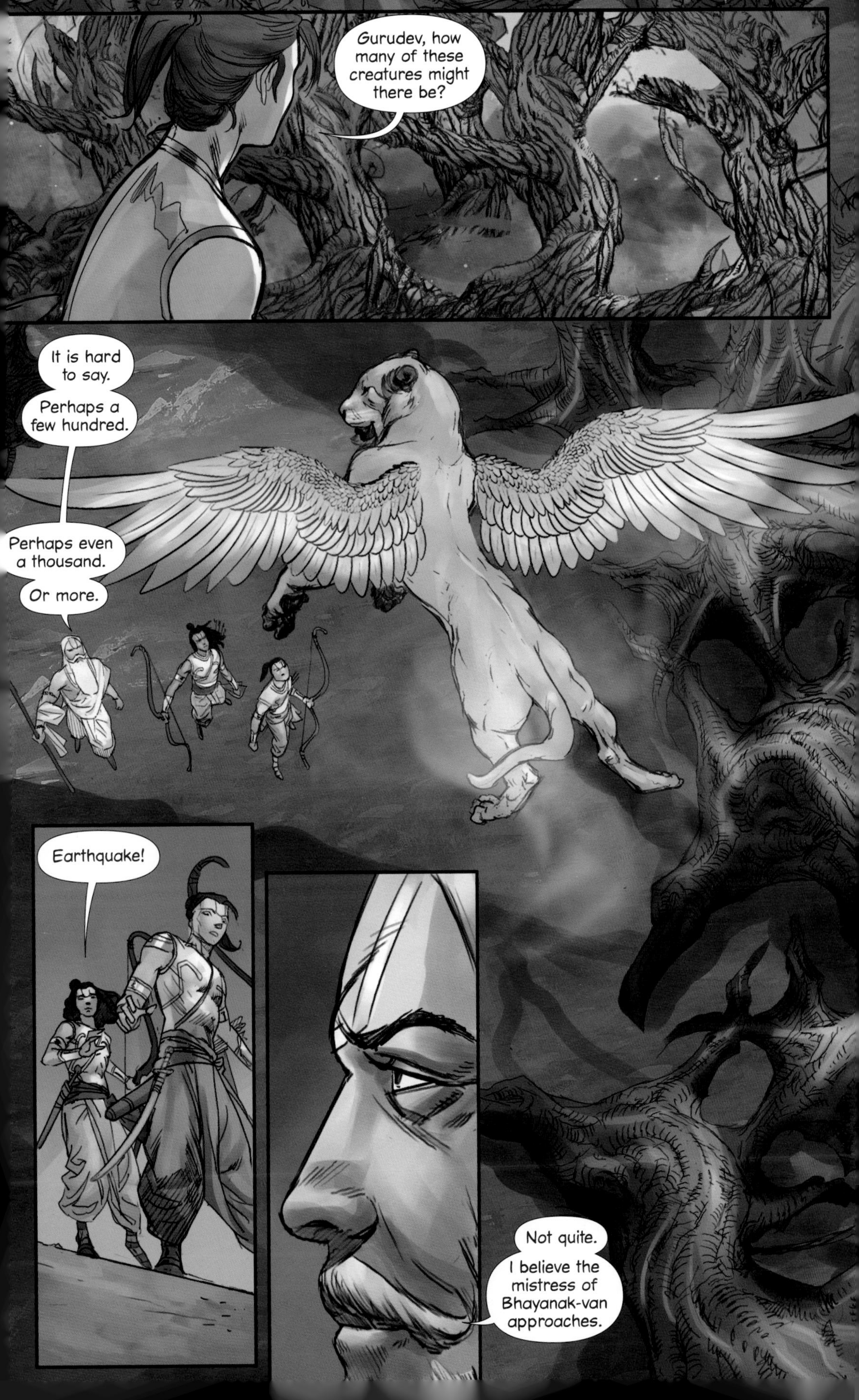

Gurudev, how many of these creatures might there be?
It is hard to say.
Perhaps a few hundred.
Perhaps even a thousand.
Or more.
Earthquake!
Not quite.
I believe the mistress of Bhayanak-van approaches.

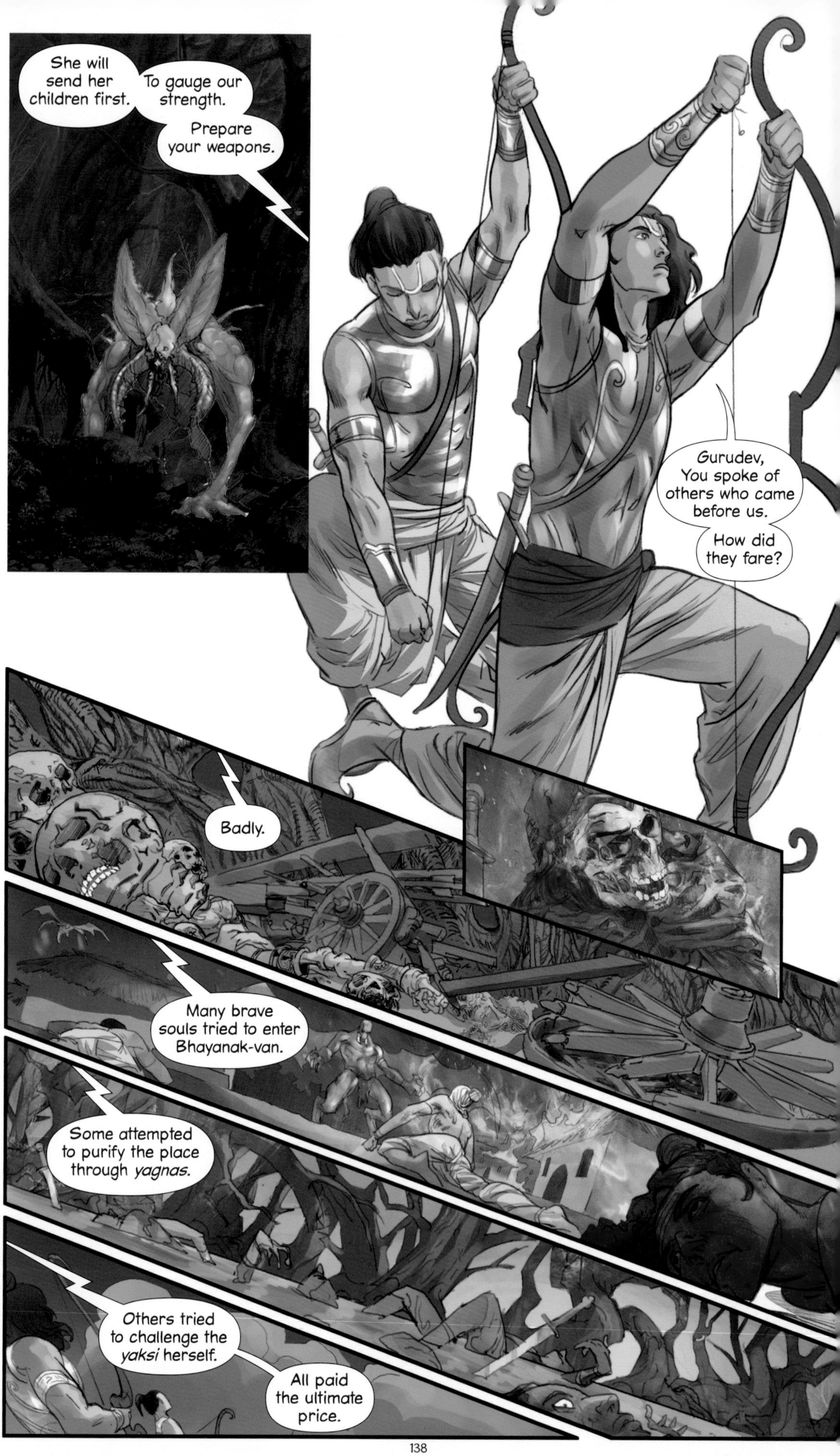
She will send her children first.
To gauge our strength.
Prepare your weapons.
Gurudev, You spoke of others who came before us.
How did they fare?
Badly.
Many brave souls tried to enter Bhayanak-van.
Some attempted to purify the place through *yagnas*.
Others tried to challenge the *yaksi* herself.
All paid the ultimate price.

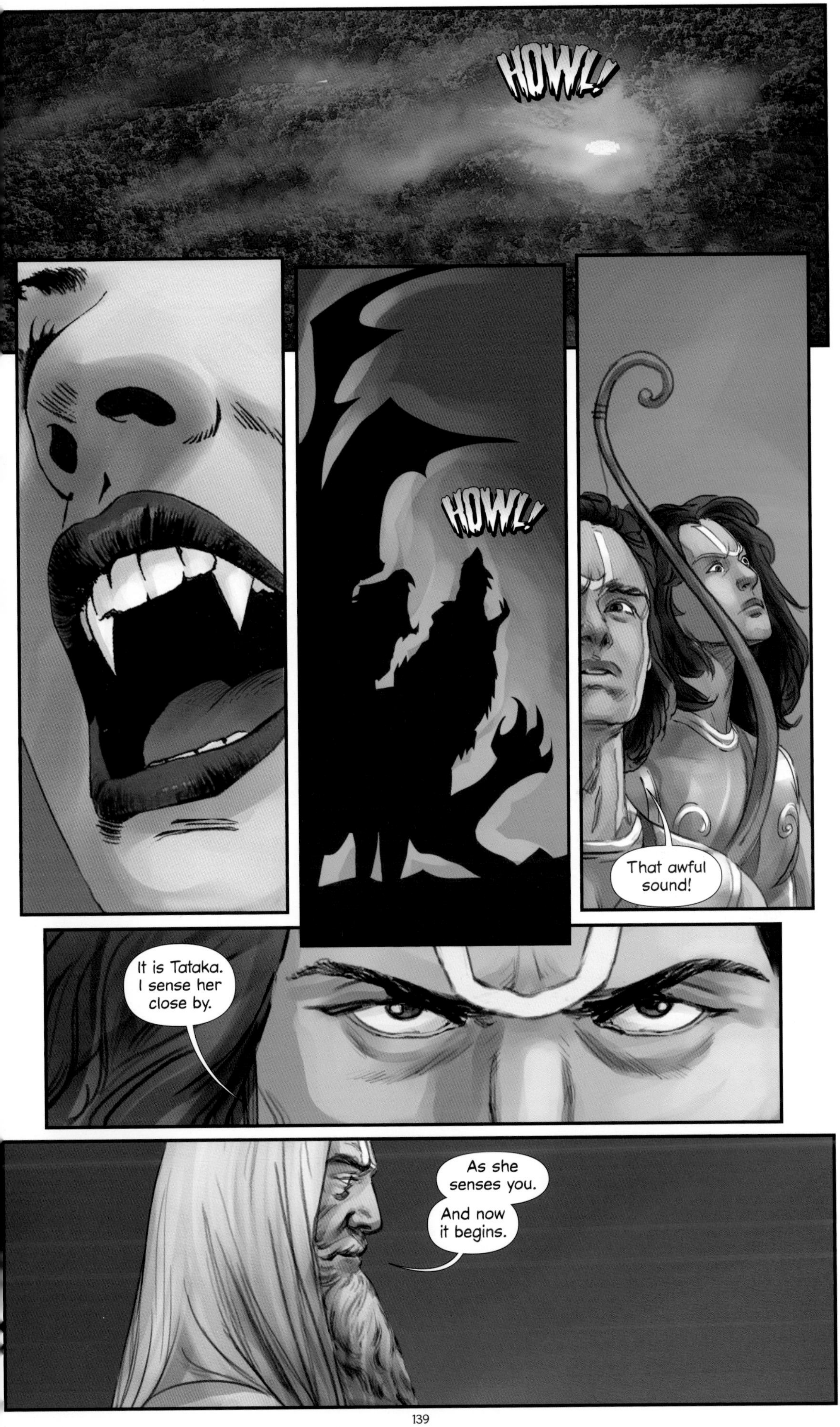
HOWL!
HOWL!
That awful sound!
It is Tataka. I sense her close by.
As she senses you.
And now it begins.

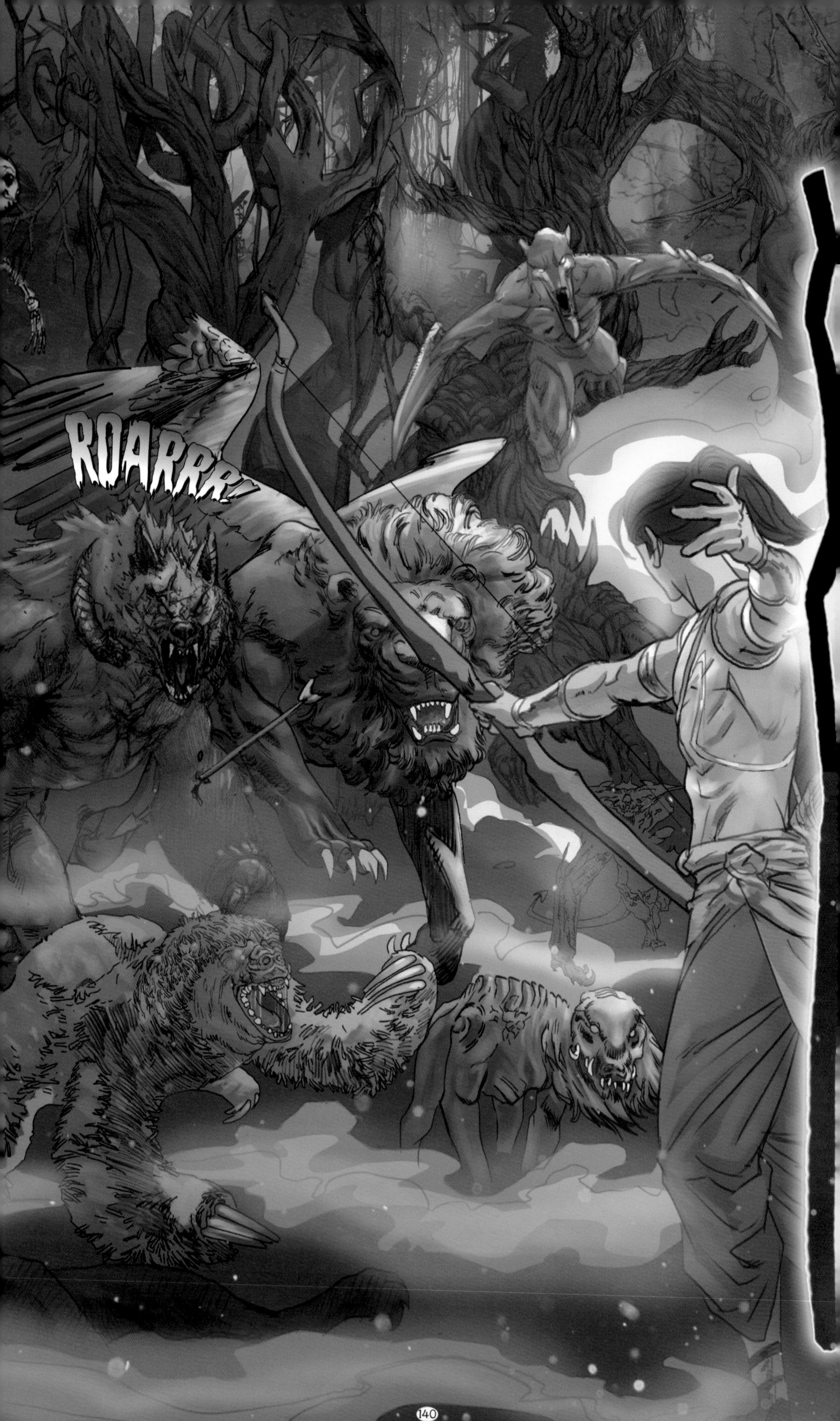
ROARRR!

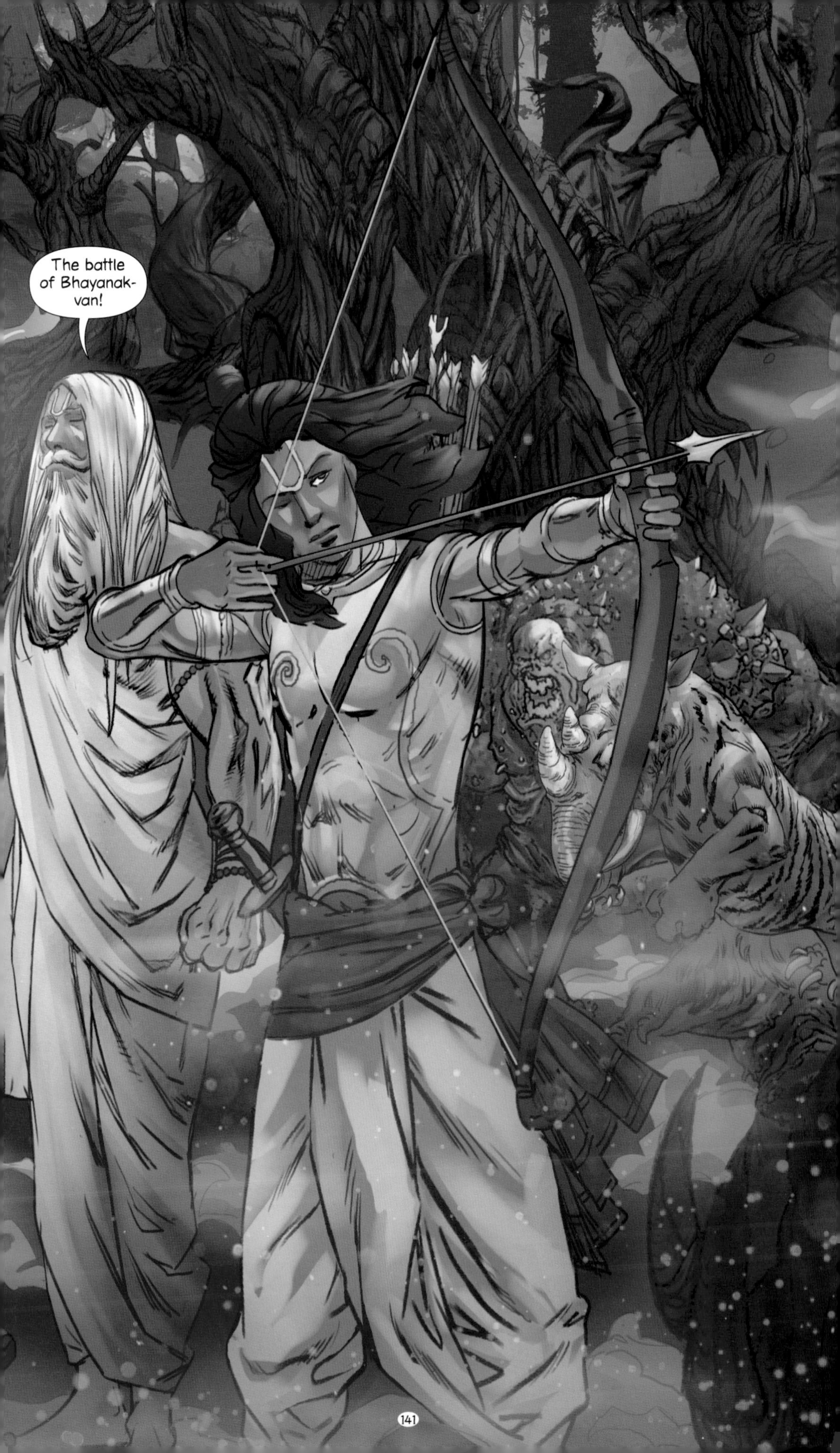
The battle of Bhayanak-van!

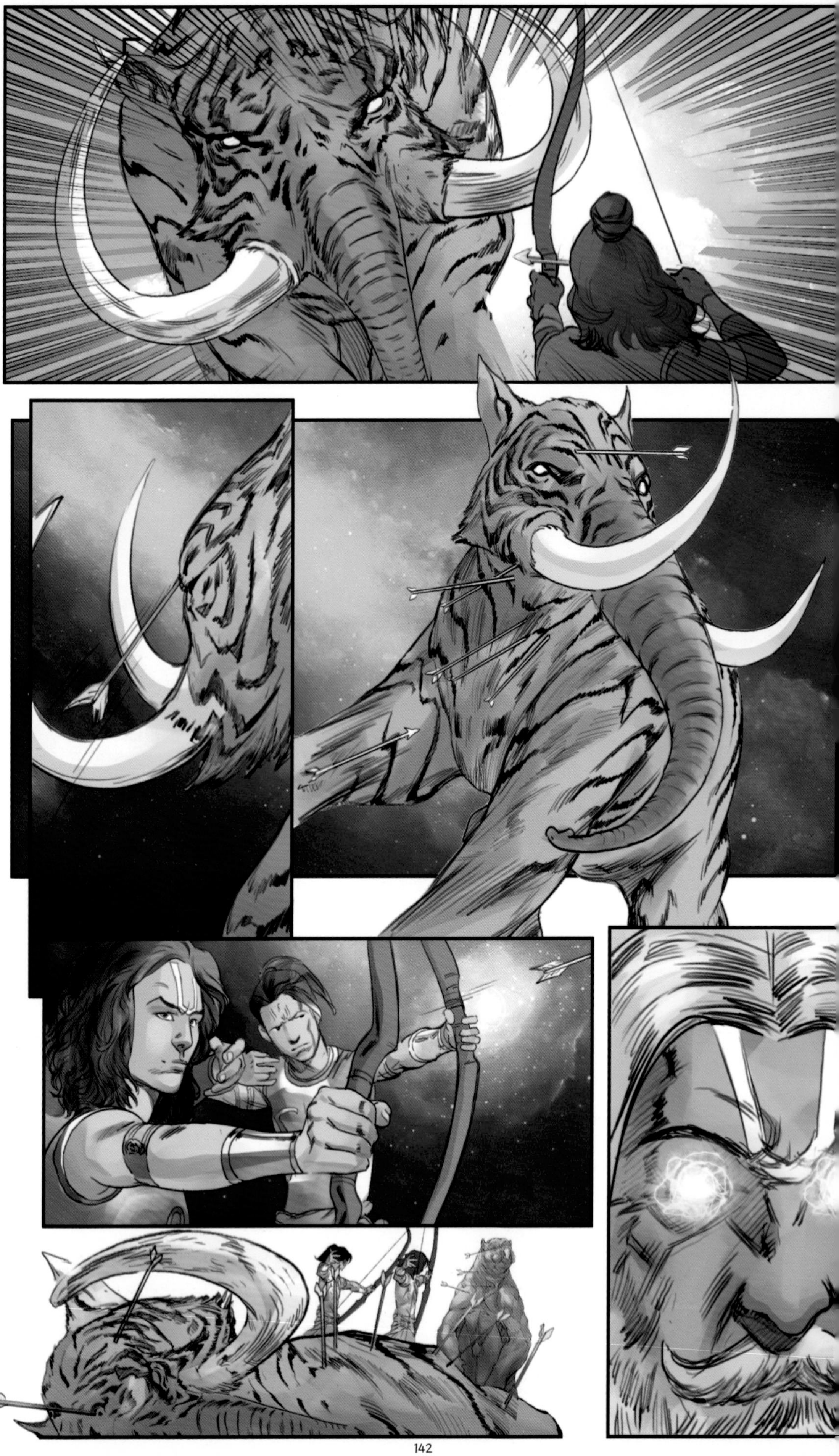

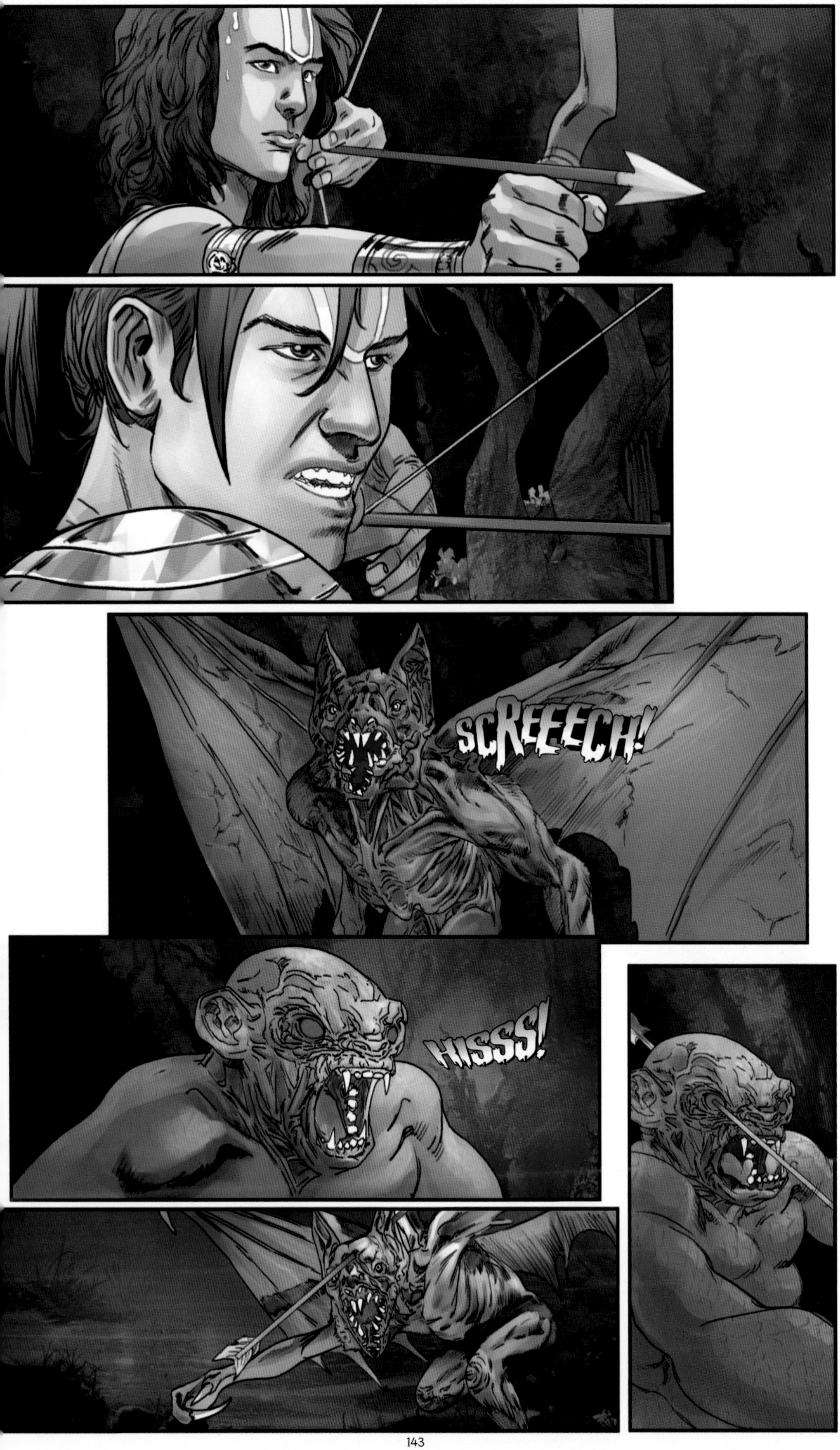
SCREEECH!
HISSS!

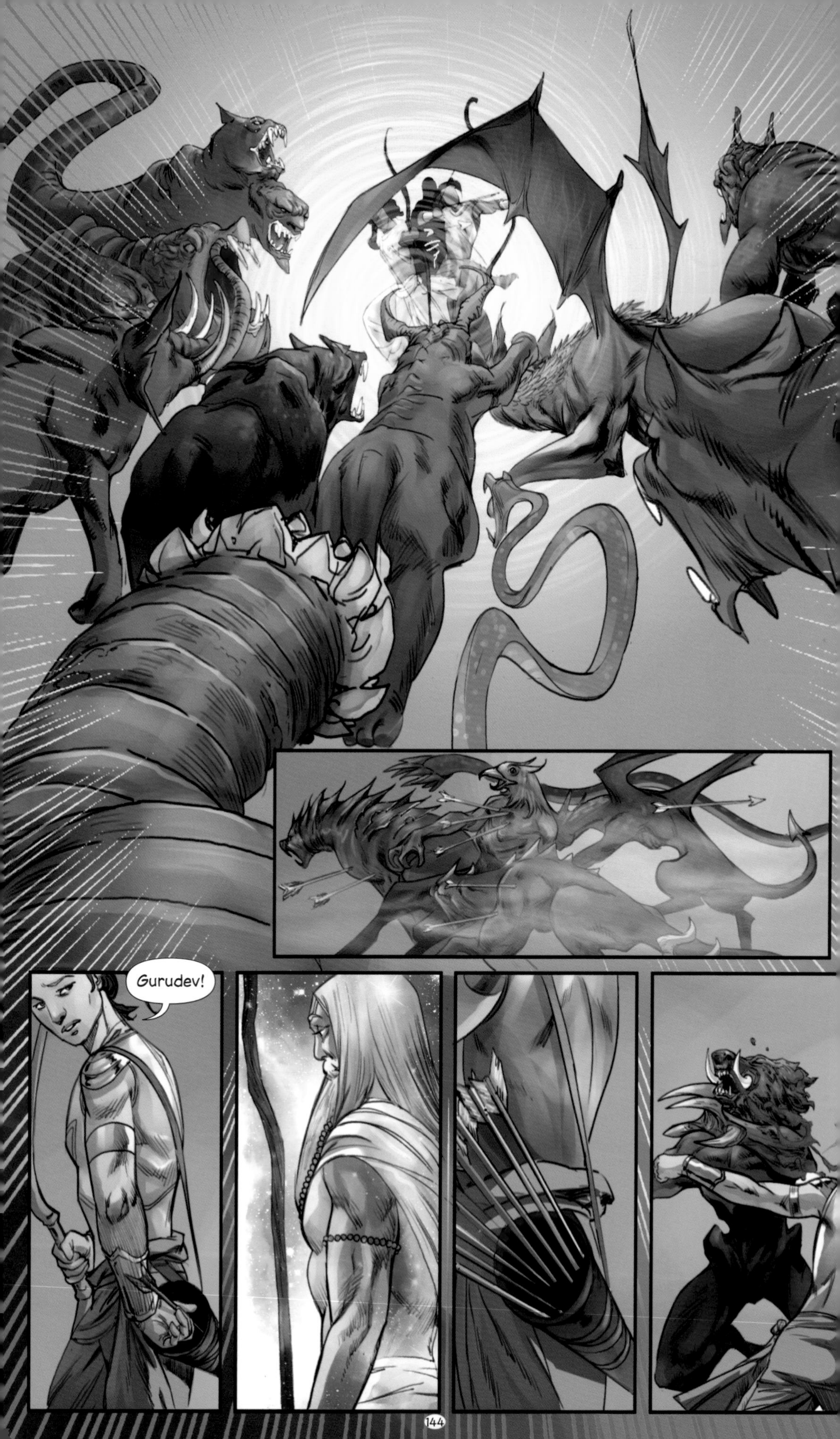
Gurudev!

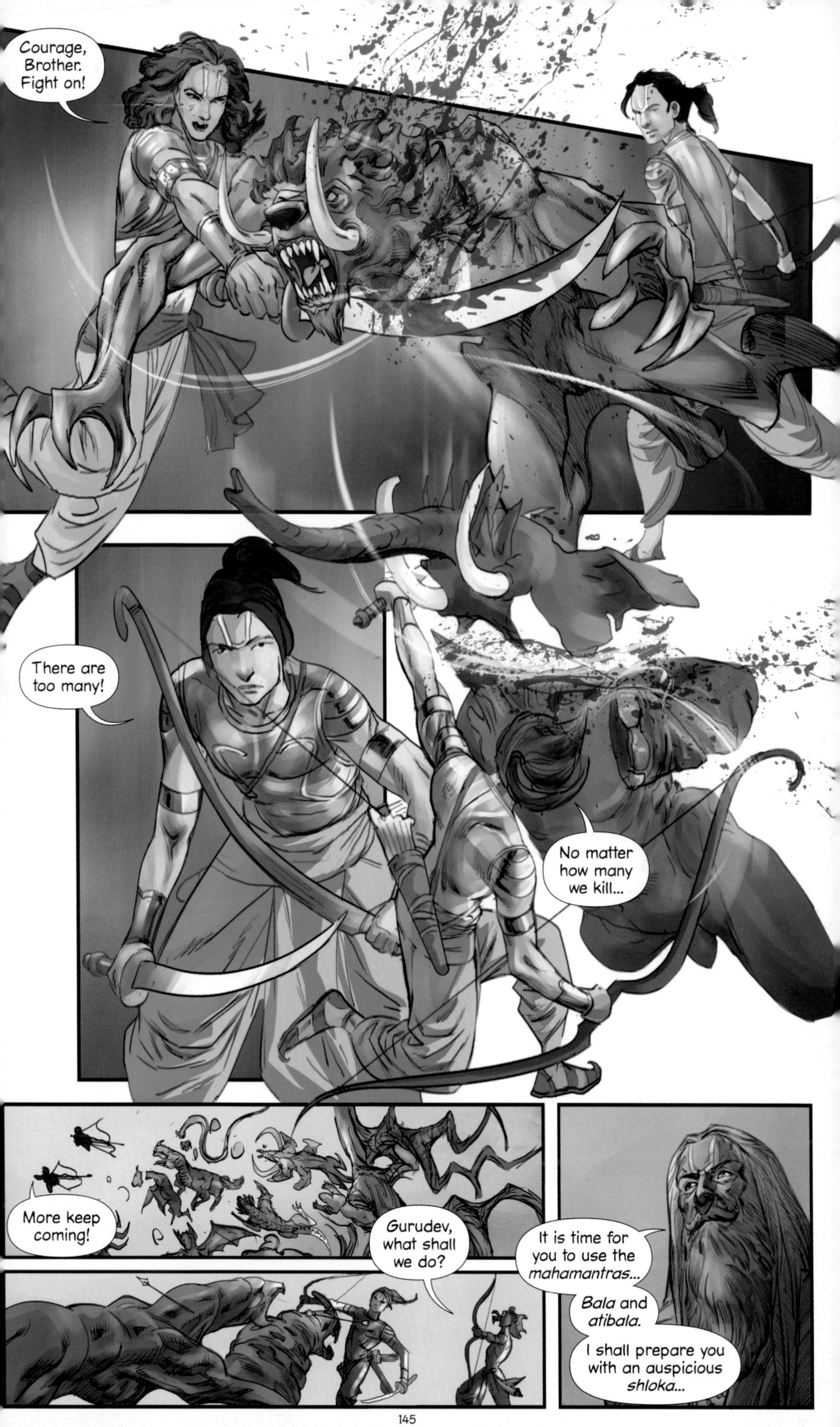
Courage, Brother. Fight on!
There are too many!
No matter how many we kill...
More keep coming!
Gurudev, what shall we do?
It is time for you to use the *mahamantras*...
Bala and *atibala*.
I shall prepare you with an auspicious *shloka*...

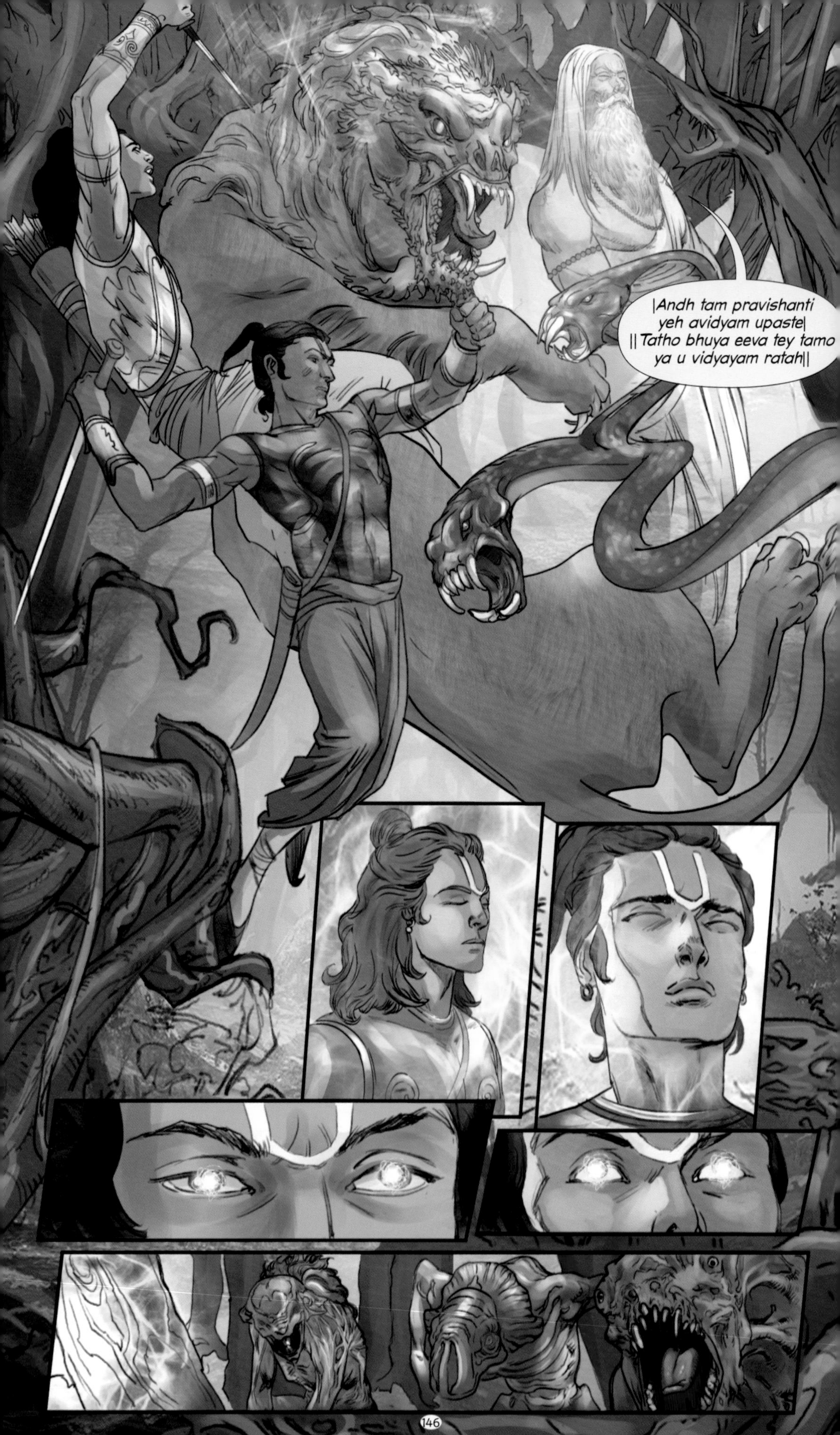
|Andh tam pravishanti yeh avidyam upaste| ||Tatho bhuya eeva tey tamo ya u vidyayam ratah||

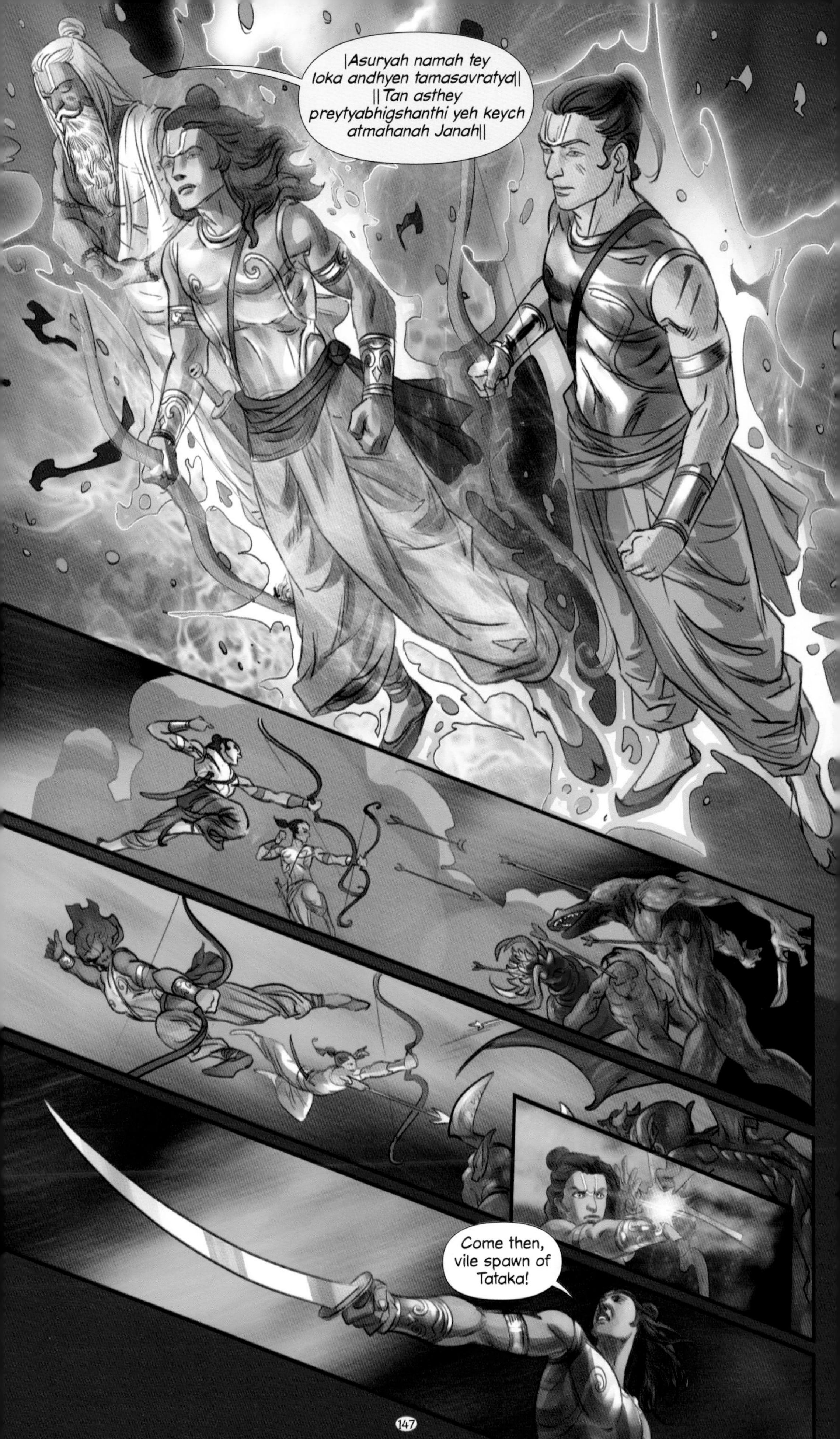
|Asuryah namah tey loka andhyen tamasavratya|| ||Tan asthey preytyabhigshanthi yeh keych atmahanah Janah||
Come then, vile spawn of Tataka!

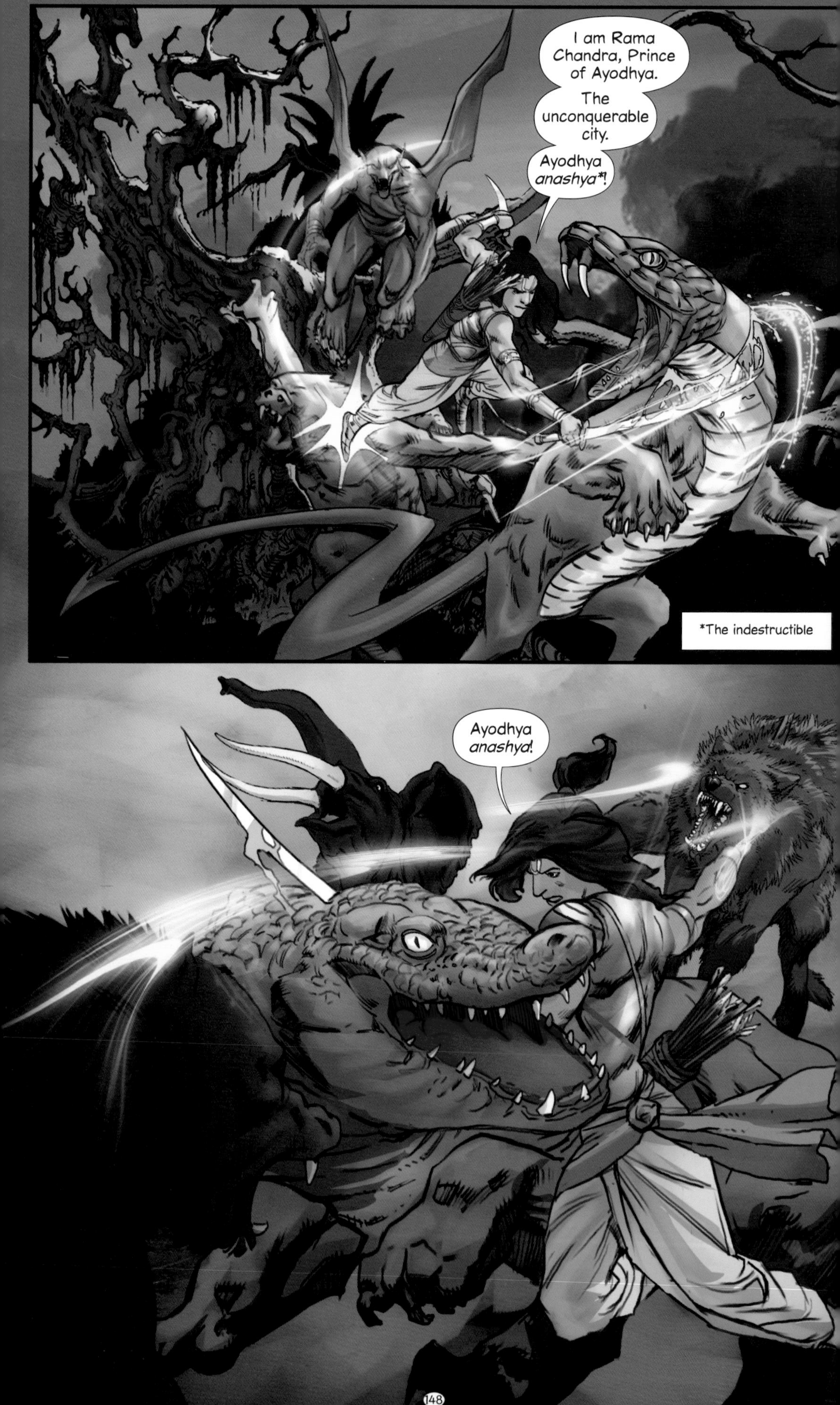
I am Rama Chandra, Prince of Ayodhya.
The unconquerable city.
Ayodhya *anashya**!
*The indestructible
Ayodhya *anashya*!

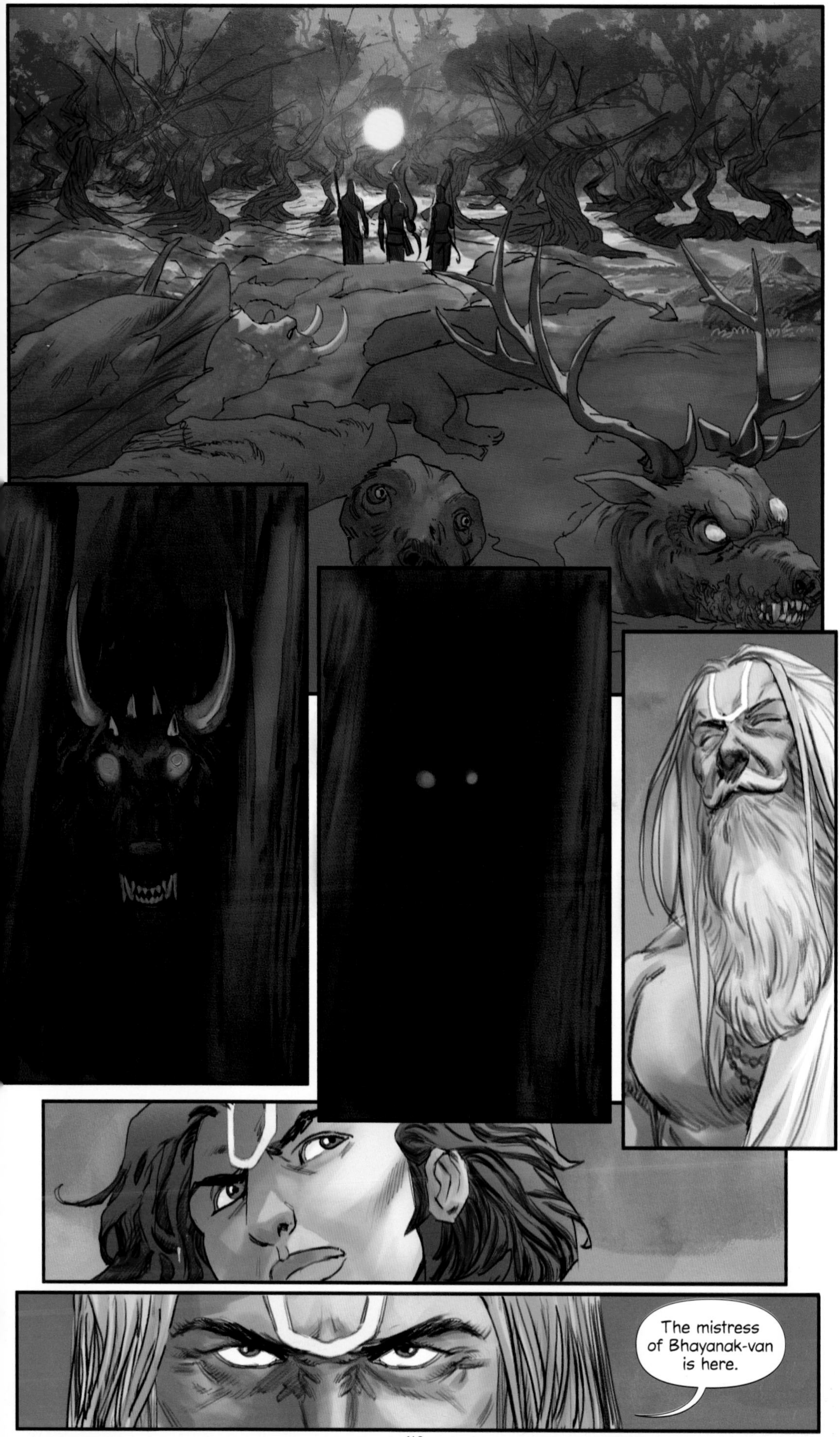
The mistress
of Bhayanak-van
is here.

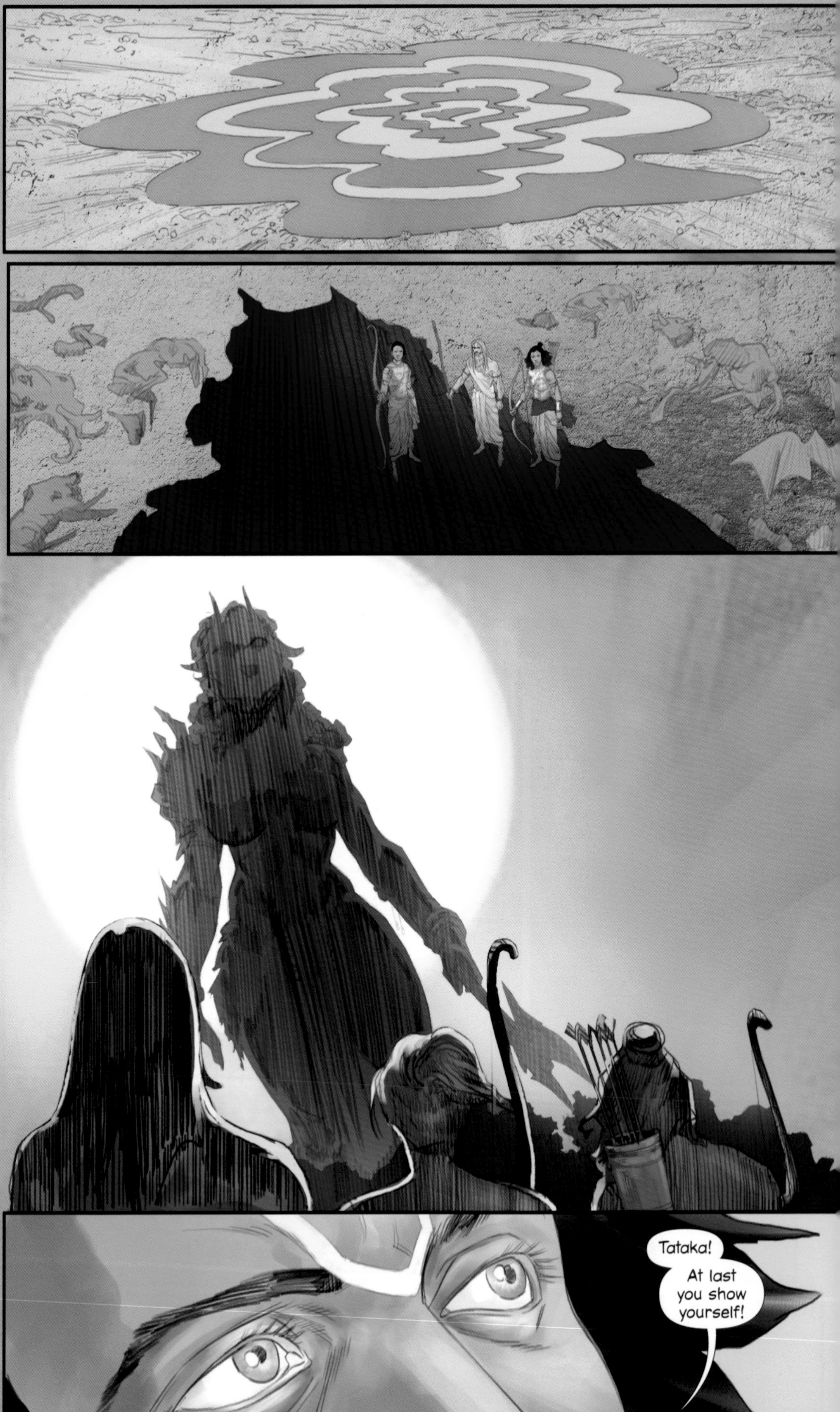
Tataka!
At last you show yourself!

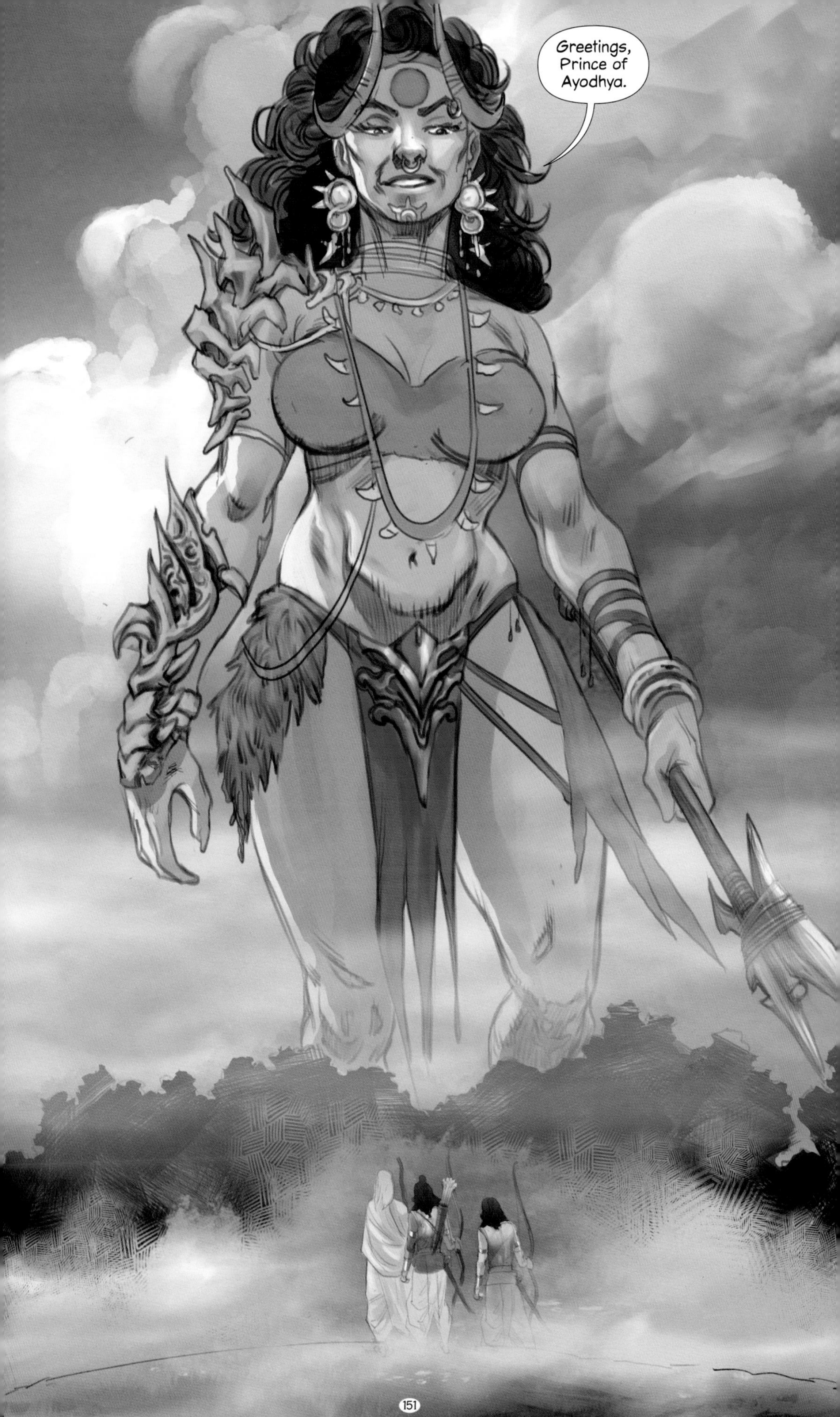
Greetings, Prince of Ayodhya.

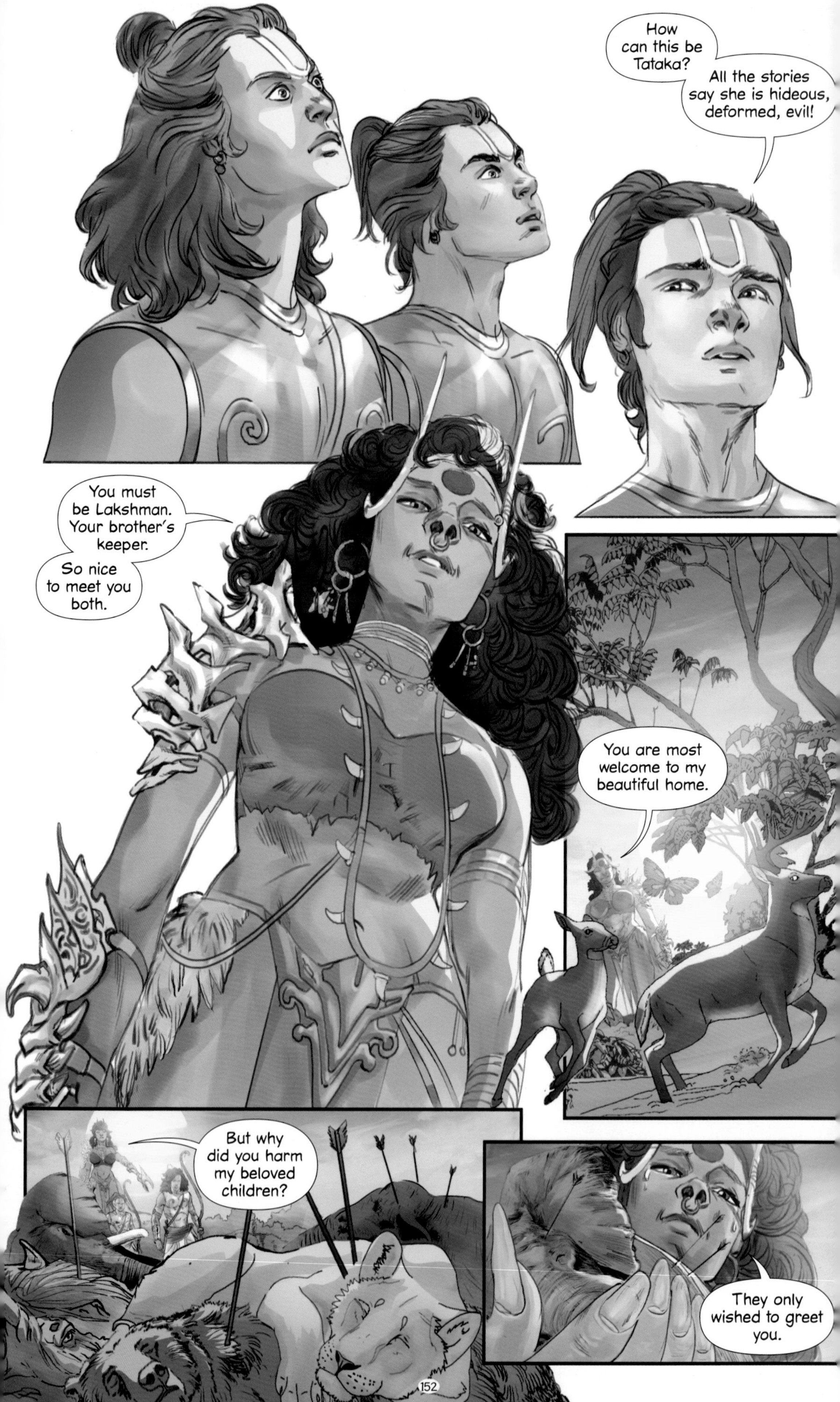
How can this be Tataka?
All the stories say she is hideous, deformed, evil!
You must be Lakshman. Your brother's keeper.
So nice to meet you both.
You are most welcome to my beautiful home.
But why did you harm my beloved children?
They only wished to greet you.

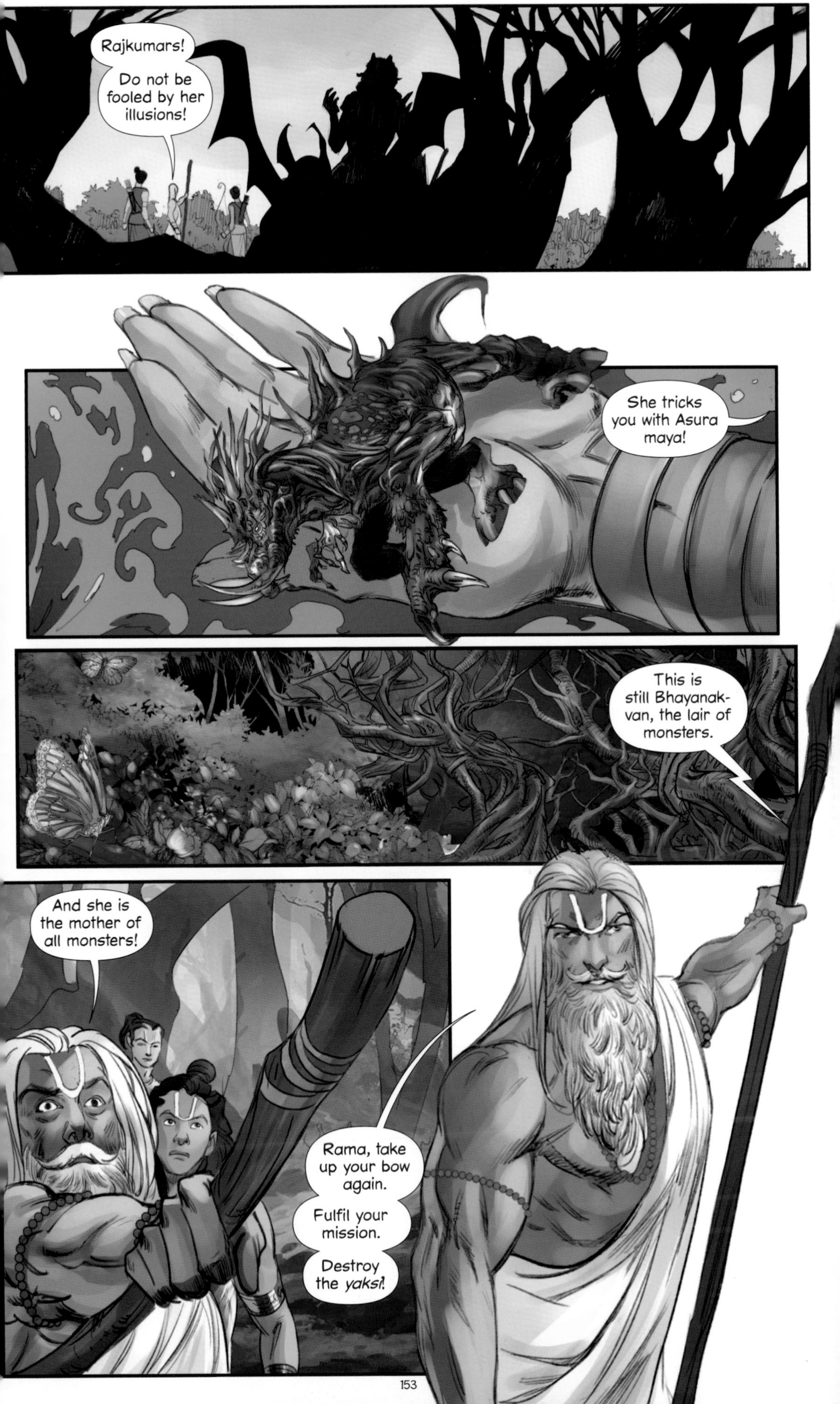
Rajkumars!
Do not be fooled by her illusions!
She tricks you with Asura maya!
This is still Bhayanak-van, the lair of monsters.
And she is the mother of all monsters!
Rama, take up your bow again.
Fulfil your mission.
Destroy the *yaksi*!

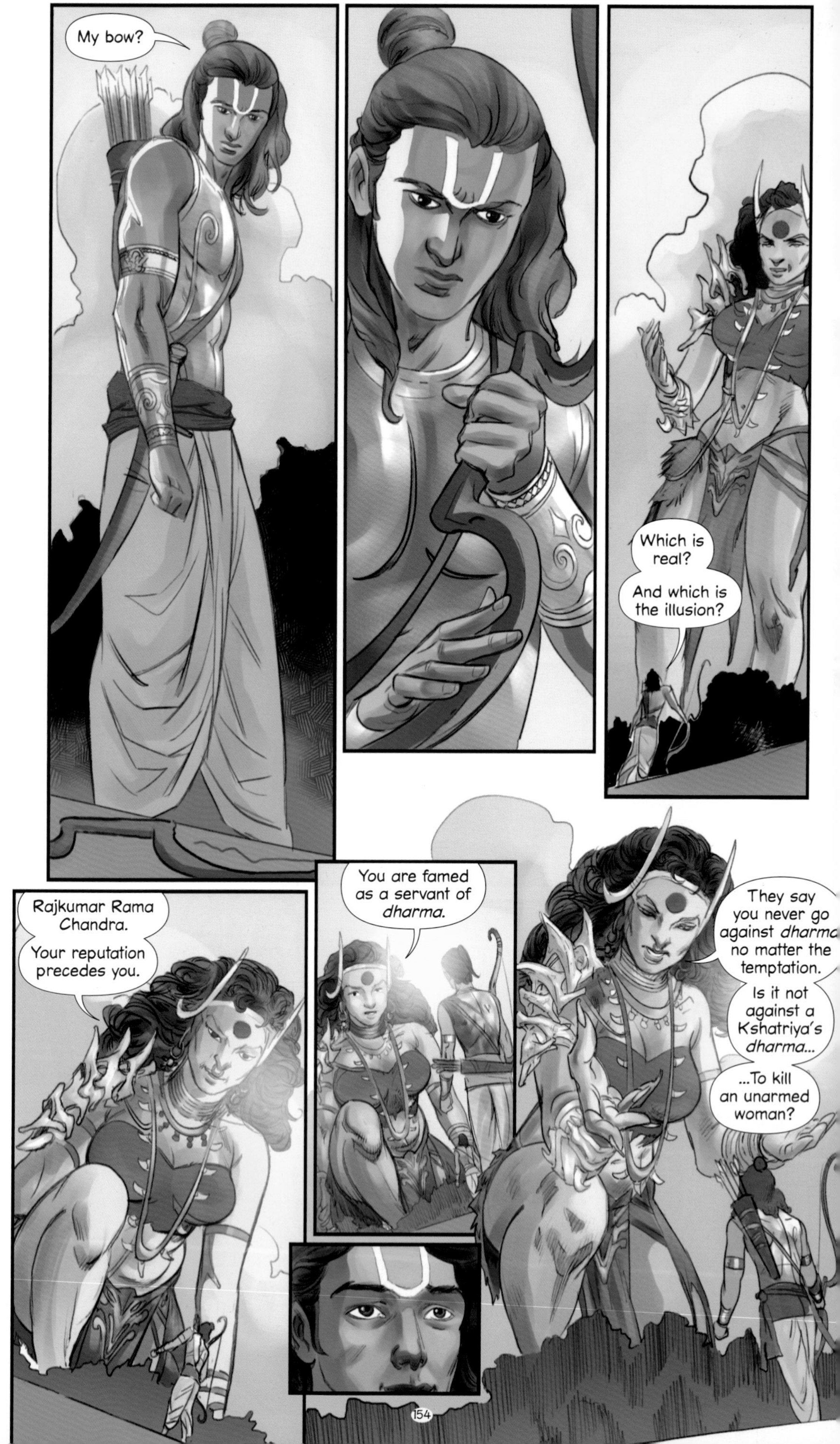

My bow?
Which is real?
And which is the illusion?
Rajkumar Rama Chandra.
Your reputation precedes you.
You are famed as a servant of *dharma.*
They say you never go against *dharma* no matter the temptation.
Is it not against a Kshatriya's *dharma*...
...To kill an unarmed woman?

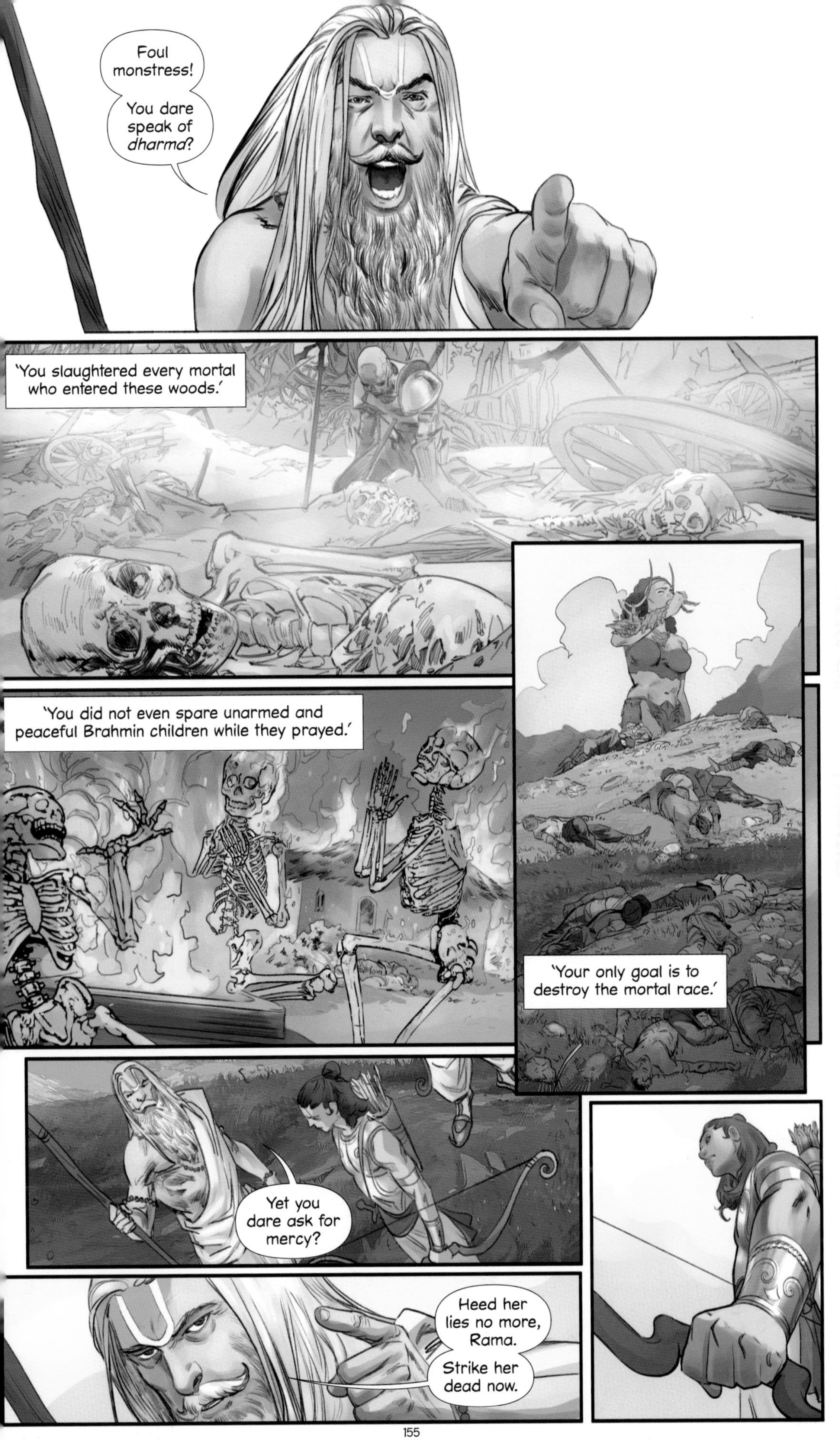
Foul monstress!
You dare speak of *dharma*?
'You slaughtered every mortal who entered these woods.'
'You did not even spare unarmed and peaceful Brahmin children while they prayed.'
'Your only goal is to destroy the mortal race.'
Yet you dare ask for mercy?
Heed her lies no more, Rama.
Strike her dead now.

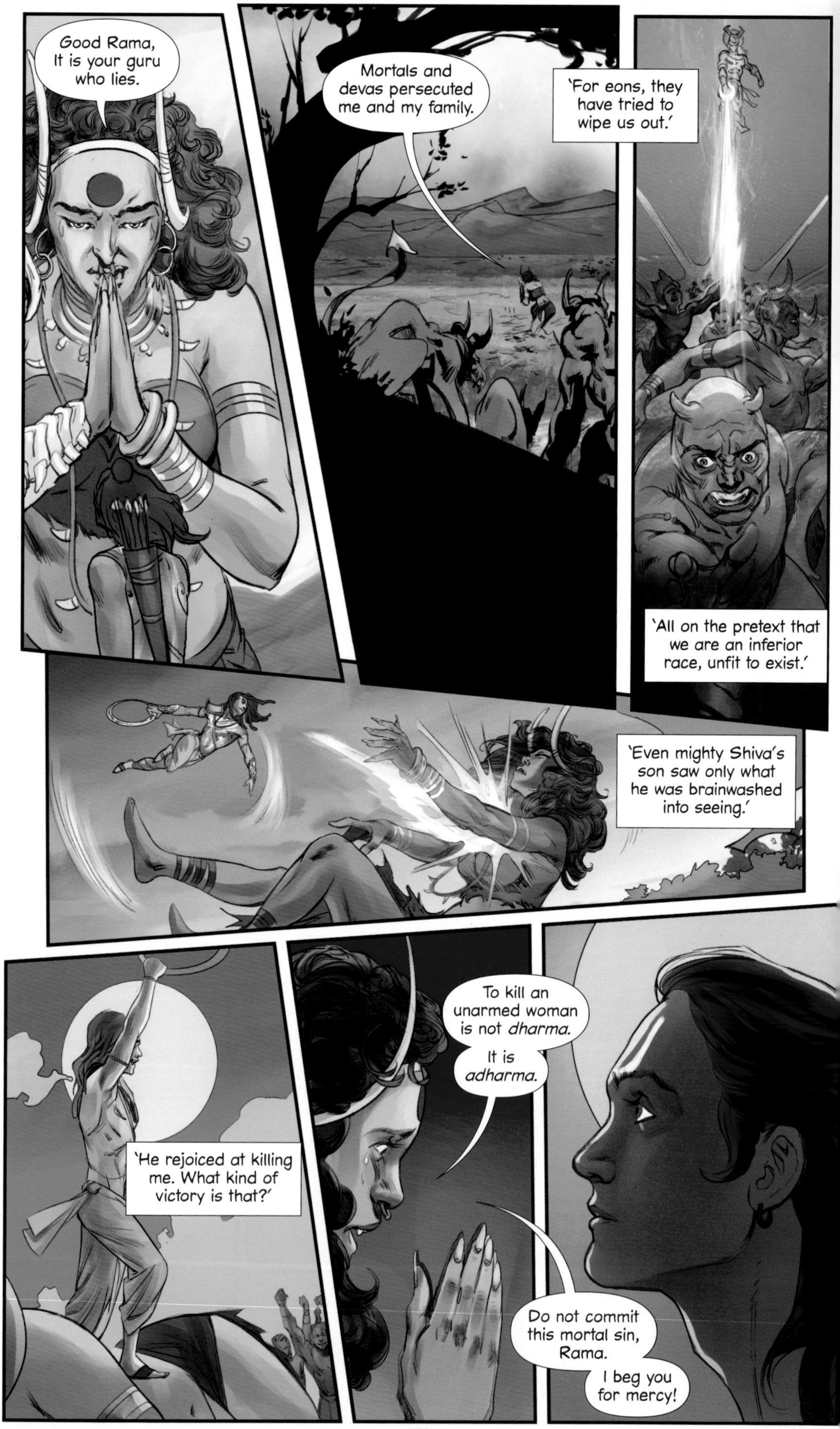
Good Rama, It is your guru who lies.
Mortals and devas persecuted me and my family.
'For eons, they have tried to wipe us out.'
'All on the pretext that we are an inferior race, unfit to exist.'
'Even mighty Shiva's son saw only what he was brainwashed into seeing.'
'He rejoiced at killing me. What kind of victory is that?'
To kill an unarmed woman is not *dharma*.
It is *adharma*.
Do not commit this mortal sin, Rama.
I beg you for mercy!

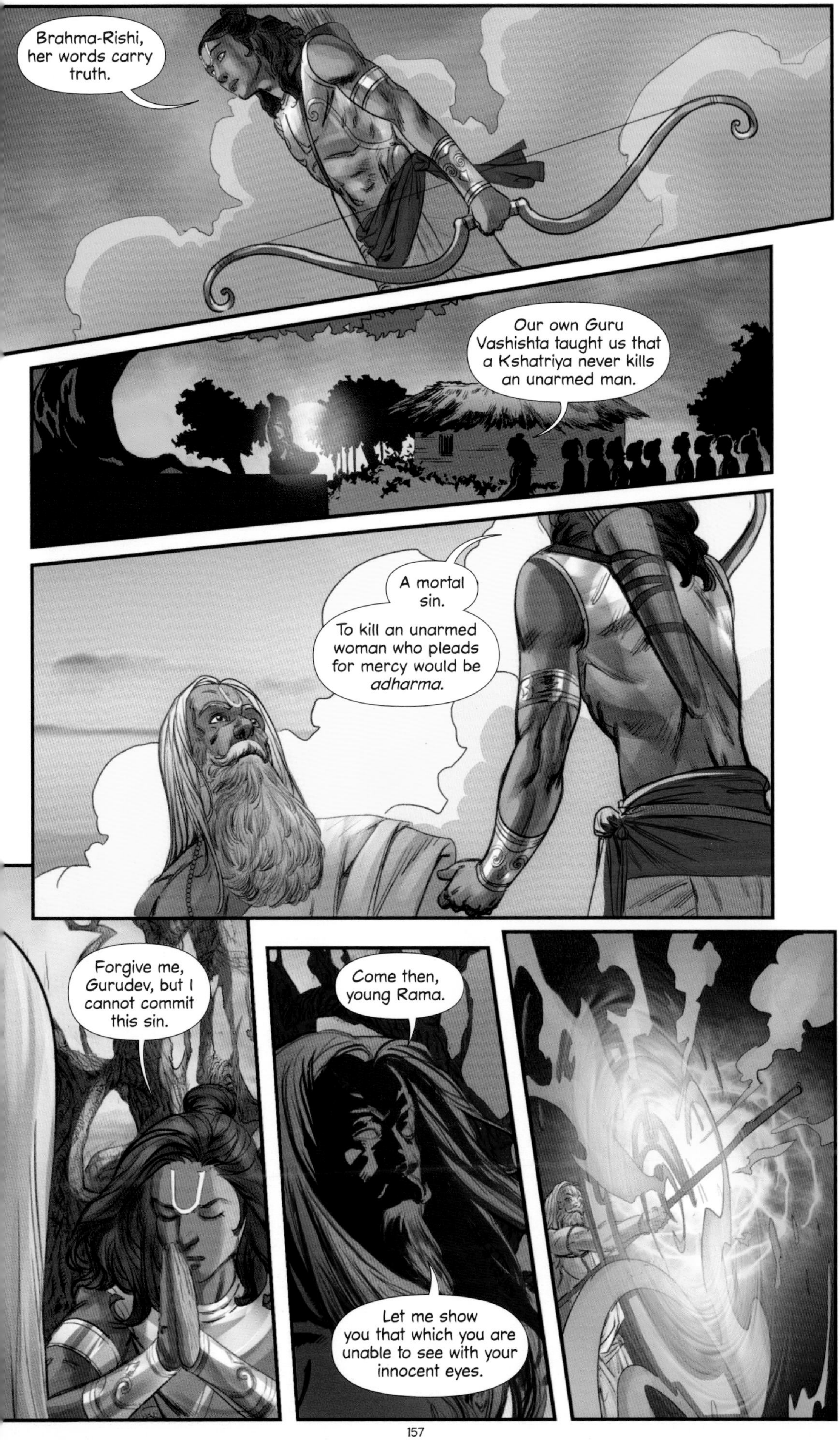
Brahma-Rishi, her words carry truth.
Our own Guru Vashishta taught us that a Kshatriya never kills an unarmed man.
A mortal sin.
To kill an unarmed woman who pleads for mercy would be *adharma*.
Forgive me, Gurudev, but I cannot commit this sin.
Come then, young Rama.
Let me show you that which you are unable to see with your innocent eyes.

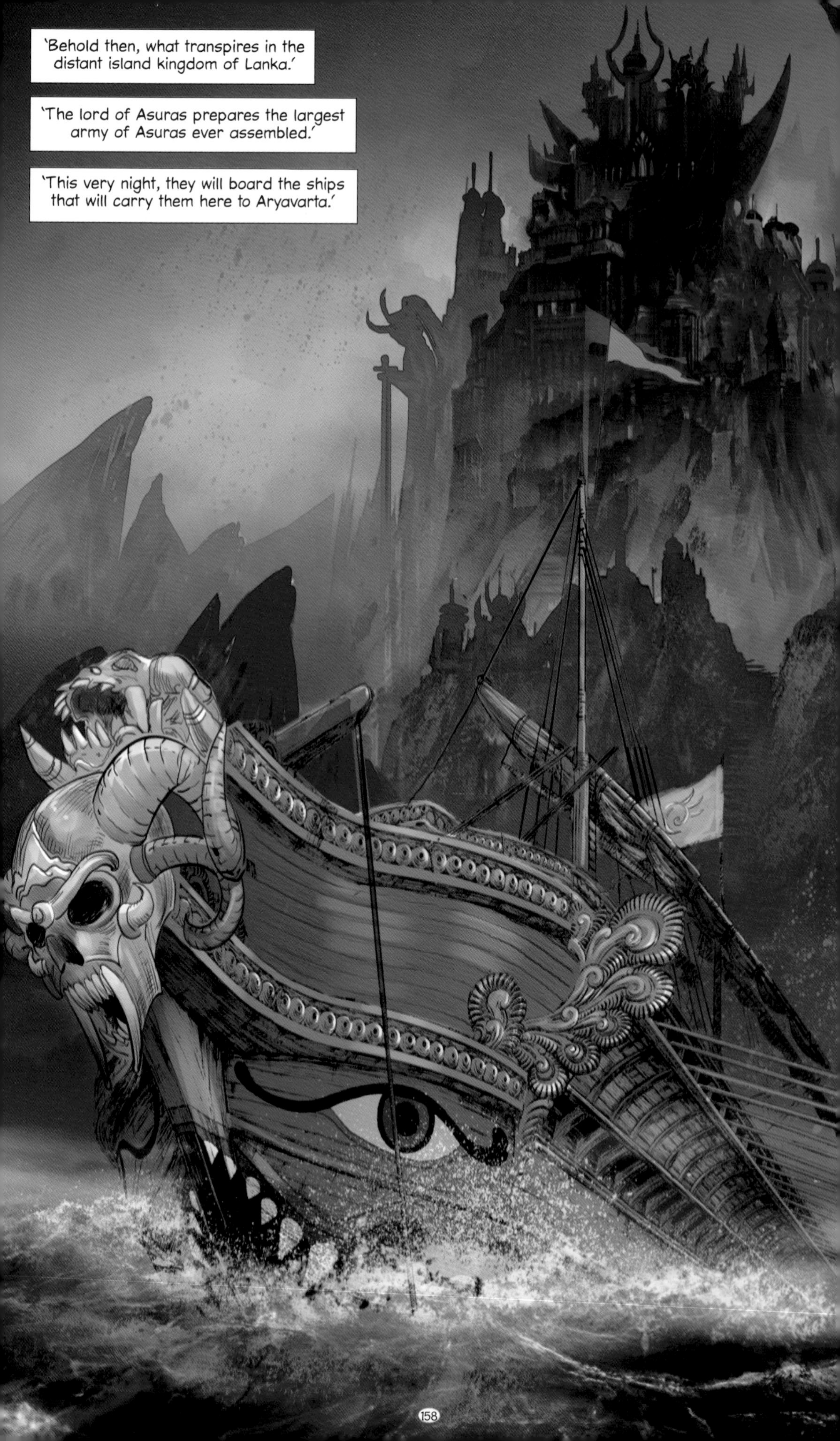
'Behold then, what transpires in the distant island kingdom of Lanka.'
'The lord of Asuras prepares the largest army of Asuras ever assembled.'
'This very night, they will board the ships that will carry them here to Aryavarta.'

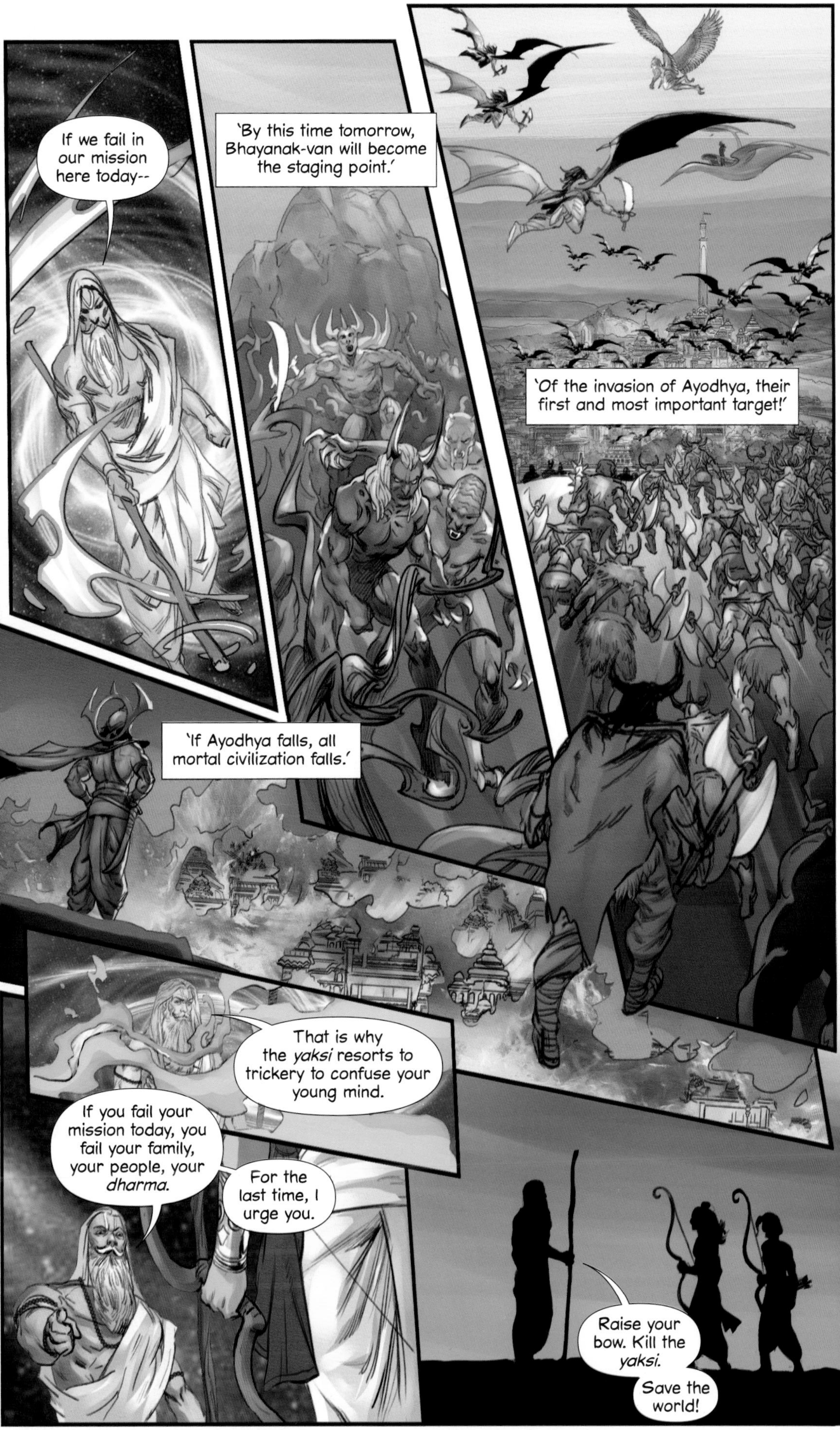
If we fail in our mission here today--
'By this time tomorrow, Bhayanak-van will become the staging point.'
'Of the invasion of Ayodhya, their first and most important target!'
'If Ayodhya falls, all mortal civilization falls.'
That is why the *yaksi* resorts to trickery to confuse your young mind.
If you fail your mission today, you fail your family, your people, your *dharma*.
For the last time, I urge you.
Raise your bow. Kill the *yaksi*.
Save the world!

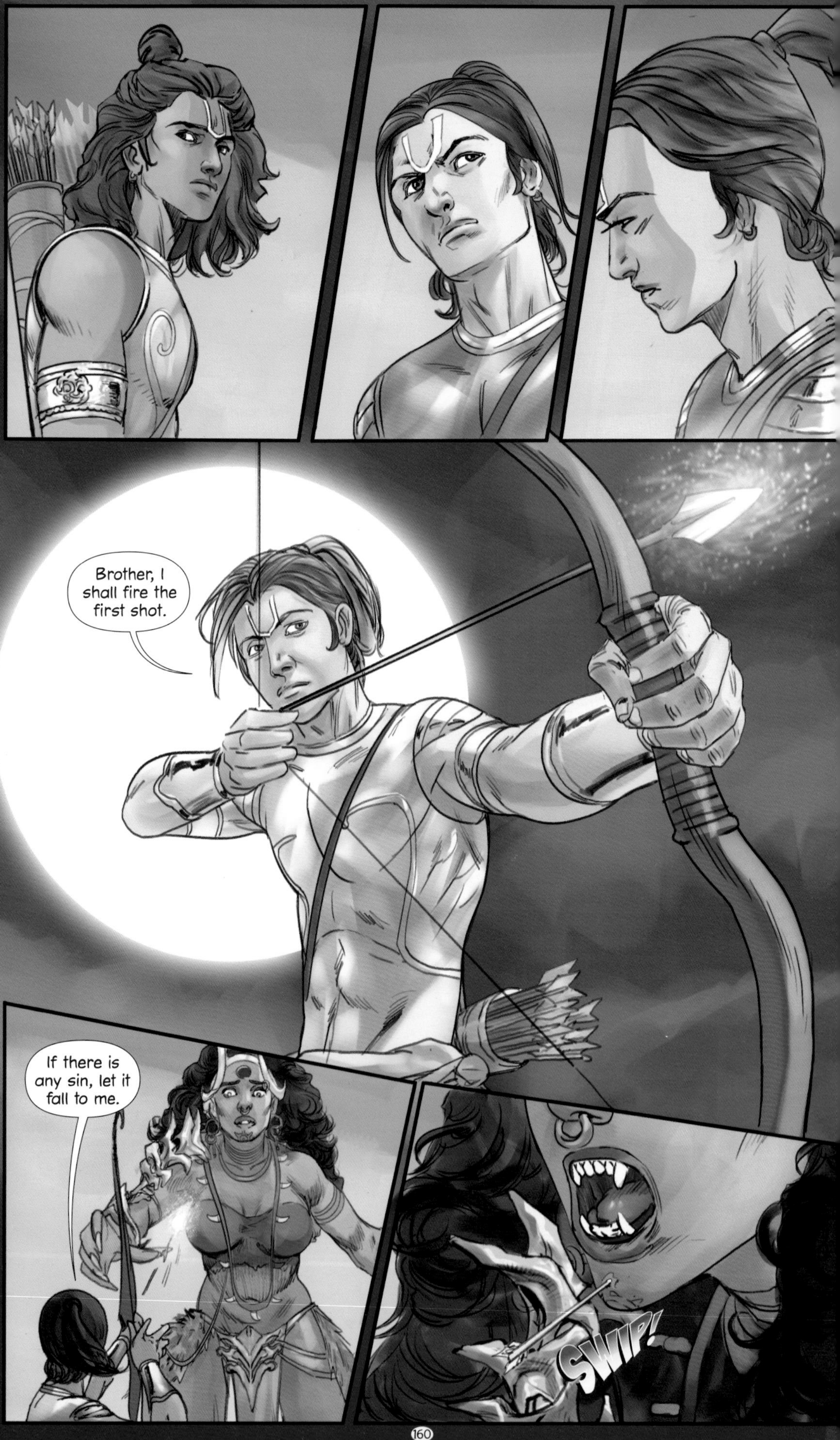
Brother, I shall fire the first shot.
If there is any sin, let it fall to me.
SWIP!

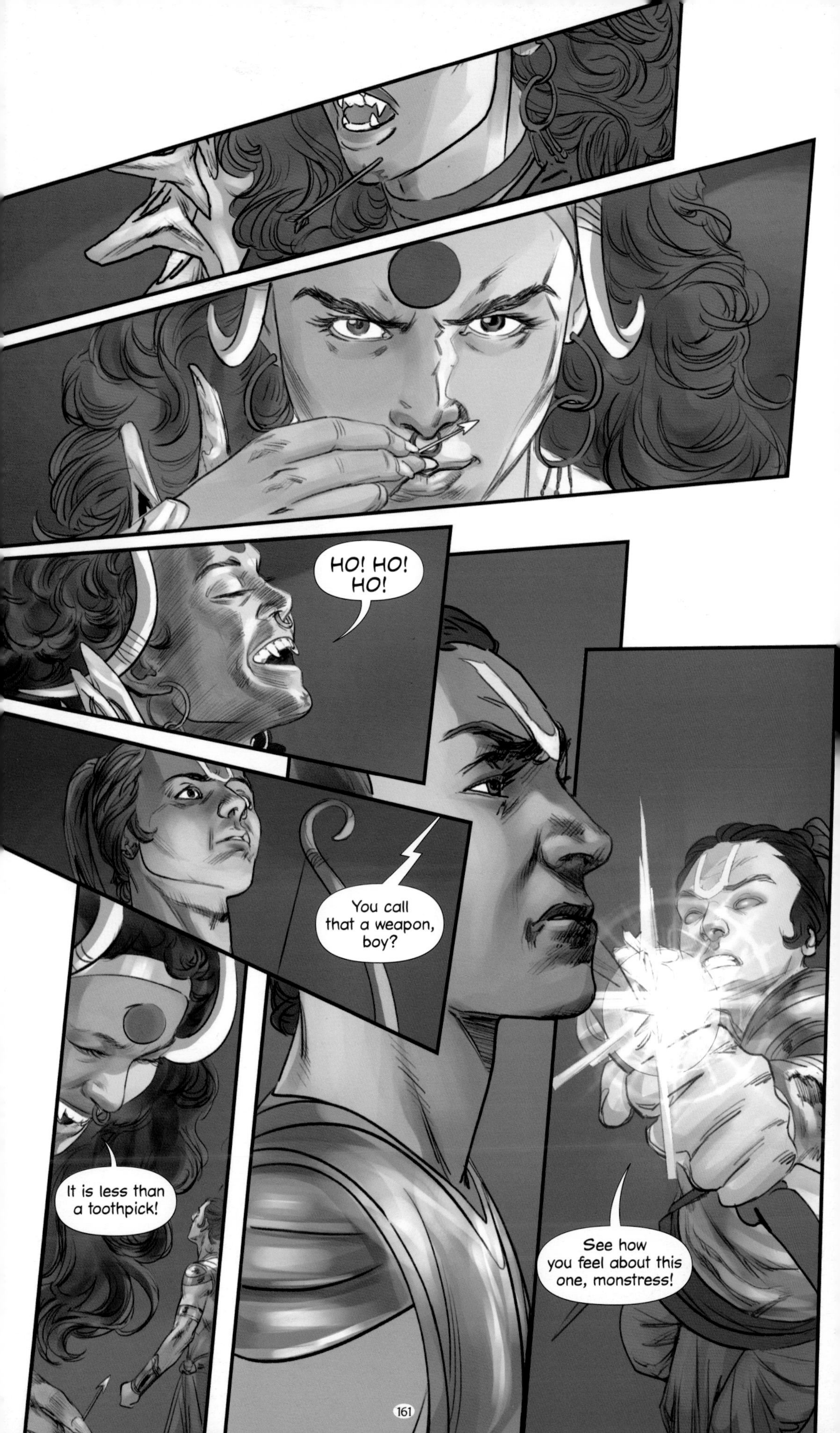
HO! HO! HO!
You call that a weapon, boy?
It is less than a toothpick!
See how you feel about this one, monstress!

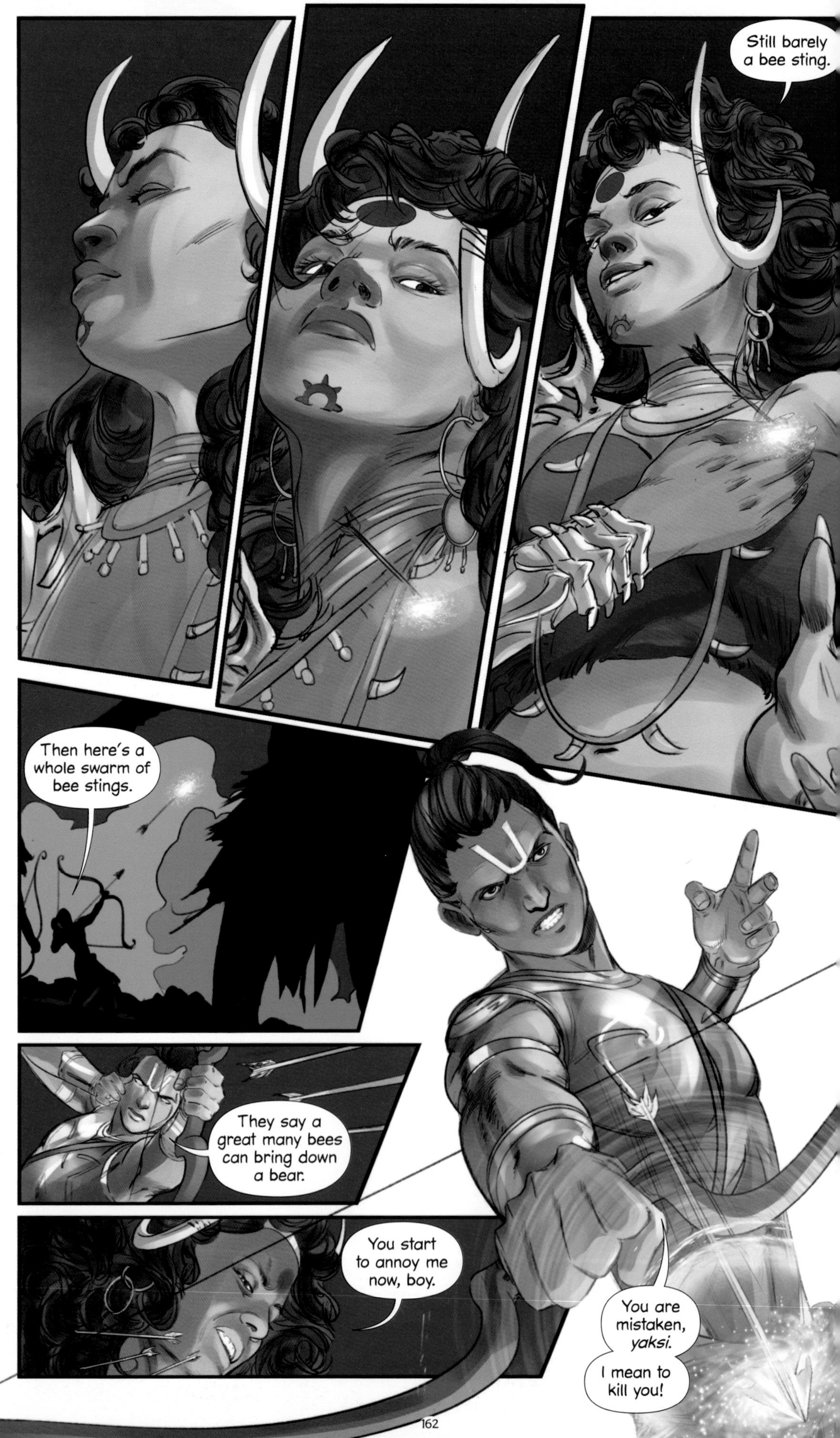
Still barely a bee sting.
Then here's a whole swarm of bee stings.
They say a great many bees can bring down a bear.
You start to annoy me now, boy.
You are mistaken, *yaksi.*
I mean to kill you!

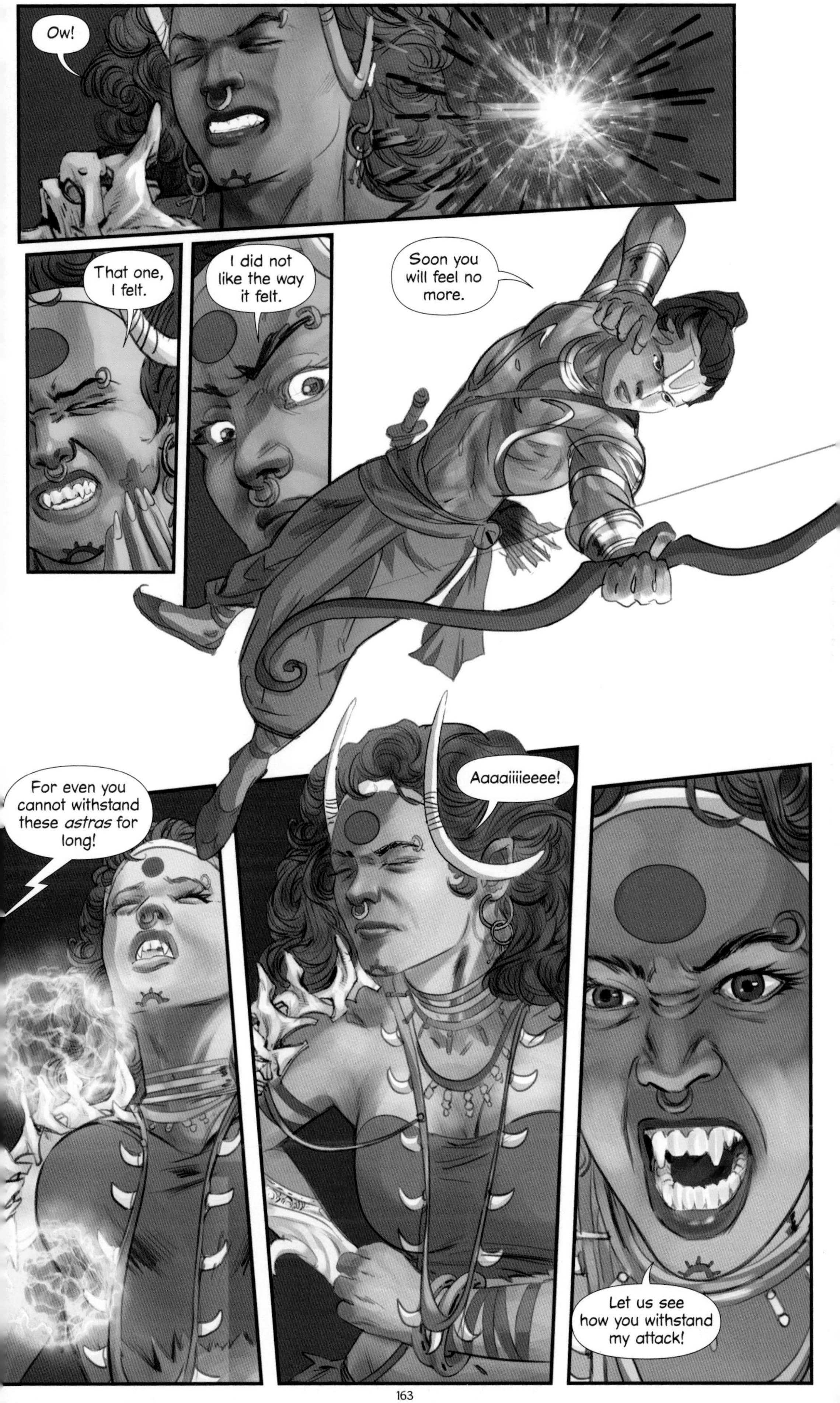
Ow!
That one, I felt.
I did not like the way it felt.
Soon you will feel no more.
For even you cannot withstand these *astras* for long!
Aaaaiiiieeee!
Let us see how you withstand my attack!

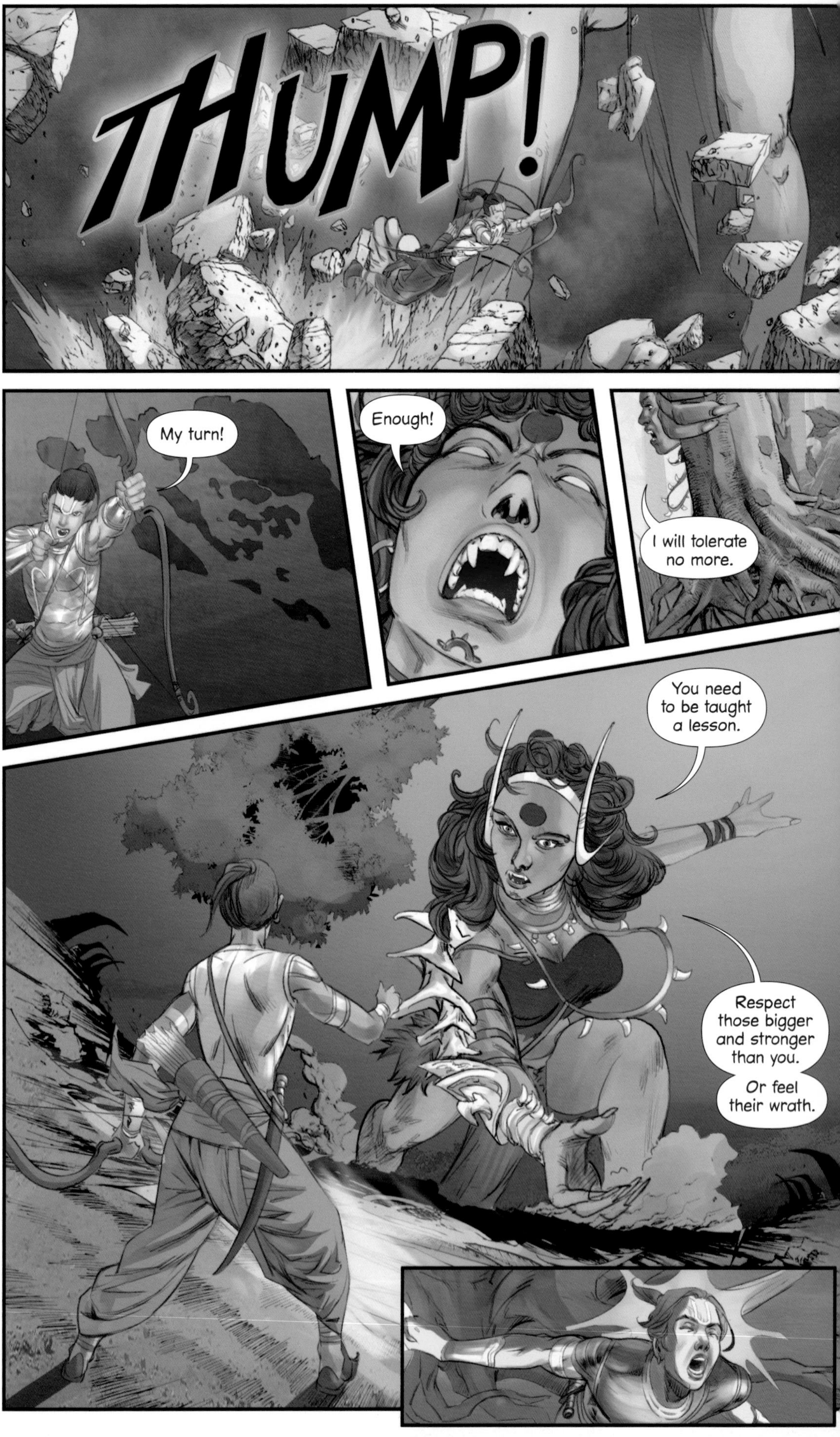
THUMP!
My turn!
Enough!
I will tolerate no more.
You need to be taught a lesson.
Respect those bigger and stronger than you.
Or feel their wrath.

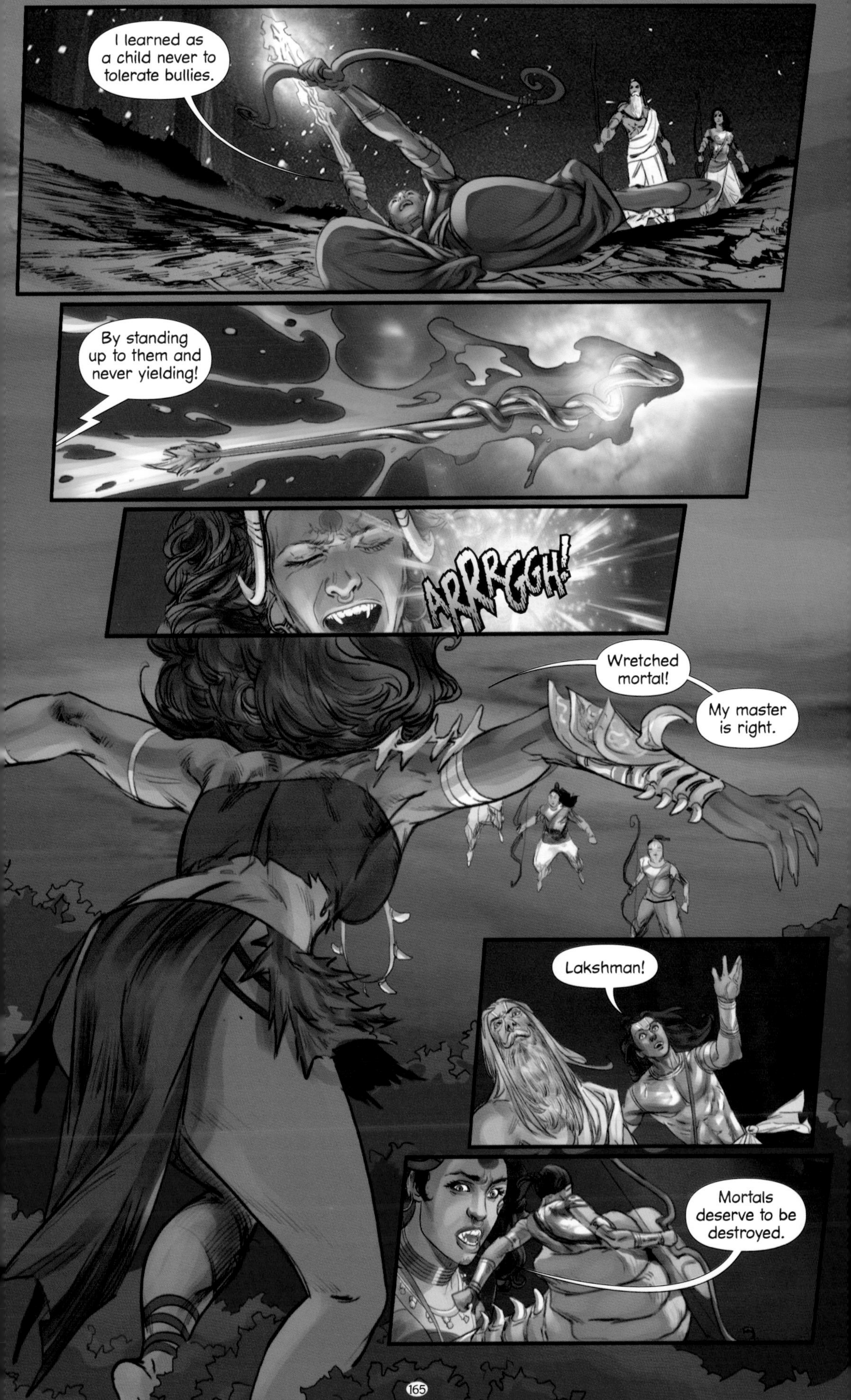
I learned as a child never to tolerate bullies.
By standing up to them and never yielding!
ARRRGGH!
Wretched mortal!
My master is right.
Lakshman!
Mortals deserve to be destroyed.

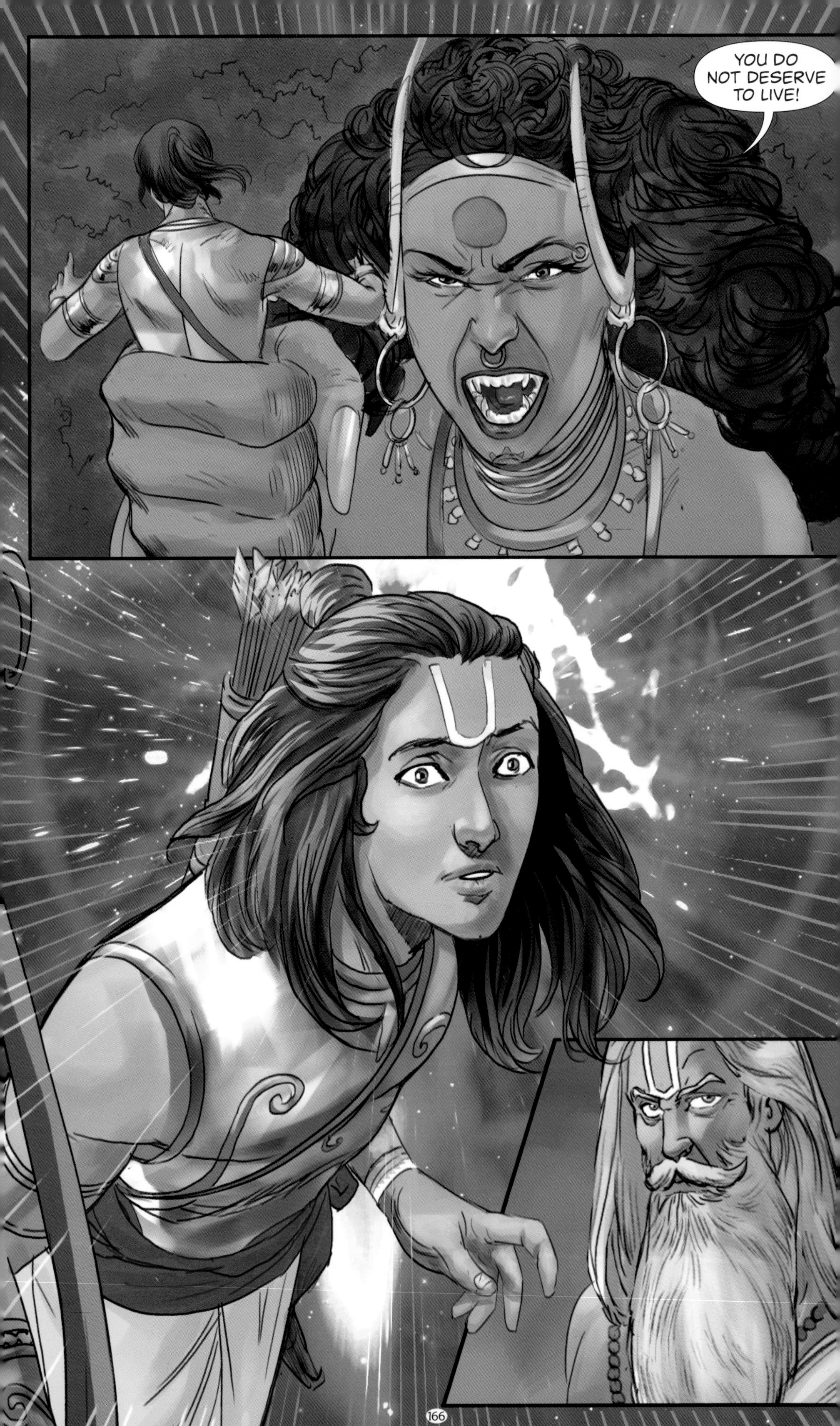
YOU DO NOT DESERVE TO LIVE!

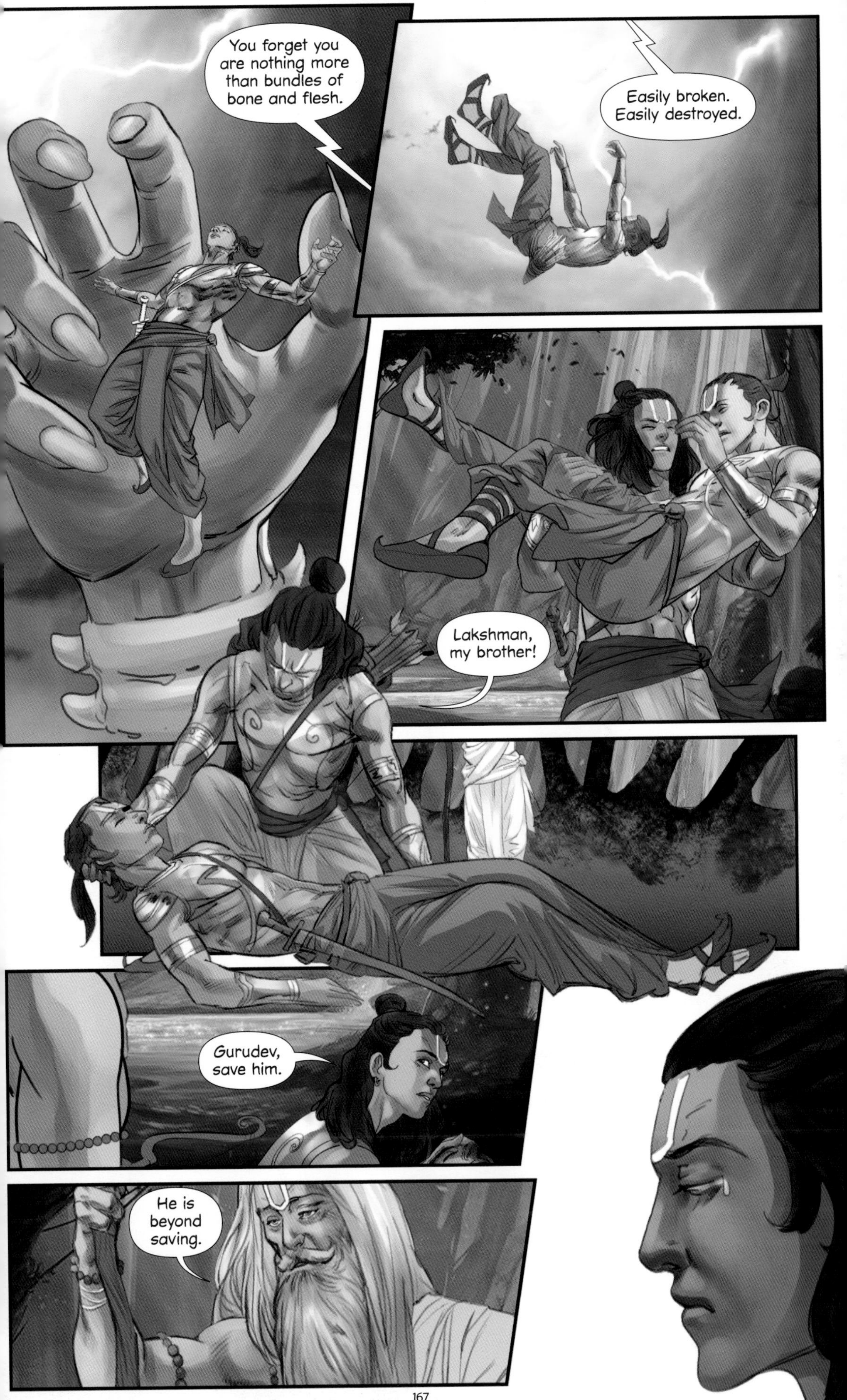
You forget you are nothing more than bundles of bone and flesh.
Easily broken. Easily destroyed.
Lakshman, my brother!
Gurudev, save him.
He is beyond saving.

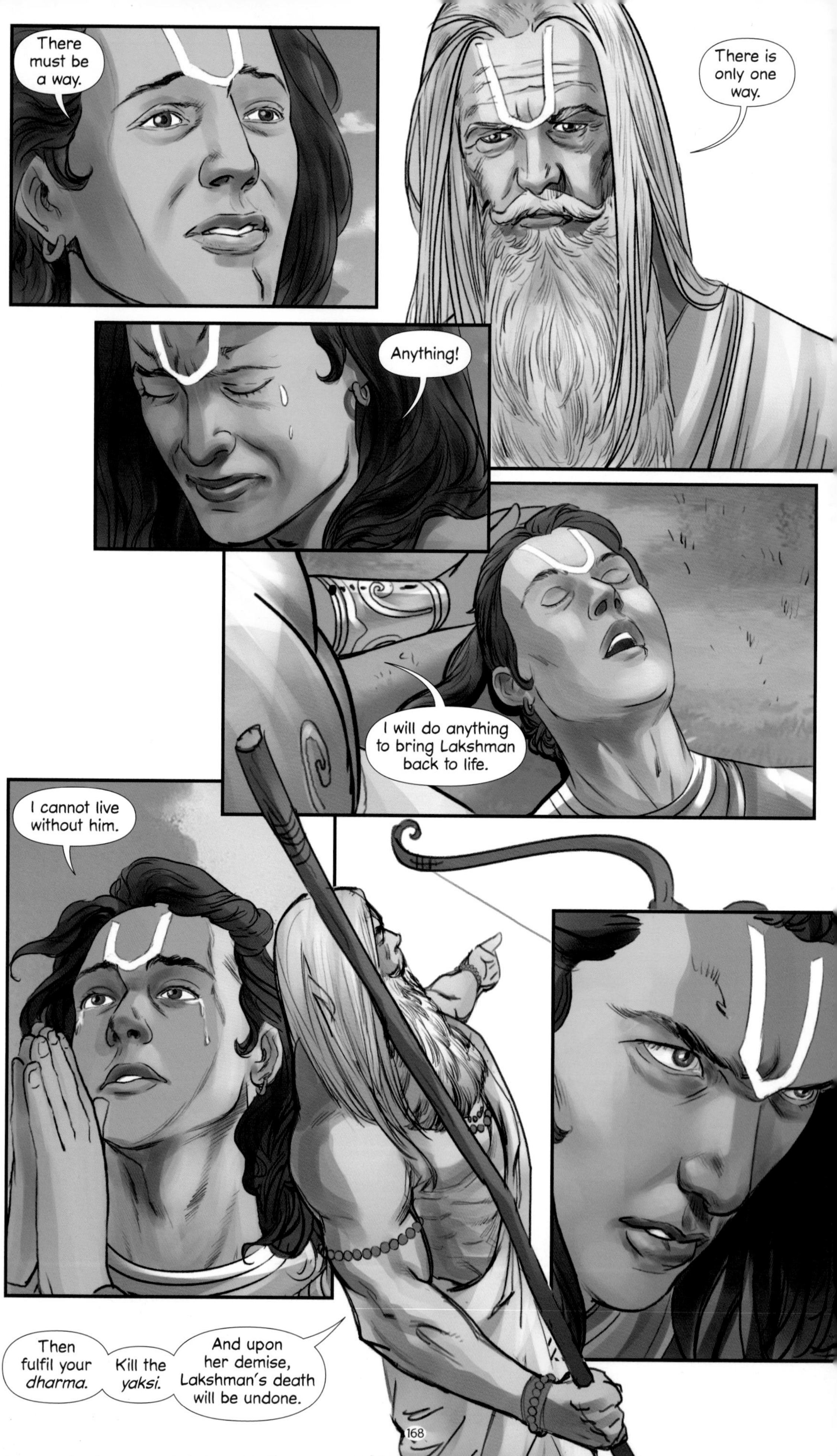
There must be a way.
There is only one way.
Anything!
I will do anything to bring Lakshman back to life.
I cannot live without him.
Then fulfil your *dharma*.
Kill the *yaksi*.
And upon her demise, Lakshman's death will be undone.

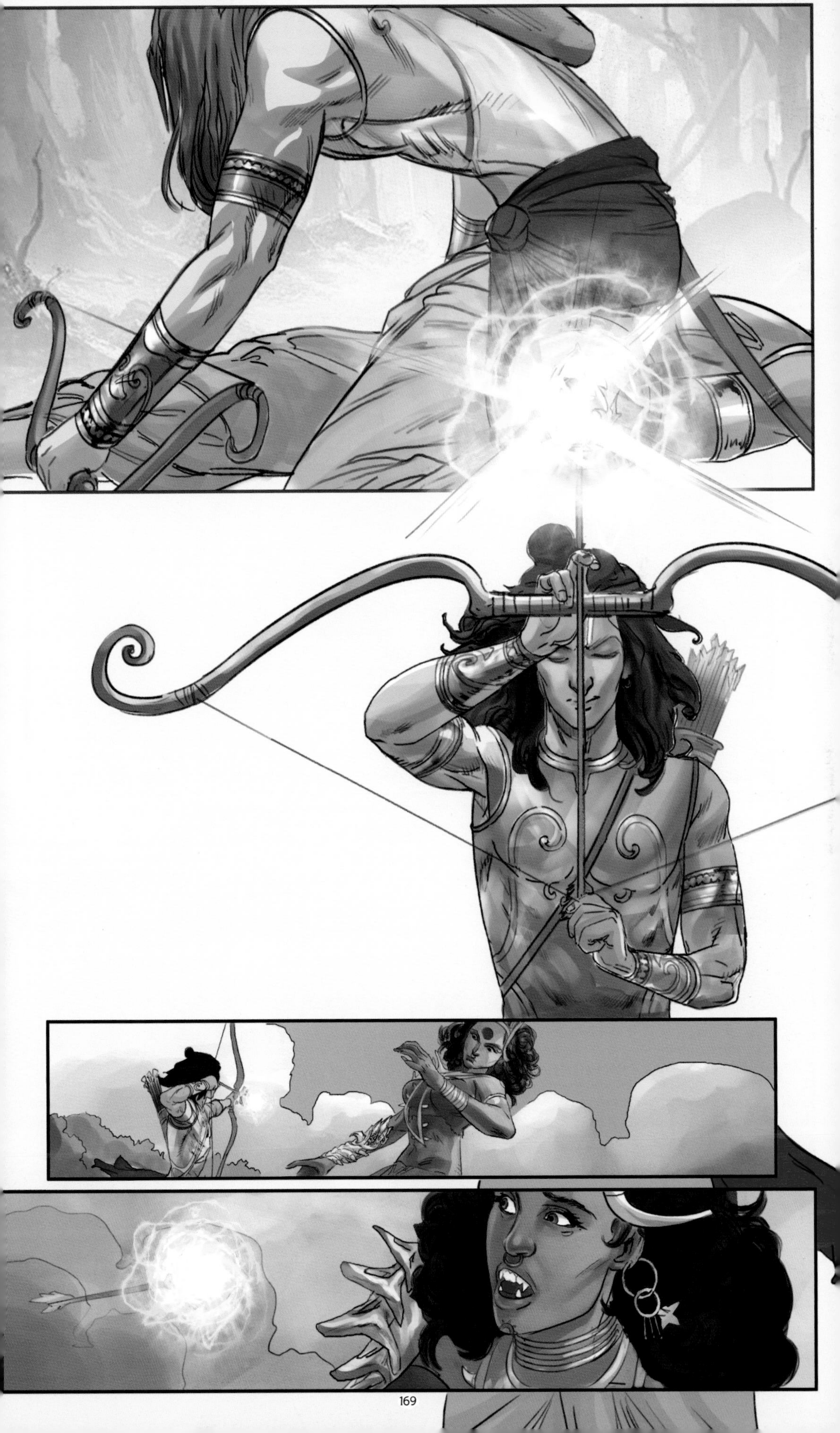

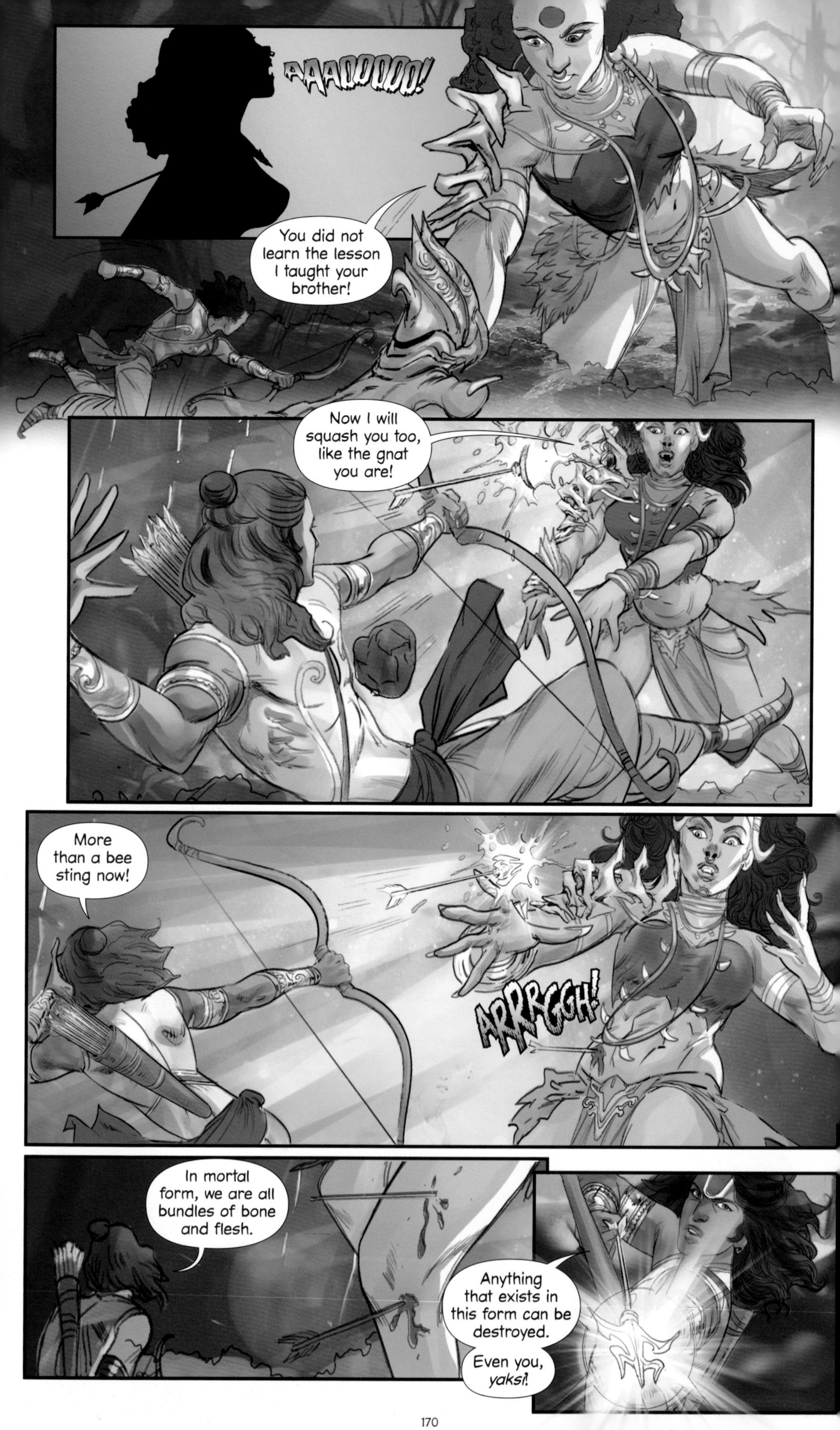
AAAOOOOO!
You did not learn the lesson I taught your brother!
Now I will squash you too, like the gnat you are!
More than a bee sting now!
ARRRGGH!
In mortal form, we are all bundles of bone and flesh.
Anything that exists in this form can be destroyed.
Even you, *yaksi*!

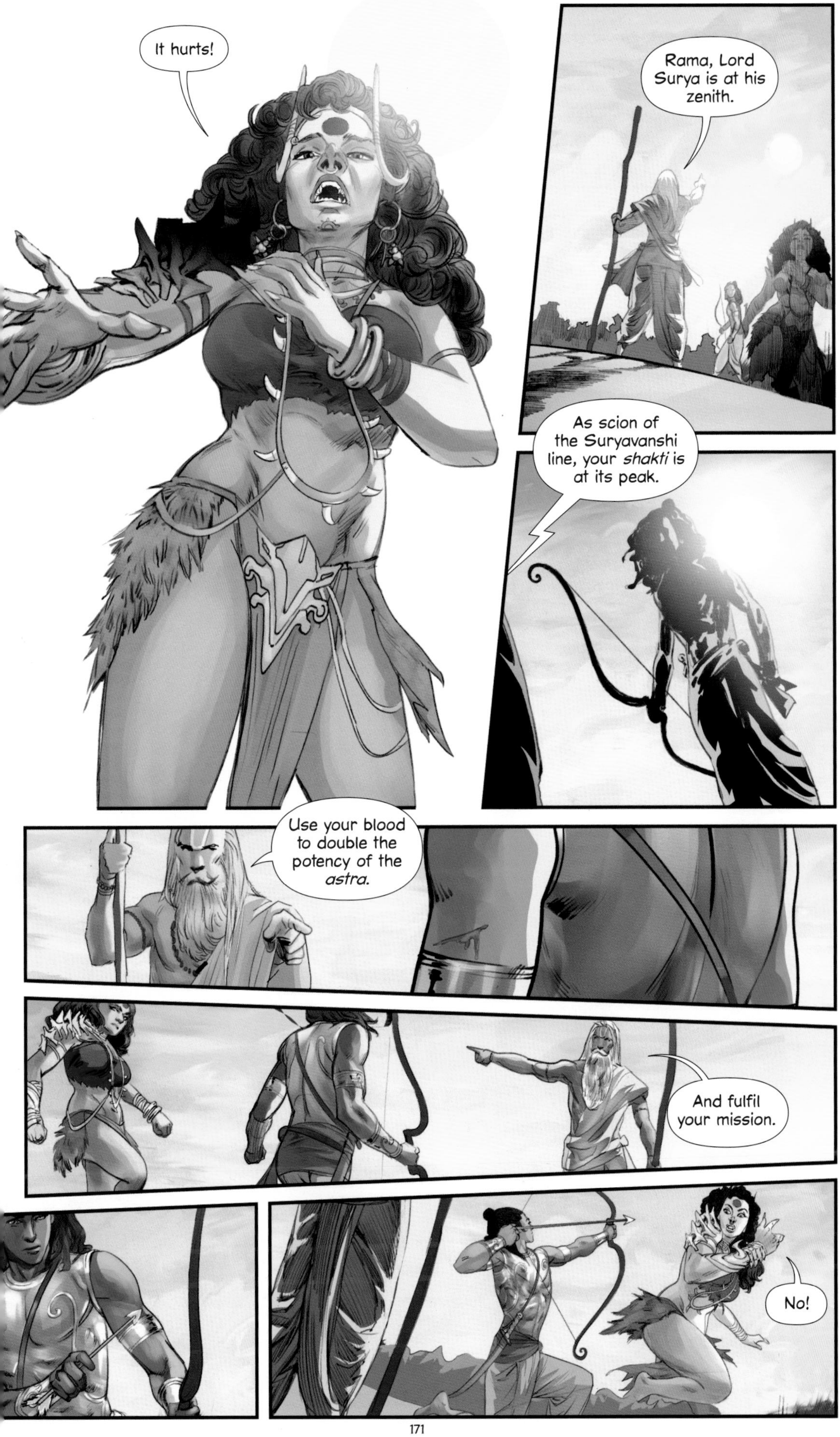
It hurts!
Rama, Lord Surya is at his zenith.
As scion of the Suryavanshi line, your *shakti* is at its peak.
Use your blood to double the potency of the *astra.*
And fulfil your mission.
No!

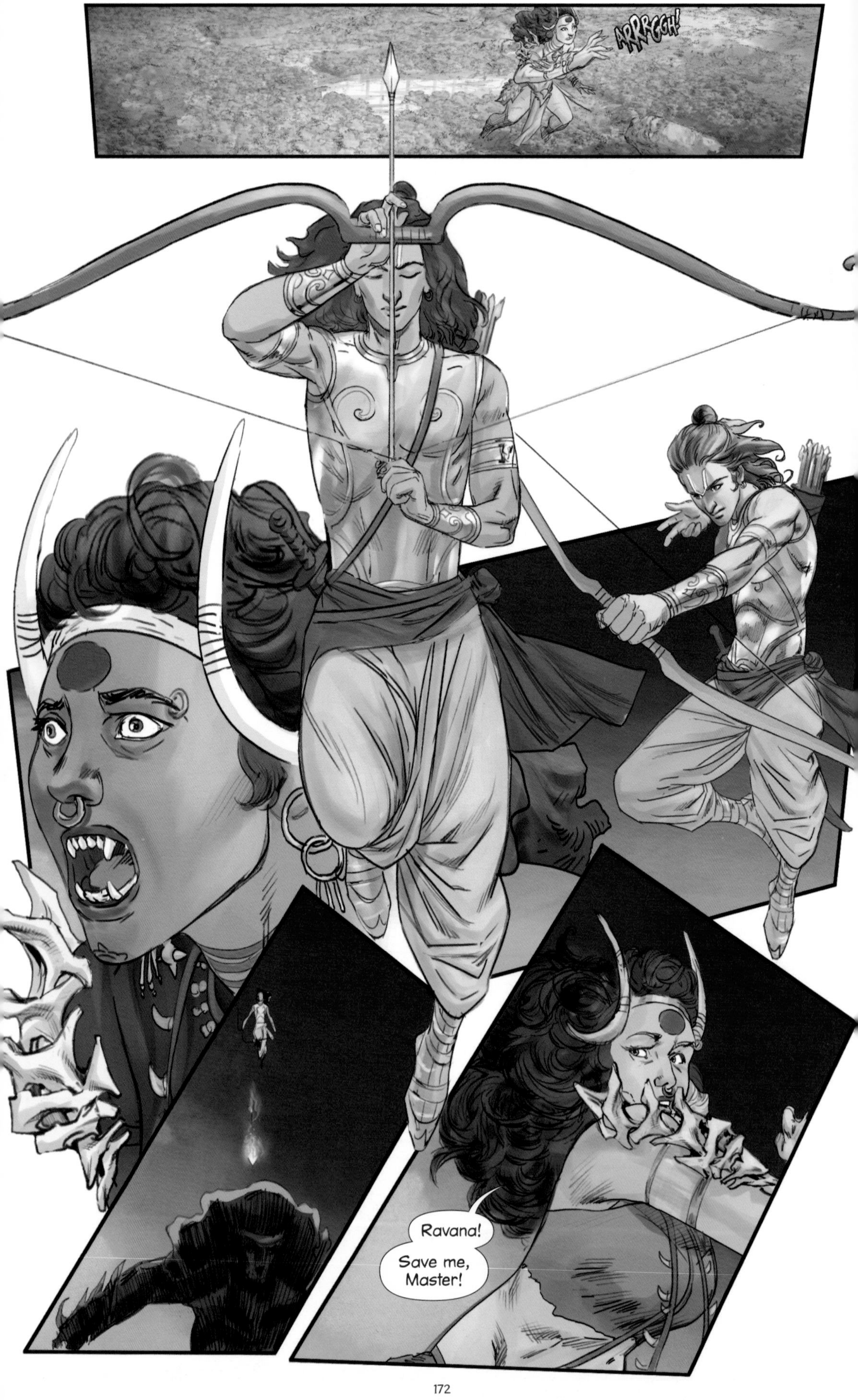
ARRRGGH!
Ravana!
Save me, Master!

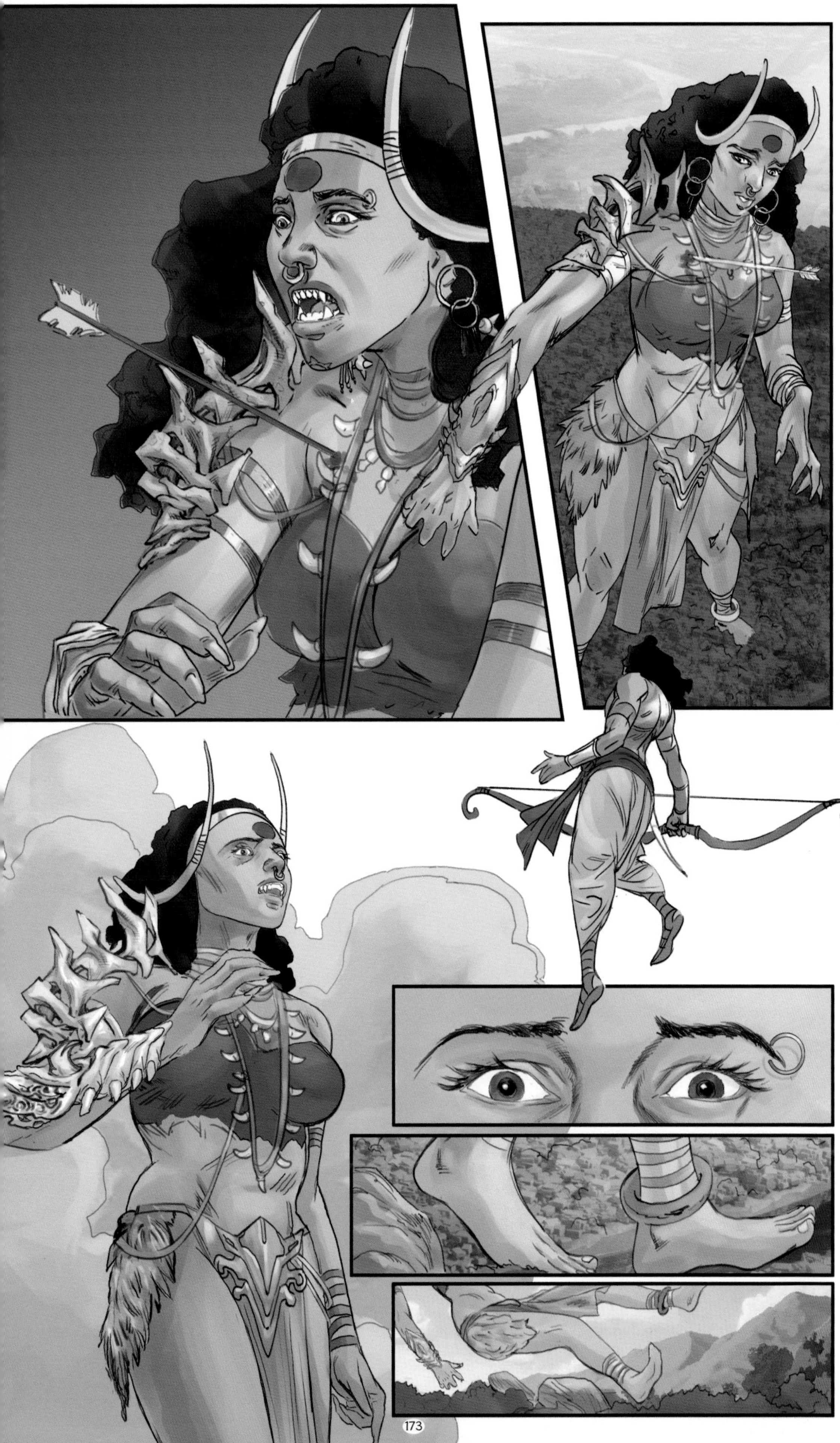

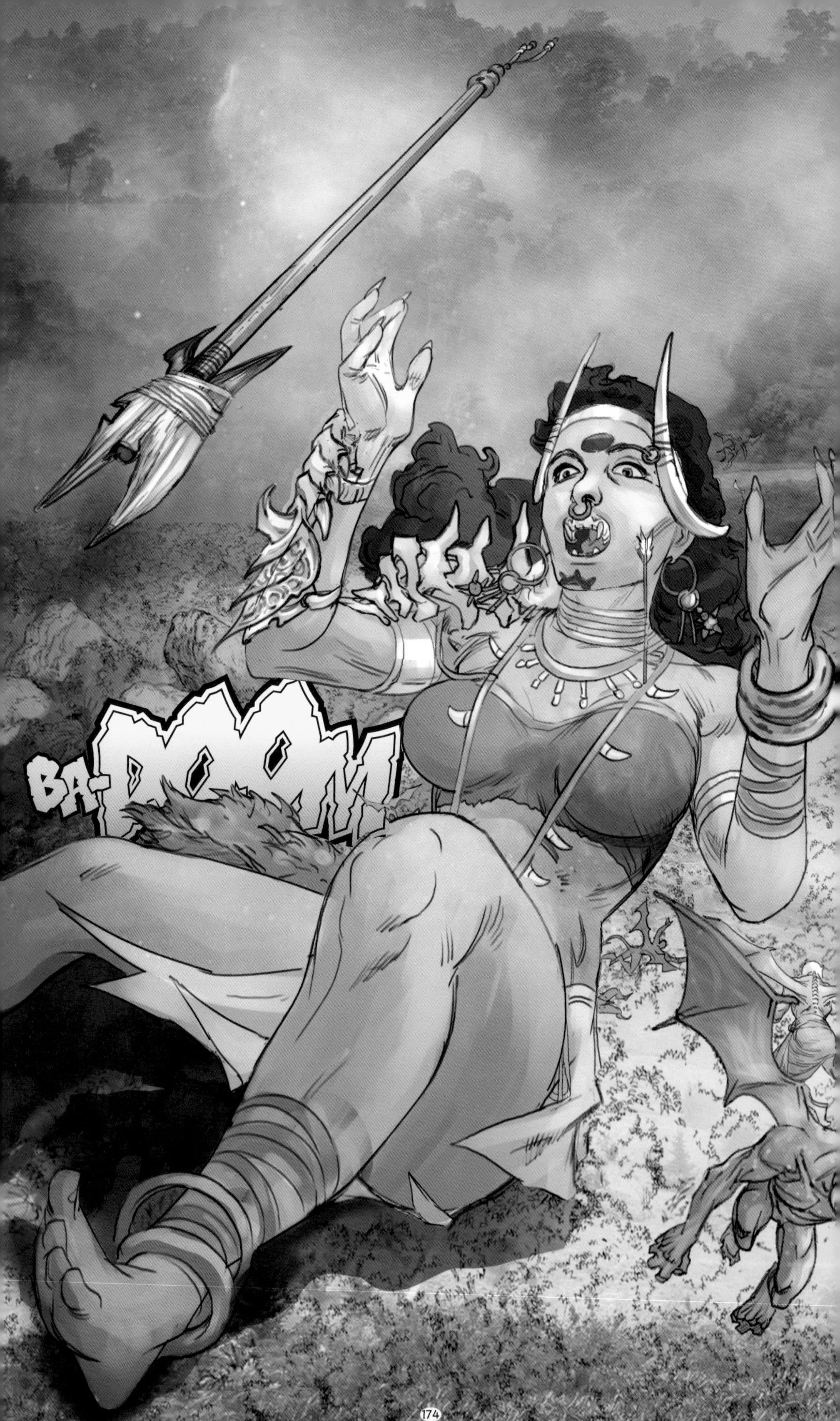
BA-BOOM

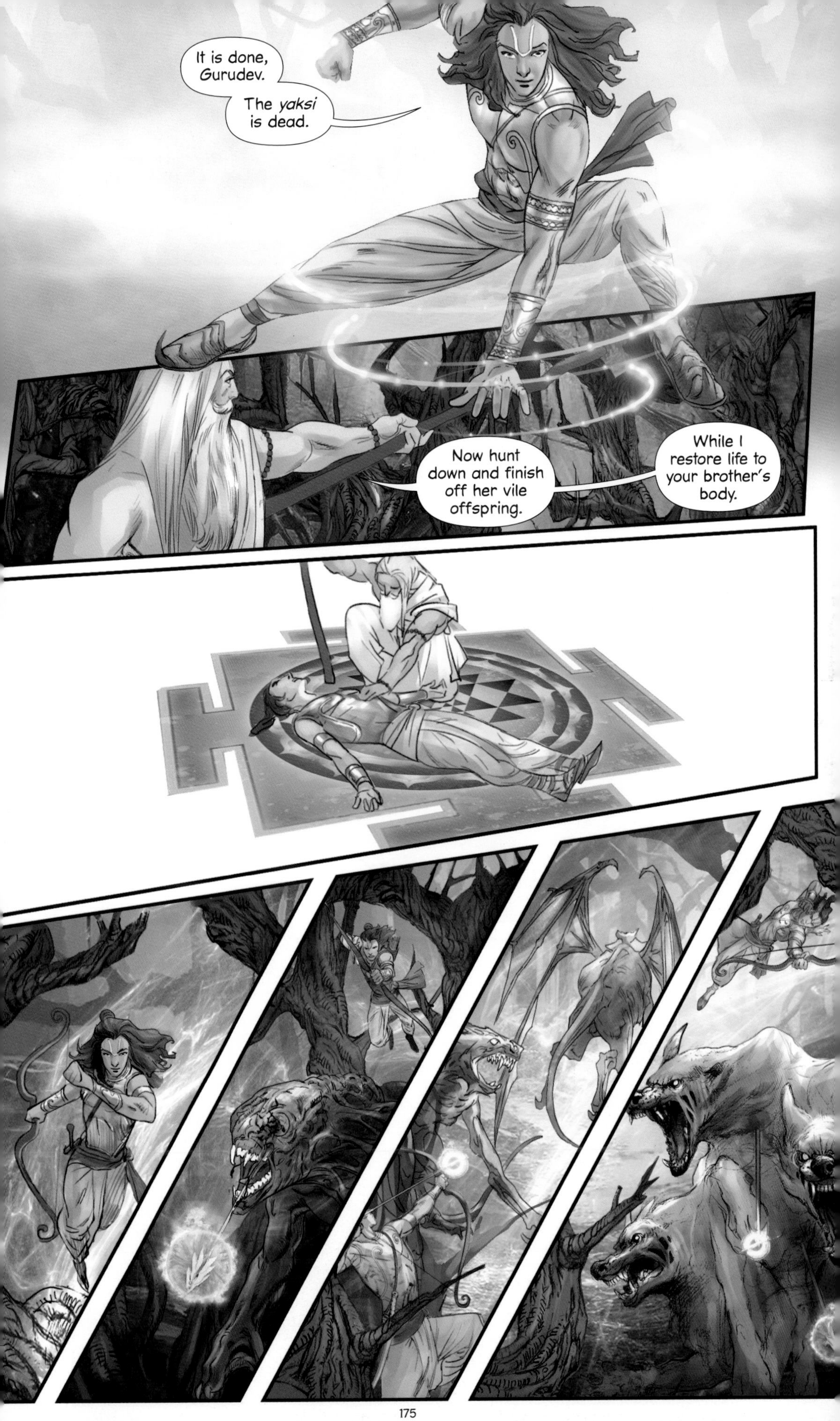
It is done, Gurudev.
The *yaksi* is dead.
Now hunt down and finish off her vile offspring.
While I restore life to your brother's body.

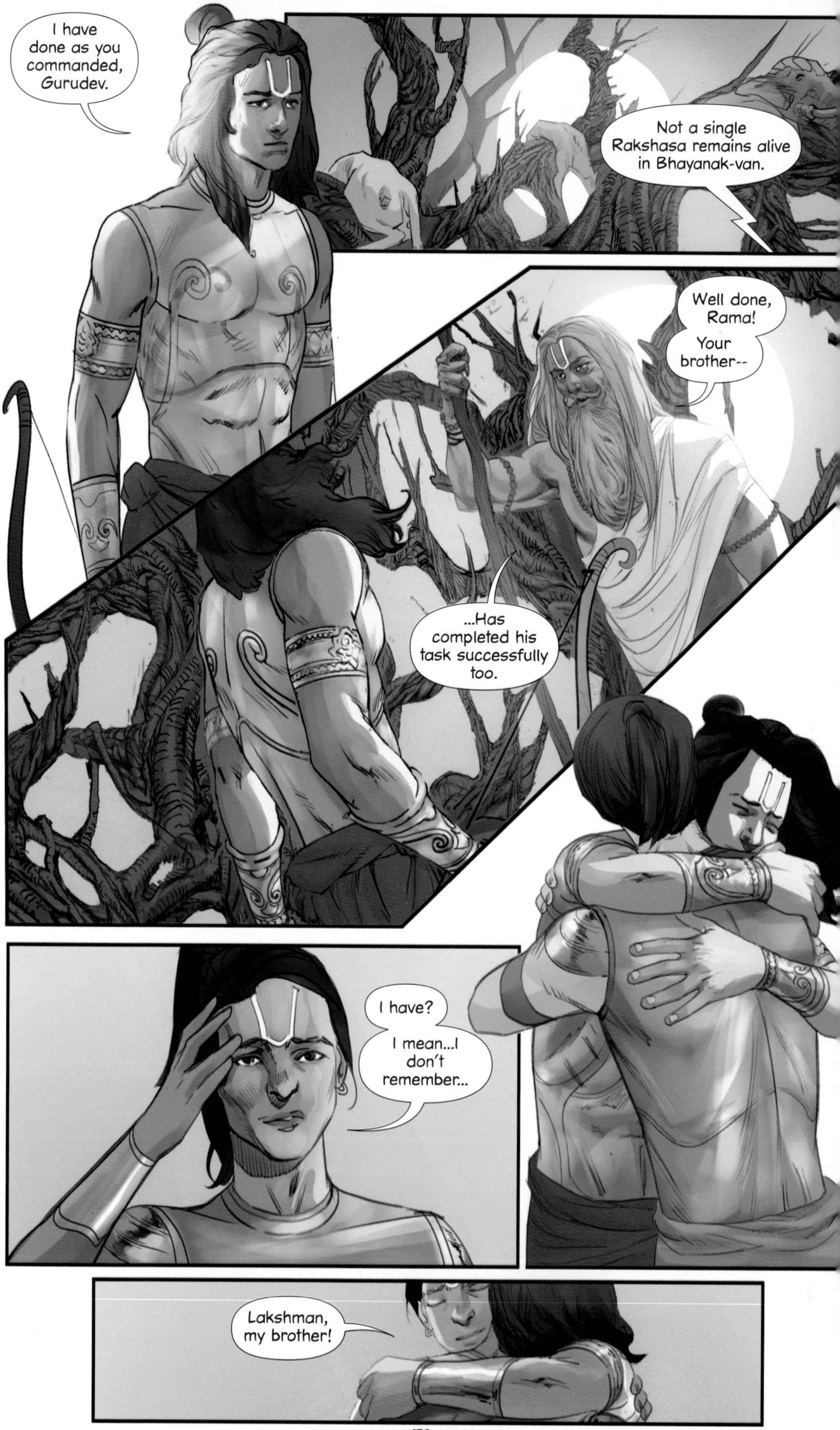
I have done as you commanded, Gurudev.
Not a single Rakshasa remains alive in Bhayanak-van.
Well done, Rama!
Your brother--
...Has completed his task successfully too.
I have?
I mean...I don't remember...
Lakshman, my brother!

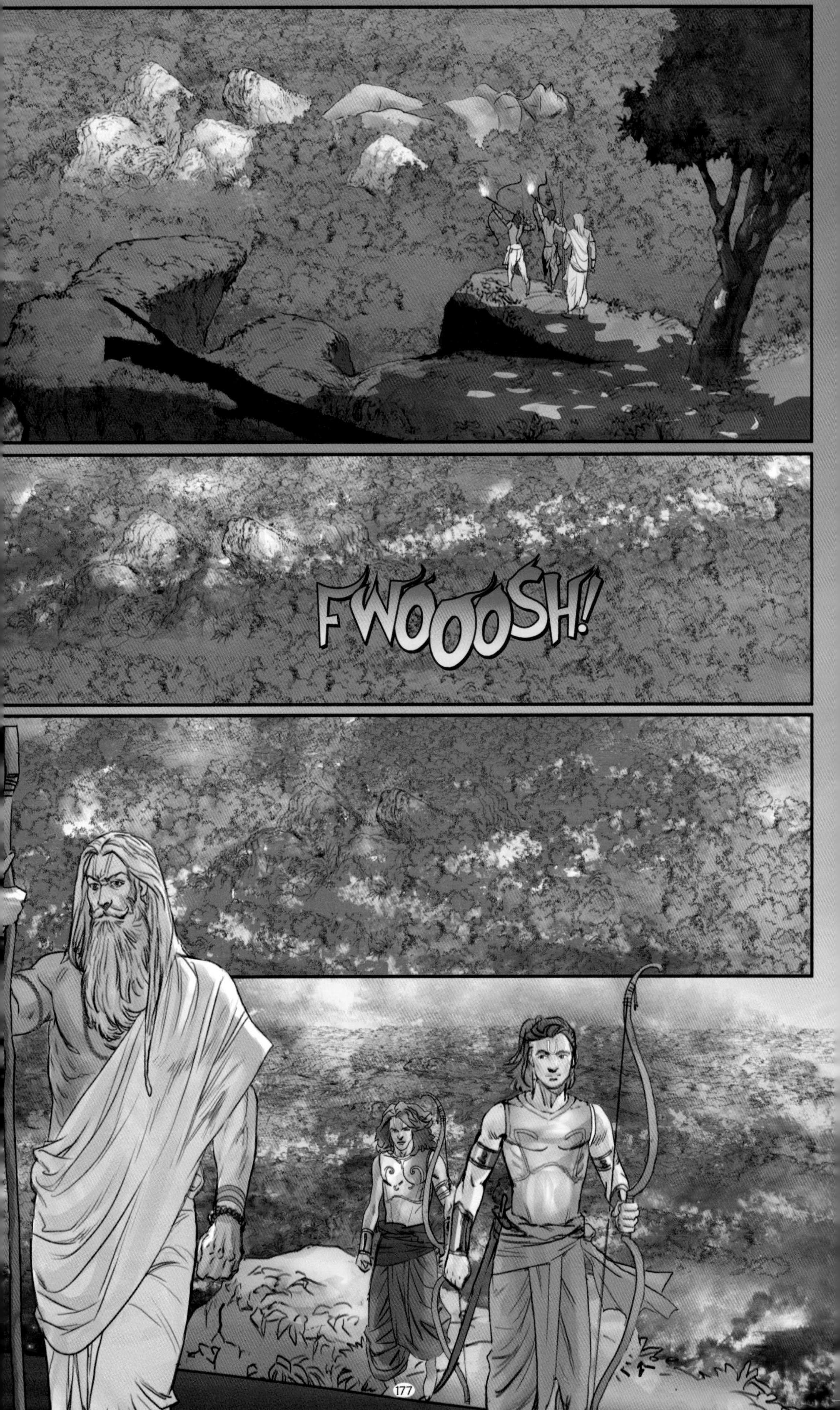
FWOOOSH!

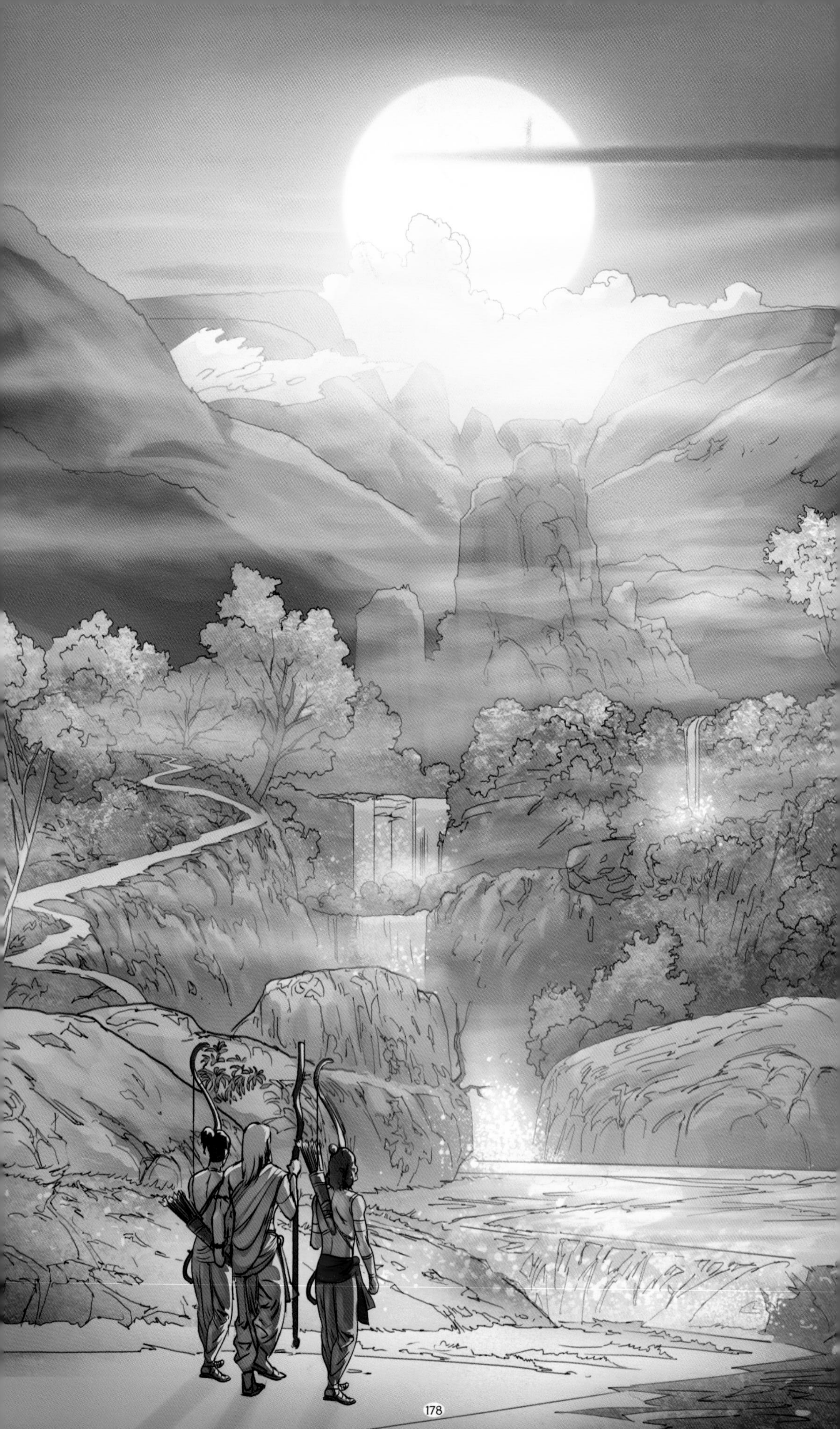

Campfire is happy to collaborate with popular author Ashok K. Banker for the graphic novel adaptation of his best-selling Ramayana series. Banker was among the first of the new wave of Indian writers in English to explore the rich legacy of Indian epics and mythology and to make them accessible to modern readers in a style and language that they can relate to. Both the author and Campfire agreed that a graphic novel adaptation of the popular series would be a great idea to project the Ramayana for first time readers of India's great epic, and Campfire was privileged to accept the author's suggestion to do a graphic version of his work.

We at Campfire believe that the graphic novel medium is a very effective technique for telling a story, due to its combination of text and sequential art. We have published award-winning graphic novel adaptations of several episodes from both the Ramayana and the Mahabharata, as well as stories from Greek mythology and Western classics. Campfire's style of presentation of a graphic novel adaptation is to use art to fully complement the text. We chose veteran artist Sachin Nagar, who has previously illustrated our adaptations of the stories of Karna, Ravana and Sundarkaand, as well futuristic sci-fi adaptations of several episodes from the Mahabharata in a series called *The Kaurava Empire*. His lush artwork makes the grand vision of the story come alive, filling up that imaginative space that may not be experienced when reading a text-only narrative. We thought he would be perfect for our adaptation of this version.

We hope our readers enjoy this graphic novel, *Prince of Ayodhya*, the first in Ashok K. Banker's Ramayana series, describing Rama's early years. There is also palace intrigue, the slaying of monsters, but above all, what is looming ahead is a far greater threat, one that can destroy the city of Ayodhya itself.

— Girija Jhunjhunwala
Director, Campfire